THE HAUNTER OF THE RING
and Other Tales

The Haunter of the Ring

and Other Tales

Robert E. Howard

*Compiled and introduced
by M. J. Elliott*

WORDSWORTH EDITIONS

For my husband
ANTHONY JOHN RANSON
with love from your wife, the publisher.
Eternally grateful for your unconditional love,
not just for me but for our children,
Simon, Andrew and Nichola Trayler

2

Readers who are interested in other titles from
Wordsworth Editions are invited to visit our website at
www.wordsworth-editions.com

For our latest list and a full mail-order service contact
Bibliophile Books, Unit 5 Datapoint,
South Crescent, London E16 4TL
Tel: +44 020 74 74 24 74
Fax: +44 020 74 74 85 89
orders@bibliophilebooks.com
www.bibliophilebooks.com

This edition published 2008 by
Wordsworth Editions Limited
8B East Street, Ware, Hertfordshire SG12 9HJ

ISBN 978 1 84022 085 8

Typeset in Great Britain by Roperford Editorial
Printed by Clays Ltd, St Ives plc

CONTENTS

For Gill

INTRODUCTION

Robert E. Howard and Conan the Barbarian – associating the author's name with that of his most famous creation is an automatic response, like connecting Sir Arthur Conan Doyle with Sherlock Holmes or Ian Fleming with James Bond. But though Howard's greatest literary achievement is certainly deserving of recognition, such familiarity comes at a cost; namely, that the Texan author's many other works are almost always overlooked. This volume is dedicated to redressing that balance to some degree.

Spear and Fang, Howard's first story for *Weird Tales*, was published in their July 1925 issue. The pulp magazine proudly described the author as one of their 'literary discoveries', and his suicide in 1936 at the age of 30 left a void no other contributor could fill.

In the Forest of Villefore and *Wolfshead* are the first two stories in a trilogy concerning the character of reluctant werewolf de Montour. The last part of the saga, *Wolfsdung*, was not published until many decades after Howard's premature death. Though they appeared eight months apart in *Weird Tales* during the mid-1920s, *Villefore* serves as little more than a prologue for *Wolfshead*, which may go some way towards explaining its surprisingly abrupt ending. When de Montour comes to explain the events of the earlier chapter to the narrator of *Wolfshead*, note that for some reason the forest's name has changed from Villefore to Ville*fere*.

For the second de Montour story, Howard was granted the front-cover illustration of *Weird Tales* for the first time, but this honour came at an unexpectedly high price – artist E. M. Stevenson had the only copy of the manuscript, necessitating a complete rewrite from memory.

Howard had an inexplicable fondness for certain character names, and used them throughout his writings. Thus you will find within these pages more than one heroic Steve, and several individuals bearing the surname Gordon. The French werewolf Le Loup from *In the Forest of Villefore* bestows his name upon a bandit who appears in Howard's first Solomon Kane adventure, *Red Shadows* (aka *Solomon Kane*).

Several of R. E. H.'s stories wear their influences upon their sleeves. *The Hyena*, from the March 1928 issue of *Weird Tales*, is suggestive of the works of Edgar Rice Burroughs and H. Rider Haggard, while *Skull-Face* – serialised in *Weird Tales* from the October to the December of 1929 – is clearly inspired by the Fu Manchu novels of Sax Rohmer, one of Howard's favourite authors. Here, Kathulos, the Skull-Faced criminal mastermind of the title, takes the place of the villainous Fu Manchu (though rather than being Chinese, Kathulos is an Atlantean posing as an Egyptian). The fair Zuleika mirrors Rohmer's heroine Karamaneh. Similarly, John Gordon is surely Sir Denis Nayland Smith by another name; even Gordon's job description matches that of Fu Manchu's arch-enemy: 'My position with the British government is a unique and peculiar one,' Gordon states. 'I hold what might be called a roving commission – an office created solely for the purpose of suiting my special needs.' The character of Li Kung no doubt obtained his name in a spooneristic manner from Kai Lung, the Chinese traveller and storyteller featured in six novels by Ernest Bramah.

The hero of *Skull-Face*, recovering opium addict Stephen Costigan, should not be confused with another Howard character, Sailor Steve Costigan, of over 30 boxing tales including *Fist and Fang*, *Circus Fists*, *Texas Fists* and *Waterfront Fists*. It is interesting (and somewhat disturbing) to read Stephen Costigan's contemplation of suicide, given his creator's own fate some seven years later. Howard/Costigan writes: 'Naught remained now but to drown this dream as I had drowned all my others – swiftly and with hope that I should soon attain that Ultimate Ocean which lies beyond all dreams.' The villain Kathulos likens Costigan to a barbarian, an accurate description given that Howard once claimed: 'My study of history has been a continual search for newer barbarians, from age to age.' The unfinished Gordon and Costigan story *The Return of Skull-Face* (aka *Taveral Manor*) was completed by Richard A. Lupoff in 1977.

In May 1928, the same year in which Howard's Puritan adventurer Solomon Kane made his first appearance, the second instalment in his Faring Town saga, *Sea Curse*, appeared in the pages of *Weird Tales*. The first in the cycle of strange stories concerning the coastal district is a poem entitled *The Legend of Faring Town*. Of the two others chapters, little is known about *The Horror at the Window*, while another, *Out of the Deep*, first saw print in the *Magazine of Horror* over 30 years after Howard's death.

Published in *Weird Tales* over the April and May of 1931, *The Children of the Night* is Howard's first real reincarnation story, doubtless drawing inspiration from Jack London's 1915 novel *The Star Rover* (known in the UK as *The Jacket*). R. E. H. would continue to explore the theme of a twentieth-century narrator experiencing a previous – and bloodier – existence throughout his writing career, each time with a significant twist. He also used it as the basis of his James Allison series (not to be confused with Jim Allison from 1936's *Graveyard Rats*, boxer Kid Allison, or cowboy Steve Allison, alias the Sonora Kid). The earlier *The Dream Snake* (*Weird Tales*, February 1928), falls somewhere between past-life and premonition, and in *The Black Stone* (*Weird Tales*, November 1931) the protagonist witnesses an unholy ritual of a bygone age which, surprisingly, turns out *not* to be a case of regression.

The Children of the Night is the first of several Howard stories to incorporate references to H. P. Lovecraft's Cthulhu Mythos – R. E. H. was put in touch with his fellow *Weird Tales* scribe in 1930, and the two became regular correspondents. Howard penned *Children* in the same month that he wrote to Lovecraft about his birthplace, Dark Valley Creek, Texas. The story begins with a discussion on genealogy, a subject close to Lovecraft's heart, and includes mention of one of H. P. L.'s favourite authors, the British fantasist Arthur Machen. Howard presents a roster of 'Great Old Ones' – the ancient and impossibly powerful beings who once ruled our planet and may yet do so again – including Cthulhu, Yog-Sothoth, Tsathoggua, and Gol-goroth. No Lovecraft pastiche would be complete without reference to Lovecraft's all-purpose forbidden tome the *Necronomicon*. Oddly, Howard refers to the volume being read in 'the original Greek', when, as any Mythos addict will tell you, it was written by the mad Arab Abdul Alhazred (Lovecraft's childhood alias). The error is corrected in the later *The Fire of Asshurbanipal*. To this already tangled web, Howard adds his own ancient and mysterious volume *Unaussprechlichen Kulten* (also to be found in the 1931 story *The Black Stone*), written by Friedrich Wilhelm Von Junzt, whose fate is similar to that suffered by Abdul Alhazred in Lovecraft's famous essay *The History of the Necronomicon*. H. P. L. returned Howard's compliment by incorporating *Unaussprechlichen Kulten* into several of his own works, including *The Man of Stone*, *The Shadow Out of Time* and *Dreams in the Witch-House*. In the latter tale, H. P. L.

suggested an English translation of Von Junzt's title might be *Nameless Cults*. After reading it, Howard wrote to Lovecraft: 'I feel honored that you should refer to Von Junzt's accursed document and thanks for the German of *Nameless Cults* which I'll use in referring to it.'

Children of the Night is one of two stories in this volume to feature academics John Kirowan and Eliot O'Donnel, both of which bear significant connections to Howard's ancient fantasy sagas. The Pictish king Bran Mak Morn, also known as 'The Dark Man' (the title of a yarn from the issue of *Weird Tales* for December 1931) does not actually appear in *Children*, but the story is nevertheless accepted as a part of the Bran canon. Lovecraft made a sly reference to Bran in his 1930 science fiction/Mythos tale *The Whisperer in Darkness*.

The Haunter of the Ring (*Weird Tales*, June 1934), is tied to the Conan series via the evil sorcerer, Thoth-Amon. In his first appearance in 1932's *The Phoenix on the Sword*, he is described as 'Thoth-Amon of the Ring'. The ring in question is the Serpent Ring of Set, discovered by Thoth-Amon 'in a nighted tomb a league beneath the earth, forgotten before the first man crawled out of the slimy sea' and used by its fiendish owner to gain influence over King Ctesphon of Stygia. Here, the ring plays a sinister part in a tale of modern marital disharmony. Many pastiche writers have presented Thoth-Amon as an arch-enemy for the famous barbarian, but *Phoenix* marks his only proper appearance in the Conan series; he is mentioned briefly in *The God in the Bowl* and the only Conan novel, *The Hour of the Dragon*.

Despite its close connections to the Cthulhu Mythos, it is unlikely that the excessively prudish Lovecraft would have described the erotic ritual from *The Black Stone* in such detail as his equally famous pen-friend. The essential plot is familiar to Lovecraft devotees – an unnamed narrator (who might or might not be John Kirowan) goes in search of an ancient legend, only to find that it is in fact the literal truth and that a cult of worshippers has built up around an aquatic beast. Indeed, this would serve as a description of both Howard's *The Black Stone* and Lovecraft's *The Call of Cthulhu* (a story praised by the characters in *Children of the Night*). In a letter to H.P.L., Howard said of *The Black Stone*: 'The story sounds as if I were trying, in my feeble and blunderingly crude way, to deliberately copy your style. Your literary influence on that particular tale, while unconscious on my part, was nonetheless strong. And indeed, many writers of the bizarre are showing your influence in their work, not only in *Weird Tales* but in other magazines as well; earlier evidence of an influence which will grow greater as time goes on, for it is inevitable that your work and art will influence the whole stream of American weird literature, and eventually the weird literature of the world'. Of the same story, he said to author August Derleth: '*The Black Stone* and other kindred yarns of mine...were written more as experiments than anything else, and I soon saw that they were not my natural style.'

1932 was a difficult year for Howard, with *Fight Stories and Action Stories,* one of the regular venues for his work, folding. Unsurprisingly, *The Thing on the Roof* – a sequel of sorts to *The Black Stone* – appeared in the February edition of *Weird Tales,* which at least published his fiction with incredible regularity, although they were not so reliable when it came to making payments. The story was initially rejected by editor Farnsworth Wright as 'too erudite for the general reader', though in truth it was Wright's habit to turn down a submission before purchasing it at a later date. Three months later, the magazine presented its readers with Howard's *The Horror from the Mound,* a far more personal work incorporating both the writer's own background and a vivid description of his phobia concerning snakes. In a letter to Lovecraft written a month before its publication, he claimed 'I'm trying to invest my native regions with surreal atmosphere, etched against a realistic setting.' The story falls into the category of Howard's 'Weird Southwest' sequence, along with *Pigeons From Hell,* an elaboration on the 'spooky old house' theme touched upon in *The Fearsome Touch of Death* (aka simply *The Touch of Death* – *Weird Tales,* February 1930). *Pigeons,* published two years after Howard's death is, to date, the only one of Howard's non-sword-and-sorcery works to have been adapted for the screen, in this case as an episode of the 1961 TV series *Thriller,* hosted by Boris Karloff.

After seeing Dark Valley again as an adult, Howard wrote perhaps his most famous and important reincarnation story, *People of the Dark,* which appeared not in his usual arena, but in *Strange Tales* magazine for June 1932. Editor Harry Bates purchased from Howard both *People* and another reincarnation story, *The Cairn on the Headland* (published in January 1933), and unlike *Weird Tales,* Bates's title paid extremely well, 'although,' R.E.H. complained, 'they kept me waiting awhile for the dough.' *People of the Dark* is sometimes erroneously considered as a Conan story in the way that *Children of the Night* is a Bran Mak Morn story, but 'Conan of the Reavers', the barbarian in whose body the narrator finds himself during his past-life experience, is certainly not the Conan of Howard's famous series. It is interesting, however, that upon his first appearance in *The Phoenix on the Sword* (written in March of 1932, and printed by *Weird*

Tales in the December of that same year), Conan the Cimmerian is described in the opening paragraph as 'a reaver'. The reptilian race featured here is clearly the same race described by Howard in both *The Children of the Night* and the Cthulhu-csque Bran Mak Morn story *Worms of the Earth*, published over a year later in the pages of *Weird* Tales, and described by H. P. Lovecraft in his essay *In Memoriam: Robert Ervin Howard* as a 'macabre masterpiece'.

In the spring of 1933, Otis Adelbert Kline became Howard's agent, and advised the young writer to attempt stories in different styles, in the hope of breaking new markets. Though not a lover of the detective genre, the writer nevertheless turned his hand to it, always, of course, incorporating an exotic twist of the sort common to his fantasy and horror tales. The effort paid off – *Black Talons*, aka *Talons in the Dark*, ran in the December 1933 issue of *Strange Detective Stories*. Steve Harrison, a tough cop with a Chinatown beat, appears in ten Howard detective tales, three of which are included in this edition. *Fangs of Gold* (*aka People of the Serpent*) was published in the February 1934 edition of *Strange Detective Stories*. Another Harrison mystery, known both as *The Tomb's Secret* and *Teeth of Doom*, appeared in the same pulp title credited to 'Patrick Ervin'. Like the earlier *Skull-Face, Names in the Black Book* (the May 1934 issue of *Super-Detective Stories*) has much in common with the Fu Manchu adventures, with the equally mysterious Erlik Khan taking the place of Kathulos as lord of the criminal underworld. Peculiarly, *Names* is a sequel to a story which had not appeared in print; Howard sold *Lord of the Dead* to *Strange Detective*, but the publication folded before it could appear. Thus, Erlik Khan (who has no apparent connection to Howard's 1934 Oriental adventure *The Daughter of Erlik Khan*) is back from the dead, despite the fact that readers had not witnessed his apparent demise.

In *Black Wind Blowing* (*Thrilling Mystery*, June 1936), heroic farmer Emmett Glanton takes on the worshippers of Ahriman, the evil god of Mazdaism or Zoroastrianism (also known as *angra mainyu*). In the novel *The Hour of the Dragon*, Conan seeks the magical jewel known as the Heart of Ahriman, guarded in the 1984 film *Conan the Destroyer* by the wizard Thoth-Amon.

With its striking *Weird Tales* cover illustration by J. Allen St John, The Cthulhu Mythos story *The Fire of Asshurbanipal* (December 1936) could not be more different in mood and setting from *Black Wind Blowing*, but where Glanton's strange experience has a tenuous link to R. E. H.'s Conan series, Steve Clarney's lost city adventures might easily be mistaken for one of the Cimmerian's outings, its shopping-list of Lovecraftian elements notwithstanding. L Sprague de Camp, author and Howard expert, rewrote a number of Howard's historical and Oriental adventure tales – *The Three-Bladed Doom*, *The Trail of the Bloodstained God*, *Hawks Over Shem* – as Conan stories, and it is somewhat surprising that *Asshurbanipal* did not receive the same treatment since it resembles to some extent the final Conan tale, *Red Nails*.

It seems inevitable, then, that any consideration of Howard's fiction must include reference to his most famous creation. This is only fitting, as Conan is one of the iconic characters of twentieth-century fiction. However, as a result the Conan stories tend to overshadow the author's other work, its range and imagination, and to do a disservice to his readers, who have for far too long been unaware of the many other worlds and works of Robert E. Howard.

M. J. ELLIOTT

M. J. Elliott is a member of the Crime Writers Association of Great Britain. His articles, fiction and reviews have appeared in *SHERLOCK Magazine*, *Scarlet Street* and *Total DVD*. For the radio, he has scripted episodes of *The Further Adventures of Sherlock Holmes*, *The Classic Adventures of Sherlock Holmes*, *The Father Brown Mysteries*, *Raffles the Gentleman Thief*, *The Adventures of Harry Nile* and *Kincaid the Strangeseeker*. He is the creator of *The Hilary Caine Mysteries*, which first aired in 2005. For Wordsworth, he has also edited *The Whisperer in Darkness* and *The Loved Dead* by H. P. Lovecraft, and *The Right Hand of Doom* by Robert E. Howard.

http://www.myspace.com/matthewjelliott

THE HAUNTER OF THE RING

and other tales

In the Forest of Villefore

The sun had set. The great shadows came striding over the forest. In the weird twilight of a late summer day, I saw the path ahead glide on among the mighty trees and disappear. And I shuddered and glanced fearfully over my shoulder. Miles behind lay the nearest village . . . miles ahead the next.

I looked to left and to right as I strode on, and anon I looked behind me. And anon I stopped short, grasping my rapier, as a breaking twig betokened the going of some small beast. Or was it a beast?

But the path led on and I followed, because, forsooth, I had naught else to do.

As I went I bethought me, 'My own thoughts will rout me, if I be not aware. What is there in this forest, except perhaps the creatures that roam it, deer and the like? Tush, the foolish legends of those villagers!'

And so I went and the twilight faded into dusk. Stars began to blink and the leaves of the trees murmured in the faint breeze. And then I stopped short, my sword leaping to my hand, for just ahead, around a curve of the path, someone was singing. The words I could not distinguish, but the accent was strange, almost barbaric.

I stepped behind a great tree, and the cold sweat beaded my forehead. Then the singer came in sight, a tall, thin man, vague in the twilight. I shrugged my shoulders. A *man* I did not fear. I sprang out, my point raised.

'Stand!'

He showed no surprise. 'I prithee, handle thy blade with care, friend,' he said.

Somewhat ashamed, I lowered my sword.

'I am new to this forest,' I quoth, apologetically. 'I heard talk of bandits. I crave pardon. Where lies the road to Villefore?'

'*Corbleu*, you've missed it,' he answered. 'You should have branched off to the right some distance back. I am going there myself. If you may abide my company, I will direct you.'

I hesitated. Yet why should I hesitate?

'Why, certainly. My name is de Montour, of Normandy.'

'And I am Carolus le Loup.'

'No!' I started back.

He looked at me in astonishment.

'Pardon,' said I; 'the name is strange. Does not *loup* mean wolf?'

'My family were always great hunters,' he answered. He did not offer his hand.

'You will pardon my staring,' said I as we walked down the path, 'but I can hardly see your face in the dusk.'

I sensed that he was laughing, though he made no sound.

'It is little to look upon,' he answered.

I stepped closer and then leaped away, my hair bristling.

'A mask!' I exclaimed. 'Why do you wear a mask, *m'sieu*?'

'It is a vow,' he exclaimed. 'In fleeing a pack of hounds I vowed that if I escaped I would wear a mask for a certain time.'

'Hounds, *m'sieu*?'

'Wolves,' he answered quickly; 'I said wolves.'

We walked in silence for awhile and then my companion said, 'I am surprised that you walk these woods by night. Few people come these ways even in the day.'

'I am in haste to reach the border,' I answered. 'A treaty has been signed with the English, and the Duke of Burgundy should know of it. The people at the village sought to dissuade me. They spoke of . . . a wolf that was purported to roam these woods.'

'Here the path branches to Villefore,' said he, and I saw a narrow, crooked path that I had not seen when I passed it before. It led in amid the darkness of the trees. I shuddered.

'You wish to return to the village?'

'No!' I exclaimed. 'No, no! Lead on.'

So narrow was the path that we walked single file, he leading. I looked well at him. He was taller, much taller than I, and thin, wiry. He was dressed in a costume that smacked of Spain. A long rapier swung at his hip. He walked with long easy strides, noiselessly.

Then he began to talk of travel and adventure. He spoke of many lands and seas he had seen and many strange things. So we talked and went farther and farther into the forest.

I presumed that he was French, and yet he had a very strange accent, that was neither French nor Spanish nor English, not like any language I had ever heard. Some words he slurred strangely and some he could not pronounce at all.

'This path is often used, is it?' I asked.

'Not by many,' he answered and laughed silently. I shuddered. It was very dark and the leaves whispered together among the branches.

'A fiend haunts this forest,' I said.

'So the peasants say,' he answered, 'but I have roamed it oft and have never seen his face.'

Then he began to speak of strange creatures of darkness, and the moon rose and shadows glided among the trees. He looked up at the moon.

'Haste!' said he. 'We must reach our destination before the moon reaches her zenith.'

We hurried along the trail.

'They say,' said I, 'that a werewolf haunts these woodlands.'

'It might be,' said he, and we argued much upon the subject.

'The old women say,' said he, 'that if a werewolf is slain while a wolf, then he is slain, but if he is slain as a man, then his half-soul will haunt his slayer forever. But haste thee, the moon nears her zenith.'

We came into a small moonlit glade and the stranger stopped.

'Let us pause a while,' said he.

'Nay, let us be gone,' I urged; 'I like not this place.'

He laughed without sound. 'Why,' said he, 'this is a fair glade. As good as a banquet hall it is, and many times have I feasted here. Ha, ha, ha! Look ye, I will show you a dance.' And he began bounding here and there, anon flinging back his head and laughing silently. Thought I, the man is mad.

As he danced his weird dance I looked about me. *The trail went not on but stopped in the glade.*

'Come,' said I, 'we must on. Do you not smell the rank, hairy scent that hovers about the glade? Wolves den here. Perhaps they are about us and are gliding upon us even now.'

He dropped upon all fours, bounded higher than my head, and came toward me with a strange slinking motion.

'That dance is called the Dance of the Wolf,' said he, and my hair bristled.

'Keep off!' I stepped back, and with a screech that set the echoes shuddering he leaped for me, and though a sword hung at his belt he did not draw it. My rapier was half out when he grasped my arm and flung me headlong. I dragged him with me and we struck the ground together. Wrenching a hand free I jerked off the mask. A shriek of horror broke from my lips. Beast eyes glittered beneath that mask, white fangs flashed in the moonlight. *The face was that of a wolf.*

In an instant those fangs were at my throat. Taloned hands tore the sword from my grasp. I beat at that horrible face with my clenched fists, but his jaws were fastened on my shoulders, his talons tore at my throat. Then I was on my back. The world was fading. Blindly I struck out. My hand dropped, then closed automatically about the hilt of my dagger, which I had been unable to get at. I drew and stabbed. A terrible, half-bestial bellowing screech. Then I reeled to my feet, free. At my feet lay the werewolf.

I stooped, raised the dagger, then paused, looked up. The moon hovered close to her zenith. *If I slew the thing as a man its frightful spirit would haunt me for ever.* I sat down waiting. The *thing* watched me with flaming wolf eyes. The long wiry limbs seemed to shrink, to crook; hair seemed to grow upon them. Fearing madness, I snatched up the *thing*'s own sword and hacked it to pieces. Then I flung the sword away and fled.

Wolfshead

Fear? Your pardon, Messieurs, but the meaning of fear you do not know. No, I hold to my statement. You are soldiers, adventurers. You have known the charges of regiments of dragoons, the frenzy of wind-lashed seas. But fear, real hair-raising, horror-crawling fear, you have not known. I myself have known such fear; but until the legions of darkness swirl from hell's gate and the world flames to ruin, will never such fear again be known to men.

Hark, I will tell you the tale; for it was many years ago and half across the world; and none of you will ever see the man of whom I tell you, or seeing, know.

Return, then, with me across the years to a day when I, a reckless young cavalier, stepped from the small boat that had landed me from the ship floating in the harbour, cursed the mud that littered the crude wharf, and strode up the landing toward the castle, in answer to the invitation of an old friend, Dom Vincente da Lusto.

Dom Vincente was a strange, far-sighted man – a strong man, one who saw visions beyond the ken of his time. In his veins, perhaps, ran the blood of those old Phoenicians who, the priests tell us, ruled the seas and built cities in far lands, in the dim ages. His plan of fortune was strange and yet successful; few men would have thought of it; fewer could have succeeded. For his estate was upon the western coast of that dark, mystic continent, that baffler of explorers . . . Africa.

There by a small bay had he cleared away the sullen jungle, built his castle and his storehouses, and with ruthless hand had he wrested the riches of the land. Four ships he had: three smaller craft and one great galleon. These plied between his domains and the cities of Spain, Portugal, France, and even England, laden with rare woods, ivory, slaves; the thousand strange riches that Dom Vincente had gained by trade and by conquest.

Aye, a wild venture, a wilder commerce. And yet might he have shaped an empire from the dark land, had it not been for the rat-faced Carlos, his nephew – but I run ahead of my tale.

Look, Messieurs, I draw a map on the table, thus, with finger dipped in wine. Here lay the small, shallow harbour, and here the wide wharves: a landing ran thus, up the slight slope with hut-like warehouses on each side, and here it stopped at a wide, shallow moat. Over it went a narrow drawbridge, and then one was confronted with a high palisade of logs set in the ground. This extended entirely around the castle. The castle itself was built on the model of another, earlier age; being more for strength than beauty. Built of stone brought from a great distance, years of labour and a thousand Negroes toiling beneath the lash had reared its walls, and now, completely, it offered an almost impregnable appearance. Such was the intention of its builders, for Barbary pirates ranged the coasts, and the horror of a native uprising lurked ever near.

A space of about a half-mile on every side of the castle was kept cleared away and roads had been built through the marshy land. All this had required an immense amount of labour, but manpower was plentiful. A present to a chief, and he furnished all that was needed. And Portuguese know how to make men work!

Less than three hundred yards to the east of the castle ran a wide, shallow river, which emptied into the harbour. The name has entirely slipt my mind. It was a heathenish title and I could never lay my tongue to it.

I found that I was not the only friend invited to the castle. It seems that once a year or some such matter, Dom Vincente brought a host of jolly companions to his lonely estate and made merry for some weeks, to make up for the work and solitude of the rest of the year.

In fact, it was nearly night, and a great banquet was in progress when I entered. I was acclaimed with great delight, greeted boisterously by friends and introduced to such strangers as were there.

Entirely too weary to take much part in the revelry, I ate, drank quietly, listened to the toasts and songs, and studied the feasters.

Dom Vincente, of course, I knew, as I had been intimate with him for years; also his pretty niece, Ysabel, who was one reason I had accepted his invitation to come to that stinking wilderness. Her second cousin, Carlos, I knew and disliked – a sly, mincing fellow with a face like a mink's. Then there was my old friend, Luigi Verenza, an Italian; and his flirt of a sister, Marcita, making eyes at the men as usual. Then there was a short, stocky German who called himself Baron von Schiller; and Jean Desmarte, an out-at-the-elbows nobleman of Gascony; and Don Florenzo de Seville, a lean, dark, silent man, who called himself a Spaniard and wore a rapier nearly as long as himself.

There were others, men and women, but it was long ago and all their names and faces I do not remember. But there was one man whose face somehow drew my gaze as an alchemist's magnet draws steel. He was a leanly-built man of slightly more than medium height, dressed plainly, almost austerely, and he wore a sword almost as long as the Spaniard's.

But it was neither his clothes nor his sword which attracted my attention. It was his face. A refined, high-bred face, it was furrowed deep with lines that gave it a weary, haggard expression. Tiny scars flecked jaw and forehead as if torn by savage claws; I could have sworn the narrow grey eyes had a fleeting, haunted look in their expression at times.

I leaned over to that flirt, Marcita, and asked the name of the man, as it had slipt my mind that we had been introduced.

'De Montour, from Normandy,' she answered. 'A strange man. I don't think I like him.'

'Then he resists your snares, my little enchantress?' I murmured, long friendship making me as immune from her anger as from her wiles. But she chose not to be angry and answered coyly, glancing from under demurely lowered lashes.

I watched de Montour much, feeling somehow a strange fascination. He ate lightly, drank much, seldom spoke, and then only to answer questions.

Presently, toasts making the rounds, I noticed his companions urging him to rise and give a health. At first he refused, then rose, upon their repeated urgings, and stood silent for a moment, goblet raised. He seemed to dominate, to overawe the group of revellers. Then with a mocking, savage laugh, he lifted the goblet above his head.

'To Solomon,' he exclaimed, 'who bound all devils! And thrice cursed be he for that some escaped!'

A toast and a curse in one! It was drunk silently, and with many sidelong, doubting glances.

That night I retired early, weary of the long sea voyage and my head spinning from the strength of the wine, of which Dom Vincente kept such great stores.

My room was near the top of the castle and looked out toward the forests of the south and the river. The room was furnished in crude, barbaric splendour, as was all the rest of the castle.

Going to the window, I gazed out at the arquebusier pacing the castle grounds just inside the palisade; at the cleared space lying unsightly and barren in the moonlight; at the forest beyond; at the silent river.

From the native quarters close to the river bank came the weird twanging of some rude lute, sounding a barbaric melody.

In the dark shadows of the forest some uncanny nightbird lifted a mocking voice. A thousand minor notes sounded – birds, and beasts, and the devil knows what else! Some great jungle cat began a hair-lifting yowling. I shrugged my shoulders and turned from the windows. Surely devils lurked in those sombre depths.

There came a knock at my door and I opened it, to admit de Montour. He strode to the window and gazed at the moon, which rode resplendent and glorious.

'The moon is almost full, is it not, Monsieur?' he remarked, turning to me. I nodded, and I could have sworn that he shuddered.

'Your pardon, Monsieur. I will not annoy you further.' He turned to go, but at the door turned and retraced his steps.

'Monsieur,' he almost whispered, with a fierce intensity, 'whatever you do, be sure you bar and bolt your door tonight!'

Then he was gone, leaving me to stare after him bewilderedly.

I dozed off to sleep, the distant shouts of the revellers in my ears, and though I was weary, or perhaps because of it, I slept lightly. While I never really awoke until morning, sounds and noises seemed to drift to me through my veil of slumber, and once it seemed that something was prying and shoving against the bolted door.

As is to be supposed, most of the guests were in a beastly humour the following day and remained in their rooms most of the morning or else straggled down late. Besides Dom Vincente there were really only three of the masculine members sober: de Montour, the Spaniard, de Seville (as he called himself), and myself. The Spaniard never touched wine, and though de Montour consumed incredible quantities of it, it never affected him in any way.

The ladies greeted us most graciously.

'S'truth, Signor,' remarked that minx Marcita, giving me her hand with a gracious air that was like to make me snicker, 'I am glad to see there are gentlemen among us who care more for our company than for the wine cup; for most of them are most surprisingly befuddled this morning.'

Then with a most outrageous turning of her wondrous eyes, 'Methinks someone was too drunk to be discreet last night . . . or not

drunk enough. For unless my poor senses deceive me much, someone came fumbling at my door late in the night.'

'Ha!' I exclaimed in quick anger, 'some – !'

'No. Hush.' She glanced about as if to see that we were alone, then:
'Is it not strange that Signor de Montour, before he retired last
night, instructed me to fasten my door firmly?'

'Strange,' I murmured, but did not tell her that he had told me the
same thing.

'And is it not strange, Pierre, that though Signor de Montour left
the banquet hall even before you did, yet he has the appearance of
one who has been up all night?' I shrugged. A woman's fancies are
often strange.

'Tonight,' she said roguishly, 'I will leave my door unbolted and
see whom I catch.'

'You will do no such thing.'

She showed her little teeth in a contemptuous smile and displayed
a small, wicked dagger.

'Listen, imp. De Montour gave me the same warning he did
you. Whatever he knew, whoever prowled the halls last night, the
object was more apt murder than amorous adventure. Keep
you your doors bolted. The lady Ysabel shares your room, does
she not?'

'Not she. And I send my woman to the slave quarters at night,'
she murmured, gazing mischievously at me from beneath drooping
eyelids.

'One would think you a girl of no character from your talk,' I told
her, with the frankness of youth and of long friendship. 'Walk with
care, young lady, else I tell your brother to spank you.'

And I walked away to pay my respects to Ysabel. The Portuguese
girl was the very opposite of Marcita, being a shy, modest young
thing, not so beautiful as the Italian, but exquisitely pretty in an
appealing, almost childish air. I once had thoughts – Hi ho! to be
young and foolish!

Your pardon, Messieurs. An old man's mind wanders. It was of de
Montour that I meant to tell you . . . de Montour and Dom Vincente's mink-faced cousin.

A band of armed natives were thronged about the gates, kept at a
distance by the Portuguese soldiers. Among them were some score
of young men and women all naked, chained neck to neck. Slaves
they were, captured by some warlike tribe and brought for sale. Dom
Vincente looked them over personally.

Followed a long haggling and bartering, of which I quickly wearied and turned away, wondering that a man of Dom Vincente's rank could so demean himself as to stoop to trade.

But I strolled back when one of the natives of the village nearby came up and interrupted the sale with a long harangue to Dom Vincente.

While they talked de Montour came up, and presently Dom Vincente turned to us and said, 'One of the woodcutters of the village was torn to pieces by a leopard or some such beast last night. A strong young man and unmarried.'

'A leopard? Did they, see it?' suddenly asked de Montour, and when Dom Vincente said no, that it came and went in the night, de Montour lifted a trembling hand and drew it across his forehead, as if to brush away cold sweat.

'Look you, Pierre,' quoth Dom Vincente, 'I have here a slave who, wonder of wonders, desires to be your man. Though the devil only knows why.'

He led up a slim young Jakri, a mere youth, whose main asset seemed a merry grin.

'He is yours,' said Dom Vincente. 'He is goodly trained and will make a fine servant. And look ye, a slave is of an advantage over a servant, for all he requires is food and a loincloth or so with a touch of the whip to keep him in his place.'

It was not long before I learned why Gola wished to be 'my man', choosing me among all the rest. It was because of my hair. Like many dandies of that day, I wore it long and curled, the strands falling to my shoulders. As it happened, I was the only man of the party who so wore my hair, and Gola would sit and gaze at it in silent admiration for hours at a time, or until, growing nervous under his unblinking scrutiny, I would boot him forth.

It was that night that a brooding animosity, hardly apparent, between Baron von Schiller and Jean Desmarie broke out into a flame.

As usual, woman was the cause. Marcita carried on a most outrageous flirtation with both of them.

That was not wise. Desmarte was a wild young fool. Von Schiller was a lustful beast. But when, Messieurs, did woman ever use wisdom?

Their hate flamed to a murderous fury when the German sought to kiss Marcita.

Swords were clashing in an instant. But before Dom Vincente could thunder a command to halt, Luigi was between the combatants, and had beaten their swords down, hurling them back viciously.

'Signori,' said he softly, but with a fierce intensity, 'is it the part of high-bred signori to fight over my sister? Ha, by the toenails of Satan, for the toss of a coin I would call you both out! You, Marcita, go to your chamber, instantly, nor leave until I give you permission.'

And she went, for, independent though she was, none cared to face the slim, effeminate-appearing youth when a tigerish snarl curled his lips, a murderous gleam lightened his dark eyes.

Apologies were made, but from the glances the two rivals threw at each other, we knew that the quarrel was not forgotten and would blaze forth again at the slightest pretext.

Late that night I woke suddenly with a strange, eerie feeling of horror. Why, I could not say. I rose, saw that the door was firmly bolted, and seeing Gola asleep on the floor, kicked him awake irritably.

And just as he got up, hastily, rubbing himself, the silence was broken by a wild scream, a scream that rang through the castle and brought a startled shout from the arquebusier pacing the palisade; a scream from the mouth of a girl, frenzied with terror.

Gola squawked and dived behind the divan. I jerked the door open and raced down the dark corridor. Dashing down a winding stair, I cannoned into someone at the bottom and we tumbled headlong.

He rasped something and I recognised the voice of Jean Desmarte. I hauled him to his feet, and raced along, he following; the screams had ceased, but the whole castle was in an uproar, voices shouting, the clank of weapons, lights flashing up, Dom Vincente's voice shouting for the soldiers, the noise of armed men rushing through the rooms and falling over each other. With all the confusion, Desmarte, the Spaniard, and I reached Marcita's room just as Luigi darted inside and snatched his sister into his arms.

Others rushed in, carrying lights and weapons, shouting, demanding to know what was occurring.

The girl lay quietly in her brother's arms, her dark hair loose and rippling over her shoulders, her dainty night-garments torn to shreds and exposing her lovely body. Long scratches showed upon her arms, breasts and shoulders.

Presently, she opened her eyes, shuddered, then shrieked wildly and clung frantically to Luigi, begging him not to let something take her.

'The door!' she whimpered. 'I left it unbarred. And something crept into my room through the darkness. I struck at it with my dagger and it hurled me to the floor, tearing, tearing at me. Then I fainted.'

'Where is von Schiller?' asked the Spaniard, a fierce glint in his dark eyes. Every man glanced at his neighbour. All the guests were there except the German. I noted de Montour gazing at the terrified girl, his face more haggard than usual. And I thought it strange that he wore no weapon.

'Aye, von Schiller!' exclaimed Desmarte fiercely. And half of us followed Dom Vincente out into the corridor. We began a vengeful search through the castle, and in a small, dark hallway we found von Schiller. On his face he lay, in a crimson, ever-widening stain.

'This is the work of some native!' exclaimed Desmarte, face aghast.

'Nonsense,' bellowed Dom Vincente. 'No native from the outside could pass the soldiers. All slaves, von Schiller's among them, were barred and bolted in the slave quarters, except Cola, who sleeps in Pierre's room, and Ysabel's woman.'

'But who else could have done this deed?' exclaimed Desmarte in a fury.

'You!' I said abruptly; 'else why ran you so swiftly away from the room of Marcita?'

'Curse you, you lie!' he shouted, and his swift-drawn sword leaped for my breast; but quick as he was, the Spaniard was quicker. Desmarte's rapier clattered against the wall and Desmarte stood like a statue, the Spaniard's motionless point just touching his throat.

'Bind him,' said the Spaniard without passion. 'Put down your blade, Don Florenzo,' commanded Dom Vincente, striding forward and dominating the scene. 'Signor Desmarte, you are one of my best friends, but I am the only law here and duty must be done. Give your word that you will not seek to escape.'

'I give it,' replied the Gascon calmly. 'I acted hastily. I apologise. I was not intentionally running away, but the halls and corridors of this cursed castle confuse me.' Of us all, probably but one man believed him.

'Messieurs!' De Montour stepped forward. 'This youth is not guilty. Turn the German over.'

Two soldiers did as he asked. De Montour shuddered, pointing. The rest of us glanced once, then recoiled in horror.

'Could man have done that thing?'

'With a dagger . . . ' began someone.

'No dagger makes wounds like that,' said the Spaniard: 'The German was torn to pieces by the talons of some frightful beast.'

We glanced about us, half expecting some hideous monster to leap upon us from the shadows.

We searched that castle; every foot, every inch of it. And we found no trace of any beast.

Dawn was breaking when I returned to my room, to find that Gola had barred himself in; and it took me nearly a half-hour to convince him to let me in. Having smacked him soundly and berated him for his cowardice, I told him what had taken place, as he could understand French and could speak a weird mixture which he proudly called French.

His mouth gaped and only the whites of his eyes showed as the tale reached its climax.

'Ju ju!' he whispered fearsomely. 'Fetish man!' Suddenly an idea came to me. I had heard vague tales, little more than hints of legends, of the devilish leopard cult that existed on the West Coast. No white man had ever seen one of its votaries, but Dom Vincente had told us tales of beast-men, disguised in skins of leopards, who stole through the midnight jungle and slew and devoured. A ghastly thrill travelled up and down my spine, and in an instant I had Gola in a grasp which made him veil.

'Was that a leopard-man?' I hissed, shaking him viciously.

'Me good boy! Ju ju man get! More besser no tell!'

'You'll tell me!' I gritted, renewing my endeavours, until, his hands waving feeble protests, he promised to tell me what he knew.

'No leopard-man!' he whispered. 'Moon, he full, woodcutter find, him heap clawed. Find 'nother woodcutter. Big Massa (Dom Vincente) say "leopard". No leopard. But leopard-man, he come to kill. Something kill leopard-man! Heap claw! Hai, hai! Moon full again. Something come in, lonely hut; claw um woman, claw um pick'nin. I am find um claw up. Big Massa say "leopard". Full moon again, and woodcutter find, heap clawed. Now come in castle. No leopard. But always footmarks of a man.'

I gave a startled, incredulous exclamation.

It was true, Gola averred. Always the footprints of a man led away from the scene of the murder. Then why did the natives not tell the Big Massa, that he might hunt down the fiend? Here Gola assumed a crafty expression and whispered in my ear, the footprints were of a man who wore shoes!

Even assuming that Gola was lying, I felt a thrill of unexplainable horror. Who, then, did the natives believe was doing these frightful murders?

And he answered: Dom Vincente!

By this time, Messieurs, my mind was in a whirl. What was the meaning of all this? Who slew the German and sought to ravish Marcita? And as I reviewed the crime, it appeared to me that murder rather than rape was the object of the attack.

Why did de Montour warn us, and then appear to have knowledge of the crime, telling us that Desmarte was innocent and then proving it?

It was all beyond me.

The tale of the slaughter got among the natives, in spite of all we could do, and they appeared restless and nervous. A brooding atmosphere pervaded the castle.

I considered going to Dom Vincente with Gola's tale, but decided to wait awhile.

The women kept their chambers that day, the men were restless and moody. Dom Vincente announced that the sentries would be doubled and some would patrol the corridors of the castle itself. I found myself musing cynically that if Gola's suspicions were true, sentries would be of little good.

I am not, Messieurs, a man to brook such a situation with patience. And I was young then. So as we drank before retiring, I flung my goblet on the table and angrily announced that in spite of man, beast or devil, I slept that night with doors flung wide. And I tramped angrily to my chamber.

Again, as on the first night, de Montour came. And his face was as a man who has looked into the gaping gates of hell.

'I have come,' he said, 'to ask you . . . nay, Monsieur, to implore you – to reconsider your rash determination.' I shook my head impatiently..

'You are resolved? Yes? Then I ask you do to this for me, that after I enter my chamber, you will bolt my doors from the outside.'

I did as he asked, and then made my way back to my chamber, my mind in a maze of wonderment. I had sent Gola to the slave quarters, and I laid rapier and dagger close at hand. Nor did I go to bed, but crouched in a great chair, in the darkness. Then I had much ado to keep from sleeping. To keep myself awake, I fell to musing on the strange words of de Montour. He seemed to be labouring under great excitement; his eyes hinted of ghastly mysteries known to him alone. And yet his face was not that of a wicked man.

Suddenly the notion took me to go to his chamber and talk with him.

Walking those dark passages was a shuddersome task, but eventually I stood before de Montour's door. I called softly. Silence. I reached out a hand and felt splintered fragments of wood. Hastily I struck flint and steel which I carried, and the flaming tinder showed the great oaken door sagging on its mighty hinges; showed a door smashed and splintered from the inside: And the chamber of de Montour was unoccupied.

Some instinct prompted me to hurry back to my room, swiftly but silently, shoeless feet treading softly. And as I neared the door, I was aware of something in the darkness before me. Something which crept in from a side corridor and glided stealthily along.

In a wild panic of fear I leaped, striking wildly and aimlessly in the darkness. All my clenched fist encountered a human head, and something went down with a crash. Again I struck a light; a man lay senseless on the floor, and he was de Montour.

I thrust a candle into a niche in the Wall, and just then de Montour's eyes opened and he rose uncertainly. 'You!' I exclaimed, hardly knowing what I said. 'You, of all men!'

He merely nodded.

'You killed von Schiller?'

'Yes.'

I recoiled with a gasp of horror.

'Listen.' He raised his hand. 'Take your rapier and run me through. No man will touch you.'

'No,' I exclaimed. 'I can not.'

'Then, quick,' he said hurriedly, 'get into your chamber and bolt the door. Haste! It will return!'

'What will return?' I asked, with a thrill of horror. 'If it will harm me, it will harm you. Come into the chamber with me.'

'No, no!' he fairly shrieked, springing back from my outstretched arm. 'Haste, haste! It left me for an instant, but it will return.' Then in a low-pitched voice of indescribable horror: 'It is returning. It is here now!'

And I felt a something, a formless, shapeless presence near. A thing of frightfulness.

De Montour was standing, legs braced, arms thrown back, fists clenched. The muscles bulged beneath his skin, his eyes widened and narrowed, the veins stood out upon his forehead as if in great physical effort. As I looked, to my horror, out of nothing, a shapeless, nameless something took vague form! Like a shadow it moved upon de Montour.

It was hovering about him! Good God, it was merging, becoming one with the man!

De Montour swayed; a great gasp escaped him. The dim thing vanished. De Montour wavered. Then he turned toward me, and may God grant that I never look on a face like that again!

It was a hideous, a bestial face. The eyes gleamed with a frightful ferocity; the snarling lips were drawn back from gleaming teeth, which to my startled gaze appeared more like bestial fangs than human teeth.

Silently the thing (I can not call it a human) slunk toward me. Gasping with horror I sprang back and through the door, just as the thing launched itself through the air, with a sinuous motion which even then made me think of a leaping wolf. I slammed the door, holding it against the frightful thing which hurled itself again and again against it.

Finally it desisted and I heard it slink stealthily off down the corridor. Faint and exhausted I sat down, waiting, listening. Through the open window wafted the breeze, bearing all the scents of Africa, the spicy and the foul. From the native village came the sound of a native drum. Other drums answered farther up the river and back in the bush. Then from somewhere in the jungle, horridly incongruous, sounded the long, high-pitched call of a timber wolf. My soul revolted.

Dawn brought a tale of terrified villagers, of a woman torn by some fiend of the night, barely escaping. And to de Montour I went.

On the way I met Dom Vincente. He was perplexed and angry.

'Some hellish thing is at work in this castle,' he said. 'Last night, though I have said naught of it to anyone, something leaped upon the back of one of the arquebusiers, tore the leather jerkin from his shoulders and pursued him to the barbican. More, someone locked de Montour into his room last night, and he was forced to smash the door to get out.'

He strode on, muttering to himself, and I proceeded down the stairs, more puzzled than ever.

De Montour sat upon a stool, gazing out the window. An indescribable air of weariness was about him.

His long hair was uncombed and tousled, his garments were tattered. With a shudder I saw faint crimson stains upon his hands, and noted that the nails were torn and broken.

He looked up as I came in, and waved me to a seat. His face was worn and haggard, but was that of a man.

After a moment's silence, he spoke.

'I will tell you my strange tale. Never before has it passed my lips, and why I tell you, knowing that you will not believe me, I can not say.'

And then I listened to what was surely the wildest, the most fantastic, the weirdest tale ever heard by man.

'Years ago,' said de Montour, 'I was upon a military mission in northern France. Alone, I was forced to pass through the fiend-haunted woodlands of Villefere. In those frightful forests I was beset by an inhuman, a ghastly thing – a werewolf. Beneath a midnight moon we fought, and I slew it. Now this is the truth: that if a werewolf is slain in the half-form of a man, its ghost will haunt its slayer through eternity. But if it is slain as a wolf, hell gapes to receive it. The true werewolf is not (as many think) a man who may take the form of a wolf, but a wolf who takes the form of a man!

'Now listen, my friend, and I will tell you of the wisdom, the hellish knowledge that is mine, gained through many a frightful deed, imparted to me amid the ghastly shadows of midnight forests where fiends and half-beasts roamed.

'In the beginning, the world was strange, misshapen. Grotesque beasts wandered through its jungles. Driven from another world, ancient demons and fiends came in great numbers and settled upon this newer, younger world. Long the forces of good and evil warred.

'A strange beast, known as man, wandered among the other beasts, and since good or bad must have a concrete form ere either accomplishes its desire, the spirits of good entered man. The fiends entered other beasts, reptiles and birds; and long and fiercely waged the age-old battle. But man conquered. The great dragons and serpents were slain and with them the demons. Finally, Solomon, wise beyond the ken of man, made great war upon them, and by virtue of his wisdom, slew, seized and bound. But there were some which were the fiercest, the boldest, and though Solomon drove them out he could not conquer them. Those had taken the form of wolves. As the ages passed, wolf and demon became merged. No longer could the fiend leave the body of the wolf at will. In many instances, the savagery of the wolf overcame the subtlety of the demon and enslaved him, so the wolf became again only a beast, a fierce, cunning beast, but merely a beast. But of the werewolves, there are many, even yet.

'And during the time of the full moon, the wolf may take the form, or the half-form, of a man. When the moon hovers at her zenith, however, the wolf-spirit again takes ascendancy and the werewolf becomes a true wolf once more. But if it is slain in the form of a man, then the spirit is free to haunt its slayer through the ages.

'Hearken now. I had thought to have slain the thing after it had changed to its true shape. But I slew it an instant too soon. The moon, though it approached the zenith, had not yet reached it, nor had the thing taken on fully the wolf-form.

'Of this I knew nothing and went my way. But when the next time approached for the full moon, I began to be aware of a strange, malicious influence. An atmosphere of horror hovered in the air and I was aware of inexplicable, uncanny impulses.

'One night in a small village in the centre of a great forest, the influence came upon me with full power. It was night, and the moon, nearly full, was rising over the forest. And between the moon and me, I saw, floating in the upper air, ghostly and barely discernible, the outline of a wolf's head!

'I remember little of what happened thereafter. I remember, dimly, clambering into the silent street, remember struggling, resisting briefly, vainly, and the rest is a crimson haze, until I came to myself the next morning and found my garments and hands caked and stained crimson; and heard the horrified chattering of the villagers, telling of a pair of clandestine lovers, slaughtered in a ghastly manner, scarcely outside the village, torn to pieces as if by wild beasts, as if by wolves.

'From that village I fled aghast, but I fled not alone. In the day I could not feel the drive of my fearful captor, but when night fell and the moon rose, I ranged the silent forest, a frightful thing, a slayer of humans, a fiend in a man's body.

'God, the battles I have fought! But always it overcame me and drove me ravening after some new victim. But after the moon had passed its fullness, the thing's power over me ceased suddenly. Nor did it return until three nights before the moon was full again.

'Since then I have roamed the world – fleeing, fleeing, seeking to escape. Always the thing follows, taking possession of my body when the moon is full. Gods, the frightful deeds I have done!

'I would have slain myself long ago, but I dare not. For the soul of a suicide is accursed, and my soul would be forever hunted through the flames of hell. And hearken, most frightful of all, my slain body would for ever roam the earth, moved and inhabited by the soul of the werewolf! Can any thought be more ghastly?

'And I seem immune to the weapons of man. Swords have pierced me, daggers have hacked me. I am covered with scars. Yet never have they struck me down. In Germany they bound and led me to the block. There would I have willingly placed my head, but the thing came upon me, and breaking my bonds, I slew and fled. Up and down the world I have wandered, leaving horror and slaughter in my trail. Chains, cells, cannot hold me. The thing is fastened to me through all eternity.

'In desperation I accepted Dom Vincente's invitation, for look you, none knows of my frightful double life, since no one could recognise me in the clutch of the demon; and few, seeing me, live to tell of it.

'My hands are red, my soul doomed to everlasting flames, my mind is torn with remorse for my crimes. And yet I can do nothing to help myself. Surely, Pierre, no man ever knew the hell that I have known.

'Yes, I slew von Schiller, and I sought to destroy the girl Marcita. Why I did not, I can not say, for I have slain both women and men.

'Now, if you will, take your sword and slay me, and with my last breath I will give you the good God's blessing. No?

'You know now my tale and you see before you a man, fiend-haunted for all eternity.'

My mind was spinning with wonderment as I left the room of de Montour. What to do, I knew not. It seemed likely that he would yet murder us all, and yet I could not bring myself to tell Dom Vincente all. From the bottom of my soul I pitied de Montour.

So I kept my peace, and in the days that followed I made occasion to seek him out and converse with him. A real friendship sprang up between us.

About this time that black devil, Gola, began to wear an air of suppressed excitement, as if he knew something he wished desperately to tell, but would not or else dared not.

So the days passed in feasting, drinking and hunting, until one night de Montour came to my chamber and pointed silently at the moon which was just rising.

'Look ye,' he said, 'I have a plan. I will give it out that I am going into the jungle for hunting and will go forth, apparently for several days. But at night I will return to the castle, and you must lock me into the dungeon which is used as a storeroom.'

This we did, and I managed to slip down twice a day and carry food and drink to my friend. He insisted on remaining in the dungeon even in the day, for though the fiend had never exerted its influence over him in the daytime, and he believed it powerless then, yet he would take no chances.

It was during this time that I began to notice that Dom Vincente's mink-faced cousin, Carlos, was forcing his attentions upon

Ysabel, who was his second cousin, and who seemed to resent those attentions.

Myself, I would have challenged him for a duel for the toss of a coin, for I despised him, but it was really none of my affair. However, it seemed that Ysabel feared him.

My friend Luigi, by the way, had become enamoured of the dainty Portuguese girl, and was making swift love to her daily.

And de Montour sat in his cell and reviewed his ghastly deeds until he battered the bars with his bare hands.

And Don Florenzo wandered about the castle grounds like a dour Mephistopheles.

And the other guests rode and quarrelled and drank.

And Gola slithered about, eyeing me as if always on the point of imparting momentous information. What wonder if my nerves became rasped to the shrieking point?

Each day the natives grew surlier and more and more sullen and intractable.

One night, not long before the full of the moon, I entered the dungeon where de Montour sat.

He looked up quickly.

'You dare much, coming to me in the night.'

I shrugged my shoulders, seating myself.

A small barred window let in the night scents and sounds of Africa.

'Hark to the native drums,' I said. 'For the past week they have sounded almost incessantly.'

De Montour assented.

'The natives are restless. Methinks 'tis deviltry they are planning. Have you noticed that Carlos is much among them?'

'No,' I answered, 'but 'tis like there will be a break between him and Luigi. Luigi is paying court to Ysabel.'

So we talked, when suddenly de Montour became silent and moody, answering only in monosyllables.

The moon rose and peered in at the barred windows. De Montour's face was illuminated by its beams.

And then the hand of horror grasped me. On the wall behind de Montour appeared a shadow, a shadow clearly defined of a wolf's head!

At the same instant de Montour felt its influence. With a shriek he bounded from his stool.

He pointed fiercely, and as with trembling hands I slammed and bolted the door behind me, I felt him hurl his weight against it.

As I fled up the stairway I heard a wild raving and battering at the iron-bound door. But with all the werewolf's might the great door held.

As I entered my room, Gola dashed in and gasped out the tale he had been keeping for days.

I listened, incredulously, and then dashed forth to find Dom Vincente.

I was told that Carlos had asked him to accompany him to the village to arrange a sale of slaves.

My informer was Don Florenzo of Seville, and when I gave him a brief outline of Gola's tale, he accompanied me.

Together we dashed through the castle gate, flinging a word to the guards, and down the landing toward the village.

Dom Vincente, Dom Vincente, walk with care, keep sword loosened in its sheath! Fool, fool, to walk in the night with Carlos, the traitor!

They were nearing the village when we caught up with them. 'Dom Vincente!' I exclaimed; 'return instantly to the castle. Carlos is selling you into the hands of the natives! Gola has told me that he lusts for your wealth and for Ysabel! A terrified native babbled to him of booted footprints near the places where the woodcutters were murdered, and Carlos has made the blacks believe that the slayer was you! Tonight the natives were to rise and slay every man in the castle except Carlos! Do you not believe me, Dom Vincente?'

'Is this the truth, Carlos?' asked Dom Vincente, in amaze.

Carlos laughed mockingly. 'The fool speaks truth,' he said, 'but it accomplishes you nothing. Ho!'

He shouted as he leaped for Dom Vincente. Steel flashed in the moonlight and the Spaniard's sword was through Carlos ere he could move.

And the shadows rose about us. Then it was back to back, sword and dagger, three men against a hundred. Spears flashed, and a fiendish yell went up from savage throats. I spitted three natives in as many thrusts and then went down from a stunning swing from a war-club, and an instant later Dom Vincente fell upon me, with a spear in one arm and another through the leg. Don Florenzo was standing above us, sword leaping like a live thing, when a charge of the arquebusiers swept the river bank clear and we were borne into the castle.

The hordes came with a rush, spears flashing like a wave of steel, a thunderous roar of savagery going up to the skies.

Time and again they swept up the slopes bounding the moat, until they were swarming over the palisades. And time and again the fire of the hundred-odd defenders hurled them back.

They had set fire to the plundered warehouses, and their light vied with the light of the moon. Just across the river there was a larger storehouse, and about this hordes of the natives gathered, tearing it apart for plunder.

'Would that they would drop a torch upon it,' said Dom Vincente, 'for naught is stored therein save some thousand pounds of gun-powder. I dared not store the treacherous stuff this side of the river. All the tribes of the river and coast have gathered for our slaughter and all my ships are upon the seas. We may hold out awhile, but eventually they will swarm the palisade and put us to the slaughter.'

I hastened to the dungeon wherein de Montour sat. Outside the door I called to him and he bade me enter in voice which told me the fiend had left him for an instant.

'How goes the battle?'

I gave him the details of the betrayal and the fight, and mentioned the powder-house across the river. He sprang to his feet.

'Now by my hag-ridden soul!' he exclaimed. 'I will fling the dice once more with hell! Swift, let me out of the castle! I will essay to swim the river and set off yon powder!'

'It is insanity!' I exclaimed. 'A thousand lurk between the palis-ades and the river, and thrice that number beyond! The river itself swarms with crocodiles!'

'I will attempt it!' he answered, a great light in his face. 'If I can reach it, some thousand natives will lighten the siege; if I am slain, then my soul is free and mayhap will gain some forgiveness for that I gave my life to atone for my crimes.'

Then, 'Haste,' he exclaimed, 'for the demon is returning! Already I feel his influence! Haste ye!'

For the castle gates we sped, and as de Montour ran he gasped as a man in a terrific battle.

At the gate he pitched headlong, then rose, to spring through it. Wild yells greeted him from the natives.

The arquebusiers shouted curses at him and at me. Peering down from the top of the palisades I saw him turn from side to side uncert-ainly. A score of natives were rushing recklessly forward, spears raised.

Then the eerie wolf-yell rose to the skies, and de Montour bounded forward. Aghast, the natives paused, and before a man of them could move he was among them. Wild shrieks, not of rage, but of terror.

In amazement the arquebusiers held their fire.

Straight through the group de Montour charged, and when they broke and fled, three of them fled not.

A dozen steps de Montour took in pursuit; then stopped stock-still. A moment he stood so while spears flew about him, then turned and ran swiftly in the direction of the river.

A few steps from the river another band barred his way. In the fading light of the burning houses the scene was clearly illuminated. A thrown spear tore through de Montour's shoulder. Without pausing in his stride he tore it forth and drove it through a native, leaping over his body to get among the others. They could not face the fiend-driven white man. With shrieks they fled, and de Montour, bounding upon the back of one, brought him down.

Then he rose, staggered and sprang to the river bank. An instant he paused there and then vanished in the shadows.

'Name of the devil!' gasped Dom Vincente at my shoulder. 'What manner of man is that? Was that de Montour?'

I nodded. The wild yells of the natives rose above the crackle of the arquebus fire. They were massed thick about the great warehouse across the river.

'They plan a great rush,' said Dom Vincente. 'They will swarm clear over the palisade, methinks. Ha!'

A crash that seemed to rip the skies apart! A burst of flame that mounted to the stars! The castle rocked with the explosion. Then silence, as the smoke, drifting away, showed only a great crater where the warehouse had stood.

I could tell of how Dom Vincente led a charge, crippled as he was, out of the castle gate and, down the slope, to fall upon the terrified blacks who had escaped the explosion. I could tell of the slaughter, of the victory and the pursuit of the fleeing natives.

I could tell, too, Messieurs, of how I became separated from the band and of how I wandered far into the jungle, unable to find my way back to the coast.

I could tell how I was captured by a wandering band of slave raiders, and of how I escaped. But such is not my intention. In itself it would make a long tale; and it is of de Montour that I am speaking.

I thought much of the things that had passed and wondered if indeed de Montour reached the storehouse to blow it to the skies or whether it was but the deed of chance.

That a man could swim that reptile-swarming river, fiend-driven though he was, seemed impossible. And if he blew up the storehouse, he must have gone up with it.

So one night I pushed my way wearily through the jungle and sighted the coast, and close to the shore a small, tumbledown hut of thatch. To it I went, thinking to sleep therein if insects and reptiles would allow.

I entered the doorway and then stopped short. Upon a makeshift stool sat a man. He looked up as I entered and the rays of the moon fell across his face.

I started back with a ghastly thrill of horror. It was de Montour, and the moon was full!

Then as I stood, unable to flee, he rose and came toward me. And his face, though haggard as of a man who has looked into hell, was the face of a sane man.

'Come in, my friend,' he said, and there was a great peace in his voice. 'Come in and fear me not. The fiend has left me forever.'

'But tell me, how conquered you?' I exclaimed as I grasped his hand.

'I fought a frightful battle, as I ran to the river,' he answered, 'for the fiend had me in its grasp and drove me to fall upon the natives. But for the first time my soul and mind gained ascendancy for an instant, an instant just long enough to hold me to my purpose. And I believe the good saints came to my aid, for I was giving my life to save life.

'I leaped into the river and swam, and in an instant the crocodiles were swarming about me. Again in the clutch of the fiend I fought them, there in the river. Then suddenly the thing left me. I climbed from the river and fired the warehouse. The explosion hurled me hundreds of feet, and for days I wandered witless through the jungle. But the full moon came, and came again, and I felt not the influence of the fiend. I am free, free!' And a wondrous note of exultation, nay, exaltation, thrilled his words.

'My soul is free. Incredible as it seems, the demon lies drowned upon the bed of the river, or else inhabits the body of one of the savage reptiles that swim the ways of the Niger.'

The Dream Snake

The night was strangely still. As we sat upon the wide veranda, gazing out over the broad, shadowy lawns, the silence of the hour entered our spirits and for a long while no one spoke.

Then far across the dim mountains that fringed the eastern sky-line, a faint haze began to glow, and presently a great golden moon came up, making a ghostly radiance over the land and etching boldly the dark clumps of shadows that were trees. A light breeze came whispering out of the east, and the unmowed grass swayed before it in long, sinuous waves, dimly visible in the moonlight; and from among the group upon the veranda there came a swift gasp, a sharp intake of breath that caused us all to turn and gaze.

Faming was leaning forward, clutching the arms of his chair, his face strange and pallid in the spectral light; a thin trickle of blood seeping from the lip in which he had set his teeth. Amazed, we looked at him, and suddenly he jerked about with a short, snarling laugh.

'There's no need of gawking at me like a flock of sheep!' he said irritably and stopped short. We sat bewildered, scarcely knowing what sort of reply to make, and suddenly he burst out again.

'Now I guess I'd better tell the whole thing or you'll be going off and putting me down as a lunatic. Don't interrupt me, any of you! I want to get this thing off my mind. You all know that I'm not a very imaginative man; but there's a thing, purely a figment of imagin-ation, that has haunted me since babyhood. A dream!' He fairly cringed back in his chair as he muttered, 'A dream! And God, what a dream! The first time . . . no, I can't remember the first time I ever dreamed it . . . I've been dreaming the hellish thing ever since I can remember. Now it's this way: there is a sort of bungalow, set upon a hill in the midst of wide grasslands – not unlike this estate; but this scene is in Africa. And I am living there with a sort of servant, a Hindu. Just why I am there is never clear to my waking mind, though I am always aware of the reason in my dreams. As a man of a dream,

I remember my past life (a life which in no way corresponds with my waking life), but when I am awake my subconscious mind fails to transmit these impressions. However, I think that I am a fugitive from justice and the Hindu is also a fugitive. How the bungalow came to be there I can never remember, nor do I know in what part of Africa it is, though all these things are known to my dream self. But the bungalow is a small one of a very few rooms, and is situated upon the top of the hill, as I said. There are no other hills about and the grasslands stretch to the horizon in every direction; knee-high in some places, waist-high in others.

'Now the dream always opens as I am coming up the hill, just as the sun is beginning to set. I am carrying a broken rifle and I have been on a hunting trip; how the rifle was broken, and the full details of the trip, I clearly remember . . . dreaming. But never upon waking. It is just as if a curtain were suddenly raised and a drama began; or just as if I were suddenly transferred to another man's body and life, remembering past years of that life, and not cognisant of any other existence. And that is the hellish part of it! As you know, most of us, dreaming, are, at the back of our consciousness, aware that we are dreaming. No matter how horrible the dream may become, we know that it is a dream, and thus insanity or possible death is staved off. But in this particular dream, there is no such knowledge. I tell you it is so vivid, so complete in every detail, that I wonder sometimes if that is not my real existence and this a dream! But no; for then I should have been dead years ago.

'As I was saying, I come up the hill and the first thing I am cognisant of that it is out of the ordinary is a sort of track leading up the hill in an irregular way; that is, the grass is mashed down as if something heavy had been dragged over it. But I pay no especial attention to it, for I am thinking, with some irritation, that the broken rifle I carry is my only arm and that now I must forgo hunting until I can send for another.

'You see, I remember thoughts and impressions of the dream itself, of the occurrences of the dream; it is the memories that the dream "I" had, of that other dream existence that I can not remember. So. I come up the hill and enter the bungalow. The doors are open and the Hindu is not there. But the main room is in confusion; chairs are broken, a table is overturned. The Hindu's dagger is lying upon the floor, but there is no blood anywhere.

'Now, in my dreams, I never remember the other dreams, as sometimes one does. Always it is the first dream, the first time. I always experience the same sensations, in my dreams, with as vivid a force as the first time I ever dreamed. So. I am not able to understand this. The Hindu is gone, but (thus I ruminate, standing in the centre of the disordered room) what did away with him? Had it been a raiding party they would have looted the bungalow and probably burned it. Had it been a lion, the place would have been smeared with blood. Then suddenly I remember the track I saw going up the hill, and a cold hand touches my spine; for instantly the whole thing is clear: the thing that came up from the grasslands and wrought havoc in the little bungalow could be naught else except a giant serpent. And as I think or the size of the spoor, cold sweat beads my forehead and the broken rifle shakes in my hand.

'Then I rush to the door in a wild panic, my only thought to make a dash for the coast. But the sun has set and dusk is stealing across the grasslands. And out there somewhere, lurking in the tall grass is that grisly thing . . . that horror. God!' The ejaculation broke from his lips with such feeling that all of us started, not realising the tension we had reached. There was a second's silence, then he continued.

'So I bolt the doors and windows, light the lamp I have and take my stand in the middle of the room. And I stand like a statue . . . waiting . . . listening. After a while the moon comes up and her haggard light drifts though the windows. And I stand still in the centre of the room; the night is very still . . . something like this night; the breeze occasionally whispers through the grass, and each time I start and clench my hands until the nails bite into the flesh and the blood trickles down my wrists . . . and I stand there and wait and listen but it does not come that night!' The sentence came suddenly and explosively, and an involuntary sigh came from the rest; a relaxing of tension.

'I am determined, if I live the night through, to start for the coast early the next morning, taking my chance out there in the grim grasslands with it. But with morning, I dare not. I do not know in which direction the monster went; and I dare not risk coming upon him in the open, unarmed as I am. So, as in a maze, I remain at the bungalow, and ever my eyes turn toward the sun, lurching relentless down the sky toward the horizon. Ah, God! if I could but halt the sun in the sky!'

The man was in the clutch of some terrific power; his words fairly leaped at us.

'Then the sun rides down the sky and the long grey shadows come stalking across the grasslands. Dizzy with fear, I have bolted the doors and windows and lighted the lamp long before the last faint glow of twilight fades. The light from the windows may attract the monster, but I dare not stay in the dark. And again I take my stand in the centre of the room . . . waiting.'

There was a shuddersome halt. Then he continued, barely above a whisper, moistening his lips: 'There is no knowing how long I stand there. Time has ceased to be and each second is an aeon; each minute is an eternity, stretching into endless eternities. Then, God! but what is that?' He leaned forward, the moonlight etching his face into such a mask of horrified listening that each of us shivered and flung a hasty glance over our shoulders.

'Not the night breeze this time,' he whispered. 'Something makes the grasses swish-swish . . . as if a great, long, pliant weight were being dragged through them. Above the bungalow it swishes and then ceases in front of the door; then the hinges creak . . . creak! The door begins to bulge inward . . . a small bit . . . then some more!' The man's arms were held in front of him, as if braced strongly against something, and his breath came in quick gasps. 'And I know I should lean against the door and hold it shut, but I do not, I cannot move. I stand there, like a sheep waiting to be slaughtered . . . but the door holds!' Again that sigh expressive of pent-up feeling.

He drew a shaky hand across his brow. 'And all night I stand in the centre of that room, as motionless as an image, except to turn slowly, as the swish-swish of the grass marks the fiend's course about the house. Ever I keep my eyes in the direction of the soft, sinister sound. Sometimes it ceases for an instant, or for several minutes, and then I stand scarcely breathing, for a horrible obsession has it that the serpent has in some way made entrance into the bungalow, and I start and whirl this way and that, frightfully fearful of making a noise, though I know not why, but ever with the feeling that the thing is at my back. Then the sounds commence again and I freeze motionless.

'Now here is the only time that my consciousness, which guides my waking hours, ever in any way pierces the veil of dreams. I am, in the dream, in no way conscious that it is a dream, but, in a detached sort of way, my other mind recognises certain facts and passes them on to my sleeping . . . shall I say "ego"? That is to say, my personality is for an instant truly dual and separate to an extent, as the right and left arms are separate, while making up parts in the same entity. My dreaming mind has no cognisance of my higher mind; for the time being the other mind is subordinated and the subconscious mind is in full control, to such an extent that it does not even recognise the existence of the other. But the conscious mind, now sleeping, is cognisant of dim thought-waves emanating from the dream mind. I know that I have not made this entirely clear, but the fact remains that I know that my mind, conscious and subconscious, is near to ruin. My obsession of fear, as I stand there in my dream, is that the serpent will raise itself and peer into the window at me. And I know, in my dream, that if this occurs I shall go insane. And so vivid is the impression imparted to my conscious, now sleeping mind that the thought-waves stir the dim seas of sleep, and somehow I can feel my sanity rocking as my sanity rocks in my dream. Back and forth it totters and sways until the motion takes on a physical aspect and I in my dream am swaying from side to side. Not always is the sensation the same, but I tell you, if that horror ever raises its terrible shape and leers at me, if I ever see the fearful thing in my dream, I shall become stark, wild insane.' There was a restless movement among the rest.

'God! but what a prospect!' he muttered. 'To be insane and forever dreaming that same dream, night and day! But there I stand, and centuries go by, but at last a dim grey light begins to steal through the windows, the swishing dies away in the distance and presently a red, haggard sun climbs the eastern sky. Then I turn about and gaze into a mirror . . . and my hair has become perfectly white. I stagger to the door and fling it wide. There is nothing in sight but a wide track leading away down the hill through the grasslands . . . in the opposite direction from that which I would take toward the coast. And with a shriek of maniacal laughter, I dash down the hill and race across the grasslands. I race until I drop from exhaustion, then I lie until I can stagger up and go on.

'All day I keep this up, with superhuman effort, spurred on by the horror behind me. And ever as I hurl myself forward on weakening legs, ever as I lie gasping for breath, I watch the sun with a terrible eagerness. How swiftly the sun travels when a man races it for life! A losing race it is, as I know when I watch the sun sinking toward the skyline, and the hills which I had to gain ere sundown seemingly as far away as ever.'

His voice was lowered and instinctively we leaned toward him; he was gripping the chair arms and the blood was seeping from his lip.

'Then the sun sets and the shadows come and I stagger on and fall and rise and reel on again. And I laugh, laugh, laugh! Then I cease, for the moon comes up and throws the grasslands in ghostly and silvery relief. The light is white across the land, though the moon itself is like blood. And I look back the way I have come . . . and far back . . . ' All of us leaned farther toward him, our hair a-prickle; his voice came like a ghostly whisper . . . 'far back . . . I . . . see . . . the . . . grass . . . waving. There is no breeze, but the tall grass parts and sways in the moonlight, in a narrow, sinuous line . . . far away, but nearing every instant.' His voice died away.

Somebody broke the ensuing stillness: 'And then . . . ?'

'Then I awake. Never yet have I seen the foul monster. But that is the dream that haunts me, and from which I have wakened, in my childhood screaming, in my manhood in cold sweat. At irregular intervals I dream it, and each time, lately' . . . he hesitated and then went on . . . 'each time lately, the thing has been getting closer . . . closer . . . the waving of the grass marks his progress and he nears me with each dream; and when he reaches me, then . . . '

He stopped short, then without a word rose abruptly and entered the house. The rest of us sat silent for awhile, then followed him, for it was late.

How long I slept I do not know, but I woke suddenly with the impression that somewhere in the house someone had laughed long, loud and hideously, as a maniac laughs. Starting up, wondering if I had been dreaming, I rushed from my room, just as a truly horrible shriek echoed through the house. The place was now alive with other people who had been awakened, and all of us rushed to Famings's room, whence the sounds had seemed to come.

Faming lay dead upon the floor, where it seemed he had fallen in some terrific struggle. There was no mark upon him, but his face was terribly distorted; as the face of a man who had been crushed by some superhuman force . . . such as some gigantic snake.

The Hyena

From the time when I first saw Senecoza, the fetish-man, I distrusted him, and from vague distrust the idea eventually grew into hatred.

I was but newly come to the East Coast, new to African ways, somewhat inclined to follow my impulses, and possessed of a large amount of curiosity.

Because I came from Virginia, race instinct and prejudice were strong in me, and doubtless the feeling of inferiority which Senecoza constantly inspired in me had a great deal to do with my antipathy for him.

He was surprisingly tall, and leanly built. Six inches above six feet he stood, and so muscular was his spare frame that he weighed a good two hundred pounds. His weight seemed incredible when one looked at his lanky build, but he was all muscle . . . a lean giant. His features more resembled Berber than Bantu, with the high, bulging forehead, thin nose and thin, straight lips. But his hair was as kinky as a Bushman's and his colour was blacker even than the Masai. In fact, his glossy hide had a different hue from those of the native tribesmen, and I believe that he was of a different tribe.

It was seldom that we of the ranch saw him. Then without warning he would be among us, or we would see him striding through the shoulder-high grass of the veldt, sometimes alone, sometimes followed at a respectful distance by several of the wilder Masai, who bunched up at a distance from the buildings, grasping their spears nervously and eyeing everyone suspiciously. He would make his greetings with a courtly grace; his manner was deferentially courteous, but somehow it 'rubbed me the wrong way', so to speak. He would stand before us, a naked bronze giant; make trade for a few simple articles, such as a copper kettle, beads or a trade musket; repeat words of some chief, and take his departure.

I did not like him. And being young and impetuous, I spoke my opinion to Ludtvik Strolvaus, a very distant relative, tenth cousin or suchlike, on whose trading-post ranch I was staying.

But Ludtvik chuckled in his blond beard and said that the fetish-man was all right.

'A power he is among the natives, true. They all fear him. But a friend he is to the whites. *Ja*.'

Ludtvik was long a resident on the East Coast; he knew natives and he knew the fat Australian cattle he raised, but he had little imagination.

The ranch buildings were in the midst of a stockade, on a kind of slope, overlooking countless miles on miles of the finest grazing land in Africa. The stockade was large, well suited for defence. Most of the thousand cattle could be driven inside in case of an uprising of the Masai. Ludtvik was inordinately proud of his cattle.

'One thousand now,' he would tell me, his round face beaming, 'one thousand now. But later, ah! Ten thousand and another ten thousand. This is a good beginning, but only a beginning. *Ja*.'

I must confess that I got little thrill out of the cattle. Natives herded and corralled them; all Ludtvik and I had to do was to ride about and give orders. That was the work he liked best, and I left it mostly to him.

My chief sport was in riding away across the veldt, alone or attended by a gun-bearer, with a rifle. Not that I ever bagged much game. In the first place I was an execrable marksman; I could hardly have hit an elephant at close range. In the second place, it seemed to me a shame to shoot so many things. A bush-antelope would bound up in front of me and race away, and I would sit watching him, admiring the slim, lithe figure, thrilled with the graceful beauty of the creature, my rifle lying idle across my saddle horn.

The native boy who served as my gun-bearer began to suspect that I was deliberately refraining from shooting, and he began in a covert way to throw sneering hints about my womanishness. I was young and valued even the opinion of a native; which is very foolish. His remarks stung my pride, and one day I hauled him off his horse and pounded him until he yelled for mercy. Thereafter my doings were not questioned.

But still I felt inferior when in the presence of the fetish-man. I could not get the other natives to talk about him. All I could get out of them was a gesticulation indicative of fear, and vague information that the fetish-man dwelt among the tribes some distance in the interior. General opinion seemed to be that Senecoza was a good man to let alone.

One incident made the mystery about the fetish-man take on, it seemed, a rather sinister form.

In the mysterious way that news travels in Africa, and which white men so seldom hear of, we learned that Senecoza and a minor chief had had a falling out of some kind. It was vague and seemed to have no especial basis of fact. But shortly afterward that chief was found half-devoured by hyenas. That, in itself, was not unusual, but the fright with which the natives heard the news was. The chief was nothing to them; in fact he was something of a villain, but his killing seemed to inspire them with a fright that was little short of homicidal. The next time Senecoza called, they rose and fled en masse and did not return until he had taken his departure.

Between the fear of the blacks, the tearing to pieces of the chief by the hyenas, and the fetish-man, I seemed to sense vaguely a connection of some kind. But I could not grasp the intangible thought.

Not long thereafter, that thought was intensified by another incident. I had ridden far out on the veldt, accompanied by my servant. As we paused to rest our horses close to a kopje, I saw, upon the top, a hyena eying us. Rather surprised, for the beasts are not in the habit of thus boldly approaching man in the daytime, I raised my rifle and was taking a steady aim, for I always hated the things, when my servant caught my arm.

'No shoot, *bwana*! No shoot!' he exclaimed hastily, jabbering a great deal in his own language, with which I was not familiar.

'What's up?' I asked impatiently.

He kept on jabbering and pulling my arm, until I gathered that the hyena was a fetish-beast of some kind.

'Oh, all right,' I conceded, lowering my rifle just as the hyena turned and sauntered out of sight.

Something about the lank, repulsive beast and his shambling yet gracefully lithe walk struck my sense of humour with a ludicrous comparison.

Laughing, I pointed toward the beast and said, 'That fellow looks like a hyena-imitation of Senecoza, the fetish-man.' My simple statement seemed to throw the native into a more abject fear than ever.

He turned his pony and dashed off in the general direction of the ranch, looking back at me with a scared face.

I followed, annoyed. And as I rode I pondered. Hyenas, a fetish-man, a chief torn to pieces, a countryside of natives in fear; what was the connection? I puzzled and puzzled, but I was new to Africa; I was young and impatient, and presently with a shrug of annoyance I discarded the whole problem.

The next time Senecoza came to the ranch, he managed to stop directly in front of me. For a fleeting instant his glittering eyes looked into mine. And in spite of myself, I shuddered and stepped back, involuntarily, feeling much as a man feels who looks unaware into the eyes of a serpent. There was nothing tangible, nothing on which I could base a quarrel, but there was a distinct threat. Before my Nordic pugnacity could reassert itself, he was gone. I said nothing. But I knew that Senecoza hated me for some reason and that he plotted my killing. Why, I did not know.

As for me, my distrust grew into bewildered rage, which in turn became hate.

And then Ellen Farel came to the ranch. Why she should choose a trading-ranch in East Africa for a place to rest from the society life of New York, I do not know. Africa is no place for a woman. That is what Ludtvik, also a cousin of hers, told her, but he was overjoyed to see her. As for me, girls never interested me much; usually I felt like a fool in their presence and was glad to be out. But there were few whites in the vicinity and I tired of the company of Ludtvik.

Ellen was standing on the wide veranda when I first saw her, a slim, pretty young thing, with rosy cheeks and hair like gold and large grey eyes. She was surprisingly winsome in her costume of riding-breeches, puttees, jacket and light helmet.

I felt extremely awkward, dusty and stupid as I sat on my wiry African pony and stared at her.

She saw a stocky youth of medium height, with sandy hair, eyes in which a kind of grey predominated; an ordinary, unhandsome youth, clad in dusty riding-clothes and a cartridge belt on one side of which was slung an ancient Colt of big calibre, and on the other a long, wicked hunting-knife.

I dismounted, and she came forward, hand outstretched.

'I'm Ellen,' she said, 'and I know you're Steve. Cousin Ludtvik has been telling me about you.'

I shook hands, surprised at the thrill the mere touch of her hand gave me.

She was enthusiastic about the ranch. She was enthusiastic about everything. Seldom have I seen anyone who had more vigour and vim, more enjoyment of everything done. She fairly scintillated with mirth and gaiety.

Ludtvik gave her the best horse on the place, and we rode much about the ranch and over the veldt.

She couldn't understand why she should treat the black people as dust beneath her feet. We had long arguments about it. I could not convince her, so I told her bluntly that she didn't know anything about it and she must do as I told her.

She pouted her pretty lips and called me a tyrant, and then was off over the veldt like an antelope, laughing at me over her shoulder, her hair blowing free in the breeze.

Tyrant! I was her slave from the first. Somehow the idea of becoming a lover never enter my mind. It was not the fact that she was several years older than I, or that she had a sweetheart (several of them, I think) back in New York. Simply, I worshipped her; her presence intoxicated me, and I could think of no more enjoyable existence than serving her as a devoted slave.

I was mending a saddle one day when she came running in.

'Oh, Steve!' she called; 'there's the most romantic-looking savage! Come quick and tell me what his name is.'

She led me out of the veranda.

'There he is,' she said, naively pointing. Arms folded, haughty head thrown back, stood Senecoza.

Ludtvik who was talking to him, paid no attention to the girl until he had completed his business with the fetish-man; and then, turning, he took her arm and they went into the house together.

Again I was face to face with the savage; but this time he was not looking at me. With a rage amounting almost to madness, I saw that he was gazing after the girl. There was an expression in his serpent-like eyes . . .

On the instant my gun was out and levelled. My hand shook like a leaf with the intensity of my fury. Surely I must shoot Senecoza down like the snake he was, shoot him down and riddle him, shoot him into a shredded heap!

The fleeting expression left his eyes and they were fixed on me. Detached they seemed, inhuman in their sardonic calm. And I could not pull the trigger.

For a moment we stood, and then he turned and strode away, a magnificent figure, while I glared after him and snarled with helpless fury.

I sat down on the veranda. What a man of mystery was that savage! What strange power did he possess? Was I right, I wondered, in interpreting the fleeting expression as he gazed after the girl? It seemed to me, in my youth and folly, incredible that a black man, no matter what his rank, should look at a white woman as he did. Most astonishing of all, why could I not shoot him down?

I started as a hand touched my arm.

'What are thinking about, Steve?' asked Ellen, laughing. Then before I could say anything, 'Wasn't that chief, or whatever he was, a fine specimen of a savage? He invited us to come to his kraal; is that what you call it? It's away off in the veldt somewhere, and we're going.'

'No!' I exclaimed violently, springing up.

'Why Steve,' she gasped recoiling, 'how rude! He's a perfect gentleman, isn't he, Cousin Ludtvik?'

'*Ja*,' nodded Ludtvik, placidly, 'we go to his kraal sometime soon, maybe. A strong chief, that savage. His chief has perhaps good trade.'

'No!' I repeated furiously. '*I'll* go if somebody has to! Ellen's not going near that beast!'

'Well, that's nice!' remarked Ellen, somewhat indignantly. 'I guess you're my boss, mister man?'

With all her sweetness, she had a mind of her own. In spite of all I could do, they arranged to go to the fetish-man's village the next day.

That night the girl came out to me, where I sat on the veranda in the moonlight, and she sat down on the arm of my chair.

'You're not angry at me, are you, Steve?' she said, wistfully, putting her arm around my shoulders. 'Not mad, are you?'

Mad? Yes, maddened by the touch of her soft body – such mad devotion as a slave feels. I wanted to grovel in the dust at her feet and kiss her dainty shoes. Will women never learn the effect they have on men?

I took her hand hesitantly and pressed it to my lips. I think she must have sensed some of my devotion.

'Dear Steve,' she murmured, and the words were like a caress, 'come, let's walk in the moonlight.'

We walked outside the stockade. I should have known better, for I had no weapon but the big Turkish dagger I carried and used for a hunting-knife, but she wished to.

'Tell me about this Senecoza,' she asked, and I welcomed the opportunity. And then I thought: what could I tell her? That hyenas had eaten a small chief of the Masai? That the natives feared the fetish-man? That he had looked at her?

And then the girl screamed as out of the tall grass leaped a vague shape, half-seen in the moonlight.

I felt a heavy, hairy form crash against my shoulders; keen fangs ripped my upflung arm. I went to the earth, fighting with frenzied horror. My jacket was slit to ribbons and the fangs were at my throat before I found and drew my knife and stabbed, blindly and savagely. I felt my blade rip into my foe, and then, like a shadow, it was gone. I staggered to my feet, somewhat shaken. The girl caught and steadied me.

'What was it?' she gasped, leading me toward the stockade.

'A hyena,' I answered. 'I could tell by the scent. But I never heard of one attacking like that.'

She shuddered. Later on, after my torn arm had been bandaged, she came close to me and said in a wondrously subdued voice, 'Steve, I've decided not to go to the village, if you don't want me to.'

After the wounds on my arm had become scars Ellen and I resumed our rides, as might be expected. One day we had wandered rather far out on the veldt, and she challenged me to a race. Her horse easily distanced mine, and she stopped and waited for me, laughing.

She had stopped on a sort of kopje, and she pointed to a clump of trees some distance away.

'Trees!' she said gleefully. 'Let's ride down there. There are so few trees on the veldt.'

And she dashed away. I followed some instinctive caution, loosening my pistol in its holster, and, drawing my knife, I thrust it down in my boot so that it was entirely concealed.

We were perhaps halfway to the trees when from the tall grass about us leaped Senecoza and some twenty warriors.

One seized the girl's bridle and the others rushed me. The one who caught at Ellen went down with a bullet between his eyes, and another crumpled at my second shot. Then a thrown war-club hurled me from the saddle, half-senseless, and as the blacks closed in on me I saw Ellen's horse, driven frantic by the prick of a carelessly handled spear, scream and rear, scattering the blacks who held her, and dash away at headlong speed, the bit in her teeth.

I saw Senecoza leap on my horse and give chase, flinging a savage command over his shoulder; and both vanished over the kopje.

The warriors bound me hand and foot and carried me into the trees. A hut stood among them – a native hut of thatch and bark. Somehow the sight of it set me shuddering. It seemed to lurk, repellent and indescribably malevolent amongst the trees; to hint of horrid and obscene rites; of voodoo.

I know not why it is, but the sight of a native hut, alone and hidden, far from a village or tribe, always has to me a suggestion of nameless horror.

In front of the hut they threw me down.

'When Senecoza returns with the girl,' said they, 'you will enter.' And they laughed like fiends. Then, leaving one to see that I did not escape, they left.

The black who remained kicked me viciously; he was armed with a trade-musket.

'They go to kill, fool!' he mocked me. 'They go to the ranches and trading-posts, first to that fool of an Englishman.' Meaning Smith, the owner of a neighbouring ranch.

And he went on giving details. Senecoza had made the plot, he boasted. They would chase all the white men to the coast.

'Senecoza is more than a man,' he boasted. 'You shall see, white man,' lowering his voice and glancing about him, from beneath his low, beetling brows; 'you shall see the magic of Senecoza.'

And meantime Ellen was riding like mad, gaining on the fetish-man, but unable to ride toward the ranch, for he had gotten between and was forcing her steadily out upon the veldt.

The black unfastened my bonds. His line of reasoning was easy to see; absurdly easy. He could not kill a prisoner of the fetish-man, but he could kill him to prevent his escape. And he was maddened with the blood-lust. Stepping back, he half-raised his trade-musket, watching me as a snake watches a rabbit.

It must have been about that time, as she afterward told me, that Ellen's horse stumbled and threw her. Before she could rise, the black had leaped from his horse and seized her in his arms. She screamed and fought, but he gripped her, held her helpless and laughed at her. Tearing her jacket to pieces, he bound her arms and legs, remounted and started back, carrying the half-fainting girl in front of him.

Back in front of the hut I rose slowly. I rubbed my arms where the ropes had been, moved a little closer, stretched, stooped and rubbed my legs; then with a catlike bound I was on him, my knife flashing from my boot. The trade-musket crashed and the charge whizzed above my head as I knocked up the barrel and closed with him. Hand to hand, I would have been no match for the giant; but I had the knife. Clinched close together we were too close for him to use the trade-musket for a club. He wasted time trying to do that, and with a desperate effort I threw him off his balance and drove the dagger to the hilt in his chest.

I wrenched it out again; I had no other weapon, for I could find no more ammunition for the trade-musket.

I had no idea which way Ellen had fled. I assumed she had gone toward the ranch, and in that direction I took my way. Smith must be warned. The warriors were far ahead of me. Even then they might be creeping up about the unsuspecting ranch.

I had not covered a fourth of the distance, when a drumming of hoofs behind me caused me to turn my head. Ellen's horse was thundering toward me, riderless. I caught her as she raced past me, and managed to stop her. The story was plain. The girl had either reached a place of safety and had turned the horse loose, or what was much more likely, had been captured, the horse escaping and fleeing toward the ranch, as a horse will do. I gripped the saddle, torn with indecision. Finally I leaped on the horse and sent her flying toward Smith's ranch. It was not many miles; Smith must not be massacred by those devils, and I must find a gun if I escaped to rescue the girl from Senecoza.

A half-mile from Smith's I overtook the raiders and went through them like drifting smoke. The workers at Smith's place were startled by a wild-riding horseman charging headlong into the stockade, shouting, 'Masai! Masai! A raid, you fools!' snatching a gun and flying out again.

So when the savages arrived they found everybody ready for them, and they got such a warm reception that after one attempt they turned tail and fled back across the veldt.

And I was riding as I never rode before. The mare was almost exhausted, but I pushed her mercilessly. On, on!

I aimed for the only place I knew likely. The hut among the trees. I assumed that the fetish-man would return there.

And long before the hut came into sight, a horseman dashed from the grass, going at right angles to my course, and our horses, colliding, sent both tired animals to the ground.

'Steve!' It was a cry of joy mingled with fear. Ellen lay, tied hand and foot, gazing up at me wildly as I regained my feet.

Senecoza came with a rush, his long knife flashing in the sunlight. Back and forth we fought – slash, ward and parry, my ferocity and agility matching his savagery and skill.

A terrific lunge which he aimed at me, I caught on my point, laying his arm open, and then with a quick engage and wrench, disarmed him. But before I could use my advantage, he sprang away into the grass and vanished.

I caught up the girl, slashing her bonds, and she clung to me, poor child, until I lifted her and carried her toward the horses. But we were not yet through with Senecoza. He must have had a rifle cached away somewhere in the bush, for the first I knew of him was when a bullet spat within a foot above my head.

I caught at the bridles, and then I saw that the mare had done all she could, temporarily. She was exhausted. I swung Ellen up on the horse.

'Ride for our ranch,' I ordered her. 'The raiders are out, but you can get through. Ride low and ride fast!'

'But you, Steve!'

'Go, go!' I ordered, swinging her horse around and starting it. She dashed away, looking at me wistfully over her shoulder. Then I snatched the rifle and a handful of cartridges I had gotten at Smith's, and took to the bush. And through the hot African day, Senecoza and I played a game of hide-and-seek. Crawling, slipping in and out of the scanty veldt-bushes, crouching in the tall grass, we traded shots back and forth. A movement of the grass, a snapping twig, the rasp of grass-blades, and a bullet came questing, another answering it.

I had but a few cartridges and I fired carefully, but presently I pushed my one remaining cartridge into the rifle – a big, six-bore, single-barrel breech-loader, for I had not had time to pick when I snatched it up.

I crouched in my covert and watched. Not a sound, not a whisper among the grasses. Away off over the veldt a hyena sounded his fiendish laugh and another answered, closer at hand. The cold sweat broke out on my brow.

What was that? A drumming of many horses' hoofs! Raiders returning? I ventured a look and could have shouted for joy. At least twenty men were sweeping toward me, and ahead of them all rode Ellen! They were still some distance away. I darted behind a tall bush and rose, waving my hand to attract their attention.

They shouted and pointed to something beyond me. I whirled and saw, some thirty yards away, a huge hyena slinking toward me, rapidly. I glanced carefully across the veldt. Somewhere out there, hidden by the billowing grasses, lurked Senecoza. A shot would betray to him my position – and I had but one cartridge. The rescue party was still out of range.

I looked again at the hyena. He was still rushing toward me. There was no doubt as to his intentions. His eyes glittered like a fiend's from Hell, and a scar on his shoulder showed him to be the same beast that had once before attacked me. Then a kind of horror took hold of me, and resting the old elephant rifle over my elbow, I sent my last bullet crashing through the bestial thing. With a scream that seemed to have a horribly human note in it, the hyena turned and fled back into the bush, reeling as it ran.

And the rescue party swept up around me.

A fusillade of bullets crashed through the bush from which Senecoza had sent his last shot. There was no reply.

'Ve hunt ter snake down,' quoth Cousin Ludtvik, his Boer accent increasing with his excitement. And we scattered through the veldt in a skirmish line, combing every inch of it warily.

Not a trace of the fetish-man did we find. A rifle we found, empty, with empty shells scattered about, and (which was very strange) *hyena tracks leading away from the rifle.*

I felt the short hairs of my neck bristle with intangible horror. We looked at each other, and said not a word, as with a tacit agreement we took up the trail of the hyena.

We followed it as it wound in and out in the shoulder-high grass, showing how it had slipped up on me, stalking me as a tiger stalks its victim. We struck the trail the thing had made, returning to the bush after I had shot it. Splashes of blood marked the way it had taken. We followed.

'It leads toward the fetish-hut,' muttered an Englishman. 'Here, sirs, is a damnable mystery.'

And Cousin Ludtvik ordered Ellen to stay back, leaving two men with her.

We followed the trail over the kopje and into the clump of trees. Straight to the door of the hut it led. We circled the hut cautiously, but no tracks led away. It was inside the hut. Rifles ready, we forced the rude door.

No tracks led away from the hut and no tracks led to it except the tracks of the hyena. Yet there was no hyena within that hut; and on the dirt floor, a bullet through his breast, lay Senecoza, the fetish-man.

Sea Curse

And some return by the failing light
And some in the waking dream.
For she hears the heels of the dripping ghosts
That ride the rough roofbeam.

KIPLING

They were the brawlers and braggarts, the loud boasters and hard drinkers of Faring town, John Kulrek and his crony Lie-lip Canool. Many a time have I, a tousle-haired lad, stolen to the tavern door to listen to their curses, their profane arguments and wild sea songs; half fearful and half in admiration of these wild rovers. Aye, all the people of Faring town gazed on them with fear and admiration, for they were not like the rest of the Faring men; they were not content to ply their trade along the coasts and among the shark-teeth shoals. No yawls, no skiffs for them! They fared far, farther than any other man in the village, for they shipped on the great sailing-ships that went out on the white tides to brave the restless grey ocean and make ports in strange lands.

Ah, I mind it was swift times in the little sea-coast village of Faring when John Kulrek came home, with the furtive Lie-lip at his side, swaggering down the gang-plank, in his tarry sea-clothes and the broad leather belt that held his ever-ready dagger; shouting condescending greeting to some favoured acquaintance, kissing some maiden who ventured too near; then up the street, roaring some scarcely decent song of the sea. How the cringers and the idlers, the hangers-on, would swarm about the two desperate heroes, flattering and smirking, guffawing hilariously at each nasty jest. For to the tavern loafers and to some of the weaker among the straightforward villagers, these men with their wild talk and their brutal deeds, their tales of the Seven Seas and the far countries, these men, I say, were valiant knights, nature's noblemen who dared to be men of blood and brawn.

And all feared them, so that when a man was beaten or a woman insulted, the villagers muttered . . . and did nothing. And so when

Moll Farrell's niece was put to shame by John Kulrek, none dared even to put into words what all thought. Moll had never married, and she and the girl lived alone in a little hut down close to the beach, so close that in high tide the waves came almost to the door.

The people of the village accounted old Moll something of a witch, and she was a grim, gaunt old dame who had little to say to anyone. But she minded her own business, and eked out a slim living by gathering clams, and picking up bits of driftwood.

The girl was a pretty, foolish little thing, vain and easily befooled, else she had never yielded to the shark-like blandishments of John Kulrek.

I mind the day was a cold winter day with a sharp breeze out of the east when the old dame came into the village street shrieking that the girl had vanished. All scattered over the beach and back among the bleak inland hills to search for her . . . all save John Kulrek and his cronies who sat in the tavern dicing and toping. All the while beyond the shoals, we heard the never-ceasing droning of the heaving, restless grey monster, and in the dim light of the ghostly dawn Moll Farrell's girl came home.

The tides bore her gently across the wet sands and laid her almost at her own door. Virgin-white she was, and her arms were folded across her still bosom; calm was her face, and the grey tides sighed about her slender limbs. Moll Farrell's eyes were stones, yet she stood above her dead girl and spoke no word till John Kulrek and his crony came reeling down from the tavern, their drinking-jacks still in their hands. Drunk was John Kulrek, and the people gave back for him, murder in their souls; so he came and laughed at Moll Farrell across the body of her girl.

'Zounds!' swore John Kulrek; 'the wench has drowned herself, Lie-lip!'

Lie-lip laughed, with the twist of his thin mouth. He always hated Moll Farrell, for it was she that had given him the name of Lie-lip.

Then John Kulrek lifted his drinking-jack, swaying on his uncertain legs. 'A health to the wench's ghost!' he bellowed, while all stood aghast.

Then Moll Farrell spoke, and the words broke from her in a scream which sent ripples of cold up and down the spines of the throng.

'The curse of the Foul Fiend upon you, John Kulrek!' she screamed. 'The curse of God rest upon your vile soul throughout eternity! May you gaze on sights that shall sear the eyes of you and scorch the soul of you! May you die a bloody death and writhe in hell's flames for a million and a million and yet a million years! I curse you by sea and by land, by earth and by air, by the demons of the swamplands, the fiends of the forest and the goblins of the hills! And you' – her lean finger stabbed at Lie-lip Canool and he started backward, his face paling – 'you shall be the death of John Kulrek and he shall be the death of you! You shall bring John Kulrek to the doors of hell and John Kulrek shall bring you to the gallows-tree! I set the seal of death upon your brow, John Kulrek! You shall live in terror and die in horror far out upon the cold grey sea! But the sea that took the soul of innocence to her bosom shall not take you, but shall fling forth your vile carcass to the sands! Aye, John Kulrek' – and she spoke with such a terrible intensity that the drunken mockery on the man's face changed to one of swinish stupidity – 'the sea roars for the victim it will not keep! There is snow upon the hills, John Kulrek, and ere it melts your corpse will lie at my feet. And I shall spit upon it and be content.'

Kulrek and his crony sailed at dawn for a long voyage, and Moll went back to her hut and her clam-gathering. She seemed to grow leaner and more grim than ever and her eyes smouldered with a light not sane. The days glided by and people whispered among themselves that Moll's days were numbered, for she faded to a ghost of a woman; but she went her way, refusing all aid.

That was a short, cold summer and the snow on the barren inland hills never melted; a thing very unusual, which caused much comment among the villagers. At dusk and at dawn Moll would come up on the beach, gaze up at the snow which glittered on the hills, then out to sea with a fierce intensity in her gaze.

Then the days grew shorter, the nights longer and darker, and the cold grey tides came sweeping along the bleak strands, bearing the rain and sleet of the sharp east breezes.

And upon a bleak day a trading-vessel sailed into the bay and anchored. And all the idlers and the wastrels flocked to the wharfs, for that was the ship upon which John Kulrek and Lie-lip Canool had sailed. Down the gang-plank came Lie-lip, more furtive than ever, but John Kulrek was not there.

To shouted queries, Canool shook his head. 'Kulrek deserted ship at a port of Sumatra,' said he. 'He had a row with the skipper, lads; wanted me to desert, too, but no! I had to see you fine lads again, eh boys?'

Almost cringing was Lie-lip Canool, and suddenly he recoiled as Moll Farrell came through the throng. A moment they stood eying each other; then Moll's grim lips bent in a terrible smile.

'There's blood on your hand, Canool!' she lashed out suddenly –
so suddenly that Lie-lip started and rubbed his right hand across his
left sleeve.

'Stand aside, witch!' he snarled in sudden anger, striding through
the crowd which gave back for him. His admirers followed him to
the tavern.

Now, I mind that the next day was even colder; grey fogs came
drifting out of the east and veiled the sea and the beaches. There
would be no sailing that day, and so all the villagers were in their
snug houses or matching tales at the tavern. So it came that Joe, my
friend, a lad of my own age, and I, were the ones who saw the first of
the strange things that happened.

Being harum-scarum lads of no wisdom, we were sitting in a small
rowboat, floating at the end of the wharfs, each shivering and wishing the other would suggest leaving, there being no reason whatever
for our being there, save that it was a good place to build air-castles
undisturbed.

Suddenly Joe raised his hand. 'Say,' he said, 'd'ye hear? Who can
be out on the bay upon a day like this?'

'Nobody. What d'ye hear?'

'Oars. Or I'm a lubber. Listen.'

There was no seeing anything in that fog, and I heard nothing. Yet
Joe swore he did, and suddenly his face assumed a strange look.

'Somebody rowing out there, I tell you! The bay is alive with
oars from the sound! A score of boats at the least! Ye dolt, can ye
not hear?'

Then, as I shook my head, he leaped and began to undo the
painter.

'I'm off to see. Name me liar if the bay is not full of boats, all
together like a close fleet. Are you with me?'

Yes, I was with him, though I heard nothing. Then out in the
greyness we went, and the fog closed behind and before so that we
drifted in a vague world of smoke, seeing naught and hearing naught.
We were lost in no time, and I cursed Joe for leading us upon a wild
goose chase that was like to end with our being swept out to sea. I
thought of Moll Farrell's girl and shuddered.

How long we drifted I know not. Minutes faded into hours, hours
into centuries. Still Joe swore he heard the oars, now close at hand,
now far away, and for hours we followed them, steering our course
toward the sound, as the noise grew or receded. This I later thought
of, and could not understand.

Then, when my hands were so numb that I could no longer hold the oar, and the forerunning drowsiness of cold and exhaustion was stealing over me, weak white stars broke through the fog which glided suddenly away, fading like a ghost of smoke, and we found ourselves afloat just outside the mouth of the bay. The waters lay smooth as a pond, all dark green and silver in the starlight, and the cold came crisper than ever. I was swinging the boat about, to put back into the bay, when Joe gave a shout, and for the first time I heard the clack of oar-locks. I glanced over my shoulder and my blood went cold.

A great beaked prow loomed above us, a weird, unfamiliar shape against the stars, and as I caught my breath, sheered sharply and swept by us, with a curious swishing I never heard any other craft make. Joe screamed and backed oars frantically, and the boat wallowed out of the way just in time; for though the prow missed us, still otherwise we had died. For from the sides of the ship stood long oars, bank upon bank which swept her along. Though I had never seen such a craft, I knew her for a galley. But what was she doing upon our coasts? They said, the far-farers, that such ships were still in use among the heathens of Barbary; but it was many a long, heaving mile to Barbary, and even so she did not resemble the ships described by those who had sailed far.

We started in pursuit, and this was strange, for though the waters broke about her prow, and she seemed fairly to fly through the waves, yet she was making little speed, and it was no time before we caught up with her. Making our painter fast to a chain far back beyond the reach of the swishing oars, we hailed those on deck. But there came no answer, and at last, conquering our fears, we clambered up the chain and found ourselves upon the strangest deck man has trod for many a long, roaring century.

Joe muttered fearsomely. 'Look, how old it seems! Almost ready to fall to pieces. Why, 'tis fairly rotten!'

There was no one on deck, no one at the long sweep with which the craft was steered. We stole to the hold and looked down the stair. Then and there, if ever men were on the verge of insanity, it was we. For there were rowers there, it is true; they sat upon the rowers' benches and drove the creaking oars through the grey waters. And they that rowed were skeletons!

Shrieking, we plunged across the deck, to fling ourselves into the sea. But at the rail I tripped upon something and fell headlong, and as I lay, I saw a thing which vanquished my fear of the horrors below for an instant. The thing upon which I had tripped was a human body, and in the dim grey light that was beginning to steal across the eastern waves I saw a dagger hilt standing up between his shoulders. Joe was at the rail, urging me to haste, and together we slid down the chain and cut the painter.

Then we stood off into the bay. Straight on kept the grim galley, and we followed, slowly, wondering. She seemed to be heading straight for the beach beside the wharfs, and as we approached, we saw the wharfs thronged with people. They had missed us, no doubt, and now they stood, there in the early dawn light, struck dumb by the apparition which had come up out of the night and the grim ocean.

Straight on swept the galley, her oars a-swish; then ere she reached the shallow water – crash! – a terrific reverberation shook the bay. Before our eyes the grim craft seemed to melt away; then she vanished, and the green waters seethed where she had ridden, but there floated no driftwood there, nor did there ever float any ashore. Aye, something floated ashore, but it was grim driftwood!

We made the landing amid a hum of excited conversation that stopped suddenly. Moll Farrell stood before her hut, limned gauntly against the ghostly dawn, her lean hand pointing sea-ward. And across the sighing wet sands, borne by the grey tide, something came floating; something that the waves dropped at Moll Farrell's feet. And there looked up at us, as we crowded about, a pair of unseeing eyes set in a still, white face. John Kulrek had come home.

Still and grim he lay, rocked by the tide, and as he lurched side-ways, all saw the dagger hilt that stood from his back . . . the dagger all of us had seen a thousand times at the belt of Lie-lip Canool.

'Aye, I killed him!' came Canool's shriek, as he writhed and grovelled before our gaze. 'At sea on a still night in a drunken brawl I slew him and hurled him overboard! And from the far seas he has followed me' – his voice sank to a hideous whisper – 'because of the curse the sea would not keep his body!'

And the wretch sank down, trembling, the shadow of the gallows already in his eyes.

'Aye!' Strong, deep and exultant was Moll Farrell's voice. 'From the hell of lost craft Satan sent a ship of bygone ages! A ship red with gore and stained with the memory of horrid crimes! None other would bear such a vile carcass! The sea has taken vengeance and has given me mine. See now, how I spit upon the face of John Kulrek.'

And with a ghastly laugh, she pitched forward, the blood starting to her lips. And the sun came up across the restless sea.

Skull-Face

Chapter 1. The face in the mist

We are no other than a moving row
Of Magic Shadow-shapes that come and go.

OMAR KHAYYAM

The horror first took concrete form amid that most unconcrete of all things – a hashish dream. I was off on a timeless, spaceless journey through the strange lands that belong to this state of being, a million miles away from earth and all things earthly; yet I became cognisant that something was reaching across the unknown voids – something that tore ruthlessly at the separating curtains of my illusions and intruded itself into my visions.

I did not exactly return to ordinary waking life, yet I was conscious of a seeing and a recognising that was unpleasant and seemed out of keeping with the dream I was at that time enjoying. To one who has never known the delights of hashish, my explanation must seem chaotic and impossible. Still, I was aware of a rending of mists and then the Face intruded itself into my sight. I thought at first it was merely a skull; then I saw that it was a hideous yellow instead of white, and was endowed with some horrid form of life. Eyes glimmered deep in the sockets and the jaws moved as if in speech. The body, except for the high, thin shoulders, was vague and indistinct, but the hands, which floated in the mists before and below the skull, were horribly vivid and filled me with crawling fears. They were like the hands of a mummy, long, lean and yellow, with knobby joints and cruel curving talons.

Then, to complete the vague horror which was swiftly taking possession of me, a voice spoke – imagine a man so long dead that his vocal organ had grown rusty and unaccustomed to speech. This was the thought which struck me and made my flesh crawl as I listened.

'A strong brute and one who might be useful somehow. See that he is given all the hashish he requires.'

Then the face began to recede, even as I sensed that I was the subject of conversation, and the mists billowed and began to close again. Yet for a single instant a scene stood out with startling clarity. I gasped — or sought to. For over the high, strange shoulder of the apparition another face stood out clearly for an instant, as if the owner peered at me. Red lips, half-parted, long dark eyelashes shading vivid eyes, a shimmery cloud of hair. Over the shoulder of Horror, breathtaking beauty for an instant looked at me.

Chapter 2. The hashish slave

Up from Earth's centre through the Seventh Gate
I rose, and on the Throne of Saturn sate.

OMAR KHAYYAM

My dream of the skull-face was borne over that usually uncrossable gap that lies between hashish enchantment and humdrum reality. I sat cross-legged on a mat in Yun Shatu's Temple of Dreams and gathered the fading forces of my decaying brain to the task of re-membering events and faces.

This last dream was so entirely different from any I had ever had before, that my waning interest was roused to the point of inquiring as to its origin. When I first began to experiment with hashish, I sought to find a physical or psychic basis for the wild flights of illusion pertaining thereto, but of late I had been content to enjoy without seeking cause and effect.

Whence this unaccountable sensation of familiarity in regard to that vision? I took my throbbing head between my hands and labor-iously sought a clue. A living dead man and a girl of rare beauty who had looked over his shoulder. Then I remembered.

Back in the fog of days and nights which veils a hashish addict's memory, my money had given out. It seemed years or possibly centuries, but my stagnant reason told me that it had probably been only a few days. At any rate, I had presented myself at Yun Shatu's sordid dive as usual and had been thrown out when it was learned I had no more money.

My universe crashing to pieces about me, and my nerves humming like taut piano wires for the vital need that was mine, I crouched in the gutter and gibbered bestially, till Hassim swaggered out and stilled my yammerings with a blow that felled me, half-stunned.

Then as I presently rose, staggeringly and with no thought save of the river which flowed with cool murmur so near me – as I rose, a light hand was laid like the touch of a rose on my arm. I turned with a frightened start, and stood spellbound before the vision of loveliness which met my gaze. Dark eyes limpid with pity surveyed me and the little hand on my ragged sleeve drew me toward the door of the Dream Temple. I shrank back, but a low voice, soft and musical, urged me, and filled with a trust that was strange, I shambled along with my beautiful guide.

At the door Hassim met us, cruel hands lifted and a dark scowl on his brow, but as I cowered there, expecting a blow, he halted before the girl's upraised hand and her word of command which had taken on an imperious note.

I did not understand what she said, but I saw dimly, as in a fog, that she gave the man money, and she led me to a couch where she had me recline and arranged the cushions as if I were king of Egypt instead of a ragged, dirty renegade who lived only for hashish. Her slim hand was cool on my brow for a moment, and then she was gone and Yussef Ali came bearing the stuff for which my very soul shrieked . . . and soon I was wandering again through those strange and exotic countries that only a hashish slave knows.

Now as I sat on the mat and pondered the dream of the skull-face I wondered more. Since the unknown girl had led me back into the dive, I had come and gone as before, when I had plenty of money to pay Yun Shatu. Someone certainly was paying him for me, and while my subconscious mind had told me it was the girl, my rusty brain had failed to grasp the fact entirely, or to wonder why. What need of wondering? So someone paid and the vivid-hued dreams continued, what cared I? But now I wondered. For the girl who had protected me from Hassim and had bought the hashish for me was the same girl I had seen in the skull-face dream.

Through the soddenness of my degradation the lure of her struck like a knife piercing my heart and strangely revived the memories of the days when I was a man like other men – not yet a sullen, cringing slave of dreams. Far and dim they were, shimmery islands in the mist of years – and what a dark sea lay between!

I looked at my ragged sleeve and the dirty, claw-like hand protruding from it; I gazed through the hanging smoke which fogged the sordid room, at the low bunks along the wall whereon lay the blankly staring dreamers – slaves, like me, of hashish or of opium. I gazed at the slippered Chinamen gliding softly to and fro bearing pipes or roasting balls of concentrated purgatory over tiny flickering fires. I gazed at Hassim standing, arms folded, beside the door like a great statue of black basalt.

And I shuddered and hid my face in my hands because with the faint dawning of returning manhood, I knew that this last and most cruel dream was futile – I had crossed an ocean over which I could never return, had cut myself off from the world of normal men or women. Naught remained now but to drown this dream as I had drowned all my others – swiftly and with hope that I should soon attain that Ultimate Ocean which lies beyond all dreams.

So these fleeting moments of lucidity, of longing, that tear aside the veils of all dope slaves – unexplainable, without hope of attainment.

So I went back to my empty dreams, to my phantasmagoria of illusions; but sometimes, like a sword cleaving a mist, through the highlands and the lowlands and seas of my visions floated, like half-forgotten music, the sheen of dark eyes and shimmery hair.

You ask how I, Stephen Costigan, American and a man of some attainments and culture, came to lie in a filthy dive of London's Limehouse? The answer is simple – no jaded debauchee, I, seeking new sensations in the mysteries of the Orient. I answer – Argonne! Heavens, what deeps and heights of horror lurk in that one word alone! Shell-shocked – shell-torn. Endless days and nights without end and roaring red hell over No Man's Land where I lay shot and bayoneted to shreds of gory flesh. My body recovered, how I know not; my mind never did.

And the leaping fires and shifting shadows in my tortured brain drove me down and down, along the stairs of degradation, uncaring until at last I found surcease in Yun Shatu's Temple of Dreams, where I slew my red dreams in other dreams – the dreams of hashish whereby a man may descend to the lower pits of the reddest hells or soar into those unnameable heights where the stars are diamond pinpoints beneath his feet.

Not the visions of the sot, the beast, were mine. I attained the unattainable, stood face to face with the unknown and in cosmic calmness knew the unguessable. And was content after a fashion, until the sight of burnished hair and scarlet lips swept away my dream-built universe and left me shuddering among its ruins.

Chapter 3. The Master of Doom

And He that toss'd you down into the Field,
He knows about it all – He knows! He knows!

OMAR KHAYYAM

A hand shook me roughly as I emerged languidly from my latest debauch. 'The Master wishes you! Up, swine!'

Hassim it was who shook me and who spoke.

'To Hell with the Master!' I answered, for I hated Hassim – and feared him.

'Up with you or you get no more hashish,' was the brutal response, and I rose in trembling haste.

I followed the huge man and he led the way to the rear of the building, stepping in and out among the wretched dreamers on the floor.

'Muster all hands on deck!' droned a sailor in a bunk. 'All hands!'

Hassim flung open the door at the rear and motioned me to enter. I had never before passed through that door and had supposed it led into Yun Shatu's private quarters. But it was furnished only with a cot, a bronze idol of some sort before which incense burned, and a heavy table.

Hassim gave me a sinister glance and seized the table as if to spin it about. It turned as if it stood on a revolving platform and a section of the floor turned with it, revealing a hidden doorway in the floor. Steps led downward in the darkness.

Hassim lighted a candle and with a brusque gesture invited me to descend. I did so, with the sluggish obedience of the dope addict, and he followed, closing the door above us by means of an iron lever fastened to the underside of the floor. In the semi-darkness we went down the rickety steps, some nine or ten I should say, and then came upon a narrow corridor.

Here Hassim again took the lead, holding the candle high in front of him. I could scarcely see the sides of this cave-like passageway but knew that it was not wide. The flickering light showed it to be bare of any sort of furnishings save for a number of strange-looking chests which lined the walls – receptacles containing opium and other dope, I thought.

A continuous scurrying and the occasional glint of small red eyes haunted the shadows, betraying the presence of vast numbers of the great rats which infest the Thames waterfront of that section.

Then more steps loomed out of the dark in front of us as the corridor came to an abrupt end. Hassim led the way up and at the top knocked four times against what seemed the underside of a floor. A hidden door opened and a flood of soft, illusive light streamed through.

Hassim hustled me up roughly and I stood blinking in such a setting as I had never seen in my wildest flights of vision. I stood in a jungle of palm trees through which wriggled a million vivid-hued dragons! Then, as my startled eyes became accustomed to the light, I saw that I had not been suddenly transferred to some other planet, as I had at first thought. The palm trees were there, and the dragons, but the trees were artificial and stood in great pots and the dragons writhed across heavy tapestries which hid the walls.

The room itself was a monstrous affair – inhumanly large, it seemed to me. A thick smoke, yellowish and tropical in suggestion, seemed to hang over all, veiling the ceiling and baffling upward glances. This smoke, I saw, emanated from an altar in front of the wall to my left. I started. Through the saffron-billowing fog two eyes, hideously large and vivid, glittered at me. The vague outlines of some bestial idol took indistinct shape. I flung an uneasy glance about, marking the oriental divans and couches and the bizarre furnishings, and then my eyes halted and rested on a lacquer screen just in front of me.

I could not pierce it and no sound came from beyond it, yet I felt eyes searing into my consciousness through it, eyes that burned through my very soul. A strange aura of evil flowed from that strange screen with its weird carvings and unholy decorations.

Hassim salaamed profoundly before it and then, without speaking, stepped back and folded his arms, statue-like.

A voice suddenly broke the heavy and oppressive silence.

'You who are a swine, would you like to be a man again?'

I started. The tone was inhuman, cold – more, there was a suggestion of long disuse of the vocal organs – the voice I had heard in my dream!

'Yes,' I replied, trance-like, 'I would like to be a man again.'

Silence ensued for a space; then the voice came again with a sinister whispering undertone at the back of its sound like bats flying through a cavern.

'I shall make you a man again because I am a friend to all broken men. Not for a price shall I do it, nor for gratitude. And I give you a sign to seal my promise and my vow. Thrust your hand through the screen.'

At these strange and almost unintelligible words I stood perplexed, and then, as the unseen voice repeated the last command, I stepped forward and thrust my hand through a slit which opened silently in the screen. I felt my wrist seized in an iron grip and something seven times colder than ice touched the inside of my hand. Then my wrist was released, and drawing forth my hand I saw a strange symbol traced in blue close to the base of my thumb – a thing like a scorpion.

The voice spoke again in a sibilant language I did not understand, and Hassim stepped forward deferentially. He reached about the screen and then turned to me, holding a goblet of some amber-coloured liquid which he proffered me with an ironical bow. I took it hesitatingly.

'Drink and fear not,' said the unseen voice. 'It is only an Egyptian wine with life-giving qualities.'

So I raised the goblet and emptied it; the taste was not unpleasant, and even as I handed the beaker to Hassim again, I seemed to feel new life and vigour whip along my jaded veins.

'Remain at Yun Shatu's house,' said the voice. 'You will be given food and a bed until you are strong enough to work for yourself. You will use no hashish nor will you require any. Go!'

As in a daze, I followed Hassim back through the hidden door, down the steps, along the dark corridor and up through the other door that let us into the Temple of Dreams.

As we stepped from the rear chamber into the main room of the dreamers, I turned wonderingly.

'Master? Master of what? Of Life?'

Hassim laughed, fiercely and sardonically. 'Master of Doom!'

Chapter 4. The spider and the fly

There was a door to which I found no key;
There was a Veil through which I might not see.

OMAR KHAYYAM

I sat on Yun Shatu's cushions and pondered with a clearness of mind new and strange to me. As for that, all my sensations were new and strange. I felt as if I had wakened from a monstrously long sleep, and though my thoughts were sluggish, I felt as though the cobwebs which had dogged them for so long had been partly brushed away.

I drew my hand across my brow, noting how it trembled. I was weak and shaky and felt the stirrings of hunger – not for dope but for food. What had been in the draft I had quenched in the chamber of mystery? And why had the 'Master' chosen me, out of all the other wretches of Yun Shatu's, for regeneration?

And who was this Master? Somehow the word sounded vaguely familiar – I sought laboriously to remember. Yes . . . I had heard it, lying half-waking in the bunks or on the floor – whispered sibilantly by Yun Shatu or by Hassim or by Yussef Ali, the Moor, muttered in their low-voiced conversations and mingled always with words I could not understand. Was not Yun Shatu, then, master of the Temple of Dreams? I had thought and the other addicts thought that the withered Chinaman held undisputed sway over this drab kingdom and that Hassim and Yussef Ali were his servants. And the four China boys who roasted opium with Yun Shatu and Yar Khan the Afghan and Santiago the Haitian and Ganra Singh, the renegade Sikh – all in the pay of Yun Shatu, we supposed – bound to the opium lord by bonds of gold or fear.

For Yun Shatu was a power in London's Chinatown and I had heard that his tentacles reached across the seas into high places of mighty and mysterious tongs. Was that Yun Shatu behind the lacquer screen? No; I knew the Chinaman's voice and besides I had seen him puttering about in the front of the Temple just as I went through the back door.

Another thought came to me. Often, lying half-torpid, in the late hours of night or in the early greyness of dawn, I had seen men and women steal into the Temple, whose dress and bearing were strangely out of place and incongruous. Tall, erect men, often in evening dress, with their hats drawn low about their brows, and fine ladies, veiled, in silks and furs. Never two of them came together, but always they came separately and, hiding their features, hurried to the rear door, where they entered and presently came forth again, hours later sometimes. Knowing that the lust for dope finds resting-place in high positions sometimes, I had never wondered overmuch, supposing that these were wealthy men and women of society who had fallen victims to the craving, and that somewhere in the back of the building there was a private chamber for such. Yet now I wondered – sometimes these persons had remained only a few moments – was it always opium for which they came, or did they, too, traverse that strange corridor and converse with the One behind the screen?

My mind dallied with the idea of a great specialist to whom came all classes of people to find surcease from the dope habit. Yet it was strange that such a one should select a dope-joint from which to work – strange, too, that the owner of that house should apparently look on him with so much reverence.

I gave it up as my head began to hurt with the unwonted effort of thinking, and shouted for food. Yussef Ali brought it to me on a tray, with a promptness which was surprising. More, he salaamed as he departed, leaving me to ruminate on the strange shift of my status in the Temple of Dreams.

I ate, wondering what the One of the screen wanted with me. Not for an instant did I suppose that his actions had been prompted by the reasons he pretended; the life of the underworld had taught me that none of its denizens leaned toward philanthropy. And underworld the chamber of mystery had been, in spite of its elaborate and bizarre nature. And where could it be located? How far had I walked along the corridor? I shrugged my shoulders, wondering if it were not all a hashish-induced dream; then my eye fell upon my hand – and the scorpion traced thereon.

'Muster all hands!' droned the sailor in the bunk. 'All hands!'

To tell in detail of the next few days would be boresome to any who have not tasted the dire slavery of dope. I waited for the craving to strike me again – waited with sure sardonic hopelessness. All day, all night . . . another day . . . then the miracle was forced upon my doubting brain. Contrary to all theories and supposed facts of science and common sense, the craving had left me as suddenly and completely as a bad dream! At first I could not credit my senses but believed myself to be still in the grip of a dope nightmare. But it was true. From the time I quaffed the goblet in the room of mystery, I felt not the slightest desire for the stuff which had been life itself to me. This, I felt vaguely, was somehow unholy and certainly opposed to all rules of nature. If the dread being behind the screen had discovered the secret of breaking hashish's terrible power, what other monstrous secrets had he discovered and what unthinkable dominance was his? The suggestion of evil crawled serpent-like through my mind.

I remained at Yun Shatu's house, lounging in a bunk or on cushions spread upon the floor, eating and drinking at will, but now that I was becoming a normal man again, the atmosphere became most revolting to me and the sight of the wretches writhing in their dreams reminded me unpleasantly of what I myself had been, and it repelled, nauseated me.

So one day, when no one was watching me, I rose and went out on the street and walked along the waterfront. The air, burdened though it was with smoke and foul scents, filled my lungs with strange freshness and aroused new vigour in what had once been a powerful frame. I took new interest in the sounds of men living and working, and the sight of a vessel being unloaded at one of the wharfs actually thrilled me. The force of longshoremen was short, and presently I found myself heaving and lifting and carrying, and though the sweat coursed down my brow and my limbs trembled at the effort, I exulted in the thought that at last I was able to labour for myself again, no matter how low or drab the work might be.

As I returned to the door of Yun Shatu's that evening – hideously weary but with the renewed feeling of manhood that comes of honest toil – Hassim met me at the door.

'You been where?' he demanded roughly.

'I've been working on the docks,' I answered shortly.

'You don't need to work on docks,' he snarled. 'The Master got work for you.'

He led the way, and again I traversed the dark stairs and the corridor under the earth. This time my faculties were alert and I decided that the passageway could not be over thirty or forty feet in length. Again I stood before the lacquer screen and again I heard the inhuman voice of living death.

'I can give you work,' said the voice. 'Are you willing to work for me?'

I quickly assented. After all, in spite of the fear which the voice inspired, I was deeply indebted to the owner.

'Good. Take these.'

As I started toward the screen a sharp command halted me and Hassim stepped forward and reaching behind took what was offered. This was a bundle of pictures and papers, apparently.

'Study these,' said the One behind the screen, 'and learn all you can about the man portrayed thereby. Yun Shatu will give you money; buy yourself such clothes as seamen wear and take a room at the front of the Temple. At the end of two days, Hassim will bring you to me again. Go!'

The last impression I had, as the hidden door closed above me, was that the eyes of the idol, blinking through the everlasting smoke, leered mockingly at me.

The front of the Temple of Dreams consisted of rooms for rent, masking the true purpose of the building under the guise of a waterfront boarding house. The police had made several visits to Yun Shatu but had never got any incriminating evidence against him.

So in one of these rooms I took up my abode and set to work studying the material given me.

The pictures were all of one man, a large man, not unlike me in build and general facial outline, except that he wore a heavy beard and was inclined to blondness whereas I am dark. The name, as written on the accompanying papers, was Major Fairlan Morley, special commissioner to Natal and the Transvaal. This office and title were new to me and I wondered at the connection between an African commissioner and an opium house on the Thames waterfront.

The papers consisted of extensive data evidently copied from authentic sources and all dealing with Major Morley, and a number of private documents, considerably illuminating, on the major's private life.

An exhaustive description was given of the man's personal appearance and habits, some of which seemed very trivial to me. I wondered what the purpose could be, and how the One behind the screen had come in possession of papers of such intimate nature.

I could find no clue in answer to this question but bent all my energies to the task set out for me. I owed a deep debt of gratitude to the unknown man who required this of me and I was determined to repay him to the best of my ability. Nothing, at this time, suggested a snare to me.

Chapter 5. The man on the couch

What dam of lances sent thee forth to jest at dawn with Death?

KIPLING

At the expiration of two days, Hassim beckoned me as I stood in the opium room. I advanced with a springy, resilient tread, secure in the confidence that I had culled the Morley papers of all their worth. I was a new man; my mental swiftness and physical readiness surprised me – sometimes it seemed unnatural.

Hassim eyed me through narrowed lids and motioned me to follow, as usual. As we crossed the room, my gaze fell upon a man who lay on a couch close to the wall, smoking opium. There was nothing at all suspicious about his ragged, unkempt clothes, his dirty, bearded face or the blank stare, but my eyes, sharpened to an abnormal point, seemed to sense a certain incongruity in the clean-cut limbs which not even the slouchy garments could efface.

Hassim spoke impatiently and I turned away. We entered the rear room, and as he shut the door and turned to the table, it moved of itself and a figure bulked up through the hidden doorway. The Sikh, Ganra Singh, a lean sinister-eyed giant, emerged and proceeded to the door opening into the opium room, where he halted until we should have descended and closed the secret doorway.

Again I stood amid the billowing yellow smoke and listened to the hidden voice.

'Do you think you know enough about Major Morley to impersonate him successfully?'

Startled, I answered, 'No doubt I could, unless I met someone who was intimate with him.'

'I will take care of that. Follow me closely. Tomorrow you sail on the first boat for Calais. There you will meet an agent of mine who will accost you the instant you step upon the wharfs, and give you further instructions. You will sail second-class and avoid all conversation with strangers or anyone. Take the papers with you. The agent will aid you in making up and your masquerade will start in Calais. That is all. Go!'

I departed, my wonder growing. All this rigmarole evidently had a meaning, but one which I could not fathom. Back in the opium room Hassim bade me be seated on some cushions to await his return. To my question he snarled that he was going forth as he had been ordered, to buy me a ticket on the Channel boat. He departed and I sat down, leaning my back against the wall. As I ruminated, it seemed suddenly that eyes were fixed on me so intensely as to disturb my sub-mind. I glanced up quickly but no one seemed to be looking at me. The smoke drifted through the hot atmosphere as usual; Yussef Ali and the Chinese glided back and forth tending to the wants of the sleepers.

Suddenly the door to the rear room opened and a strange and hideous figure came haltingly out. Not all of those who found entrance to Yun Shatu's back room were aristocrats and society members. This was one of the exceptions, and one whom I remembered as having often entered and emerged therefrom. A tall, gaunt figure, shapeless and ragged wrappings and nondescript garments, face entirely hidden. Better that the face be hidden, I thought, for without doubt the wrapping concealed a grisly sight. The man was a leper, who had somehow managed to escape the attention of the public guardians and who was occasionally seen haunting the lower and more mysterious regions of East End . . . a mystery even to the lowest denizens of Limehouse.

Suddenly my supersensitive mind was aware of a swift tension in the air. The leper hobbled out the door, closed it behind him. My eyes instinctively sought the couch whereon lay the man who had aroused my suspicions earlier in the day. I could have sworn that cold steely eyes glared menacingly before they flickered shut. I crossed to the couch in one stride and bent over the prostrate man. Something about his face seemed unnatural . . . a healthy bronze seemed to underlie the pallor of complexion.

'Yun Shatu!' I shouted. 'A spy is in the house!'

Things happened then with bewildering speed. The man on the couch with one tigerish movement leaped erect and a revolver gleamed in his hand. One sinewy arm flung me aside as I sought to grapple with him and a sharp decisive voice sounded over the babble which broke forth.

'You there! Halt! Halt!'

The pistol in the stranger's hand was levelled at the leper, who was making for the door in long strides!

All about was confusion; Yun Shatu was shrieking volubly in Chinese and the four China boys and Yussef Ali were rushing in from all sides, knives glittering in their hands.

All this I saw with unnatural clearness even as I marked the stranger's face. As the fleeing leper gave no evidence of halting, I saw the eyes harden to steely points of determination, sighting along the pistol barrel – the features set with the grim purpose of the slayer. The leper was almost to the outer door, but death would strike him down ere he could reach it.

And then, just as the finger of the stranger tightened on the trigger, I hurled myself forward and my right fist crashed against his chin. He went down as though struck by a trip-hammer, the revolver exploding harmlessly in the air.

In that instant, with the blinding flare of light that sometimes comes to one, I knew that the leper was none other than the Man Behind the Screen!

I bent over the fallen man, who though not entirely senseless had been rendered temporarily helpless by that terrific blow. He was struggling dazedly to rise but I shoved him roughly down again and seizing the false beard he wore, tore it away. A lean bronzed face was revealed, the strong lines of which not even the artificial dirt and grease-paint could alter.

Yussef Ali leaned above him now, dagger in hand, eyes slits of murder. The brown sinewy hand went up – I caught the wrist.

'Not so fast! What are you about to do?'

'This is John Gordon,' he hissed, 'the Master's greatest foe! He must die, curse you!'

John Gordon! The name was familiar somehow, and yet I did not seem to connect it with the London police nor account for the man's presence in Yun Shatu's dope-joint. However, on one point I was determined.

'You don't kill him, at any rate. Up with you!' This last to Gordon, who with my aid staggered up, still very dizzy.

'That punch would have dropped a bull,' I said in wonderment; 'I didn't know I had it in me.'

The false leper had vanished. Yun Shatu stood gazing at me as immobile as an idol, hands in his wide sleeves, and Yussef Ali stood back, muttering murderously and thumbing his dagger edge, as I led Gordon out of the opium room and through the innocent-appearing bar which lay between that room and the street.

Out in the street I said to him: 'I have no idea as to who you are or what you are doing here, but you see what an unhealthful place it is for you. Hereafter be advised by me and stay away.'

His only answer was a searching glance, and then he turned and walked swiftly though somewhat unsteadily up the street.

Chapter 6. The dream-girl

I have reached these lands but newly
From an ultimate dim Thule.

EDGAR ALLAN POE

Outside my room sounded a light footstep. The doorknob turned cautiously and slowly; the door opened. I sprang erect with a gasp. Red lips, half-parted, dark eyes like limpid seas of wonder, a mass of shimmering hair – framed in my drab doorway stood the girl of my dreams!

She entered, and half-turning with a sinuous motion, closed the door. I sprang forward, my hands outstretched, then halted as she put a finger to her lips.

'You must not talk loudly,' she almost whispered. 'He did not say I could not come; yet – '

Her voice was soft and musical, with just a touch of foreign accent which I found delightful. As for the girl herself, every intonation, every movement proclaimed the Orient. She was a fragrant breath from the East. From her night-black hair, piled high above her alabaster forehead, to her little feet, encased in high-heeled pointed slippers, she portrayed the highest ideal of Asiatic loveliness – an effect which was heightened rather than lessened by the English blouse and skirt which she wore.

'You are beautiful!' I said dazedly. 'Who are you?'

'I am Zuleika,' she answered with a shy smile. 'I – I am glad you like me. I am glad you no longer dream hashish dreams.'

Strange that so small a thing should set my heart to leaping wildly!

'I owe it all to you, Zuleika,' I said huskily. 'Had not I dreamed of you every hour since you first lifted me from the gutter, I had lacked the power of even hoping to be freed from my curse.'

She blushed prettily and intertwined her white fingers as if in nervousness.

'You leave England tomorrow?' she said suddenly.

'Yes. Hassim has not returned with my ticket . . . ' I hesitated suddenly, remembering the command of silence.

'Yes, I know, I know!' she whispered swiftly, her eyes widening. 'And John Gordon has been here! He saw you!'

'Yes!'

She came close to me with a quick lithe movement.

'You are to impersonate some man! Listen, while you are doing this, you must not ever let Gordon see you! He would know you, no matter what your disguise! He is a terrible man!'

'I don't understand,' I said, completely bewildered. 'How did the Master break me of my hashish craving? Who is this Gordon and why did he come here? Why does the Master go disguised as a leper – and who is he? Above all, why am I to impersonate a man I never saw or heard of?'

'I cannot . . . I dare not tell you!' she whispered, her face paling. 'I . . .'

Somewhere in the house sounded the faint tones of a Chinese gong. The girl started like a frightened gazelle.

'I must go! *He* summons me!'

She opened the door, darted through, halted a moment to electrify me with her passionate exclamation: 'Oh, be careful, be very careful, sahib!'

Then she was gone.

Chapter 7. The man of the skull

What the hammer? What the chain?
In what furnace was thy brain?
What the anvil? What dread grasp
Dare its deadly terrors clasp?

BLAKE

A while after my beautiful and mysterious visitor had left, I sat in meditation. I believed that I had at last stumbled on to an explanation of a part of the enigma, at any rate. This was the conclusion I had reached: Yun Shatu, the opium lord, was simply the agent or servant of some organisation or individual whose work was on a far larger scale than merely supplying dope addicts in the Temple of Dreams. This man or these men needed co-workers among all classes of people; in other words, I was being let in with a group of opium smugglers on a gigantic scale. Gordon no doubt had been investigating the case, and his presence alone showed that it was no ordinary one, for I knew that he held a high position with the English government, though just what, I did not know.

Opium or not, I determined to carry out my obligation to the Master. My moral sense had been blunted by the dark ways I had travelled, and the thought of despicable crime did not enter my head. I was indeed hardened. More, the mere debt of gratitude was increased a thousand-fold by the thought of the girl. To the Master I owed it that I was able to stand up on my feet and look into her clear eyes as a man should. So if he wished my services as a smuggler of dope, he should have them. No doubt I was to impersonate some man so high in governmental esteem that the usual actions of the customs officers would be deemed unnecessary; was I to bring some rare dream-producer into England?

These thoughts were in my mind as I went downstairs, but ever back of them hovered other and more alluring suppositions – what was the reason for the girl, here in this vile dive – a rose in a garbage-heap – and who was she?

As I entered the outer bar, Hassim came in, his brows set in a dark scowl of anger, and, I believed, fear. He carried a newspaper in his hand, folded.

'I told you to wait in opium room,' he snarled.

'You were gone so long that I went up to my room. Have you the ticket?'

He merely grunted and pushed on past me into the opium room, and standing at the door I saw him cross the floor and disappear into the rear room. I stood there, my bewilderment increasing. For as Hassim had brushed past me, I had noted an item on the face of the paper, against which his black thumb was tightly pressed as if to mark that special column of news.

And with the unnatural celerity of action and judgment which seemed to be mine those days, I had in that fleeting instant read:

AFRICAN SPECIAL COMMISSIONER FOUND MURDERED!

The body of Major Fairlan Morley was yesterday discovered in a rotting ship's hold at Bordeaux . . .

No more I saw of the details, but that alone was enough to make me think! The affair seemed to be taking on an ugly aspect. Yet . . .

Another day passed. To my inquiries, Hassim snarled that the plans had been changed and I was not to go to France. Then, late in the evening, he came to bid me once more to the room of mystery.

I stood before the lacquer screen, the yellow smoke acrid in my nostrils, the woven dragons writhing along the tapestries, the palm trees rearing thick and oppressive.

'A change has come in our plans,' said the hidden voice. 'You will not sail as was decided before. But I have other work that you may do. Mayhap this will be more to your type of usefulness, for I admit you have somewhat disappointed me in regard to subtlety. You interfered the other day in such manner as will no doubt cause me great inconvenience in the future.'

I said nothing, but a feeling of resentment began to stir in me.

'Even after the assurance of one of my most trusted servants,' the toneless voice continued, with no mark of any emotion save a slightly rising note, 'you insisted on releasing my most deadly enemy. Be more circumspect in the future.'

'I saved your life!' I said angrily.

'And for that reason alone I overlook your mistake – this time!'

A slow fury suddenly surged up in me.

'This time! Make the best of it this time, for I assure you there will be no next time. I owe you a greater debt than I can ever hope to pay, but that does not make me your slave. I have saved your life the debt is as near paid as a man can pay it. Go your way and I go mine!'

A low, hideous laugh answered me, like a reptilian hiss.

'You fool! You will pay with your whole life's toil! You say you are not my slave? I say you are – just as Hassim there beside you is my slave . . . just as the girl Zuleika is my slave, who has bewitched you with her beauty.'

These words sent a wave of hot blood to my brain and I was conscious of a flood of fury which completely engulfed my reason for a second. Just as all my moods and senses seemed sharpened and exaggerated those days, so now this burst of rage transcended every moment of anger I had ever had before.

'Hell's fiends!' I shrieked. 'You devil – who are you and what is your hold on me? I'll see you or die!'

Hassim sprang at me, but I hurled him backward and with one stride reached the screen and flung it aside with an incredible effort of strength. Then I shrank back, hands outflung, shrieking. A tall, gaunt figure stood before me, a figure arrayed grotesquely in a silk brocaded gown which fell to the floor.

From the sleeves of this gown protruded hands which filled me with crawling horror – long, predatory hands, with thin bony fingers and curved talons – withered skin of a parchment brownish-yellow, like the hands of a man long dead.

The hands . . . but, oh God, the face! A skull to which no vestige of flesh seemed to remain but on which taut brownish-yellow skin grew fast, etching out every detail of that terrible death's-head. The forehead was high and in a way magnificent, but the head was curiously narrow through the temples, and from under penthouse brows great eyes glimmered like pools of yellow fire. The nose was high-bridged and very thin; the mouth was a mere colourless gash between thin, cruel lips. A long, bony neck supported this frightful vision and completed the effect of a reptilian demon from some medieval hell.

I was face to face with the skull-faced man of my dreams!

Chapter 8. Black wisdom

By thought a crawling ruin,
By life a leaping mire.
By a broken heart in the breast of the world
And the end of the world's desire.

CHESTERTON

The terrible spectacle drove for the instant all thought of rebellion from my mind. My very blood froze in my veins and I stood motionless. I heard Hassim laugh grimly behind me. The eyes in the cadaverous face blazed fiendishly at me and I blanched from the concentrated satanic fury in them.

Then the horror laughed sibilantly.

'I do you a great honour, Mr Costigan; among a very few, even of my own servants, you may say that you saw my face and lived. I think you will be more useful to me living than dead.'

I was silent, completely unnerved. It was difficult to believe that this man lived, for his appearance certainly belied the thought. He seemed horribly like a mummy. Yet his lips moved when he spoke and his eyes flamed with hideous life.

'You will do as I say,' he said abruptly, and his voice had taken on a note of command. 'You doubtless know, or know of, Sir Haldred Frenton?'

'Yes.'

Every man of culture in Europe and America was familiar with the travel books of Sir Haldred Frenton, author and soldier of fortune.

'You will go to Sir Haldred's estate tonight . . . '

'Yes?'

'*And kill him!*'

I staggered, literally. This order was incredible – unspeakable! I had sunk low, low enough to smuggle opium, but to deliberately murder a man I had never seen, a man noted for his kindly deeds! That was too monstrous even to contemplate.

'You do not refuse?'

The tone was as loathly and as mocking as the hiss of a serpent.

'Refuse?' I screamed, finding my voice at last. 'Refuse? You incarnate devil! Of course I refuse! You . . . '

Something in the cold assurance of his manner halted me – froze me into apprehensive silence.

'You fool!' he said calmly. 'I broke the hashish chains – do you know how? Four minutes from now you will know and curse the day you were born! Have you not thought it strange, the swiftness of brain, the resilience of body – the brain that should be rusty and slow, the body that should be weak and sluggish from years of abuse? That blow that felled John Gordon – have you not wondered at its might? The ease with which you mastered Major Morley's records – have you not wondered at that? You fool, you are bound to me by chains of steel and blood and fire! I have kept you alive and sane – I alone. Each day the life-saving elixir has been given you in your wine. You could not live and keep your reason without it. And I and only I know its secret!'

He glanced at a queer timepiece which stood on a table at his elbow.

'This time I had Yun Shatu leave the elixir out . . . I anticipated rebellion. The time is near – ha, it strikes!'

Something else he said, but I did not hear. I did not see, nor did I feel in the human sense of the word. I was writhing at his feet, screaming and gibbering in the flames of such hells as men have never dreamed of.

Aye, I knew now! He had simply given me a dope so much stronger that it drowned the hashish. My unnatural ability was explainable now – I had simply been acting under the stimulus of something which combined all the hells in its makeup, which stimulated, something like heroin, but whose effect was unnoticed by the victim. What it was, I had no idea, nor did I believe anyone knew save that hellish being who stood watching me with grim amusement. But it had held my brain together, instilling into my system a need for it, and now my frightful craving tore my soul asunder.

Never, in my moments of worst shell-shock or my moments of hashish-craving, have I ever experienced anything like that. I burned with the heat of a thousand hells and froze with an iciness that was colder than any ice, a hundred times. I swept down to the deepest pits of torture and up to the highest crags of torment – a million yelling devils hemmed me in, shrieking and stabbing. Bone by bone, vein by vein, cell by cell I felt my body disintegrate and fly in bloody atoms all over the universe . . . and each separate cell was an entire system of quivering, screaming nerves. And they gathered from far voids and reunited with a greater torment.

Through the fiery bloody mists I heard my own voice screaming, a monotonous yammering. Then with distended eyes I saw a golden goblet, held by a claw-like hand, swim into view – a goblet filled with an amber liquid.

With a bestial screech, I seized it with both hands, being dimly aware that the metal stem gave beneath my fingers, and brought the brim to my lips. I drank in frenzied haste, the liquid slopping down onto my breast.

Chapter 9. Kathulos of Egypt

Night shall be thrice night over you,
And Heaven an iron cope.

CHESTERTON

The Skull-faced One stood watching me critically as I sat panting on a couch, completely exhausted. He held in his hand the goblet and surveyed the golden stem, which was crushed out of all shape. This my maniac fingers had done in the instant of drinking.

'Superhuman strength, even for a man in your condition,' he said with a sort of creaky pedantry. 'I doubt if even Hassim here could equal it. Are you ready for your instructions now?'

I nodded, wordless. Already the hellish strength of the elixir was flowing through my veins, renewing my burnt-out force. I wondered how long a man could live as I lived, being constantly burned out and artificially rebuilt.

'You will be given a disguise and will go alone to the Frenton estate. No one suspects any design against Sir Haldred and your entrance into the estate and the house itself should be a matter of comparative ease. You will not don the disguise – which will be of unique nature – until you are ready to enter the estate. You will then proceed to Sir Haldred's room and kill him, breaking his neck with your bare hands – this is essential . . . '

The voice droned on, giving the ghastly orders in a frightfully casual and matter-of-fact way. The cold sweat beaded my brow.

'You will then leave the estate, taking care to leave the imprint of your hand somewhere plainly visible, and the automobile, which will be waiting for you at some safe place nearby, will bring you back here, you having first removed the disguise. I have, in case of complications, any amount of men who will swear that you spent the entire night in the Temple of Dreams and never left it. But there must be no detection! Go warily and perform your task surely, for you know the alternative.'

I did not return to the opium house but was taken through winding corridors, hung with heavy tapestries, to a small room containing only an oriental couch. Hassim gave me to understand that I was to remain here until after nightfall, and then left me. The door was closed but I made no effort to discover if it was locked. The Skull-faced Master held me with stronger shackles than locks and bolts.

Seated upon the couch in the bizarre setting of a chamber which might have been a room in an Indian zenana, I faced fact squarely and fought out my battle. There was still in me some trace of manhood left . . . more than the fiend had reckoned, and added to this were black despair and desperation. I chose and determined on my only course.

Suddenly the door opened softly. Some intuition told me whom to expect, nor was I disappointed. Zuleika stood, a glorious vision before me – a vision which mocked me, made blacker my despair and yet thrilled me with wild yearning and reasonless joy.

She bore a tray of food which she set beside me, and then she seated herself on the couch, her large eyes fixed upon my face. A flower in a serpent den she was, and the beauty of her took hold of my heart.

'Steephen!' she whispered, and I thrilled as she spoke my name for the first time.

Her luminous eyes suddenly shone with tears and she laid her little hand on my arm. I seized it in both my rough hands.

'They have set you a task which you fear and hate!' she faltered.

'Aye,' I almost laughed, 'but I'll fool them yet! Zuleika, tell me – what is the meaning of all this?'

She glanced fearfully around her.

'I do not know all' – she hesitated – 'your plight is all my fault but I – I hoped . . . Steephen, I have watched you every time you came to Yun Shatu's for months. You did not see me but I saw you, and I saw in you, not the broken sot your rags proclaimed, but a wounded soul, a soul bruised terribly on the ramparts of life. And from my heart I pitied you. Then when Hassim abused you that day' – again tears started to her eyes – 'I could not bear it and I knew how you suffered for want of hashish. So I paid Yun Shatu, and going to the Master I – I – oh, you will hate me for this!' she sobbed.

'No . . . no . . . never . . . '

'I told him that you were a man who might be of use to him and begged him to have Yun Shatu supply you with what you needed. He had already noticed you, for his is the eye of the slaver and all the world is his slave market! So he bade Yun Shatu do as I asked; and now . . . better if you had remained as you were, my friend.'

'No! No!' I exclaimed. 'I have known a few days of regeneration, even if it was false! I have stood before you as a man, and that is worth all else!'

And all that I felt for her must have looked forth from my eyes, for she dropped hers and flushed. Ask me not how love comes to a man; but I knew that I loved Zuleika – had loved this mysterious oriental girl since first I saw her – and somehow I felt that she, in a measure, returned my affection. This realisation made blacker and more barren the road I had chosen; yet – for pure love must ever strengthen a man – it nerved me to what I must do.

'Zuleika,' I said, speaking hurriedly, 'time flies and there are things I must learn; tell me – who are you and why do you remain in this den of Hades?'

'I am Zuleika – that is all I know. I am Circassian by blood and birth; when I was very little I was captured in a Turkish raid and raised in a Stamboul harem; while I was yet too young to marry, my master gave me as a present to – to *Him*.'

'And who is he – this skull-faced man?'

'He is Kathulos of Egypt – that is all I know. My master.'

'An Egyptian? Then what is he doing in London – why all this mystery?'

She intertwined her fingers nervously.

'Steephen, please speak lower; always there is someone listening everywhere. I do not know who the Master is or why he is here or why he does these things. I swear by Allah! if I knew I would tell you. Sometimes distinguished-looking men come here to the room where the Master receives them – not the room where you saw him – and he makes me dance before them and afterward flirt with them a little. And always I must repeat exactly what they say to me. That is what I must always do – in Turkey, in the Barbary States, in Egypt, in France and in England. The Master taught me French and English and educated me in many ways himself. He is the greatest sorcerer in all the world and knows all ancient magic and everything.'

'Zuleika,' I said, 'my race is soon run, but let me get you out of this – come with me and I swear I'll get you away from this fiend!'

She shuddered and hid her face.

'No, no, I cannot!'

'Zuleika,' I asked gently, 'what hold has he over you, child – dope also?'

'No, no!' she whimpered. 'I do not know . . . I do not know . . . but I cannot . . . I never can escape him!'

I sat, baffled for a few moments; then I asked, 'Zuleika, where are we right now?'

'This building is a deserted storehouse back of the Temple of Silence.'

'I thought so. What is in the chests in the tunnel?'

'I do not know.'

Then suddenly she began weeping softly. 'You too, a slave, like me – you who are so strong and kind – oh Steephen, I cannot bear it!'

I smiled. 'Lean closer, Zuleika, and I will tell you how I am going to fool this Kathulos.'

She glanced apprehensively at the door.

'You must speak low. I will lie in your arms and while you pretend to caress me, whisper your words to me.'

She glided into my embrace, and there on the dragon-worked couch in that house of horror I first knew the glory of Zuleika's slender form nestling in my arms – of Zuleika's soft cheek pressing my breast. The fragrance of her was in my nostrils, her hair in my eyes, and my senses reeled; then with my lips hidden by her silky hair I whispered, swiftly: 'I am going first to warn Sir Haldred Frenton – then to find John Gordon and tell him of this den. I will lead the police here and you must watch closely and be ready to hide from *Him* – until we can break through and kill or capture him. Then you will be free.'

'But you!' she gasped, paling. 'You must have the elixir, and only he – '

'I have a way of outdoing him, child,' I answered.

She went pitifully white and her woman's intuition sprang at the right conclusion.

'You are going to kill yourself!'

And much as it hurt me to see her emotion, I yet felt a torturing thrill that she should feel so on my account. Her arms tightened about my neck.

'Don't, Steephen!' she begged. 'It is better to live, even – '

'No, not at that price. Better to go out clean while I have the manhood left.'

She stared at me wildly for an instant; then, pressing her red lips suddenly to mine, she sprang up and fled from the room. Strange,

strange are the ways of love. Two stranded ships on the shores of life, we had drifted inevitably together, and though no word of love had passed between us, we knew each other's heart – through grime and rags, and through accoutrements of the slave, we knew each other's heart and from the first loved as naturally and as purely as it was intended from the beginning of Time.

The beginning of life now and the end for me, for as soon as I had completed my task, ere I felt again the torments of my curse, love and life and beauty and torture should be blotted out together in the stark finality of a pistol ball scattering my rotting brain. Better a clean death than –

The door opened again and Yussef Ali entered.

'The hour arrives for departure,' he said briefly. 'Rise and follow.'

I had no idea, of course, as to the time. No window opened from the room I occupied – I had seen no outer window whatever. The rooms were lighted by tapers in censers swinging from the ceiling. As I rose the slim young Moor slanted a sinister glance in my direction.

'This lies between you and me,' he said sibilantly. 'Servants of the same Master we – but this concerns ourselves alone. Keep your distance from Zuleika – the Master has promised her to me in the days of the empire.'

My eyes narrowed to slits as I looked into the frowning, handsome face of the Oriental, and such hate surged up in me as I have seldom known. My fingers involuntarily opened and closed, and the Moor, marking the action, stepped back, hand in his girdle.

'Not now – there is work for us both – later perhaps.' Then in a sudden cold gust of hatred, 'Swine! Ape-man! When the Master is finished with you I shall quench my dagger in your heart!'

I laughed grimly.

'Make it soon, desert-snake, or I'll crush your spine between my hands.'

Chapter 10. The dark house

Against all man-made shackles and a man-made hell –
Alone . . . at last . . . unaided – I rebel!

MUNDY

I followed Yussef Ali along the winding hallways, down the steps – Kathulos was not in the idol room – and along the tunnel, then through the rooms of the Temple of Dreams and out into the street, where the street lamps gleamed drearily through the fogs and a slight drizzle. Across the street stood an automobile, curtains closely drawn.

'That is yours,' said Hassim, who had joined us. 'Saunter across natural-like. Don't act suspicious. The place may be watched. The driver knows what to do.'

Then he and Yussef Ali drifted back into the bar and I took a single step toward the curb.

'Steephen!'

A voice that made my heart leap spoke my name! A white hand beckoned from the shadows of a doorway. I stepped quickly there.

'Zuleika!'

'Shhh!'

She clutched my arm, slipped something into my hand; I made out vaguely a small flask of gold.

'Hide this, quick!' came her urgent whisper. 'Don't come back but go away and hide. This is full of elixir – I will try to get you some more before that is all gone. You must find a way of communicating with me.'

'Yes, but how did you get this?' I asked amazedly.

'I stole it from the Master! Now please, I must go before he misses me.'

And she sprang back into the doorway and vanished. I stood undecided. I was sure that she had risked nothing less than her life in doing this and I was torn by the fear of what Kathulos might do to her, were the theft discovered. But to return to the house of mystery would certainly invite suspicion, and I might carry out my plan and strike back before the Skull-faced One learned of his slave's duplicity.

So I crossed the street to the waiting automobile. The driver was a lanky man of medium height. I stared hard at him, wondering how much he had seen. He gave no evidence of having seen anything, and I decided that even if he had noticed me step back into the shadows he could not have seen what passed there nor have been able to recognise the girl.

He merely nodded as I climbed in the back seat, and a moment later we were speeding away down the deserted and fog-haunted streets. A bundle beside me I concluded to be the disguise mentioned by the Egyptian.

To recapture the sensations I experienced as I rode through the rainy, misty night would be impossible. I felt as if I were already dead and the bare and dreary streets about me were the roads of death over which my ghost had been doomed to roam forever. A torturing joy was in my heart, and bleak despair – the despair of a doomed man. Not that death itself was so repellent – a dope victim dies too many deaths to shrink from the last – but it was hard to go out just as love had entered my barren life. And I was still young.

A sardonic smile crossed my lips . . . they were young, too, the men who died beside me in No Man's Land. I drew back my sleeve and clenched my fists, tensing my muscles. There was no surplus weight on my frame, and much of the firm flesh had wasted away, but the cords of the great biceps still stood out like knots of iron, seeming to indicate massive strength. But I knew my might was false, that in reality I was a broken hulk of a man, animated only by the artificial fire of the elixir, without which a frail girl might topple me over.

The automobile came to a halt among some trees. We were on the outskirts of an exclusive suburb and the hour was past midnight. Through the trees I saw a large house looming darkly against the distant flares of night-time London.

Holding a match so that its light could not be detected outside the car, I examined the 'disguise' and was hard put to restrain an insane laugh. The disguise was the complete hide of a gorilla! Gathering the bundle under my arm I trudged toward the wall which surrounded the Frenton estate. For safety's sake I made, not for the high iron gate at the front, but for the wall at the side where there was no gate.

No light showed in the house. Sir Haldred was a bachelor and I was sure that the servants were all in bed long ago. I negotiated the wall with ease and stole across the dark lawn to a side door, still carrying the grisly 'disguise' under my arm. The door was locked, as I had anticipated, and I did not wish to arouse anyone until I was safely in the house, where the sound of voices would not carry to one who might have followed me. I took hold of the knob with both hands, and, exerting slowly the inhuman strength that was mine, began to twist. The shaft turned in my hands and the lock within shattered suddenly, with a noise that was like the crash of a cannon in the stillness. An instant more and I was inside and had closed the door behind me.

I took a single stride in the darkness in the direction I believed the stair to be, then halted as a beam of light flashed into my face. At the side of the beam I caught the glimmer of a pistol muzzle. Beyond a lean shadowy face floated.

'Stand where you are and put up your hands!'

I lifted my hands, allowing the bundle to slip to the floor. I had heard that voice only once but I recognised it – knew instantly that the man who held that light was John Gordon.

'How many are with you?'

His voice was sharp, commanding.

'I am alone,' I answered. 'Take me into a room where a light cannot be seen from the outside and I'll tell you some things you want to know.'

He was silent; then, bidding me take up the bundle I had dropped, he stepped to one side and motioned me to precede him into the next room. There he directed me to a stairway and at the top landing opened a door and switched on lights.

I found myself in a room whose curtains were closely drawn. During this journey Gordon's alertness had not relaxed, and now he stood, still covering me with his revolver. Clad in conventional garments, he stood revealed a tall, leanly but powerfully built man, taller than I but not so heavy – with steel-grey eyes and clean-cut features. Something about the man attracted me, even as I noted a bruise on his jawbone where my fist had struck in our last meeting.

'I cannot believe,' he said crisply, 'that this apparent clumsiness and lack of subtlety is real. Doubtless you have your own reasons for wishing me to be in a secluded room at this time, but Sir Haldred is efficiently protected even now. Stand still.'

Muzzle pressed against my chest, he ran his hand over my garments for concealed weapons, seeming slightly surprised when he found none.

'Still,' he murmured as if to himself, 'a man who can burst an iron lock with his bare hands has scant need of weapons.'

'You are wasting valuable time,' I said impatiently. 'I was sent here tonight to kill Sir Haldred Frenton – '

'By whom?' the question was shot at me.

'By the man who sometimes goes disguised as a leper.'

He nodded, a gleam in his scintillant eyes.

'My suspicions were correct, then.'

'Doubtless. Listen to me closely – do you desire the death or arrest of that man?'

Gordon laughed grimly.

'To one who wears the mark of the scorpion on his hand, my answer would be superfluous.'

'Then follow my directions and your wish shall be granted.'

His eyes narrowed suspiciously.

'So that was the meaning of this open entry and non-resistance,' he said slowly. 'Does the dope which dilates your eyeballs so warp your mind that you think to lead me into ambush?'

I pressed my hands against my temples. Time was racing and every moment was precious – how could I convince this man of my honesty?

'Listen; my name is Stephen Costigan of America. I was a frequenter of Yun Shatu's dive and a hashish addict – as you have guessed, but just now a slave of stronger dope. By virtue of this slavery, the man you know as a false leper, whom Yun Shatu and his friends call "Master", gained dominance over me and sent me here to murder Sir Haldred – why, God only knows. But I have gained a space of respite by coming into possession of some of this dope which I must have in order to live, and I fear and hate this Master. Listen to me and I swear, by all things holy and unholy, that before the sun rises the false leper shall be in your power!'

I could tell that Gordon was impressed in spite of himself.

'Speak fast!' he rapped.

Still I could sense his disbelief and a wave of futility swept over me.

'If you will not act with me,' I said, 'let me go and somehow I'll find a way to get to the Master and kill him. My time is short – my hours are numbered and my vengeance is yet to be realised.'

'Let me hear your plan, and talk fast,' Gordon answered.

'It is simple enough. I will return to the Master's lair and tell him I have accomplished that which he sent me to do. You must follow closely with your men and while I engage the Master in conversation, surround the house. Then, at the signal, break in and kill or seize him.'

Gordon frowned. 'Where is this house?'

'The warehouse back of Yun Shatu's has been converted into a veritable oriental palace.'

'The warehouse!' he exclaimed. 'How can that be? I had thought of that first, but I have carefully examined it from without. The windows are closely barred and spiders have built webs across them. The doors are nailed fast on the outside and the seals that mark the warehouse as deserted have never been broken or disturbed in any way.'

'They tunnelled up from beneath,' I answered. 'The Temple of Dreams is directly connected with the warehouse.'

'I have traversed the alley between the two buildings,' said Gordon, 'and the doors of the warehouse opening into that alley are, as I have said, nailed shut from without just as the owners left them. There is apparently no rear exit of any kind from the Temple of Dreams.'

'A tunnel connects the buildings, with one door in the rear room of Yun Shatu's and the other in the idol room of the warehouse.'

'I have been in Yun Shatu's back room and found no such door.'

'The table rests upon it. You noted the heavy table in the centre of the room? Had you turned it around the secret door would have opened in the floor. Now this is my plan: I will go in through the Temple of Dreams and meet the Master in the idol room. You will have men secretly stationed in front of the warehouse and others upon the other street, in front of the Temple of Dreams. Yun Shatu's building, as you know, faces the waterfront, while the warehouse, fronting the opposite direction, faces a narrow street running parallel with the river. At the signal let the men in this street break open the front of the warehouse and rush in, while simultaneously those in front of Yun Shatu's make an invasion through the Temple of Dreams. Let these make for the rear room, shooting without mercy any who may seek to deter them, and there open the secret door as I have said. There being, to the best of my knowledge, no other exit from the Master's lair, he and his servants will necessarily seek to make their escape through the tunnel. Thus we will have them on both sides.'

Gordon ruminated while I studied his face with breathless interest.

'This may be a snare,' he muttered, 'or an attempt to draw me away from Sir Haldred, but – '

I held my breath.

'I am a gambler by nature,' he said slowly. 'I am going to follow what you Americans call a hunch – but God help you if you are lying to me!'

I sprang erect.

'Thank God! Now aid me with this suit, for I must be wearing it when I return to the automobile waiting for me.'

His eyes narrowed as I shook out the horrible masquerade and prepared to don it.

'This shows, as always, the touch of the master hand. You were doubtless instructed to leave marks of your hands, encased in those hideous gauntlets?'

'Yes, though I have no idea why.'

'I think I have – the Master is famed for leaving no real clues to mark his crimes – a great ape escaped from a neighbouring zoo earlier in the evening and it seems too obvious for mere chance, in the light of this disguise. The ape would have gotten the blame of Sir Haldred's death.'

The thing was easily gotten into and the illusion of reality it created was so perfect as to draw a shudder from me as I viewed myself in a mirror.

'It is now two o'clock,' said Gordon.' Allowing for the time it will take you to get back to Limehouse and the time it will take me to get my men stationed, I promise you that at half-past four the house will be closely surrounded. Give me a start – wait here until I have left this house, so I will arrive at least as soon as you.'

'Good!' I impulsively grasped his hand. 'There will doubtless be a girl there who is in no way implicated with the Master's evildoings, but only a victim of circumstances such as I have been. Deal gently with her.'

'It shall be done. What signal shall I look for?'

'I have no way of signalling for you and I doubt if any sound in the house could be heard on the street. Let your men make their raid on the stroke of five.'

I turned to go.

'A man is waiting for you with a car, I take it? Is he likely to suspect anything?'

'I have a way of finding out, and if he does,' I replied grimly, 'I will return alone to the Temple of Dreams.'

Chapter 11. Four thirty-four

Doubting, dreaming dreams no mortal ever dared to dream before.

EDGAR ALLAN POE

The door closed softly behind me, the great dark house looming up more starkly than ever. Stooping, I crossed the wet lawn at a run, a grotesque and unholy figure, I doubt not, since any man had at a glance sworn me to be not a man but a giant ape. So craftily had the Master devised!

I clambered the wall, dropped to the earth beyond and made my way through the darkness and the drizzle to the group of trees which masked the automobile.

The driver leaned out of the front seat. I was breathing hard and sought in various ways to simulate the actions of a man who has just murdered in cold blood and fled the scene of his crime.

'You heard nothing, no sound, no scream?' I hissed, gripping his arm.

'No noise except a slight crash when you first went in,' he answered. 'You did a good job – nobody passing along the road could have suspected anything.'

'Have you remained in the car all the time?' I asked. And when he replied that he had, I seized his ankle and ran my hand over the soles of his shoe, it was perfectly dry, as was the cuff of his trouser leg. Satisfied, I climbed into the back seat. Had he taken a step on the earth, shoe and garment would have showed it by the telltale dampness.

I ordered him to refrain from starting the engine until I had removed the ape skin, and then we sped through the night and I fell victim to doubts and uncertainties. Why should Gordon put any trust in the word of a stranger and a former ally of the Master's? Would he not put my tale down as the ravings of a dope-crazed addict, or a lie to ensnare or befool him? Still, if he had not believed me, why had he let me go?

I could but trust. At any rate, what Gordon did or did not do would scarcely affect my fortunes ultimately, even though Zuleika had furnished me with that which would merely extend the number of my days. My thought centred on her, and more than my hope of vengeance on Kathulos was the hope that Gordon might be able to save her from the clutches of the fiend. At any rate, I thought grimly, if Gordon failed me, I still had my hands and if I might lay them upon the bony frame of the Skull-faced One –

Abruptly I found myself thinking of Yussef Ali and his strange words, the import of which just occurred to me, '*The Master has promised her to me in the days of the empire!*'

The days of the empire – what could that mean?

The automobile at last drew up in front of the building which hid the Temple of Silence – now dark and still. The ride had seemed interminable and as I dismounted I glanced at the timepiece on the dashboard of the car. My heart leaped – it was four thirty-four, and unless my eyes tricked me I saw a movement in the shadows across the street, out of the flare of the street lamp. At this time of night it could mean only one of two things – some menial of the Master watching for my return or else Gordon had kept his word. I opened the door, crossed the deserted bar and entered the opium room. The bunks and the floor were littered with the dreamers, for such places as these know nothing of day or night as normal people know, but all lay deep in sottish slumber.

The lamps glimmered through the smoke and a silence hung mist-like over all.

Chapter 12. The stroke of five

He saw gigantic tracks of death,
And many a shape of doom.

CHESTERTON

Two of the China-boys squatted among the smudge fires, staring at me unwinkingly as I threaded my way among the recumbent bodies and made my way to the rear door. For the first time I traversed the corridor alone and found time to wonder again as to the contents of the strange chests which lined the walls.

Four raps on the underside of the floor, and a moment later I stood in the idol room. I gasped in amazement – the fact that across a table from me sat Kathulos in all his horror was not the cause of my exclamation. Except for the table, the chair on which the Skull-faced One sat and the altar – now bare of incense – the room was perfectly bare! Drab, unlovely walls of the unused warehouse met my gaze instead of the costly tapestries I had become accustomed to. The palms, the idol, the lacquered screen – all were gone.

'Ah, Mr Costigan, you wonder, no doubt.'

The dead voice of the Master broke in on my thoughts. His serpent eyes glittered balefully. The long yellow fingers twined sinuously upon the table.

'You thought me to be a trusting fool, no doubt!' he rapped suddenly. 'Did you think I would not have you followed? You fool, Yussef Ali was at your heels every moment!'

An instant I stood speechless, frozen by the crash of these words against my brain; then as their import sank home, I launched myself forward with a roar. At the same instant, before my clutching fingers could close on the mocking horror on the other side of the table, men rushed from every side. I whirled, and with the clarity of hate, from the swirl of savage faces I singled out Yussef Ali, and crashed my right fist against his temple with every ounce of my strength. Even as he dropped, Hassim struck me to my knees and a Chinaman flung a man-net over my shoulders. I heaved erect, bursting the stout cords as if they were strings, and then a blackjack in the hands of Ganra Singh stretched me stunned and bleeding on the floor.

Lean sinewy hands seized and bound me with cords that cut cruelly into my flesh. Emerging from the mists of semi-unconsciousness, I found myself lying on the altar with the masked Kathulos towering over me like a gaunt ivory tower. About in a semicircle stood Ganra Singh, Yar Khan, Yun Shatu and several others whom I knew as frequenters of the Temple of Dreams. Beyond them – and the sight cut me to the heart – I saw Zuleika crouching in a doorway, her face white and her hands pressed against her cheeks, in an attitude of abject terror.

'I did not fully trust you,' said Kathulos sibilantly, 'so I sent Yussef Ali to follow you. He reached the group of trees before you and following you into the estate heard your very interesting conversation with John Gordon – for he scaled the house-wall like a cat and clung to the window ledge! Your driver delayed purposely so as to give Yussef Ali plenty of time to get back – I have decided to change my abode anyway. My furnishings are already on their way to another house, and as soon as we have disposed of the traitor – you! – we shall depart also, leaving a little surprise for your friend Gordon when he arrives at five-thirty.'

My heart gave a sudden leap of hope. Yussef Ali had misunderstood, and Kathulos lingered here in false security while the London detective force had already silently surrounded the house. Over my shoulder I saw Zuleika vanish from the door.

I eyed Kathulos, absolutely unaware of what he was saying. It was not long until five – if he dallied longer – then I froze as the Egyptian spoke a word and Li Kung, a gaunt, cadaverous Chinaman, stepped from the silent semicircle and drew from his sleeve a long thin dagger. My eyes sought the timepiece that still rested on the table and my heart sank. It was still ten minutes until five. My death did not matter so much, since it simply hastened the inevitable, but in my mind's eye I could see Kathulos and his murderers escaping while the police awaited the stroke of five.

The Skull-face halted in some harangue, and stood in a listening attitude. I believe his uncanny intuition warned him of danger. He spoke a quick staccato command to Li Kung and the Chinaman sprang forward, dagger lifted above my breast.

The air was suddenly supercharged with dynamic tension. The keen dagger-point hovered high above me – loud and clear sounded the skirl of a police whistle and on the heels of the sound there came a terrific crash from the front of the warehouse!

Kathulos leaped into frenzied activity. Hissing orders like a cat spitting, he sprang for the hidden door and the rest followed him. Things happened with the speed of a nightmare. Li Kung had followed the rest, but Kathulos flung a command over his shoulder and the Chinaman turned back and came rushing toward the altar where I lay, dagger high, desperation in his countenance.

A scream broke through the clamour and as I twisted desperately about to avoid the descending dagger, I caught a glimpse of Kathulos dragging Zuleika away. Then with a frenzied wrench I toppled from the altar just as Li Kung's dagger, grazing my breast, sank inches deep into the dark-stained surface and quivered there.

I had fallen on the side next to the wall and what was taking place in the room I could not see, but it seemed as if far away I could hear men screaming faintly and hideously. Then Li Kung wrenched his blade free and sprang, tigerishly, around the end of the altar. Simultaneously a revolver cracked from the doorway – the Chinaman spun clear around, the dagger flying from his hand – he slumped to the floor.

Gordon came running from the doorway where a few moments earlier Zuleika had stood, his pistol still smoking in his hand. At his heels were three rangy, clean-cut men in plain clothes. He cut my bonds and dragged me upright.

'Quick! Where have they gone?'

The room was empty of life save for myself, Gordon and his men, though two dead men lay on the floor.

I found the secret door and after a few seconds' search located the lever which opened it. Revolvers drawn, the men grouped about me and peered nervously into the dark stairway. Not a sound came up from the total darkness.

'This is uncanny!' muttered Gordon. 'I suppose the Master and his servants went this way when they left the building – as they are certainly not here now! – and Leary and his men should have stopped them either in the tunnel itself or in the rear room of Yun Shatu's. At any rate, in either event they should have communicated with us by this time.'

'Look out, sir!' one of the men exclaimed suddenly, and Gordon, with an ejaculation, struck out with his pistol barrel and crushed the life from a huge snake which had crawled silently up the steps from the blackness beneath.

'Let us see into this matter,' said he, straightening.

But before he could step onto the first stair, I halted him; for, flesh crawling, I began dimly to understand something of what had happened – I began to understand the silence in the tunnel, the absence of the detectives, the screams I had heard some minutes previously while I lay on the altar. Examining the lever which opened the door,

I found another smaller lever – I began to believe I knew what those mysterious chests in the tunnel contained.

'Gordon,' I said hoarsely, 'have you an electric torch?'

One of the men produced a large one.

'Direct the light into the tunnel, but as you value your life, do not put a foot upon the steps.'

The beam of light struck through the shadows, lighting the tunnel, etching out boldly a scene that will haunt my brain all the rest of my life. On the floor of the tunnel, between the chests which now gaped open, lay two men who were members of London's finest secret service. Limbs twisted and faces horribly distorted they lay, and above and about them writhed, in long glittering scaly shimmerings, scores of hideous reptiles.

The clock struck five.

Chapter 13. The blind beggar who rode

He seemed a beggar such as lags
Looking for crusts and ale.

CHESTERTON

The cold grey dawn was stealing over the river as we stood in the deserted bar of the Temple of Dreams. Gordon was questioning the two men who had remained on guard outside the building while their unfortunate companions went in to explore the tunnel.

'As soon as we heard the whistle, sir, Leary and Murken rushed the bar and broke into the opium room, while we waited here at the bar door according to orders. Right away several ragged dopers came tumbling out and we grabbed them. But no one else came out and we heard nothing from Leary and Murken; so we just waited until you came, sir.'

'You saw nothing of the Chinaman Yun Shatu?'

'No, sir. After a while the patrolmen arrived and we threw a cordon around the house, but no one was seen.'

Gordon shrugged his shoulders; a few cursory questions had satisfied him that the captives were harmless addicts and he had them released.

'You are sure no one else came out?'

'Yes, sir – no, wait a moment. A wretched old blind beggar did come out, all rags and dirt and with a ragged girl leading him. We stopped him but didn't hold him – a wretch like that couldn't be harmful.'

'No?' Gordon jerked out. 'Which way did he go?'

'The girl led him down the street to the next block and then an automobile stopped and they got in and drove off, sir.'

Gordon glared at him.

'The stupidity of the London detective has rightfully become an international jest,' he said acidly. 'No doubt it never occurred to you as being strange that a Limehouse beggar should ride about in his own automobile.'

Then impatiently waving aside the man, who sought to speak further, he turned to me and I saw the lines of weariness beneath his eyes.

'Mr Costigan, if you will come to my apartment we may be able to clear up some new things.'

Chapter 14. The black empire

Oh the new spears dipped in life-blood as the woman shrieked in vain!
Oh the days before the English! When will those days come again?

MUNDY

Gordon struck a match and absently allowed it to flicker and go out in his hand. His Turkish cigarette hung unlighted between his fingers.

'This is the most logical conclusion to be reached,' he was saying. 'The weak link in our chain was lack of men. But curse it, one cannot round up an army at two o'clock in the morning, even with the aid of Scotland Yard. I went on to Limehouse, leaving orders for a number of patrolmen to follow me as quickly as they could be got together, and to throw a cordon about the house.

'They arrived too late to prevent the Master's servants slipping out of the side doors and windows, no doubt, as they could easily do with only Finnegan and Hansen on guard at the front of the building. However, they arrived in time to prevent the Master himself from slipping out in that way – no doubt he lingered to effect his disguise and was caught in that manner. He owes his escape to his craft and boldness and to the carelessness of Finnegan and Hansen. The girl who accompanied him – '

'She was Zuleika, without doubt.'

I answered listlessly, wondering anew what shackles bound her to the Egyptian sorcerer.

'You owe your life to her,' Gordon rapped, lighting another match. 'We were standing in the shadows in front of the warehouse, waiting for the hour to strike, and of course ignorant as to what was going on in the house, when a girl appeared at one of the barred windows and begged us for God's sake to do something, that a man was being murdered. So we broke in at once. However, she was not to be seen when we entered.'

'She returned to the room, no doubt,' I muttered, 'and was forced to accompany the Master. God grant he knows nothing of her trickery.'

'I do not know,' said Gordon, dropping the charred match stem, 'whether she guessed at our true identity or whether she just made the appeal in desperation.

'However, the main point is this: evidence points to the fact that, on hearing the whistle, Leary and Murken invaded Yun Shatu's from the front at the same instant my three men and I made our attack on the warehouse front. As it took us some seconds to batter down the door, it is logical to suppose that they found the secret door and entered the tunnel before we effected an entrance into the warehouse.

'The Master, knowing our plans beforehand, and being aware that an invasion would be made through the tunnel and having long ago made preparations for such an exigency – '

An involuntary shudder shook me.

' – the Master worked the lever that opened the chest – the screams you heard as you lay upon the altar were the death shrieks of Leary and Murken. Then, leaving the Chinaman behind to finish you, the Master and the rest descended into the tunnel – incredible as it seems – and threading their way unharmed among the serpents, entered Yun Shatu's house and escaped therefrom as I have said.'

'That seems impossible. Why should not the snakes turn on them?'

Gordon finally ignited his cigarette and puffed a few seconds before replying.

'The reptiles might still have been giving their full and hideous attention to the dying men, or else . . . I have on previous occasions been confronted with indisputable proof of the Master's dominance over beasts and reptiles of even the lowest or most dangerous orders. How he and his slaves passed unhurt among those scaly fiends must remain, at present, one of the many unsolved mysteries pertaining to that strange man.'

I stirred restlessly in my chair. This brought up a point for the purpose of clearing up which I had come to Gordon's neat but bizarre apartments.

'You have not yet told me,' I said abruptly, 'who this man is and what is his mission.'

'As to who he is, I can only say that he is known as you name him – the Master. I have never seen him unmasked, nor do I know his real name nor his nationality.'

'I can enlighten you to an extent there,' I broke in. 'I have seen him unmasked and have heard the name his slaves call him.'

Gordon's eyes blazed and he leaned forward.

'His name,' I continued, 'is Kathulos and he claims to be an Egyptian.'

'Kathulos!' Gordon repeated. 'You say he claims to be an Egyptian – have you any reason for doubting his claim of that nationality?'

'He may be of Egypt,' I answered slowly, 'but he is different, somehow, from any human I ever saw or hope to see. Great age might account for some of his peculiarities, but there are certain lineal differences that my anthropological studies tell me have been present since birth – features which would be abnormal to any other man but which are perfectly normal in Kathulos. That sounds paradoxical, I admit, but to appreciate fully the horrid inhumanness of the man, you would have to see him yourself.'

Gordon sat at attention while I swiftly sketched the appearance of the Egyptian as I remembered him . . . and that appearance was indelibly etched on my brain forever.

As I finished he nodded.

'As I have said, I never saw Kathulos except when disguised as a beggar, a leper or some such thing – when he was fairly swathed in rags. Still, I too have been impressed with a strange difference about him – something that is not present in other men.'

Gordon tapped his knee with his fingers – a habit of his when deeply engrossed by a problem of some sort.

'You have asked as to the mission of this man,' he began slowly. 'I will tell you all I know.'

'My position with the British government is a unique and peculiar one. I hold what might be called a roving commission – an office created solely for the purpose of suiting my special needs. As a secret service official during the war, I convinced the powers of a need of such office and of my ability to fill it.

'Somewhat over seventeen months ago I was sent to South Africa to investigate the unrest which has been growing among the natives of the interior ever since the World War and which has of late assumed alarming proportions. There I first got on the track of this man Kathulos. I found, in roundabout ways, that Africa was a seething cauldron of rebellion from Morocco to Cape Town.

'I sensed a giant intellect and a monstrous genius behind the veil, a genius powerful enough to accomplish this union and hold it together. Working entirely on hints and vague whispered clues, I followed the trail up through Central Africa and into Egypt. There, at last, I came upon definite evidence that such a man existed. The whispers hinted of a living dead man – a *skull-faced* man. I learned that this man was the high priest of the mysterious Scorpion society of northern Africa. He was spoken of variously as Skull-face, the Master, and the Scorpion.

'Following a trail of bribed officials and filched state secrets, I at last trailed him to Alexandria, where I had my first sight of him in a dive in the native quarter – disguised as a leper. I heard him distinctly addressed as "Mighty Scorpion" by the natives, but he escaped me.

'All trace vanished then; the trail ran out entirely until rumours of strange happenings in London reached me and I came back to England to investigate an apparent leak in the War Office.

'As I thought, the Scorpion had preceded me. This man, whose education and craft transcend anything I ever met with, is simply the leader and instigator of a world-wide movement such as the world has never seen before.'

'I understand now what Yussef Ali meant when he said "the days of the empire",' I muttered.

'Exactly,' Gordon rapped with suppressed excitement. 'Kathulos' power is unlimited and unguessed. Like an octopus his tentacles stretch to the high places of civilisation and the far corners of the world. And his main weapon is – dope! He has flooded Europe and no doubt America with opium and hashish, and in spite of all efforts it has been impossible to discover the break in the barriers through which the hellish stuff is coming. With this he ensnares and enslaves men and women.

'You have told me of the aristocratic men and women you saw coming to Yun Shatu's dive. Without doubt they were dope addicts – for, as I said, the habit lurks in high places – holders of governmental positions, no doubt, coming to trade for the stuff they craved and giving in return state secrets, inside information and promise of protection for the Master's crimes.

'A steady stream of rifles and ammunition has been pouring into East Africa and it was not until I discovered the source that it was stopped. I found that a staid and reliable Scotch firm was smuggling these arms among the natives and I found more: the manager of this firm was an opium slave. That was enough. I saw Kathulos' hand in the matter. The manager was arrested and committed suicide in his cell – that is only one of the many situations with which I am called upon to deal.

'Again, the case of Major Fairlan Morley. He, like myself, held a very flexible commission and had been sent to the Transvaal to work upon the same case. He sent to London a number of secret papers for safe keeping. They arrived some weeks ago and were put in a bank vault. The letter accompanying them gave explicit instructions that they were to be delivered to no one but the major himself, when he called for them in person, or in event of his death, to myself.

'As soon as I learned that he had sailed from Africa I sent trusted men to Bordeaux, where he intended to make his first landing in Europe. They did not succeed in saving the major's life, but they certified his death, for they found his body in a deserted ship whose hulk was stranded on the beach. Efforts were made to keep the affair a secret but somehow it leaked into the papers with the result – '

'I begin to understand why I was to impersonate the unfortunate major,' I interrupted.

'Exactly. A false beard furnished you, and your black hair dyed blond, you would have presented yourself at the bank, received the papers from the banker, who knew Major Morley just intimately enough to be deceived by your appearance, and the papers would have then fallen into the hands of the Master.

'I can only guess at the contents of those papers, for events have been taking place too swiftly for me to call for and obtain them. But they must deal with subjects closely connected with the activities of Kathulos. How he learned of them and of the provisions of the letter accompanying them, I have no idea, but as I said, London is honey-combed with his spies.

'In my search for clues, I often frequented Limehouse disguised as you first saw me. I went often to the Temple of Dreams and even once managed to enter the back room, for I suspected some sort of rendezvous in the rear of the building. The absence of any exit baffled me and I had no time to search for secret doors before I was ejected by the giant Hassim, who had no suspicion of my true identity. I noticed that very often the leper entered or left Yun Shatu's, and finally it was borne on me that past a shadow of doubt this supposed leper was the Scorpion himself.

'That night you discovered me on the couch in the opium room, I had come there with no especial plan in mind. Seeing Kathulos leaving, I determined to rise and follow him, but you spoiled that.'

He fingered his chin and laughed grimly.

'I was an amateur boxing champion in Oxford,' said he, 'but Tom Cribb himself could not have withstood that blow – or have dealt it.'

'I regret it as I regret few things.'

'No need to apologise. You saved my life immediately afterward – I was stunned, but not too much to know that that devil Yussef Ali was burning to cut out my heart.'

'How did you come to be at Sir Haldred Frenton's estate? And how is it that you did not raid Yun Shatu's dive?'

'I did not have the place raided because I knew somehow Kathulos would be warned and our efforts would come to naught. I was at Sir Haldred's that night because I have contrived to spend at least part of each night with him since he returned from the Congo. I anticipated an attempt upon his life when I learned from his own lips that he was preparing, from the studies he made on this trip, a treatise on the secret native societies of West Africa. He hinted that the disclosures he intended to make therein might prove sensational, to say the least. Since it is to Kathulos' advantage to destroy such men as might be able to arouse the Western world to its danger, I knew that Sir Haldred was a marked man. Indeed, two distinct attempts were made upon his life on his journey to the coast from the African interior. So I put two trusted men on guard and they are at their post even now.

'Roaming about the darkened house, I heard the noise of your entry, and, warning my men, I stole down to intercept you. At the time of our conversation, Sir Haldred was sitting in his unlighted study, a Scotland Yard man with drawn pistol on each side of him. Their vigilance no doubt accounts for Yussef Ali's failure to attempt what you were sent to do.

'Something in your manner convinced me in spite of yourself,' he meditated. 'I will admit I had some bad moments of doubt as I waited in the darkness that precedes dawn, outside the warehouse.'

Gordon rose suddenly and going to a strong box which stood in a corner of the room, drew thence a thick envelope.

'Although Kathulos has checkmated me at almost every move,' he said, 'I have not been entirely idle. Noting the frequenters of Yun

Shatu's, I have compiled a partial list of the Egyptian's right-hand men, and their records. What you have told me has enabled me to complete that list. As we know, his henchmen are scattered all over the world, and there are possibly hundreds of them here in London. However, this is a list of those I believe to be in his closest council, now with him in England. He told you himself that few even of his followers ever saw him unmasked.'

We bent together over the list, which contained the following names: 'Yun Shatu, Hongkong Chinese, suspected opium smuggler ... keeper of Temple of Dreams . . . resident of Limehouse seven years. Hassim, ex-Senegalese Chief – wanted in French Congo for murder. Santiago – fled from Haiti under suspicion of voodoo worship atrocities. Yar Khan, Afridi, record unknown. Yussef Ali, Moor, slave-dealer in Morocco – suspected of being a German spy in the World War – an instigator of the Fellaheen Rebellion on the upper Nile. Ganra Singh, Lahore, India, Sikh – smuggler of arms into Afghanistan – took an active part in the Lahore and Delhi riots . . . suspected of murder on two occasions—a dangerous man. Stephen Costigan, American – resident in England since the war . . . hashish addict . . . man of remarkable strength. Li Kung, northern China, opium smuggler.'

Lines were drawn significantly through three names – mine, Li Kung's and Yussef Ali's. Nothing was written next to mine, but following Li Kung's name was scrawled briefly in Gordon's rambling characters: 'Shot by John Gordon during the raid on Yun Shatu's.' And following the name of Yussef Ali: 'Killed by Stephen Costigan during the Yun Shatu raid.'

I laughed mirthlessly. Yussef Ali would never hold Zuleika in his arms, for he had never risen from where I felled him.

He glanced at his watch.

'It is nearly ten. Make yourself at home here, Mr Costigan, while I visit Scotland Yard and see if any clue has been found as to Kathulos' new quarters. I believe that the webs are closing on him, and with your aid I promise you we will have the gang located within a week at most.'

Chapter 15. The mark of the tulwar

The fed wolf curls by his drowsy mate
In a tight-trod earth; but the lean wolves wait.

MUNDY

I sat alone in John Gordon's apartments and laughed mirthlessly. In spite of the elixir's stimulus, the strain of the previous night, with its loss of sleep and its heartrending actions, was telling on me. My mind was a chaotic whirl wherein the faces of Gordon, Kathulos and Zuleika shifted with numbing swiftness. All the mass of information Gordon had given to me seemed jumbled and incoherent.

Through this state of being, one fact stood out boldly. I must find the latest hiding-place of the Egyptian and get Zuleika out of his hands . . . if indeed she still lived.

A week, Gordon had said – I laughed again – a week and I would be beyond aiding anyone. I had found the proper amount of elixir to use – knew the minimum amount my system required – and knew that I could make the flask last me four days at most. Four days! Four days in which to comb the rat-holes of Limehouse and Chinatown – four days in which to ferret out, somewhere in the mazes of the East End, the lair of Kathulos.

I burned with impatience to begin, but nature rebelled, and staggering to a couch, I fell upon it and was asleep instantly.

Then someone was shaking me.

'Wake up, Mr Costigan!'

I sat up, blinking. Gordon stood over me, his face haggard.

'There's devil's work done, Costigan! The Scorpion has struck again!'

I sprang up, still half-asleep and only partly realising what he was saying. He helped me into my coat, thrust my hat at me, and then his firm grip on my arm was propelling me out of his door and down the stairs. The street lights were blazing; I had slept an incredible time.

'A logical victim!' I was aware that my companion was saying. 'He should have notified me the instant of his arrival!'

'I don't understand – ' I began dazedly.

We were at the curb now and Gordon hailed a taxi, giving the address of a small and unassuming hotel in a staid and prim section of the city.

'The Baron Rokoff,' he rapped as we whirled along at reckless speed, 'a Russian free-lance, connected with the War Office. He returned from Mongolia yesterday and apparently went into hiding. Undoubtedly he had learned something vital. He had not yet communicated with us, and I had no idea that he was in England until just now.'

'And you learned – '

'The baron was found in his room, his dead body mutilated in a frightful manner!'

The respectable and conventional hotel which the doomed baron had chosen for his hiding-place was in a state of mild uproar, suppressed by the police. The management had attempted to keep the matter quiet, but somehow the guests had learned of the atrocity and many were leaving in haste – or preparing to, as the police were holding all for investigation.

The baron's room, which was on the top floor, was in a state to defy description. Not even in the Great War have I seen a more complete shambles. Nothing had been touched; all remained just as the chambermaid had found it a half-hour since. Tables and chairs lay shattered on the floor, and the furniture, floor and walls were spattered with blood. The baron, a tall, muscular man in life, lay in the middle of the room, a fearful spectacle. His skull had been cleft to the brows, a deep gash under his left arm-pit had shorn through his ribs, and his left arm hung by a shred of flesh. The cold bearded face was set in a look of indescribable horror.

'Some heavy, curved weapon must have been used,' said Gordon, 'something like a sabre, wielded with terrific force. See where a chance blow sank inches deep into the windowsill. And again, the thick back of this heavy chair has been split like a shingle. A sabre, surely.'

'A tulwar,' I muttered, sombrely. 'Do you not recognise the handiwork of the Central Asian butcher? Yar Khan has been here.'

'He came across the roofs, of course, and descended to the window-ledge by means of a knotted rope made fast to something on the edge of the roof. About one-thirty the maid, passing through the corridor, heard a terrific commotion in the baron's room – smashing of chairs and a sudden short shriek which died abruptly into a ghastly gurgle and then ceased – to the sound of heavy blows, curiously muffled, such as a sword might make when driven deep into human flesh. Then all noises stopped suddenly.

'She called the manager and they tried the door and, finding it locked, and receiving no answer to their shouts, opened it with the desk key. Only the corpse was there, but the window was open. This is strangely unlike Kathulos' usual procedure. It lacks subtlety. Often his victims have appeared to have died from natural causes. I scarcely understand.'

'I see little difference in the outcome,' I answered. 'There is nothing that can be done to apprehend the murderer as it is.'

'True,' Gordon scowled. 'We know who did it, but there is no proof – not even a fingerprint. Even if we knew where the Afghan is hiding and arrested him, we could prove nothing – there would be a score of men to swear alibis for him. The baron returned only yesterday. Kathulos probably did not know of his arrival until to-night. He knew that on the morrow Rokoff would make known his presence to me and impart what he learned in northern Asia. The Egyptian knew he must strike quickly, and lacking time to prepare a safer and more elaborate form of murder, he sent the Afridi with his tulwar. There is nothing we can do, at least not until we discover the Scorpion's hiding-place; what the baron had learned in Mongolia, we shall never know, but that it dealt with the plans and aspirations of Kathulos, we may be sure.'

We went down the stairs again and out on the street, accompanied by one of the Scotland Yard men, Hansen. Gordon suggested that we walk back to his apartment and I greeted the opportunity to let the cool night air blow some of the cobwebs out of my mazed brain.

As we walked along the deserted streets, Gordon suddenly cursed savagely.

'This is a veritable labyrinth we are following, leading nowhere! Here, in the very heart of civilisation's metropolis, the direct enemy of that civilisation commits crimes of the most outrageous nature and goes free! We are children, wandering in the night, struggling with an unseen evil – dealing with an incarnate devil, of whose true identity we know nothing and whose true ambitions we can only guess.

'Never have we managed to arrest one of the Egyptian's direct henchmen, and the few dupes and tools of his we have apprehended have died mysteriously before they could tell us anything. Again I repeat: what strange power has Kathulos that dominates these men of different creeds and races? The men in London with him are, of course, mostly renegades, slaves of dope, but his tentacles stretch all over the East. Some dominance is his: the power that sent the Chinaman, Li Kung, back to kill you, in the face of certain death;

that sent Yar Khan over the roofs of London to do murder; that holds Zuleika the Circassian in unseen bonds of slavery.'

'Of course we know,' he continued after a brooding silence, 'that there are cults in Africa and the Orient whose origin dates back to Ophir and the fall of Atlantis. This man must be a power in some or possibly all of these societies.

'Have you ever' – he turned to me abruptly – 'heard the ocean mentioned in connection with Kathulos?'

'Never.'

'There is a widespread superstition in northern Africa, based on a very ancient legend, that the great leader would come out of the sea! And I once heard a Berber speak of the Scorpion as "the Son of the Ocean".'

'That is a term of respect among that tribe, is it not?'

'Yes; still I wonder sometimes.'

Chapter 16. The mummy who laughed

> *Laughing as littered skulls that lie*
> *After lost battles turn to the sky*
> *An everlasting laugh.*

CHESTERTON

'A shop open this late,' Gordon remarked suddenly.

A fog had descended on London and along the quiet street we were traversing the lights glimmered with the peculiar reddish haze characteristic of such atmospheric conditions. Our footfalls echoed drearily. Even in the heart of a great city there are always sections which seem overlooked and forgotten. Such a street was this. Not even a policeman was in sight.

The shop which had attracted Gordon's attention was just in front of us, on the same side of the street. There was no sign over the door, merely some sort of emblem, something like a dragon. Light flowed from the open doorway and the small show windows on each side. As it was neither a cafe nor the entrance to a hotel we found ourselves idly speculating over its reason for being open. Ordinarily, I suppose, neither of us would have given the matter a thought, but our nerves were so keyed up that we found ourselves instinctively suspicious of anything out of the ordinary. Then something occurred which was distinctly out of the ordinary.

A very tall, very thin man, considerably stooped, suddenly loomed up out of the fog in front of us, and beyond the shop. I had only a glance of him – an impression of incredible gauntness, of worn, wrinkled garments, a high silk hat drawn close over the brows, a face entirely hidden by a muffler; then he turned aside and entered the shop. A cold wind whispered down the street, twisting the fog into wispy ghosts, but the coldness that came upon me transcended the wind's.

'Gordon!' I exclaimed in a fierce, low voice; 'either my senses are no longer reliable or else Kathulos himself has just gone into that house!'

Gordon's eyes blazed. We were now close to the shop, and lengthening his strides into a run he hurled himself into the door, the detective and I close upon his heels.

A weird assortment of merchandise met our eyes. Antique weapons covered the walls, and the floor was piled high with curious things. Maori idols shouldered Chinese josses, and suits of medieval armour bulked darkly against stacks of rare oriental rugs and Latin-make shawls. The place was an antique shop. Of the figure who had aroused our interest we saw nothing.

An old man clad bizarrely in red fez, brocaded jacket and Turkish slippers came from the back of the shop.

'You wish something, sirs?'

'You keep open rather late,' Gordon said abruptly, his eyes travelling swiftly over the shop for some secret hiding-place that might conceal the object of our search.

'Yes, sir. My customers number many eccentric professors and students who keep very irregular hours. Often the night boats unload special pieces for me and very often I have customers later than this. I remain open all night, sir.'

'We are merely looking around,' Gordon returned, and in an aside to Hansen: 'Go to the back and stop anyone who tries to leave that way.'

Hansen nodded and strolled casually to the rear of the shop. The back door was clearly visible to our view, through a vista of antique furniture and tarnished hangings strung up for exhibition. We had followed the Scorpion – if he it was – so closely that I did not believe he would have had time to traverse the full length of the shop and make his exit without our having seen him as we came in. For our eyes had been on the rear door ever since we had entered.

Gordon and I browsed around casually among the curios, handling and discussing some of them but I have no idea as to their nature.

After a time Gordon whispered to me: 'There is no advantage in keeping up this pretence. We have looked everywhere the Scorpion might be hiding, in the ordinary manner. I will make known my identity and authority and we will search the entire building openly.'

Even as he spoke a truck drew up outside the door and two burly Negroes entered. The Levantine seemed to have expected them, for he merely waved them toward the back of the shop and they responded with a grunt of understanding.

Gordon and I watched them closely as they made their way to a large mummy-case which stood upright against the wall not far from the back. They lowered this to a level position and then started for the door, carrying it carefully between them.

'Halt!' Gordon stepped forward, raising his hand authoritatively.

'I represent Scotland Yard,' he said swiftly, 'and have sanction for anything I choose to do. Set that mummy down; nothing leaves this shop until we have thoroughly searched it.'

The Negroes obeyed without a word and my friend turned to the Levantine, who, apparently not perturbed or even interested, sat smoking a Turkish water-pipe.

'Who was that tall man who entered just before we did, and where did he go?'

'No one entered before you, sir. Or, if anyone did, I was at the back of the shop and did not see him. You are certainly at liberty to search my shop, sir.'

And search it we did, with the combined craft of a secret service expert and a denizen of the underworld. The whole thing had a distinct effect of unreality.

At last, baffled, we returned to the mummy-case, which was certainly long enough to conceal even a man of Kathulos' height. The thing did not appear to be sealed as is the usual custom, and Gordon opened it without difficulty. A formless shape, swathed in mouldering wrappings, met our eyes. Gordon parted some of the wrappings and revealed an inch or so of withered, brownish, leathery arm. He shuddered involuntarily as he touched it, as a man will do at the touch of a reptile or some inhumanly cold thing. Taking a small metal idol from a stand nearby, he rapped on the shrunken breast and the arm. Each gave out a solid thumping, like some sort of wood.

Gordon shrugged his shoulders. 'Dead for two thousand years anyway and I don't suppose I should risk destroying a valuable mummy simply to prove what we know to be true.'

He closed the case again.

'The mummy may have crumbled some, even from this much exposure, but perhaps it did not.'

This last was addressed to the Levantine who replied merely by a courteous gesture of his hand, and the Negroes once more lifted the case and carried it to the truck, where they loaded it on, and a moment later mummy, truck and Negroes had vanished in the fog.

Gordon still nosed about the shop, but I stood stock-still in the centre of the floor. To my chaotic and dope-ridden brain I attribute it, but the sensation had been mine, that through the wrappings of the mummy's face, great eyes had burned into mine, eyes like pools of yellow fire, that seared my soul and froze me where I stood. And as the case had been carried through the door, I knew that the lifeless thing in it, dead God only knows how many centuries, was laughing, hideously and silently.

Chapter 17. The dead man from the sea

The blind gods roar and rave and dream
Of all cities under the sea.

CHESTERTON

Gordon puffed savagely at his Turkish cigarette, staring abstractedly and unseeingly at Hansen, who sat opposite him.

'I suppose we must chalk up another failure against ourselves. Kamonos is evidently a creature of the Egyptian's and the walls and floors of his shop are probably honeycombed with secret panels and doors which would baffle a magician.'

Hansen made some answer but I said nothing. Since our return to Gordon's apartment, I had been conscious of a feeling of intense languor and sluggishness which not even my condition could account for. I knew that my system was full of the elixir – but my mind seemed strangely slow and hard of comprehension in direct contrast with the average state of my mentality when stimulated by the hellish dope.

This condition was slowly leaving me, like mist floating from the surface of a lake, and I felt as if I were waking gradually from a long and unnaturally sound sleep.

Gordon was saying: 'I would give a good deal to know if Kamonos is really one of Kathulos' slaves or if the Scorpion managed to make his escape through some natural exit as we entered.'

'Kamonos is his servant, true enough,' I found myself saying slowly, as if searching for the proper words. 'As we left, I saw his gaze light upon the scorpion which is traced on my hand. His eyes narrowed, and as we were leaving he contrived to brush close against me – and to whisper in a quick low voice: "Soho, 48".'

Gordon came erect like a loosened steel bow.

'Indeed!' he rapped. 'Why did you not tell me at the time?'

'I don't know.'

My friend eyed me sharply.

'I noticed you seemed like a man intoxicated all the way from the shop,' said he. 'I attributed it to some aftermath of hashish. But no. Kathulos is undoubtedly a masterful disciple of Mesmer – his power over venomous reptiles shows that, and I am beginning to believe it is the real source of his power over humans.

'Somehow, the Master caught you off your guard in that shop and partly asserted his dominance over your mind. From what hidden nook he sent his thought-waves to shatter your brain, I do not know, but Kathulos was somewhere in that shop, I am sure.'

'He was. He was in the mummy-case.'

'The mummy-case!' Gordon exclaimed rather impatiently. 'That is impossible! The mummy quite filled it and not even such a thin being as the Master could have found room there.'

I shrugged my shoulders, unable to argue the point but somehow sure of the truth of my statement.

'Kamonos,' Gordon continued, 'doubtless is not a member of the inner circle and does not know of your change of allegiance. Seeing the mark of the scorpion, he undoubtedly supposed you to be a spy of the Master's. The whole thing may be a plot to ensnare us, but I feel that the man was sincere – Soho 48 can be nothing less than the Scorpion's new rendezvous.'

I too felt that Gordon was right, though a suspicion lurked in my mind.

'I secured the papers of Major Morley yesterday,' be continued, 'and while you slept, I went over them. Mostly they but corroborated what I already knew – touched on the unrest of the natives and repeated the theory that one vast genius was behind all. But there was one matter which interested me greatly and which I think will interest you also.'

From his strong-box he took a manuscript written in the close, neat characters of the unfortunate major, and in a monotonous droning voice which betrayed little of his intense excitement he read the following nightmarish narrative:

This matter I consider worth jotting down – as to whether it has any bearing on the case at hand, further developments will show. At Alexandria, where I spent some weeks seeking further clues as to the identity of the man known as the Scorpion, I made the acquaintance, through my friend Ahmed Shah, of the noted Egyptologist Professor Ezra Schuyler of New York. He verified the statement made by various laymen, concerning the legend of the 'ocean-man'. This myth, handed down from generation to generation, stretches back into the very mists of antiquity and is, briefly, that some day a man shall come up out of the sea and shall lead the people of Egypt to victory over all others. Professor Schuyler gave it as his opinion that the myth was somehow connected with the lost Atlantis, which, he maintains, was located between the African and South American continents and to whose inhabitants the ancestors of the Egyptians were tributary. The reasons for his connection are too lengthy and vague to note here, but following the line of his theory he told me a strange and fantastic tale. He said that a close friend of his, Von Lorfmon of Germany, a sort of free-lance scientist, now dead, was sailing off the coast of Senegal some years ago, for the purpose of investigating and classifying the rare specimens of sea life found there. He was using for his purpose a small trading-vessel.

Some days out of sight of land, something floating was sighted, and this object, being grappled and brought aboard, proved to be a mummy-case of a most curious kind. Professor Schuyler explained to me the features whereby it differed from the ordinary Egyptian style, but from his rather technical account I merely got the impression that it was a strangely shaped affair carved with characters neither cuneiform nor hieroglyphic. The case was heavily lacquered, being watertight and airtight, and Von Lorfmon had considerable difficulty in opening it. However, he managed to do so without damaging the case, and a most unusual mummy was revealed. Schuyler said that he never saw either the mummy or the case, but that from descriptions given him by the Greek skipper who was present at the opening of the case, the mummy differed as much from the ordinary man as the case differed from the conventional type.

Examination proved that the subject had not undergone the usual procedure of mummification. All parts were intact just as in life, but the whole form was shrunk and hardened to a wood-like consistency. Cloth wrappings swathed the thing and they crumbled to dust and vanished the instant air was let in upon them.

Von Lorfmon was impressed by the effect upon the crew. As the case was hoisted on board, they all fell prostrate on the deck and raised a sort of worshipful chant, and it was necessary to use force in order to exclude them from the cabin wherein the mummy was exposed. A number of fights broke out between them and the Greek element of the crew, and the skipper and Von Lorfmon thought best to put back to the nearest port in all haste. The skipper attributed it to the natural aversion of seamen toward having a corpse on board, but Von Lorfmon seemed to sense a deeper meaning.

They made port in Lagos, and that very night Von Lorfmon was murdered in his state-room and the mummy and its case vanished. An aura of mystery hung over Von Lorfmon's death. He had taken the mummy into his state-room, and anticipating an attack from the fanatical crew, had carefully barred and bolted door and portholes. The skipper, a reliable man, swore that it was virtually impossible to effect an entrance from without. And what signs were present pointed to the fact that the locks had been worked from within. The scientist was killed by a dagger which formed part of his collection and which was left in his breast.

Schuyler gave as his opinion that the thing was the work of Atlanteans and that the man in the mummy-case was a native of lost Atlantis. How the case came to float up through the fathoms of water which cover the forgotten land, he does not venture to offer a theory.

Gordon ceased and looked up at me.

'Mummies seem to weave a weird dance through the warp of the tale,' he said. 'The German scientist took several pictures of the mummy with his camera, and it was after seeing these – which strangely enough were not stolen along with the thing – that Major Morley began to think himself on the brink of some monstrous discovery. His diary reflects his state of mind and becomes incoherent – his condition seems to have bordered on insanity. What did he learn to unbalance him so? Do you suppose that the mesmeric spells of Kathulos were used against him?'

'These pictures – ' I began.

'They fell into Schuyler's hands and he gave one to Morley. I found it among the manuscripts.'

He handed the thing to me, watching me narrowly. I stared, then rose unsteadily and poured myself a tumbler of wine.

'Not a dead idol in a voodoo hut,' I said shakily, 'but a monster animated by fearsome life, roaming the world for victims. Morley had seen the Master – that is why his brain crumbled. Gordon, as I hope to live again, *that face is the face of Kathulos* !'

Gordon stared wordlessly at me.

'The Master hand, Gordon,' I laughed. A certain grim enjoyment penetrated the mists of my horror, at the sight of the steel-nerved Englishman struck speechless, doubtless for the first time in his life.

He moistened his lips and said in a scarcely recognisable voice, 'Then, in God's name, Costigan, nothing is stable or certain, and mankind hovers at the brink of untold abysses of nameless horror. If that dead monster found by Von Lorfmon be in truth the Scorpion, brought to life in some hideous fashion, what can mortal effort do against him?'

'The mummy at Kamonos' – ' I began.

'Aye, the man whose flesh, hardened by a thousand years of non-existence – that must have been Kathulos himself! He would have just had time to strip, wrap himself in the linens and step into the case before we entered. You remember that the case, leaning upright against the wall, stood partly concealed by a large Burmese idol, which obstructed our view and doubtless gave him time to accomplish his purpose. My God, Costigan, with what horror of the prehistoric world are we dealing?'

'I have heard of Hindu fakirs who could induce a condition closely resembling death,' I began. 'Is it not possible that Kathulos, a shrewd and crafty Oriental, could have placed himself in this state and his followers have placed the case in the ocean where it was sure to be found? And might not he have been in this shape tonight at Kamonos'?'

Gordon shook his head.

'No, I have seen these fakirs. None of them ever feigned death to the extent of becoming shrivelled and hard – in a word, dried up. Morley, narrating in another place the description of the mummy-case as jotted down by Von Lorfmon and passed on to Schuyler, mentions the fact that large portions of seaweed adhered to it – seaweed of a kind found only at great depths, on the bottom of the ocean. The wood, too, was of a kind which Von Lorfmon failed to recognise or to classify, in spite of the fact that he was one of the greatest living authorities on flora. And his notes again and again emphasise the enormous age of the thing. He admitted that there was no way of telling how old the mummy was, but his hints intimate that he believed it to be, not thousands of years old, but millions of years!

'No. We must face the facts. Since you are positive that the picture of the mummy is the picture of Kathulos – and there is little room for fraud – one of two things is practically certain: the Scorpion was never dead but ages ago was placed in that mummy-case and his life preserved in some manner, or else – he was dead and has been brought to life! Either of these theories, viewed in the cold light of reason, is absolutely untenable. Are we all insane?'

'Had you ever walked the road to hashish land,' I said sombrely, 'you could believe anything to be true. Had you ever gazed into the terrible reptilian eyes of Kathulos the sorcerer, you would not doubt that he was both dead and alive.'

Gordon gazed out the window, his fine face haggard in the grey light which had begun to steal through them.

'At any rate,' said he, 'there are two places which I intend exploring thoroughly before the sun rises again – Kamonos' antique shop and Soho 48.'

Chapter 18. The grip of the Scorpion

While from a proud tower in the town
Death looks gigantically down.

EDGAR ALLAN POE

Hansen snored on the bed as I paced the room. Another day had passed over London and again the street lamps glimmered through the fog. Their lights affected me strangely. They seemed to beat, solid waves of energy, against my brain. They twisted the fog into strange sinister shapes. Footlights of the stage that is the streets of London, how many grisly scenes had they lighted? I pressed my hands hard against my throbbing temples, striving to bring my thoughts back from the chaotic labyrinth where they wandered.

Gordon I had not seen since dawn. Following the clue of 'Soho 48' he had gone forth to arrange a raid upon the place and he thought it best that I should remain under cover. He anticipated an attempt upon my life, and again he feared that if I went searching among the dives I formerly frequented it would arouse suspicion.

Hansen snored on. I seated myself and began to study the Turkish shoes which clothed my feet. Zuleika had worn Turkish slippers – how she floated through my waking dreams, gilding prosaic things with her witchery! Her face smiled at me from the fog; her eyes shone from the flickering lamps; her phantom footfalls re-echoed through the misty chambers of my skull.

They beat an endless tattoo, luring and haunting till it seemed that these echoes found echoes in the hallway outside the room where I stood, soft and stealthy. A sudden rap at the door and I started.

Hansen slept on as I crossed the room and flung the door swiftly open. A swirling wisp of fog had invaded the corridor, and through it, like a silver veil, I saw her – Zuleika stood before me with her shimmering hair and her red lips parted and her great dark eyes.

Like a speechless fool I stood and she glanced quickly down the hallway and then stepped inside and closed the door.

'Gordon!' she whispered in a thrilling undertone. 'Your friend! The Scorpion has him!'

Hansen had awakened and now sat gaping stupidly at the strange scene which met his eyes.

Zuleika did not heed him.

'And oh, Steephen!' she cried, and tears shone in her eyes, 'I have tried so hard to secure some more elixir but I could not.'

'Never mind that,' I finally found my speech. 'Tell me about Gordon.'

'He went back to Kamonos' alone, and Hassim and Ganra Singh took him captive and brought him to the Master's house. Tonight assemble a great host of the people of the Scorpion for the sacrifice.'

'Sacrifice!' A grisly thrill of horror coursed down my spine. Was there no limit to the ghastliness of this business?

'Quick, Zuleika, where is this house of the Master's?'

'Soho, 48. You must summon the police and send many men to surround it, but you must not go yourself – '

Hansen sprang up quivering for action, but I turned to him. My brain was clear now, or seemed to be, and racing unnaturally.

'Wait!' I turned back to Zuleika. 'When is this sacrifice to take place?'

'At the rising of the moon.'

'That is only a few hours before dawn. Time to save him, but if we raid the house they'll kill him before we can reach them. And God only knows how many diabolical things guard all approaches.'

'I do not know,' Zuleika whimpered. 'I must go now, or the Master will kill me.'

Something gave way in my brain at that; something like a flood of wild and terrible exultation swept over me.

'The Master will kill no one!' I shouted, flinging my arms on high. 'Before ever the east turns red for dawn, the Master dies! By all things holy and unholy I swear it!'

Hansen stared wildly at me and Zuleika shrank back as I turned on her. To my dope-inspired brain had come a sudden burst of light, true and unerring. I knew Kathulos was a mesmerist – that he understood fully the secret of dominating another's mind and soul. And I knew that at last I had hit upon the reason of his power over the girl. Mesmerism! As a snake fascinates and draws to him a bird, so the Master held Zuleika to him with unseen shackles. So absolute was his rule over her that it held even when she was out of his sight, working over great distances.

There was but one thing which would break that hold: the magnetic power of some other person whose control was stronger with her than Kathulos'. I laid my hands on her slim little shoulders and made her face me.

'Zuleika,' I said commandingly, 'here you are safe; you shall not return to Kathulos. There is no need of it. Now you are free.'

But I knew I had failed before I ever started. Her eyes held a look of amazed, unreasoning fear and she twisted timidly in my grasp.

'Steephen, please let me go!' she begged. 'I must – I must!'

I drew her over to the bed and asked Hansen for his handcuffs. He handed them to me, wonderingly, and I fastened one cuff to the bedpost and the other to her slim wrist. The girl whimpered but made no resistance, her limpid eyes seeking mine in mute appeal.

It cut me to the quick to enforce my will upon her in this apparently brutal manner but I steeled myself.

'Zuleika,' I said tenderly, 'you are now my prisoner. The Scorpion cannot blame you for not returning to him when you are unable to do so – and before dawn you shall be free of his rule entirely.'

I turned to Hansen and spoke in a tone which admitted of no argument. 'Remain here, just without the door, until I return. On no account allow any strangers to enter – that is, anyone whom you do not personally know. And I charge you, on your honour as a man, do not release this girl, no matter what she may say. If neither I nor Gordon have returned by ten o'clock tomorrow, take her to this address – that family once was friends of mine and will take care of a homeless girl. I am going to Scotland Yard.'

'Steephen,' Zuleika wailed, 'you are going to the Master's lair! You will be killed. Send the police, do not go!'

I bent, drew her into my arms, felt her lips against mine, then tore myself away.

The fog plucked at me with ghostly fingers, cold as the hands of dead men, as I raced down the street. I had no plan, but one was forming in my mind, beginning to seethe in the stimulated cauldron that was my brain. I halted at the sight of a policeman pacing his beat, and beckoning him to me, scribbled a terse note on a piece of paper torn from a notebook and handed it to him.

'Get this to Scotland Yard; it's a matter of life and death and it has to do with the business of John Gordon.'

At that name, a gloved hand came up in swift assent, but his assurance of haste died out behind me as I renewed my flight. The note stated briefly that Gordon was a prisoner at Soho 48 and advised an immediate raid in force – advised, nay, in Gordon's name, commanded it.

My reason for my actions was simple; I knew that the first noise of the raid sealed John Gordon's doom. Somehow I first must reach him and protect or free him before the police arrived.

The time seemed endless, but at last the grim gaunt outlines of the house that was Soho 48 rose up before me, a giant ghost in the fog. The hour grew late; few people dared the mists and the dampness as I came to a halt in the street before this forbidding building. No lights showed from the windows, either upstairs or down. It seemed deserted. But the lair of the scorpion often seems deserted until the silent death strikes suddenly.

Here I halted and a wild thought struck me. One way or another, the drama would be over by dawn. Tonight was the climax of my career, the ultimate top of life. Tonight I was the strongest link in the strange chain of events. Tomorrow it would not matter whether I lived or died. I drew the flask of elixir from my pocket and gazed at it. Enough for two more days if properly eked out. Two more days of life! Or – I needed stimulation as I never needed it before; the task in front of me was one no mere human could hope to accomplish.

If I drank the entire remainder of the elixir, I had no idea as to the duration of its effect, but it would last the night through. And my legs were shaky; my mind had curious periods of utter vacuity; weakness of brain and body assailed me. I raised the flask and with one draft drained it.

For an instant I thought it was death. Never had I taken such an amount.

Sky and world reeled and I felt as if I would fly into a million vibrating fragments, like the bursting of a globe of brittle steel. Like fire, like hell-fire the elixir raced along my veins and I was a giant! A monster! A superman!

Turning, I strode to the menacing, shadowy doorway. I had no plan; I felt the need of none. As a drunken man walks blithely into danger, I strode to the lair of the Scorpion, magnificently aware of my superiority, imperially confident of my stimulation and sure as the unchanging stars that the way would open before me.

Oh, there never was a superman like that who knocked commandingly on the door of Soho 48 that night in the rain and the fog!

I knocked four times, the old signal that we slaves had used to be admitted into the idol room at Yun Shatu's. An aperture opened in the centre of the door and slanted eyes looked warily out. They slightly widened as the owner recognised me, then narrowed wickedly.

'You fool!' I said angrily. 'Don't you see the mark?'

I held my hand to the aperture.

'Don't you recognise me? Let me in, curse you.'

I think the very boldness of the trick made for its success. Surely by now all the Scorpion's slaves knew of Stephen Costigan's rebellion, knew that he was marked for death. And the very fact that I came there, inviting doom, confused the doorman.

The door opened and I entered. The man who had admitted me was a tall, lank Chinaman I had known as a servant at Kathulos. He closed the door behind me and I saw we stood in a sort of vestibule, lighted by a dim lamp whose glow could not be seen from the street for the reason that the windows were heavily curtained. The Chinaman glowered at me undecided. I looked at him, tensed. Then suspicion flared in his eyes and his hand flew to his sleeve. But at the instant I was on him and his lean neck broke like a rotten bough between my hands.

I eased his corpse to the thickly carpeted floor and listened. No sound broke the silence. Stepping as stealthily as a wolf, fingers spread like talons, I stole into the next room. This was furnished in oriental style, with couches and rugs and gold-worked drapery, but was empty of human life. I crossed it and went into the next one. Light flowed softly from the censers which were swung from the ceiling, and the Eastern rugs deadened the sound of my footfalls; I seemed to be moving through a castle of enchantment.

Every moment I expected a rush of silent assassins from the door ways or from behind the curtains or screens with their writhing dragons. Utter silence reigned. Room after room I explored and at last halted at the foot of the stairs. The inevitable censer shed an uncertain light, but most of the stairs were veiled in shadows. What horrors awaited me above?

But fear and the elixir are strangers and I mounted that stair of lurking terror as boldly as I had entered that house of terror. The upper rooms I found to be much like those below and with them they had this fact in common: they were empty of human life. I sought an attic but there seemed no door letting into one. Returning to the first floor, I made a search for an entrance into the basement, but again my efforts were fruitless. The amazing truth was borne in upon me: except for myself and that dead man who lay sprawled so grotesquely in the outer vestibule, there were no men in that house, dead or living.

I could not understand it. Had the house been bare of furniture I should have reached the natural conclusion that Kathulos had fled – but no signs of flight met my eye. This was unnatural, uncanny. I stood in the great shadowy library and pondered. No, I had made no mistake in the house. Even if the broken corpse in the vestibule were not there to furnish mute testimony, everything in the room pointed toward the presence of the Master. There were the artificial palms, the lacquered screens, the tapestries, even the idol, though now no incense smoke rose before it. About the walls were ranged long shelves of books, bound in strange and costly fashion – books in every language in the world, I found from a swift examination, and on every subject – outré and bizarre, most of them.

Remembering the secret passage in the Temple of Dreams, I investigated the heavy mahogany table which stood in the centre of the room. Bur nothing resulted. A sudden blaze of fury surged up in me, primitive and unreasoning. I snatched a statuette from the table and dashed it against the shelf-covered wall. The noise of its breaking would surely bring the gang from their hiding-place. But the result was much more startling than that!

The statuette struck the edge of a shelf and instantly the whole section of shelves with their load of books swung silently outward, revealing a narrow doorway! As in the other secret door, a row of steps led downward. At another time I would have shuddered at the thought of descending, with the horrors of the other tunnel fresh in my mind, but inflamed as I was by the elixir, I strode forward without an instant's hesitancy.

Since there was no one in the house, they must be somewhere in the tunnel or in whatever lair the tunnel led to. I stepped through the doorway, leaving the door open; the police might find it that way and follow me, though somehow I felt as if mine would be a lone hand from start to grim finish.

I went down a considerable distance and then the stair debouched into a level corridor some twenty feet wide – a remarkable thing. In spite of the width, the ceiling was rather low and from it hung small, curiously shaped lamps which flung a dim light. I stalked hurriedly along the corridor like old Death seeking victims, and as I went I noted the work of the thing. The floor was of great broad flags and the walls seemed to be of huge blocks of evenly set stone. This passage was clearly no work of modern days; the slaves of Kathulos never tunnelled there. Some secret way of medieval times, I thought – and after all, who knows what catacombs lie below London, whose secrets are greater and darker than those of Babylon and Rome?

On and on I went, and now I knew that I must be far below the earth. The air was dank and heavy, and cold moisture dripped from the stones of walls and ceiling. From time to time I saw smaller passages leading away in the darkness but I determined to keep to the larger main one.

A ferocious impatience gripped me. I seemed to have been walking for hours and still only dank damp walls and bare flags and guttering lamps met my eyes. I kept a close watch for sinister-appearing chests or the like – saw no such things.

Then as I was about to burst into savage curses, another stair loomed up in the shadows in front of me.

Chapter 19. Dark fury

The ringed wolf glared the circle round
Through baleful, blue-lit eye,
Not unforgetful of his debt.
Quoth he, 'I'll do some damage yet
Or ere my turn to die!'

MUNDY

Like a lean wolf I glided up the stairs. Some twenty feet up there was a sort of landing from which other corridors diverged, much like the lower one by which I had come. The thought came to me that the earth below London must be honeycombed with such secret passages, one above the other.

Some feet above this landing the steps halted at a door, and here I hesitated, uncertain as to whether I should chance knocking or not. Even as I meditated, the door began to open. I shrank back against the wall, flattening myself out as much as possible. The door swung wide and a Moor came through. Only a glimpse I had of the room beyond, out of the corner of my eye, but my unnaturally alert senses registered the fact that the room was empty.

And on the instant, before be could turn, I smote the Moor a single deathly blow behind the angle of the jawbone and be toppled head-long down the stairs, to lie in a crumpled heap on the landing, his limbs tossed grotesquely about.

My left hand caught the door as it started to slam shut and in an instant I was through and standing in the room beyond. As I had thought, there was no occupant of this room. I crossed it swiftly and entered the next. These rooms were furnished in a manner before which the furnishings of the Soho house paled into insignificance. Barbaric, terrible, unholy – these words alone convey some slight idea of the ghastly sights which met my eyes. Skulls, bones and complete skeletons formed much of the decorations, if such they were. Mummies leered from their cases and mounted reptiles ranged the walls. Between these sinister relics hung African shields of hide and bamboo, crossed with assegais and war-daggers. Here and there reared obscene idols, black and horrible.

And in between and scattered about among these evidences of savagery and barbarism were vases, screens, rugs and hangings of the highest oriental workmanship; a strange and incongruous effect.

I had passed through two of these rooms without seeing a human being, when I came to stairs leading upward. Up these I went, several flights, until I came to a door in a ceiling. I wondered if I was still under the earth. Surely the first stairs had led into a house of some sort. I raised the door cautiously. Starlight met my eyes and I drew myself warily up and out. There I halted. A broad flat roof stretched away on all sides and beyond its rim on all sides glimmered the lights of London. Just what building I was on, I had no idea, but that it was a tall one I could tell, for I seemed to be above most of the lights I saw. Then I saw that I was not alone.

Over against the shadows of the ledge that ran around the roof's edge, a great menacing form bulked in starlight. A pair of eyes glinted at me with a light not wholly sane; the starlight glanced silver from a curving length of steel. Yar Khan the Afghan killer fronted me in the silent shadows.

A fierce wild exultation surged over me. Now I could begin to pay the debt I owed Kathulos and all his hellish band! The dope fired my veins and sent waves of inhuman power and dark fury through me. A spring and I was on my feet in a silent, deathly rush.

Yar Khan was a giant, taller and bulkier than I. He held a tulwar, and from the instant I saw him I knew that he was full of the dope to the use of which he was addicted – heroin.

As I came in he swung his heavy weapon high in the air, but ere he could strike I seized his sword wrist in an iron grip and with my free hand drove smashing blows into his midriff.

Of that hideous battle, fought in silence above the sleeping city with only the stars to see, I remember little. I remember tumbling back and forth, locked in a death embrace. I remember the stiff beard rasping my flesh as his dope-fired eyes gazed wildly into mine. I remember the taste of hot blood in my mouth, the tang of fearful exultation in my soul, the onrushing and upsurging of in-human strength and fury.

God, what a sight for a human eye, had anyone looked upon that grim roof where two human leopards, dope maniacs, tore each other to pieces!

I remember his arm breaking like rotten wood in my grip and the tulwar falling from his useless hand. Handicapped by a broken arm, the end was inevitable, and with one wild uproaring flood of might, I rushed him to the edge of the roof and bent him backward far out over the ledge. An instant we struggled there; then I tore loose his hold and hurled him over, and one single shriek came up as he hurtled into the darkness below.

I stood upright, arms hurled up toward the stars, a terrible statue of primordial triumph. And down my breast trickled streams of blood from the long wounds left by the Afghan's frantic nails, on neck and face.

Then I turned with the craft of the maniac. Had no one heard the sound of that battle? My eyes were on the door through which I had come, but a noise made me turn, and for the first time I noticed a small affair like a tower jutting up from the roof. There was no window there, but there was a door, and even as I looked that door opened and a huge black form framed itself in the light that streamed from within. Hassim!

He stepped out on the roof and closed the door, his shoulders hunched and neck outthrust as he glanced this way and that. I struck him senseless to the roof with one hate-driven smash. I crouched over him, waiting some sign of returning consciousness; then away in the sky close to the horizon, I saw a faint red tint. The rising of the moon!

Where in God's name was Gordon? Even as I stood undecided, a strange noise reached me. It was curiously like the droning of many bees.

Striding in the direction from which it seemed to come, I crossed the roof and leaned over the ledge. A sight nightmarish and incredible met my eyes.

Some twenty feet below the level of the roof on which I stood, there was another roof, of the same size and clearly a part of the same building. On one side it was bounded by the wall; on the other three sides a parapet several feet high took the place of a ledge.

A great throng of people stood, sat and squatted, close-packed on the roof! There were hundreds of them, and it was their low-voiced conversation which I had heard. But what held my gaze was that upon which their eyes were fixed.

About the centre of the roof rose a sort of teocalli some ten feet high, almost exactly like those found in Mexico and on which the priests of the Aztecs sacrificed human victims. This, allowing for its infinitely smaller scale, was an exact type of those sacrificial pyramids. On the flat top of it was a curiously carved altar, and beside it stood a lank, dusky form whom even the ghastly mask he wore could not disguise to my gaze – Santiago, the Haiti voodoo fetish man. On the altar lay John Gordon, stripped to the waist and bound hand and foot, but conscious.

I reeled back from the roof edge, rent in twain by indecision. Even the stimulus of the elixir was not equal to this. Then a sound brought me about to see Hassim struggling dizzily to his knees. I reached him with two long strides and ruthlessly smashed him down again. Then I noticed a queer sort of contrivance dangling from his girdle. I bent and examined it. It was a mask similar to that worn by Santiago. Then my mind leaped swift and sudden to a wild desperate plan, which to my dope-ridden brain seemed not at all wild or desperate. I stepped softly to the tower and, opening the door, peered inward. I saw no one who might need to be silenced, but I saw a long silken robe hanging upon a peg in the wall. The luck of the dope fiend! I snatched it and closed the door again. Hassim showed no signs of consciousness but I gave him another smash on the chin to make sure and, seizing his mask, hurried to the ledge.

A low guttural chant floated up to me, jangling, barbaric, with an undertone of maniacal blood-lust. Men and women were swaying back and forth to the wild rhythm of their death chant. On the teocalli Santiago stood like a statue of black basalt, facing the east, dagger held high – a wild and terrible sight, naked as he was save for a wide silken girdle and that inhuman mask on his face. The moon thrust a red rim above the eastern horizon and a faint breeze stirred the great black plumes which nodded above the voodoo man's mask. The chant of the worshippers dropped to a low, sinister whisper.

I hurriedly slipped on the death mask, gathered the robe close about me and prepared for the descent. I was prepared to drop the full distance, being sure in the superb confidence of my insanity that I would land unhurt, but as I climbed over the ledge I found a steel ladder leading down. Evidently Hassim, one of the voodoo priests, intended descending this way. So down I went, and in haste, for I knew that the instant the moon's lower rim cleared the city's skyline, that motionless dagger would descend into Gordon's breast.

Gathering the robe close about me so as to conceal my white skin, I stepped down upon the roof and strode forward through rows of black worshipers who shrank aside to let me through. To the foot of the teocalli I stalked and up the stair that ran about it, until I stood beside the death altar and marked the dark red stains upon it. Gordon lay on his back, his eyes open, his face drawn and haggard, but his gaze dauntless and unflinching.

Santiago's eyes blazed at me through the slits of his mask, but I read no suspicion in his gaze until I reached forward and took the dagger from his hand. He was too much astonished to resist, and the throng fell suddenly silent. He was simply struck speechless with astonishment. Moving swiftly I cut Gordon's bonds and hauled him erect. Then Santiago with a shriek leaped upon me – shrieked again and, arms flung high, pitched headlong from the teocalli with his own dagger buried to the hilt in his breast.

Then the worshippers were on us with a screech and a roar – leaping on the steps of the teocalli like black leopards in the moonlight, knives flashing, eyes gleaming whitely.

I tore mask and robe from me and answered Gordon's exclamation with a wild laugh. I had hoped that by virtue of my disguise I might get us both safely away but now I was content to die there at his side.

He tore a great metal ornament from the altar, and as the attackers came he wielded this. A moment we held them at bay and then they flowed over us like a wave. This to me was Valhalla! Knives stung me and blackjacks smashed against me, but I laughed and drove my iron fists in straight, steam-hammer smashes that shattered flesh and bone. I saw Gordon's crude weapon rise and fall, and each time a man went down. Skulls shattered and blood splashed and the dark fury swept over me. Nightmare faces swirled about me and I was on my knees; up again and the faces crumpled before my blows. Through far mists I seemed to hear a hideous familiar voice raised in imperious command.

Gordon was swept away from me but from the sounds I knew that the work of death still went on. The stars reeled through fogs of blood, but Hell's exaltation was on me and I revelled in the dark tides of fury until a darker, deeper tide swept over me and I knew no more.

Chapter 20. Ancient horror

Here now in his triumph where all things falter,
Stretched out on the spoils that his own hand spread,
As a God self-slain on his own strange altar,
Death lies dead.

SWINBURNE

Slowly I drifted back into life . . . slowly, slowly. A mist held me and in the mist I saw a Skull . . .

I lay in a steel cage like a captive wolf, and the bars were too strong, I saw, even for my strength. The cage seemed to be set in a sort of niche in the wall and I was looking into a large room.

This room was under the earth, for the floor was of stone flags and the walls and ceiling were composed of gigantic block of the same material. Shelves ranged the walls, covered with weird appliances, apparently of a scientific nature, and more were on the great table that stood in the centre of the room. Beside this sat Kathulos.

The sorcerer was clad in a snaky yellow robe, and those hideous hands and that terrible head were more pronouncedly reptilian than ever. He turned his great yellow eyes toward me, like pools of livid fire, and his parchment-thin lips moved in what probably passed for a smile.

I staggered erect and gripped the bars, cursing.

'Gordon, curse you, where is Gordon?'

Kathulos took a test-tube from the table, eyed it closely and emptied it into another.

'Ah, my friend awakes,' he murmured in his voice – the voice of a living dead man.

He thrust his hands into his long sleeves and turned fully to me.

'I think in you,' he said distinctly, 'I have created a Frankenstein monster. I made of you a superhuman creature to serve my wishes and you broke from me. You are the bane of my might, worse than Gordon even. You have killed valuable servants and interfered with my plans. However, your evil comes to an end tonight. Your friend Gordon broke away but he is being hunted through the tunnels and cannot escape.

'You,' he continued with the sincere interest of the scientist, 'are a most interesting subject. Your brain must be formed differently from any other man that ever lived. I will make a close study of it and add it to my laboratory. How a man with the apparent need of the elixir in his system, has managed to go on for two days still stimulated by the last draft is more than I can understand.'

My heart leaped. With all his wisdom, little Zuleika had tricked him and he evidently did not know that she had filched a flask of the life-giving stuff from him.

'The last draft you had from me,' he went on, 'was sufficient only for some eight hours. I repeat, it has me puzzled. Can you offer any suggestion?'

I snarled wordlessly. He sighed.

'As always the barbarian. Truly the proverb speaks: "Jest with the wounded tiger and warm the adder in your bosom before you seek to lift the savage from his savagery." '

He meditated awhile in silence. I watched him uneasily. There was about him a vague and curious difference . . . his long fingers emerging from the sleeves drummed on the chair arms and some hidden exultation strummed at the back of his voice, lending it unaccustomed vibrancy.

'And you might have been a king of the new regime,' he said suddenly. 'Aye, the new – new and inhumanly old!'

I shuddered as his dry cackling laugh rasped out.

He bent his head as if listening. From far off seemed to come a hum of guttural voices. His lips writhed in a smile.

'My children,' he murmured. 'They tear my enemy Gordon to pieces in the tunnels. They, Mr Costigan, are my real henchmen and it was for their edification tonight that I laid John Gordon on the sacrificial stone. I would have preferred to have made some experiments with him, based on certain scientific theories, but my children must be humoured. Later under my tutelage they will outgrow their childish superstitions and throw aside their foolish customs, but now they must be led gently by the hand.

'How do you like these under-the-earth corridors, Mr Costigan?' he switched suddenly. 'You thought of them – what? No doubt that the savages of your Middle Ages built them? Faugh! These tunnels are older than your world! They were brought into being by mighty kings, too many aeons ago for your mind to grasp, when an imperial city towered where this crude village of London stands. All trace of that metropolis has crumbled to dust and vanished, but these corridors were built by more than human skill – ha ha! Of all the teeming thousands who move daily above them, none knows of their existence save my servants – and not all of them. Zuleika, for instance, does not know of them, for of late I have begun to doubt her loyalty and shall doubtless soon make of her an example.'

At that I hurled myself blindly against the side of the cage, a red wave of hate and fury tossing me in its grip. I seized the bars and strained until the veins stood out on my forehead and the muscles bulged and crackled in my arms and shoulders. And the bars bent before my onslaught – a little but no more, and finally the power flowed from my limbs and I sank down trembling and weakened. Kathulos watched me imperturbably.

'The bars hold,' he announced with something almost like relief in his tone. 'Frankly, I prefer to be on the opposite side of them. You are a human ape if there was ever one.'

He laughed suddenly and wildly.

'But why do you seek to oppose me?' he shrieked unexpectedly. 'Why defy me, who am Kathulos, the Sorcerer, great even in the days of the old empire? Today, invincible! A magician, a scientist, among ignorant savages! Ha ha!'

I shuddered, and sudden blinding light broke in on me. Kathulos himself was an addict, and was fired by the stuff of his choice! What hellish concoction was strong enough, terrible enough to thrill the Master and inflame him, I do not know, nor do I wish to know. Of all the uncanny knowledge that was his, I, knowing the man as I did, count this the most weird and grisly.

'You, you paltry fool!' he was ranting, his face lit supernaturally.

'Know you who I am? Kathulos of Egypt! Bah! They knew me in the old days! I reigned in the dim misty sea lands ages and ages before the sea rose and engulfed the land. I died, not as men die; the magic draft of life everlasting was ours! I drank deep and slept. Long I slept in my lacquered case! My flesh withered and grew hard; my blood dried in my veins. I became as one dead. But still within me burned the spirit of life, sleeping but anticipating the awakening. The great cities crumbled to dust. The sea drank the land. The tall shrines and the lofty spires sank beneath the green waves. All this I knew as I slept, as a man knows in dreams. Kathulos of Egypt? Faugh! *Kathulos of Atlantis* !'

I uttered a sudden involuntary cry. This was too grisly for sanity.

'Aye, the magician, the sorcerer.

'And down the long years of savagery, through which the barbaric races struggled to rise without their masters, the legend came of the day of empire, when one of the Old Race would rise up from the sea. Aye, and lead to victory the people who were our slaves in the old days.

'These people, what care I for them? And you, you barbarians, whose ape-ancestors forever defied me, your doom is at hand!

'The day came as prophesied, when my case, breaking free from the halls where it lay – where it had lain when Atlantis was still sovereign of the world – where since her empery it had sunk into the green fathoms – when my case, I say, was smitten by the deep sea tides and moved and stirred, and thrust aside the clinging seaweed that masks temples and minarets, and came floating up past the lofty sapphire and golden spires, up through the green waters, to float upon the lazy waves of the sea.

'Then came a fool carrying out the destiny of which he was not aware. The men on his ship, true believers, knew that the time had come. And I – the air entered my nostrils and I awoke from the long, long sleep. I stirred and moved and lived. And rising in the night, I slew the fool that had lifted me from the ocean, and my servants made obeisance to me and took me into Africa, where I abode awhile and learned new languages and new ways of a new world and became strong.

'The wisdom of your dreary world – ha ha! I who delved deeper in the mysteries of the old than any man dared go! All that men know today, I know, and the knowledge beside that which I have brought down the centuries is as a grain of sand beside a mountain! You should know something of that knowledge! By it I lifted you from one hell to plunge you into a greater! You fool, here at my hand is that which would lift you from this! Aye, would strike from you the chains whereby I have bound you!'

He snatched up a golden vial and shook it before my gaze. I eyed it as men dying in the desert must eye the distant mirages. Kathulos fingered it meditatively. His unnatural excitement seemed to have passed suddenly, and when he spoke again it was in the passionless, measured tones of the scientist.

'That would indeed be an experiment worthwhile – to free you of the elixir habit and see if your dope-riddled body would sustain life. Nine times out of ten the victim, with the need and stimulus removed, would die – but you are such a giant of a brute . . . '

He sighed and set the vial down.

'The dreamer opposes the man of destiny. My time is not my own or I should choose to spend my life pent in my laboratories, carrying out my experiments. Aye, I must toil and sow the seed of glory against the full coming of the imperial days when the seas give up all their living dead.'

I shuddered. Kathulos laughed wildly again. His fingers began to drum his chair arms and his face gleamed with the unnatural light once more. The red visions had begun to seethe in his skull again.

'Under the green seas they lie, the ancient masters, in their lacquered cases, dead as men reckon death, but only sleeping. Sleeping through the long ages as hours, awaiting the day of awakening! The old masters, the wise men, who foresaw the day when the sea would gulp the land, and who made ready. Made ready that they might rise again in the barbaric days to come. As did I. Sleeping they lie, ancient kings and grim wizards, who died as men die, before Atlantis sank. Who, sleeping, sank with her but who shall arise again!

'Mine the glory! I rose first. And I sought out the site of old cities, on shores that did not sink. Vanished, long vanished. The barbarian tide swept over them thousands of years ago as the green waters swept over their elder sister of the deeps. On some, the deserts stretch bare. Over some, as here, young barbarian cities rise.'

He halted suddenly. His eyes sought one of the dark openings that marked a corridor. I think his strange intuition warned him of some impending danger but I do not believe that he had any inkling of how dramatically our scene would be interrupted.

As he looked, swift footsteps sounded and a man appeared suddenly in the doorway – a man dishevelled, tattered and bloody. John Gordon! Kathulos sprang erect with a cry, and Gordon, gasping as from superhuman exertion, brought down the revolver he held in his hand and fired point-blank. Kathulos staggered, clapping his hand to his breast, and then, groping wildly, reeled to the wall and fell against it. A doorway opened and he reeled through, but as Gordon leaped fiercely across the chamber, a blank stone surface met his gaze, which yielded not to his savage hammerings.

He whirled and ran drunkenly to the table where lay a bunch of keys the Master had dropped there.

'The vial!' I shrieked. 'Take the vial!' And he thrust it into his pocket.

Back along the corridor through which he had come sounded a faint clamour growing swiftly like a wolf-pack in full cry. A few precious seconds spent with fumbling for the right key, then the cage door swung open and I sprang out. A sight for the gods we were, the two of us! Slashed, bruised and cut, our garments hanging in tatters – my wounds had ceased to bleed, but now as I moved they began again, and from the stiffness of my hands I knew that my knuckles were shattered. As for Gordon, he was fairly drenched in blood from crown to foot.

We made off down a passage in the opposite direction from the menacing noise, which I knew to be the servants of the Master in full pursuit of us. Neither of us was in good shape for running, but we did our best. Where we were going I had no idea. My superhuman strength had deserted me and I was going now on willpower alone. We switched off into another corridor and we had not gone twenty steps until, looking back, I saw the first of the devils round the corner.

A desperate effort increased our lead a trifle. But they had seen us, were in full view now, and a yell of fury broke from them to be succeeded by a more sinister silence as they bent all efforts to overhauling us.

There a short distance in front of us we saw a stair loom suddenly in the gloom. If we might reach that . . . but we saw something else.

Against the ceiling, between us and the stairs, hung a huge thing like an iron grille, with great spikes along the bottom – a portcullis. And even as we looked, without halting in our panting strides, it began to move.

'They're lowering the portcullis!' Gordon croaked, his blood-streaked face a mask of exhaustion and will.

Now the huge grate, gaining momentum, with a creak of rusty, unused mechanism, rushed downward. A final spurt, a gasping straining nightmare of effort – and Gordon, sweeping us both along in a wild burst of pure nerve-strength, hurled us under and through, and the grate crashed behind us!

A moment we lay gasping, not heeding the frenzied horde who raved and screamed on the other side of the grate. So close had that final leap been, that the great spikes in their descent had torn shreds from our clothing.

It seemed to me that I was content to lie there and die of exhaustion. But Gordon weaved unsteadily erect and hauled me with him.

'Got to get out,' he croaked; 'go to warn . . . Scotland Yard . . . honeycombs in heart of London . . . high explosives . . . arms . . . ammunition.'

We blundered up the steps, and in front of us I seemed to hear a sound of metal grating against metal. The stairs ended abruptly, on a landing that terminated in a blank wall. Gordon hammered against this and the inevitable secret doorway opened. Light streamed in, through the bars of a sort of grille. Men in the uniform of London police were sawing at these with hacksaws, and even as they greeted us, an opening was made through which we crawled.

'You're hurt, sir!' One of the men took Gordon's arm.

My companion shook him off.

'There's no time to lose! Out of here, as quick as we can go!'

I saw that we were in a basement of some sort. We hastened up the steps and out into the early dawn which was turning the east scarlet. Over the tops of smaller houses I saw in the distance a great gaunt building on the roof of which, I felt instinctively, that wild drama had been enacted the night before.

'That building was leased some months ago by a mysterious China-man,' said Gordon, following my gaze. 'Office building originally – the neighbourhood deteriorated and the building stood vacant for some time. The new tenant added several storeys to it but left it apparently empty. Had my eye on it for some time.'

This was told in Gordon's jerky swift manner as we started hurriedly along the sidewalk. I listened mechanically, like a man in a trance. My vitality was ebbing fast and I knew that I was going to crumple at any moment.

'The people living in the vicinity had been reporting strange sights and noises. The man who owned the basement we just left heard queer sounds emanating from the wall of the basement and called the police. About that time I was racing back and forth among those cursed corridors like a hunted rat and I heard the police banging on the wall. I found the secret door and opened it but found it barred by a grating. By pure luck I found you and by pure luck managed to find the way back to the door.

'Now we must get to Scotland Yard. If we strike swiftly, we may capture the entire band of devils. Whether I killed Kathulos or not I do not know, or if he can be killed by mortal weapons. But to the best of my knowledge all of them are now in those subterranean corridors and –'

At that moment the world shook! A brain-shattering roar seemed to break the sky with its incredible detonation; houses tottered and crashed to ruins; a mighty pillar of smoke and flame burst from the earth and on its wings great masses of debris soared skyward. A black fog of smoke and dust and falling timbers enveloped the world, a prolonged thunder seemed to rumble up from the centre of the earth as of walls and ceilings falling, and amid the uproar and the screaming I sank down and knew no more.

Chapter 21. The breaking of the chain

And like a soul belated,
In heaven and hell unmated;
By cloud and mist abated;
Come out of darkness morn.

SWINBURNE

There is little need to linger on the scenes of horror of that terrible London morning. The world is familiar with and knows most of the details attendant on the great explosion which wiped out a tenth of that great city with a resultant loss of lives and property. For such a happening some reason must needs be given; the tale of the deserted building got out, and many wild stories were circulated. Finally, to still the rumours, the report was unofficially given out that this building had been the rendezvous and secret stronghold of a gang of international anarchists, who had stored its basement full of high explosives and who had supposedly ignited these accidentally. In a way there was a good deal to this tale, as you know, but the threat that had lurked there far transcended any anarchist.

All this was told to me, for when I sank unconscious, Gordon, attributing my condition to exhaustion and a need of the hashish to the use of which he thought I was addicted, lifted me and with the aid of the stunned policemen got me to his rooms before returning to the scene of the explosion. At his rooms he found Hansen, and Zuleika handcuffed to the bed as I had left her. He released her and left her to tend to me, for all London was in a terrible turmoil and he was needed elsewhere.

When I came to myself at last, I looked up into her starry eyes and lay quiet, smiling up at her. She sank down upon my bosom, nestling my head in her arms and covering my face with her kisses.

'Steephen!' she sobbed over and over, as her tears splashed hot on my face.

I was scarcely strong enough to put my arms about her but I managed it, and we lay there for a space, in silence, except for the girl's hard, racking sobs.

'Zuleika, I love you,' I murmured.

'And I love you, Steephen,' she sobbed. 'Oh, it is so hard to part now – but I'm going with you, Steephen; I can't live without you!'

'My dear child,' said John Gordon, entering the room suddenly, 'Costigan's not going to die. We will let him have enough hashish to tide him along, and when he is stronger we will take him off the habit slowly.'

'You don't understand, sahib; it is not hashish Steephen must have. It is something which only the Master knew, and now that he is dead or is fled, Steephen cannot get it and must die.'

Gordon shot a quick, uncertain glance at me. His fine face was drawn and haggard, his clothes sooty and torn from his work among the debris of the explosion.

'She's right, Gordon,' I said languidly. 'I'm dying. Kathulos killed the hashish-craving with a concoction he called the elixir. I've been keeping myself alive on some of the stuff that Zuleika stole from him and gave me, but I drank it all last night.'

I was aware of no craving of any kind, no physical or mental discomfort even. All my mechanism was slowing down fast; I had passed the stage where the need of the elixir would tear and rend me. I felt only a great lassitude and a desire to sleep. And I knew that the moment I closed my eyes, I would die.

'A strange dope, that elixir,' I said with growing languor. 'It burns and freezes and then at last the craving kills easily and without torment.'

'Costigan, curse it,' said Gordon desperately, 'you can't go like this! That vial I took from the Egyptian's table – what is in it?'

'The Master swore it would free me of my curse and probably kill me also,' I muttered. 'I'd forgotten about it. Let me have it; it can no more than kill me and I'm dying now.'

'Yes, quick, let me have it!' exclaimed Zuleika fiercely, springing to Gordon's side, her hands passionately outstretched. She returned with the vial which he had taken from his pocket, and knelt beside me, holding it to my lips, while she murmured to me gently and soothingly in her own language.

I drank, draining the vial, but feeling little interest in the whole matter. My outlook was purely impersonal, at such a low ebb was my life, and I cannot even remember how the stuff tasted. I only remember feeling a curious sluggish fire burn faintly along my veins, and the last thing I saw was Zuleika crouching over me, her great eyes fixed with a burning intensity on me. Her tense little hand rested inside her blouse, and remembering her vow to take her own life if I died I tried to lift a hand and disarm her, tried to tell Gordon to take away the dagger she had hidden in her garments. But speech and action failed me and I drifted away into a curious sea of unconsciousness.

Of that period I remember nothing. No sensation fired my sleeping brain to such an extent as to bridge the gulf over which I drifted. They say I lay like a dead man for hours, scarcely breathing, while Zuleika hovered over me, never leaving my side an instant, and fighting like a tigress when anyone tried to coax her away to rest. Her chain was broken.

As I had carried the vision of her into that dim land of nothingness, so her dear eyes were the first thing which greeted my returning consciousness. I was aware of a greater weakness than I thought possible for a man to feel, as if I had been an invalid for months, but the life in me, faint though it was, was sound and normal, caused by no artificial stimulation. I smiled up at my girl and murmured weakly: 'Throw away your dagger, little Zuleika; I'm going to live.'

She screamed and fell on her knees beside me, weeping and laughing at the same time. Women are strange beings, of mixed and powerful emotions, truly.

Gordon entered and grasped the hand which I could not lift from the bed.

'You're a case for an ordinary human physician now, Costigan,' he said. 'Even a layman like myself can tell that. For the first time since I've known you, the look in your eyes is entirely sane. You look like a man who has had a complete nervous breakdown, and needs about a year of rest and quiet. Great heavens, man, you've been through enough, outside your dope experience, to last you a lifetime.'

'Tell me first,' said I, 'was Kathulos killed in the explosion?'

'I don't know,' answered Gordon sombrely. 'Apparently the entire system of subterranean passages was destroyed. I know my last bullet – the last bullet that was in the revolver which I wrested from one of my attackers – found its mark in the Master's body, but whether he died from the wound, or whether a bullet can hurt him, I do not know. And whether in his death agonies he ignited the tons and tons of high explosives which were stored in the corridors, we shall never know.

'My God, Costigan, did you ever see such a honeycomb? And we know not how many miles in either direction the passages reached. Even now Scotland Yard men are combing the subways and basements of the town for secret openings. All known openings, such as the one through which we came and the one in Soho 48, were blocked by falling walls. The office building was simply blown to atoms.'

'What about the men who raided Soho 48?'

'The door in the library wall had been closed. They searched the house without avail. Lucky for them, too, else they had doubtless been in the tunnels when the explosion came.'

'There is no way to search among those subterranean ruins, I suppose?'

'None whatever. When the walls caved in, the tons of earth upheld by the ceilings also came crashing down, filling the corridors with dirt and broken stone, blocking them forever. And on the surface of the earth, the houses which the vibration shook down were heaped high in utter ruins. What happened in those terrible corridors must remain forever a mystery.'

My tale draws to a close. The months that followed passed uneventfully, except for the growing happiness which to me was paradise, but which would bore you were I to relate it. But one day Gordon and I again discussed the mysterious happenings that had had their being under the grim hand of the Master.

'Since that day,' said Gordon, 'the world has been quiet. There can be but one answer – living or dead, Kathulos was destroyed that morning when his world crashed about him.'

'Gordon,' said I, 'what is the answer to that greatest of all mysteries?'

My friend shrugged his shoulders.

'I have come to believe that mankind eternally hovers on the brinks of secret oceans of which it knows nothing. Races have lived and vanished before our race rose out of the slime of the primitive, and it is likely still others will live upon the earth after ours has vanished. Scientists have long upheld the theory that the Atlanteans possessed a higher civilisation than our own, and on very different lines. Certainly Kathulos himself was proof that our boasted culture and knowledge were nothing beside that of whatever fearful civilisation produced him.

'His dealings with you alone have puzzled all the scientific world, for none of them has been able to explain how he could remove the hashish craving, stimulate you with a drug so infinitely more powerful, and then produce another drug which entirely effaced the effects of the other.'

'I have him to thank for two things,' I said slowly; 'the regaining of my lost manhood – and Zuleika. Kathulos, then, is dead, as far as any mortal thing can die. But what of those others – those "ancient masters" who still sleep in the sea?'

Gordon shuddered.

'As I said, perhaps mankind loiters on the brink of unthinkable chasms of horror. But a fleet of gunboats is even now patrolling the oceans unobtrusively, with orders to destroy instantly any strange case that may be found floating – to destroy it and its contents. And if my word has any weight with the English government and the nations of the world, the seas will be so patrolled until doomsday shall let down the curtain on the races of today.'

'At night I dream of them, sometimes,' I muttered, 'sleeping in their lacquered cases, which drip with strange seaweed, far down among the green surges – where unholy spires and strange towers rise in the dark ocean.'

'We have been face to face with an ancient horror,' said Gordon sombrely, 'with a fear too dark and mysterious for the human brain to cope with. It is best that we be ever on our guard. The universe was not made for humanity alone; life takes strange phases and it is the first instinct of nature for the different species to destroy each other. No doubt we seemed as horrible to the Master as he did to us. We have scarcely tapped the chest of secrets which nature has stored, and I shudder to think of what that chest may hold for the human race.'

'That's true,' said I, inwardly rejoicing at the vigour which was beginning to course through my wasted veins, 'but men will meet obstacles as they come, as men have always risen to meet them. Now, I am beginning to know the full worth of life and love, and not all the devils from all the abysses can hold me.'

Gordon smiled.

'You have it coming to you, old comrade. The best thing is to forget all that dark interlude, for in that course lies light and happiness.'

The Fearsome Touch of Death

As long as midnight cloaks the earth
With shadows grim and stark,
God save us from the Judas kiss
Of a dead man in the dark.

Old Adam Farrel lay dead in the house wherein he had lived alone for the last twenty years. A silent, churlish recluse, in his life he had known no friends, and only two men had watched his passing.

Dr Stein rose and glanced out the window into the gathering dusk.

'You think you can spend the night here, then?' he asked his companion.

This man, Falred by name, assented.

'Yes, certainly. I guess it's up to me.'

'Rather a useless and primitive custom, sitting up with the dead,' commented the doctor, preparing to depart, 'but I suppose in common decency we will have to bow to precedence. Maybe I can find someone who'll come over here and help you with your vigil.'

Falred shrugged his shoulders. 'I doubt it. Farrel wasn't liked – wasn't known by many people. I scarcely knew him myself, but I don't mind sitting up with the corpse.'

Dr Stein was removing his rubber gloves and Falred watched the process with an interest that almost amounted to fascination. A slight, involuntary shudder shook him at the memory of touching these gloves – slick, cold, clammy things, like the touch of death.

'You may get lonely tonight, if I don't find anyone,' the doctor remarked as he opened the door. 'Not superstitious, are you?'

Falred laughed. 'Scarcely. To tell the truth, from what I hear of Farrel's disposition, I'd rather be watching his corpse than have been his guest in life.'

The door closed and Falred took up his vigil. He seated himself in the only chair the room boasted, glanced casually at the formless, sheeted bulk on the bed opposite him, and began to read by the light of the dim lamp which stood on the rough table.

Outside, the darkness gathered swiftly, and finally Falred laid down his magazine to rest his eyes. He looked again at the shape which had, in life, been the form of Adam Farrel, wondering what quirk in human nature made the sight of a corpse not so unpleasant, but such an object of fear to man. Unthinking ignorance, seeing in dead things a reminder of death to come, he decided lazily, and began idly contemplating what life had held for this grim and crabbed old man, who had neither relatives nor friends, and who had seldom left the house wherein he had died. The usual tales of miser-hoarded wealth had accumulated, but Falred felt so little interest in the whole matter that it was not even necessary for him to overcome any temptation to prey about the house for possible hidden treasure.

He returned to his reading with a shrug. The task was more boresome than he had thought for. After a while he was aware that every time he looked up from his magazine and his eyes fell upon the bed with its grim occupant, he started involuntarily as if he had, for an instant, forgotten the presence of the dead man and was unpleasantly reminded of the fact. The start was slight and instinctive, but he felt almost angered at himself. He realised, for the first time, the utter and deadening silence which enwrapped the house – a silence apparently shared by the night, for no sound came through the window. Adam Farrel lived as far apart from his neighbours as possible, and there was no other house within hearing distance.

Falred shook himself as if to rid his mind of unsavoury speculations, and went back to his reading. A sudden vagrant gust of wind whipped through the window, in which the light in the lamp flickered and went out suddenly. Falred, cursing softly, groped in the darkness for matches, burning his fingers on the lamp chimney. He struck a match, relighted the lamp, and glancing over at the bed, got a horrible mental jolt. Adam Farrel's face stared blindly at him, the dead eyes wide and blank, framed in the gnarled grey features. Even as Falred instinctively shuddered, his reason explained the apparent phenomenon: the sheet that covered the corpse had been carelessly thrown across the face and the sudden puff of wind had disarranged and flung it aside.

Yet there was something grisly about the thing, something fearsomely suggestive – as if, in the cloaking dark, a dead hand had flung aside the sheet, just as if the corpse were about to rise . . .

Falred, an imaginative man, shrugged his shoulders at these ghastly thoughts and crossed the room to replace the sheet. The dead eyes seemed to stare malevolently, with an evilness that transcended the dead man's churlishness in life. The workings of a vivid imagination, Falred knew, and he re-covered the grey face, shrinking as his hand chanced to touch the cold flesh – slick and clammy, the touch of death. He shuddered with the natural revulsion of the living for the dead, and went back to his chair and magazine.

At last, growing sleepy, he lay down upon a couch which, by some strange whim of the original owner, formed part of the room's scant furnishings, and composed himself for slumber. He decided to leave the light burning, telling himself that it was in accordance with the usual custom of leaving lights burning for the dead; for he was not willing to admit to himself that already he was conscious of a dislike for lying in the darkness with the corpse. He dozed, awoke with a start and looked at the sheeted form of the bed. Silence reigned over the house, and outside it was very dark.

The hour was approaching midnight, with its accompanying eerie domination over the human mind. Falred glanced again at the bed where the body lay and found the sight of the sheeted object most repellent. A fantastic idea had birth in his mind, and grew, that beneath the sheet, the mere lifeless body had become a strange, monstrous thing, a hideous, conscious being, that watched him with eyes which burned through the fabric of the cloth. This thought – a mere fantasy, of course – he explained to himself by the legends of vampires, undead ghosts and suchlike – the fearsome attributes with which the living have cloaked the dead for countless ages, since primitive man first recognised in death something horrid and apart from life. Man feared death, thought Falred, and some of this fear of death took hold on the dead so that they, too, were feared. And the sight of the dead engendered grisly thoughts, gave rise to dim fears of hereditary memory, lurking back in the dark corners of the brain.

At any rate, that silent, hidden thing was getting on his nerves. He thought of uncovering the face, on the principle that familiarity breeds contempt. The sight of the features, calm and still in death, would banish, he thought, all such wild conjectures as were haunting him in spite of himself. But the thought of those dead eyes staring in the lamplight was intolerable; so at last he blew out the light and lay down. This fear had been stealing upon him so insidiously and gradually that he had not been aware of its growth.

With the extinguishing of the light, however, and the blotting out of the sight of the corpse, things assumed their true character and proportions, and Falred fell asleep almost instantly, on his lips a faint smile for his previous folly.

He awakened suddenly. How long he had been asleep he did not know. He sat up, his pulse pounding frantically, the cold sweat beading his forehead. He knew instantly where he was, remembered the other occupant of the room. But what had awakened him? A dream – yes, now he remembered – a hideous dream in which the dead man had risen from the bed and stalked stiffly across the room with eyes of fire and a horrid leer frozen on his grey lips. Falred had seemed to lie motionless, helpless; then as the corpse reached out a gnarled and horrible hand, he had awakened.

He strove to pierce the gloom, but the room was all blackness and all without was so dark that no gleam of light came through the window. He reached a shaking hand toward the lamp, then recoiled as if from a hidden serpent. Sitting here in the dark with a fiendish corpse was bad enough, but he dared not light the lamp, for fear that his reason would be snuffed out like a candle at what he might see. Horror, stark and unreasoning, had full possession of his soul; he no longer questioned the instinctive fears that rose in him. All those legends he had heard came back to him and brought a belief in them. Death was a hideous thing, a brain-shattering horror, imbuing life-less men with a horrid malevolence. Adam Farrel in his life had been simply a churlish but harmless man; now he was a terror, a monster, a fiend lurking in the shadows of fear, ready to leap on mankind with talons dipped deep in death and insanity.

Falred sat there, his blood freezing, and fought out his silent battle. Faint glimmerings of reason had begun to touch his fright when a soft, stealthy sound again froze him. He did not recognise it as the whisper of the night wind across the windowsill. His frenzied fancy knew it only as the tread of death and horror. He sprang from the couch, then stood undecided. Escape was in his mind but he was too dazed to even try to formulate a plan of escape. Even his sense of direction was gone. Fear had so stultified his mind that he was not able to think consciously. The blackness spread in long waves about him, and its darkness and void entered into his brain. His motions, such as they were, were instinctive. He seemed shackled with mighty chains and his limbs responded sluggishly, like an imbecile's.

A terrible horror grew up in him and reared its grisly shape, that the dead man was behind him, was stealing upon him from the rear. He no longer thought of lighting the lamp; he no longer thought of anything. Fear filled his whole being; there was room for nothing else.

He backed slowly away in the darkness, hands behind him, in-stinctively feeling the way. With a terrific effort he partly shook the clinging mists of horror from him, and, the cold sweat clammy upon his body, strove to orient himself. He could see nothing, but the bed was across the room, in front of him. He was backing away from it. There was where the dead man was lying, according to all rules of nature; if the thing were, as he felt, behind him, then the old tales were true: death did implant in lifeless bodies an unearthly animation, and dead men did roam the shadows to work their ghastly and evil will upon the sons of men. Then – great God! – what was man but a wailing infant, lost in the night and beset by frightful things from the black abysses and the terrible unknown voids of space and time? These conclusions he did not reach by any reasoning process; they leaped full-grown into his terror-dazed brain. He worked his way slowly backward, groping, clinging to the thought that the dead man must be in front of him.

Then his back-flung hands encountered something – something slick, cold and clammy – like the touch of death. A scream shook the echoes, followed by the crash of a falling body.

The next morning they who came to the house of death found two corpses in the room. Adam Farrel's sheeted body lay motionless upon the bed, and across the room lay the body of Falred, beneath the shelf where Dr Stein had absent-mindedly left his gloves . . . rubber gloves, slick and clammy to the touch of a hand groping in the dark – a hand of one fleeing his own fear – rubber gloves, slick and clammy and cold, like the touch of death.

The Children of the Night

There were, I remember, six of us in Conrad's bizarrely fashioned study, with its queer relics from all over the world and its long rows of books which ranged from the Mandrake Press edition of Boccaccio to a *Missale Romanum*, bound in clasped oak boards and printed in Venice, 1740. Clemants and Professor Kirowan had just engaged in a somewhat testy anthropological argument: Clemants upholding the theory of a separate, distinct Alpine race, while the professor maintained that this so-called race was merely a deviation from an original Aryan stock – possibly the result of an admixture between the southern or Mediterranean races and the Nordic people.

'And how,' asked Clemants, 'do you account for their brachycephalicism? The Mediterraneans were as long-headed as the Aryans: would admixture between these dolichocephalic peoples produce a broad-headed intermediate type?'

'Special conditions might bring about a change in an originally long-headed race,' snapped Kirowan. 'Boaz has demonstrated, for instance, that in the case of immigrants to America, skull formations often change in one generation. And Flinders Petrie has shown that the Lombards changed from a long-headed to a round-headed race in a few centuries.'

'But what caused these changes?'

'Much is yet unknown to science,' answered Kirowan, 'and we need not be dogmatic. No one knows, as yet, why people of British and Irish ancestry tend to grow unusually tall in the Darling district of Australia – cornstalks, as they are called – or why people of such descent generally have thinner jaw-structures after a few generations in New England. The universe is full of the unexplainable.'

'And therefore the uninteresting, according to Machen,' laughed Taverel.

Conrad shook his head. 'I must disagree. To me, the unknowable is most tantalisingly fascinating.'

'Which accounts, no doubt, for all the works on witchcraft and demonology I see on your shelves,' said Ketrick, with a wave of his hand toward the rows of books.

And let me speak of Ketrick. Each of the six of us was of the same breed – that is to say, a Briton or an American of British descent. By British, I include all natural inhabitants of the British Isles. We represented various strains of English and Celtic blood, but basically, these strains are the same after all. But Ketrick: to me the man always seemed strangely alien. It was in his eyes that this difference showed externally. They were a sort of amber, almost yellow, and slightly oblique. At times, when one looked at his face from certain angles, they seemed to slant like a Chinaman's.

Others than I had noticed this feature, so unusual in a man of pure Anglo-Saxon descent. The usual myths ascribing his slanted eyes to some pre-natal influence had been mooted about, and I remember Professor Hendrik Brooler once remarked that Ketrick was undoubtedly an atavism, representing a reversion of type to some dim and distant ancestor of Mongolian blood – a sort of freak reversion, since none of his family showed such traces.

But Ketrick comes of the Welsh branch of the Cetrics of Sussex, and his lineage is set down in the *Book of Peers*. There you may read the line of his ancestry, which extends unbroken to the days of Canute. No slightest trace of Mongoloid intermixture appears in the genealogy, and how could there have been such intermixture in old Saxon England? For Ketrick is the modern form of Cedric, and though that branch fled into Wales before the invasion of the Danes, its male heirs consistently married with English families on the border marches, and it remains a pure line of the powerful Sussex Cedrics – almost pure Saxon. As for the man himself, this defect of his eyes, if it can be called a defect, is his only abnormality, except for a slight and occasional lisping of speech. He is highly intellectual and a good companion except for a slight aloofness and a rather callous indifference which may serve to mask an extremely sensitive nature.

Referring to his remark, I said with a laugh: 'Conrad pursues the obscure and mystic as some men pursue romance; his shelves throng with delightful nightmares of every variety.'

Our host nodded. 'You'll find there a number of delectable dishes – Machen, Poe, Blackwood, Maturin . . . look, there's a rare feast – *Horrid Mysteries*, by the Marquis of Grosse – the real eighteenth-century edition.'

Taverel scanned the shelves. 'Weird fiction seems to vie with works on witchcraft, voodoo and dark magic.'

True; historians and chronicles are often dull, tale-weavers never – the masters, I mean. A voodoo sacrifice can be described in such a dull manner as to take all the real fantasy out of it, and leave it merely a sordid murder. I will admit that few writers of fiction touch the true heights of horror – most of their stuff is too concrete, given too much earthly shape and dimensions. But in such tales as Poe's *The Fall of the House of Usher*, Machen's *Black Seal* and Lovecraft's *The Call of Cthulhu* – the three master horror-tales, to my mind – the reader is borne into dark and *outer* realms of imagination.

'But look there,' he continued, 'there, sandwiched between that nightmare of Huysmans' and Walpole's *Castle of Otranto* – Von Junzt's *Nameless Cults*. There's a book to keep you awake at night!'

'I've read it,' said Taverel, 'and I'm convinced the man is mad. His work is like the conversation of a maniac – it runs with startling clarity for awhile, then suddenly merges into vagueness and disconnected ramblings.'

Conrad shook his head. 'Have you ever thought that perhaps it is his very sanity that causes him to write in that fashion? What if he dares not put on paper all he knows? What if his vague suppositions are dark and mysterious hints, keys to the puzzle, to those who know?'

'Bosh!' This from Kirowan. 'Are you intimating that any of the nightmare cults referred to by Von Junzt survive to this day – if they ever existed save in the hag-ridden brain of a lunatic poet and philosopher?'

'Not he alone used hidden meanings,' answered Conrad. 'If you will scan various works of certain great poets you may find double meanings. Men have stumbled on to cosmic secrets in the past and given a hint of them to the world in cryptic words. Do you remember Von Junzt's hints of "a city in the waste"? What do you think of Flecker's lines:

Pass not beneath! Men say there blows in stony deserts still a rose
But with no scarlet to her leaf . . . and from whose heart no perfume flows.

'Men may stumble upon secret things, but Von Junzt dipped deep into forbidden mysteries. He was one of the few men, for instance, who could read the *Necronomicon* in the original Greek translation.'

Taverel shrugged his shoulders, and Professor Kirowan, though he snorted and puffed viciously at his pipe, made no direct reply; for he, as well as Conrad, had delved into the Latin version of the book, and had found there things not even a cold-blooded scientist could answer or refute.

'Well,' he said presently, 'suppose we admit the former existence of cults revolving about such nameless and ghastly gods and entities as Cthulhu, Yog Sothoth, Tsathoggua, Gol-goroth, and the like, I cannot find it in my mind to believe that survivals of such cults lurk in the dark corners of the world today.'

To our surprise Clemants answered. He was a tall, lean man, silent almost to the point of taciturnity, and his fierce struggles with poverty in his youth had lined his face beyond his years. Like many another artist, he lived a distinctly dual literary life, his swashbuckling novels furnishing him a generous income, and his editorial position on *The Cloven Hoof* affording him full artistic expression. *The Cloven Hoof* was a poetry magazine whose bizarre contents had often aroused the shocked interest of the conservative critics.

'You remember Von Junzt makes mention of a so-called Bran cult,' said Clemants, stuffing his pipe-bowl with a peculiarly villainous brand of shag tobacco. 'I think I heard you and Taverel discussing it once.'

'As I gather from his hints,' snapped Kirowan, 'Von Junzt includes this particular cult among those still in existence. Absurd.'

Again Clemants shook his head. 'When I was a boy working my way through a certain university, I had for room-mate a lad as poor and ambitious as I. If I told you his name, it would startle you. Though he came of an old Scotch line of Galloway, he was obviously of a non-Aryan type.

'This is in strictest confidence, you understand. But my room-mate talked in his sleep. I began to listen and put his disjointed mumbling together. And in his mutterings I first heard of the ancient cult hinted at by Von Junzt; of the king who rules the Dark Empire, which was a revival of an older, darker empire dating back into the Stone Age; and of the great, nameless cavern where stands the Dark Man – the image of Bran Mak Morn, carved in his likeness by a master-hand while the great king yet lived, and to which each worshipper of Bran makes a pilgrimage once in his or her lifetime. Yes, that cult lives today in the descendants of Bran's people – a silent, unknown current, it flows on in the great ocean of life, waiting for the stone image of the great Bran to breathe and move with sudden life, and come from the great cavern to rebuild their lost empire.'

'And who were the people of that empire?' asked Ketrick.

'Picts,' answered Taverel, 'doubtless the people known later as the wild Picts of Galloway were predominantly Celtic – a mixture of Gaelic, Cymric, aboriginal and possibly Teutonic elements. Whether they took their name from the older race or lent their own name to that race, is a matter yet to be decided. But when Von Junzt speaks of Picts, he refers specifically to the small, dark, garlic-eating peoples of Mediterranean blood who brought the Neolithic culture into Britain. The first settlers of that country, in fact, who gave rise to the tales of earth spirits and goblins.'

'I cannot agree to that last statement,' said Conrad. 'These legends ascribe a deformity and inhumanness of appearance to the characters. There was nothing about the Picts to excite such horror and repulsion in the Aryan peoples. I believe that the Mediterraneans were preceded by a Mongoloid type, very low in the scale of development, whence these tales – '

'Quite true,' broke in Kirowan, 'but I hardly think they preceded the Picts, as you call them, into Britain. We find troll and dwarf legends all over the Continent, and I am inclined to think that both the Mediterranean and Aryan people brought these tales with them from the Continent. They must have been of extremely inhuman aspect, those early Mongoloids.'

'At least,' said Conrad, 'here is a flint mallet a miner found in the Welsh hills and gave to me, which has never been fully explained. It is obviously of no ordinary Neolithic make. See how small it is, compared to most implements of that age; almost like a child's toy; yet it is surprisingly heavy and no doubt a deadly blow could be dealt with it. I fitted the handle to it myself, and you would be surprised to know how difficult it was to carve it into a shape and balance corresponding with the head.'

We looked at the thing. It was well made, polished somewhat like the other remnants of the Neolithic I had seen, yet as Conrad said, it was strangely different. Its small size was oddly disquieting, for it had no appearance of a toy, otherwise. It was as sinister in suggestion as an Aztec sacrificial dagger. Conrad had fashioned the oaken handle with rare skill, and in carving it to fit the head, had managed to give it the same unnatural appearance as the mallet itself had. He had even copied the workmanship of primal times, fixing the head into the cleft of the haft with rawhide.

'My word!' Taverel made a clumsy pass at an imaginary antagonist and nearly shattered a costly Shang vase. 'The balance of the thing is all off-centre; I'd have to readjust all my mechanics of poise and equilibrium to handle it.'

'Let me see it,' Ketrick took the thing and fumbled with it, trying to strike the secret of its proper handling. At length, somewhat irritated, he swung it up and struck a heavy blow at a shield which hung on the wall nearby. I was standing near it; I saw the hellish mallet twist in his hand like a live serpent, and his arm wrenched out of line; I heard a shout of alarmed warning – then darkness came with the impact of the mallet against my head.

Slowly I drifted back to consciousness. First there was dull sensation with blindness and total lack of knowledge as to where I was or what I was; then vague realisation of life and being, and a hard something pressing into my ribs. Then the mists cleared and I came to myself completely.

I lay on my back half-beneath some underbrush and my head throbbed fiercely. Also my hair was caked and clotted with blood, for the scalp had been laid open. But my eyes travelled down my body and limbs, naked but for a deerskin loincloth and sandals of the same material, and found no other wound. That which pressed so uncomfortably into my ribs was my axe, on which I had fallen.

Now an abhorrent babble reached my ears and stung me into clear consciousness. The noise was faintly like language, but not such language as men are accustomed to. It sounded much like the repeated hissing of many great snakes.

I stared. I lay in a great, gloomy forest. The glade was overshadowed, so that even in the daytime it was very dark. Aye – that forest was dark, cold, silent, gigantic and utterly grisly. And I looked into the glade.

I saw a shambles. Five men lay there – at least, what had been five men. Now as I marked the abhorrent mutilations my soul sickened. And about clustered the . . . Things. Humans they were, of a sort, though I did not consider them so. They were short and stocky, with broad heads too large for their scrawny bodies. Their hair was snaky and stringy, their faces broad and square, with flat noses, hideously slanted eyes, a thin gash for a mouth, and pointed ears. They wore the skins of beasts, as did I, but these hides were but crudely dressed. They bore small bows and flint-tipped arrows, flint knives and cudgels. And they conversed in a speech as hideous as themselves, a hissing, reptilian speech that filled me with dread and loathing.

Oh, I hated them as I lay there; my brain flamed with white-hot fury. And now I remembered. We had hunted, we six youths of the

Sword People, and wandered far into the grim forest which our people generally shunned. Weary of the chase, we had paused to rest; to me had been given the first watch, for in those days, no sleep was safe without a sentry. Now shame and revulsion shook my whole being. I had slept – I had betrayed my comrades. And now they lay gashed and mangled – butchered while they slept, by vermin who had never dared to stand before them on equal terms. I, Aryara, had betrayed my trust.

Aye – I remembered. I had slept and in the midst of a dream of the hunt, fire and sparks had exploded in my head and I had plunged into a deeper darkness where there were no dreams. And now the penalty. They who had stolen through the dense forest and smitten me senseless, had not paused to mutilate me. Thinking me dead they had hastened swiftly to their grisly work. Now perhaps they had forgotten me for a time. I had sat somewhat apart from the others, and when struck, had fallen half-under some bushes. But soon they would remember me. I would hunt no more, dance no more in the dances of hunt and love and war, see no more the wattle huts of the Sword People.

But I had no wish to escape back to my people. Should I slink back with my tale of infamy and disgrace? Should I hear the words of scorn my tribe would fling at me, see the girls point their contempt-uous fingers at the youth who slept and betrayed his comrades to the knives of vermin?

Tears stung my eyes, and slow hate heaved up in my bosom, and my brain. I would never bear the sword that marked the warrior. I would never triumph over worthy foes and die gloriously beneath the arrows of the Picts or the axes of the Wolf People or the River People. I would go down to death beneath a nauseous rabble, whom the Picts had long ago driven into forest dens like rats.

And mad rage gripped me and dried my tears, giving in their stead a berserk blaze of wrath. If such reptiles were to bring about my downfall, I would make it a fall long remembered – if such beasts had memories.

Moving cautiously, I shifted until my hand was on the haft of my axe; then I called on Il-marinen and bounded up as a tiger springs. And as a tiger springs I was among my enemies and mashed a flat skull as a man crushes the head of a snake. A sudden wild clamour of fear broke from my victims and for an instant they closed round me, hacking and stabbing. A knife gashed my chest but I gave no heed. A red mist waved before my eyes, and my body and limbs moved in perfect accord with my fighting brain. Snarling, hacking and smiting, I was a tiger among reptiles. In an instant they gave way and fled, leaving me bestriding half a dozen stunted bodies. But I was not satiated.

I was close on the heels of the tallest one, whose head would perhaps come to my shoulder, and who seemed to be their chief. He fled down a sort of runway, squealing like a monstrous lizard, and when I was close at his shoulder, he dived, snake-like, into the bushes. But I was too swift for him, and I dragged him forth and butchered him in a most gory fashion.

And through the bushes I saw the trail he was striving to reach – a path winding in and out among the trees, almost too narrow to allow the traversing of it by a man of normal size. I hacked off my victim's hideous head, and carrying it in my left hand, went up the serpent-path, with my red axe in my right.

Now as I strode swiftly along the path and blood splashed beside my feet at every step from the severed jugular of my foe, I thought of those I hunted. Aye – we held them in so little esteem, we hunted by day in the forest they haunted. What they called themselves, we never knew; for none of our tribe ever learned the accursed hissing sibilances they used as speech; but we called them Children of the Night. And night-things they were indeed, for they slunk in the depths of the dark forests, and in subterraneous dwellings, venturing forth into the hills only when their conquerors slept. It was at night that they did their foul deeds – the quick flight of a flint-tipped arrow to slay cattle, or perhaps a loitering human, the snatching of a child that had wandered from the village.

But it was for more than this we gave them their name; they were, in truth, people of night and darkness and the ancient horror-ridden shadows of bygone ages. For these creatures were very old, and they represented an outworn age. They had once overrun and possessed this land, and they had been driven into hiding and obscurity by the dark, fierce little Picts with whom we contested now, and who hated and loathed them as savagely as did we.

The Picts were different from us in general appearance, being shorter of stature and dark of hair, eyes and skin, whereas we were tall and powerful, with yellow hair and light eyes. But they were cast in the same mould, for all of that. These Children of the Night seemed not human to us, with their deformed dwarfish bodies, yellow skin and hideous faces. Aye, they were reptiles . . . vermin.

And my brain was like to burst with fury when I thought that it was these vermin on whom I was to glut my axe and perish. Bah! There is no glory slaying snakes or dying from their bites. All this rage and fierce disappointment turned on the objects of my hatred, and with the old red mist waving in front of me I swore by all the gods I knew, to wreak such red havoc before I died as to leave a dread memory in the minds of the survivors.

My people would not honour me, in such contempt they held the Children. But those Children that I left alive would remember me and shudder. So I swore, gripping savagely my axe, which was of bronze, set in a cleft of the oaken haft and fastened securely with rawhide.

Now I heard ahead a sibilant, abhorrent murmur, and a vile stench filtered to me through the trees, human, yet less than human. A few moments more and I emerged from the deep shadows into a wide open space. I had never before seen a village of the Children. There was a cluster of earthen domes, with low doorways sunk into the ground; squalid dwelling-places, half-above and half-below the earth. And I knew from the talk of the old warriors that these dwelling-places were connected by underground corridors, so the whole village was like an ant-bed, or a system of snake holes. And I wondered if other tunnels did not run off under the ground and emerge long distances from the villages.

Before the domes clustered a vast group of the creatures, hissing and jabbering at a great rate.

I had quickened my pace, and now as I burst from cover, I was running with the fleetness of my race. A wild clamour went up from the rabble as they saw the avenger, tall, bloodstained and blazing-eyed leap from the forest, and I cried out fiercely, flung the dripping head among them and bounded like a wounded tiger into the thick of them.

Oh, there was no escape for them now! They might have taken to their tunnels but I would have followed, even to the guts of Hell. They knew they must slay me, and they closed around, a hundred strong, to do it.

There was no wild blaze of glory in my brain as there had been against worthy foes. But the old berserk madness of my race was in my blood and the smell of blood and destruction in my nostrils.

I know not how many I slew. I only know that they thronged about me in a writhing, slashing mass, like serpents about a wolf, and I smote until the axe-edge turned and bent and the axe became no more than a bludgeon; and I smashed skulls, split heads, splintered bones, scattered blood and brains in one red sacrifice to Il-marinen, god of the Sword People.

Bleeding from half a hundred wounds, blinded by a slash across the eyes, I felt a flint knife sink deep into my groin and at the same instant a cudgel laid my scalp open. I went to my knees but reeled up again, and saw in a thick red fog a ring of leering, slant-eyed faces. I lashed out as a dying tiger strikes, and the faces broke in red ruin.

And as I sagged, overbalanced by the fury of my stroke, a taloned hand clutched my throat and a flint blade was driven into my ribs and twisted venomously. Beneath a shower of blows I went down again, but the man with the knife was beneath me, and with my left hand I found him and broke his neck before he could writhe away.

Life was waning swiftly; through the hissing and howling of the Children I could hear the voice of Il-marinen. Yet once again I rose stubbornly, through a very whirlwind of cudgels and spears. I could no longer see my foes, even in a red mist. But I could feel their blows and knew they surged about me. I braced my feet, gripped my slippery axe-haft with both hands, and calling once more on Il-marinen I heaved up the axe and struck one last terrific blow. And I must have died on my feet, for there was no sensation of falling; even as I knew, with a last thrill of savagery that slew, even as I felt the splintering of skulls beneath my axe, darkness came with oblivion.

I came suddenly to myself. I was half-reclining in a big armchair and Conrad was pouring water on me. My head ached and a trickle of blood had half-dried on my face. Kirowan, Taverel and Clemants were hovering about, anxiously, while Ketrick stood just in front of me, still holding the mallet, his face schooled to a polite perturbation which his eyes did not show. And at the sight of those cursed eyes a red madness surged up in me.

'There,' Conrad was saying, 'I told you he'd come out of it in a moment; just a light crack. He's taken harder than that. All right now, aren't you, O'Donnel?'

At that I swept them aside, and with a single low snarl of hatred launched myself at Ketrick. Taken utterly by surprise he had no opportunity to defend himself. My hands locked on his throat and we crashed together on the ruins of a divan. The others cried out in amazement and horror and sprang to separate us – or rather, to tear me from my victim, for already Ketrick's slant eyes were beginning to start from their sockets.

'For God's sake, O'Donnel,' exclaimed Conrad, seeking to break my grip, 'what's come over you? Ketrick didn't mean to hit you – let go, you idiot!'

A fierce wrath almost overcame me at these men who were my friends, men of my own tribe, and I swore at them and their blindness, as they finally managed to tear my strangling fingers from Ketrick's throat. He sat up and choked and explored the blue marks my fingers had left, while I raged and cursed, nearly defeating the combined efforts of the four to hold me.

'You fools!' I screamed. 'Let me go! Let me do my duty as a tribesman! You blind fools! I care nothing for the paltry blow he dealt me – he and his dealt stronger blows than that against me, in bygone ages. You fools, he is marked with the brand of the beast – the reptile – the vermin we exterminated centuries ago! I must crush him, stamp him out, rid the clean earth of his accursed pollution!'

So I raved and struggled and Conrad gasped to Ketrick over his shoulder: 'Get out, quick! He's out of his head! His mind is unhinged! Get away from him.'

Now I look out over the ancient dreaming downs and the hills and deep forests beyond and I ponder. Somehow, that blow from that ancient accursed mallet knocked me back into another age and another life. While I was Aryara I had no cognisance of any other life. It was no dream; it was a stray bit of reality wherein I, John O'Donnel, once lived and died, and back into which I was snatched across the voids of time and space by a chance blow. Time and times are but cogwheels, unmatched, grinding on oblivious to one another. Occasionally – oh, very rarely! – the cogs fit; the pieces of the plot snap together momentarily and give men faint glimpses beyond the veil of this everyday blindness we call reality.

I am John O'Donnel and I was Aryara, who dreamed dreams of war-glory and hunt-glory and feast-glory and who died on a red heap of his victims in some lost age. But in what age and where?

The last I can answer for you. Mountains and rivers change their contours; the landscapes alter; but the downs least of all. I look out upon them now and I remember them, not only with John O'Donnel's eyes, but with the eyes of Aryara. They are but little changed. Only the great forest has shrunk and dwindled and in many, many places vanished utterly. But here on these very downs Aryara lived and fought and loved and in yonder forest he died. Kirowan was wrong. The little, fierce, dark Picts were not the first men in the Isles. There were beings before them – aye, the Children of the Night. Legends – why, the Children were not unknown to us when we came into what is now the isle of Britain. We had encountered them before, ages before. Already we had our myths of them. But we found them in Britain. Nor had the Picts totally exterminated them.

Nor had the Picts, as so many believe, preceded us by many centuries. We drove them before us as we came, in that long drift from the East. I, Aryara, knew old men who had marched on that century-long trek; who had been borne in the arms of yellow-haired women over countless miles of forest and plain, and who as youths had walked in the vanguard of the invaders.

As to the age – that I cannot say. But I, Aryara, was surely an Aryan and my people were Aryans – members of one of the thousand unknown and unrecorded drifts that scattered yellow-haired blue-eyed tribes all over the world. The Celts were not the first to come into western Europe. I, Aryara, was of the same blood and appear-ance as the men who sacked Rome, but mine was a much older strain. Of the language spoke, no echo remains in the waking mind of John O'Donnel, but I knew that Aryara's tongue was to ancient Celtic what ancient Celtic is to modern Gaelic.

Il-marinen! I remember the god I called upon, the ancient, ancient god who worked in metals – in bronze then. For Il-marinen was one of the base gods of the Aryans from whom many gods grew; and he was Wieland and Vulcan in the ages of iron. But to Aryara he was Il-marinen.

And Aryara – he was one of many tribes and many drifts. Not alone did the Sword People come or dwell in Britain. The River People were before us and the Wolf People came later. But they were Aryans like us, light-eyed and tall and blond. We fought them, for the reason that the various drifts of Aryans have always fought each other, just as the Achaeans fought the Dorians, just as the Celts and Germans cut each other's throats; aye, just as the Hellenes and the Persians, who were once one people and of the same drift, split in two different ways on the long trek and centuries later met and flooded Greece and Asia Minor with blood.

Now understand, all this I did not know as Aryara. I, Aryara, knew nothing of all these world-wide drifts of my race. I knew only that my people were conquerors, that a century ago my ancestors had dwelt in the great plains far to the east, plains populous with fierce, yellow-haired, light-eyed people like myself; that my ancestors had come westward in a great drift; and that in that drift, when my tribesmen met tribes of other races, they trampled and destroyed them, and when they met other yellow-haired, light-eyed people, of older or newer drifts, they fought savagely and mercilessly, according to the old, illogical custom of the Aryan people. This Aryara knew, and I, John O'Donnel, who know much more and much less than I, Aryara, know, have combined the knowledge of these separate selves and have come to conclusions that would startle many noted scientists and historians.

Yet this fact is well known: Aryans deteriorate swiftly in sedentary and peaceful lives. Their proper existence is a nomadic one; when they settle down to an agricultural existence, they pave the way for their downfall; and when they pen themselves with city walls, they seal their doom. Why, I, Aryara, remember the tales of the old men – how the Sons of the Sword, on that long drift, found villages of white-skinned yellow-haired people who had drifted into the west centuries before and had quit the wandering life to dwell among the dark, garlic-eating people and gain their sustenance from the soil. And the old men told how soft and weak they were, and how easily they fell before the bronze blades of the Sword People.

Look – is not the whole history of the Sons of Aryan laid on those lines? Look – how swiftly has Persian followed Mede; Greek, Persian; Roman, Greek; and German, Roman. Aye, and the Norseman followed the Germanic tribes when they had grown flabby from a century or so of peace and idleness, and despoiled the spoils they had taken in the southland.

But let me speak of Ketrick. Ha – the short hairs at the back of my neck bristle at the very mention of his name. A reversion to type – but not to the type of some cleanly Chinaman or Mongol of recent times. The Danes drove his ancestors into the hills of Wales; and there, in what medieval century, and in what foul way did that cursed aboriginal taint creep into the clean Saxon blood of the Celtic line, there to lie dormant so long? The Celtic Welsh never mated with the Children any more than the Picts did. But there must have been survivals – vermin lurking in those grim hills, that had outlasted their time and age. In Aryara's day they were scarcely human. What must a thousand years of retrogression have done to the breed?

What foul shape stole into the Ketrick castle on some forgotten night, or rose out of the dusk to grip some woman of the line, straying in the hills?

The mind shrinks from such an image. But this I know: there must have been survivals of that foul, reptilian epoch when the Ketricks went into Wales. There still may be. But this changeling, this waif of darkness, this horror who bears the noble name of Ketrick, the brand of the serpent is upon him, and until he is destroyed there is no rest for me. Now that I know him for what he is, he pollutes the clean air and leaves the slime of the snake on the green earth. The sound of his lisping, hissing voice fills me with crawling horror and the sight of his eyes inspires me with madness.

And as my ancestors – as I, Aryara, destroyed the scum that writhed beneath our heels, so shall I, John O'Donnel, exterminate the reptilian thing, the monster bred of the snaky taint that slumbered so long unguessed in clean Saxon veins, the vestigial serpent-things left to taunt the Sons of Aryan. They say the blow I received affected my mind; I know it but opened my eyes. Mine ancient enemy walks often on the moors alone, attracted, though he may not know it, by ancestral urgings. And on one of these lonely walks I shall meet him, and when I meet him, I will break his foul neck with my hands, as I, Aryara, broke the necks of foul night-things in the long, long ago.

Then they may take me and break my neck at the end of a rope if they will. I am not blind, if my friends are. And in the sight of the old Aryan god, if not in the blinded eyes of men, I will have kept faith with my tribe.

The Black Stone

They say foul things of Old Times still lurk
In dark forgotten corners of the world,
And Gates still gape to loose, on certain nights,
Shapes pent in Hell

JUSTIN

I read of it first in the strange book of Von Junzt, the German eccentric who lived so curiously and died in such grisly and mysterious fashion. It was my fortune to have access to his *Nameless Cults* in the original edition, the so-called Black Book, published in Dusseldorf in 1839, shortly before a hounding doom overtook the author. Collectors of rare literature were familiar with *Nameless Cults* mainly through the cheap and faulty translation which was pirated in London by Bridewall in 1845, and the carefully expurgated edition put out by the Golden Goblin Press of New York, 1909. But the volume I stumbled upon was one of the unexpurgated German copies, with heavy leather covers and rusty iron hasps. I doubt if there are more than half a dozen such volumes in the entire world today, for the quantity issued was not great, and when the manner of the author's demise was bruited about, many possessors of the book burned their volumes in panic.

Von Junzt spent his entire life (1795–1840) delving into forbidden subjects; he travelled in all parts of the world, gained entrance into innumerable secret societies, and read countless little-known and esoteric books and manuscripts in the original; and in the chapters of the Black Book, which range from startling clarity of exposition to murky ambiguity, there are statements and hints to freeze the blood of a thinking man. Reading what Von Junzt dared put in print arouses uneasy speculations as to what it was that he dared not tell. What dark matters, for instance, were contained in those closely-written pages that formed the unpublished manuscript on which he worked unceasingly for months before his death, and which lay torn and scattered all over the floor of the locked and bolted chamber in which Von Junzt was found dead with the marks of taloned fingers on his throat? It will never be known, for the author's closest friend, the Frenchman Alexis Ladeau, after having spent a whole night piecing the fragments together and reading what was written, burnt them to ashes and cut his own throat with a razor.

But the contents of the published matter are shuddersome enough, even if one accepts the general view that they but represent the ravings of a madman. There among many strange things I found mention of the Black Stone, that curious, sinister monolith that broods among the mountains of Hungary, and about which so many dark legends cluster. Van Junzt did not devote much space to it – the bulk of his grim work concerns cults and objects of dark worship which he maintained existed in his day, and it would seem that the Black Stone represents some order of being lost and forgotten centuries ago. But he spoke of it as one of the keys – a phrase used many times by him, in various relations, and constituting one of the obscurities of his work. And he hinted briefly at curious sights to be seen about the monolith on midsummer's night. He mentioned Otto Dostmann's theory that this monolith was a remnant of the Hunnish invasion and had been erected to commemorate a victory of Attila over the Goths. Von Junzt contradicted this assertion without giving any refutatory facts, merely remarking that to attribute the origin of the Black Stone to the Huns was as logical as assuming that William the Conqueror reared Stonehenge.

This implication of enormous antiquity piqued my interest immensely and after some difficulty I succeeded in locating a rat-eaten and mouldering copy of Dostmann's *Remnants of Lost Empires* (Berlin, 1809, Der Drachenhaus Press). I was disappointed to find that Dostmann referred to the Black Stone even more briefly than had Von Junzt, dismissing it with a few lines as an artefact comparatively modern in contrast with the Greco-Roman ruins of Asia Minor, which were his pet theme. He admitted inability to make out the defaced characters on the monolith but pronounced them unmistakably Mongoloid. However, little as I learned from Dostmann, he did mention the name of the village adjacent to the Black Stone – Stregoicavar – meaning something like Witch-Town.

A close scrutiny of guidebooks and travel articles gave me no further information – Stregoicavar, not on any map that I could find, lay in a wild, little-frequented region, out of the path of casual tourists. But I did find subject for thought in Dornly's *Magyar Folklore*. In his chapter on Dream Myths he mentions the Black Stone and tells of some curious superstitions regarding it – especially the belief that if anyone sleeps in the vicinity of the monolith, that person will be haunted by monstrous nightmares for ever after; and he cited tales of the peasants regarding too-curious people, who ventured to visit the Stone on Midsummer Night and who died raving mad because of something they saw there.

That was all I could gleam from Dornly, but my interest was even more intensely roused as I sensed a distinctly sinister aura about the Stone. The suggestion of dark antiquity, the recurrent hint of unnatural events on Midsummer Night, touched some slumbering instinct in my being, as one senses, rather than hears, the flowing of some dark subterraneous river in the night.

And I suddenly saw a connection between this Stone and a certain weird and fantastic poem written by the mad poet, Justin Geoffrey: *The People of the Monolith*. Inquiries led to the information that Geoffrey had indeed written that poem while travelling in Hungary, and I could not doubt that the Black Stone was the very monolith to which lie referred in his strange verse. Reading his stanzas again, I felt once more the strange dim stirrings of subconscious promptings that I had noticed when first reading of the Stone.

I had been casting about for a place to spend a short vacation and I made up my mind. I went to Stregoicavar. A train of obsolete style carried me from Temesvar to within striking distance, at least, of my objective, and a three days' ride in a bouncing coach brought me to the little village which lay in a fertile valley – high up in the fir-clad mountains.

The journey itself was uneventful, but during the first day we passed the old battlefield of Schomvaal where the brave Polish-Hungarian knight, Count Boris Vladinoff, made his gallant and futile stand against the victorious hosts of Suleiman the magnificent, when the Grand Turk swept over eastern Europe in 1526.

The driver of the coach pointed out to me a great heap of crumbling stones on a hill nearby, under which, he said, the bones of the brave Count lay. I remembered a passage from Larson's Turkish Wars. 'After the skirmish' (in which the Count with his small army had beaten back the Turkish advance-guard) 'the Count was standing beneath the half-ruined walls of the old castle on the hill, giving orders as to the disposition of his forces, when an aide brought to him a small lacquered case which had been taken from the body of the famous Turkish scribe and historian, Selim Bahadur, who had fallen in the fight. The Count took therefrom a roll of parchment and began to read, but he had not read far before he turned very pale and, without saying a word, replaced the parchment in the case and thrust the case into his cloak. At that very instant a hidden Turkish battery suddenly opened fire, and the balls striking the old castle, the Hungarians were horrified to see the halls crash down in ruin, completely covering the brave Count. Without a leader the gallant little army was cut to pieces, and in the warswept years which followed, the bones of the noblemen were never recovered. Today the natives point out a huge and mouldering pile of ruins near Schomvaal beneath which, they say, still rests all that the centuries have left of Count Boris Vladinolf.'

I found the village of Stregoicavar a dreamy, drowsy little village that apparently belied its sinister cognomen – a forgotten back-eddy that Progress had passed by. The quaint houses and the quainter dress and manners of the people were those of an earlier century. They were friendly, mildly curious but not inquisitive, though visitors from the outside world were extremely rare.

'Ten years ago another American came here and stayed a few days in the villa. Aye,' said the owner of the tavern where I had put up, 'a young fellow and queer-acting – mumbled to himself – a poet, I think.'

I knew he must mean Justin Geoffrey.

'Yes, he was a poet,' I answered, 'and he wrote a poem about a bit of scenery near this very village.'

'Indeed.' Mine host's interest was aroused. 'Then, since all great poets are strange in their speech and actions, he must have achieved great fame, for his actions and conversations were the strangest of any man I ever knew.'

'As is usual with artists,' I answered, 'most of his recognition has come since his death.'

'He is dead, then?'

'He died screaming in a madhouse five years ago.'

'Too bad, too bad,' sighed mine host sympathetically. 'Poor lad – he looked too long at the Black Stone.'

My heart gave a leap, but I masked my keen interest and said casually. 'I have heard something of this Black Stone; somewhere near this village, is it not?'

'Nearer than Christian folk wish,' he responded. 'Look!' He drew me to a latticed window and pointed up at the fir-clad slopes of the brooding blue mountains. 'There beyond where you see the bare face of that jutting cliff stands that accursed Stone. Would that it were ground to powder and the powder flung into the Danube to be carried to the deepest ocean! Once men tried to destroy the thing, but each man who laid hammer or maul against it came to an evil end. So now the people shun it.'

'What is there so evil about it?' I asked curiously.

'It is a demon-haunted thing,' he answered uneasily and with the suggestion of a shudder. 'In my childhood I knew a young man who came up from below and laughed at our traditions – in his fool-hardiness he went to the Stone on Midsummer Night and at dawn stumbled into the village again, stricken dumb and mad. Something had shattered his brain and sealed his lips, for until the day of his death, which came soon after, he spoke only to utter terrible blas-phemies or to slaver gibberish.

'My own nephew when very small was lost in the mountains and slept in the woods near the Stone, and now in his manhood he is tortured by foul dreams so that at times he makes the night hideous with his screams and wakes with cold sweat upon him.

'But let us talk of something else, Herr; it is not good to dwell upon such things.'

I remarked on the evident age of the tavern and he answered with pride. 'The foundations are more than four hundred years old; the original house was the only one in the village which was not burned to the ground when Suleiman's devil swept through the mountains. Here, in the house that then stood on these same foundations, it is said, the scribe Selim Bahadur had his headquarters while ravaging the country hereabouts.'

I learned then that the present inhabitants of Stregoicavar are not descendants of the people who dwelt there before the Turkish raid of 1526. The present people of Stregoicavar are descended from hardy settlers from the lower valleys who came into the ruined village after the Turk was thrust back.

Mine host did not speak of the extermination of the original inhab-itants with any great resentment and I learned that his ancestors in the lower levels had looked on the mountaineers with even more hatred and aversion than they regarded the Turks. He was rather vague regarding the causes of this feud, but said that the original inhabitants of Stregoicavar had been in the habit of making stealthy raids on the lowlands and stealing girls and children. Moreover, he said that they were not exactly of the same blood as his own people; the sturdy, original Magyar-Slavic stock had mixed and intermarried with a degraded aboriginal race until the breeds had blended, producing an unsavoury amalgamation. Who these aborigines were, he had not the slightest idea, but maintained that they were 'pagans' and had dwelt in the mountains since time immemorial, before the coming of the conquering peoples.

I attached little importance to this tale, seeing in it merely a parallel to the amalgamation of Celtic tribes with Mediterranean aborigines in the Galloway hills, with the resultant mixed race which, as Picts, has such an extensive part in Scotch legendary. Time has a curious foreshortening effect on folklore, and just as tales of the Picts became intertwined with legends of an older Mongoloid race, so that eventually the Picts were ascribed the repulsive appearance of the squat primitives, whose individuality merged, in the telling, into Pictish tales, and was forgotten; so, I felt, the supposed inhuman attributes of the first villagers of Stregoicavar could be traced to older, outworn myths with invading Huns and Mongols.

The morning after my arrival I received directions from mine host, who gave them worriedly, and set out to find the Black Stone. A few hours' tramp up the fir-covered slopes brought me to the face of the rugged, solid stone cliff which jutted boldly from the mountainside. A narrow trail wound up it, and mounting this, I looked out over the peaceful valley of Stregoicavar, which seemed to drowse, guarded on either hand by the great blue mountains. No huts or any sign of human tenancy showed between the cliff whereon I stood and the village. I saw numbers of scattered farms in the valley but all lay on the other side of Stregoicavar, which itself seemed to shrink from the brooding slopes which masked the Black Stone.

The summit of the cliffs proved to be a sort of thickly wooded plateau. I made my way through the dense growth for a short distance and came into a wide glade; and in the centre of the glade reared a gaunt figure of black stone.

It was octagonal in shape, some sixteen feet in height and about a foot and a half thick. It had once evidently been highly polished, but now the surface was thickly dinted as if savage efforts had been made to demolish it; but the hammers had done little more than flake off small bits of stone and mutilate the characters which once had evidently marched up in a spiralling line round and round the shaft to the top. Up to ten feet from the base these characters were almost completely blotted out, so that it was very difficult to trace their direction. Higher up they were plainer, and I managed to squirm part of the way up the shaft and scan them at close range. All were more or less defaced, but I was positive that they symbolised no language now remembered on the face of the earth. I am fairly familiar with all hieroglyphics known to researchers and philologists, and I can say with certainty that those characters were like nothing of which I have ever read or heard. The nearest approach to them that I ever saw were some crude scratches on a gigantic and strangely symmetrical rock in a lost valley of Yucatan. I remember that when I pointed out these marks to the archaeologist who was my companion, he maintained that they either represented natural weathering or the idle scratching of some Indian. To my theory that the rock was really the base of a long-vanished column, he merely laughed, calling my attention to the dimensions of it, which suggested, if it were built with any natural rules of architectural symmetry, a column a thousand feet high. But I was not convinced.

I will not say that the characters on the Black Stone were similar to those on that colossal rock in Yucatan; but one suggested the other. As to the substance of the monolith, again I was baffled. The stone of which it was composed was a dully gleaming black, whose surface, where it was not dinted and roughened, created a curious illusion of semitransparency.

I spent most of the morning there and came away baffled. No connection of the Stone with any other artefact in the world suggested itself to me. It was as if the monolith had been reared by alien hands, in an age distant and apart from human ken.

I returned to the village with my interest in no way abated. Now that I had seen the curious thing, my desire was still more keenly whetted to investigate the matter further and seek to learn by what strange hands and for what strange purpose the Black Stone had been reared in the long ago.

I sought out the tavern keeper's nephew and questioned him in regard to his dreams, but he was vague, though willing to oblige. He did not mind discussing them, but was unable to describe them with any clarity. Though he dreamed the same dreams repeatedly, and though they were hideously vivid at the time, they left no distinct impression on his waking mind. He remembered them only as chaotic nightmares through which huge whirling fires shot lurid tongues of flames and a black drum bellowed incessantly. One thing only: he had seen the Black Stone, not on a mountain slope but set like a spire on a colossal black castle.

As for the rest of the villagers, I found them not inclined to talk about the Stone, with the exception of the schoolmaster, a man of surprising education, who spent much more of his time out in the world than any of the rest.

He was much interested in what I told him of Von Junzt's remarks about the Stone, and warmly agreed with the German author in the alleged age of the monolith. He believed that a coven had once existed in the vicinity and that possibly all of the original villagers had been members of that fertility cult which once threatened to undermine European civilisation and gave rise to the tales of witchcraft. He cited the very name of the village to prove his point; it had not been originally named Stregoicavar, he said; according to legends the builders had called it Xuthltan, which was the aboriginal name of the site on which the village had been built many centuries ago.

This fact roused again an indescribable feeling of uneasiness. The barbarous name did not suggest connection with any Scythic, Slavic or Mongolian race to which an aboriginal people of these mountains would, under natural circumstances, have belonged.

That the Magyars and Slavs of the lower valleys believed the original inhabitants of the village to be members of the witchcraft cult was evident, the schoolmaster said, by the name they gave it, which name continued to be used even after the older settlers had been massacred by the Turks, and the village rebuilt by a cleaner and more wholesome breed.

He did not believe that the members of the cult erected the monolith, but he did believe that they used it as a centre of their activities, and repeating vague legends which had been handed down since before the Turkish invasion, he advanced the theory that the degenerate villagers had used it as a sort of altar on which they offered human sacrifices, using as victims the girls and babies stolen from his own ancestors in the lower valleys.

He discounted the myths of weird events on Midsummer Night, as well as a curious legend of a strange deity which the witch-people of Xuthltan were said to have invoked with chants and wild rituals of flagellation and slaughter.

He had never visited the Stone on Midsummer Night, he said, but he would not fear to do so; whatever had existed or taken place there in the past, had been long engulfed in the mists of time and oblivion. The Black Stone had lost its meaning save as a link to a dead and dusty past.

It was while returning from a visit to this schoolmaster one night about a week after my arrival at Stregoicavar that a sudden recollection struck me – it was Midsummer Night! The very time that the legends linked with grisly implications to the Black Stone. I turned away from the tavern and strode swiftly through the village. Stregoicavar lay silent; the villagers retired early. I saw no one as I passed rapidly out of the village and up into the firs which masked the mountain slopes with whispering darkness. A broad silver moon hung above the valley, flooding the crags and slopes in a weird light and etching the shadows blackly. No wind blew through the firs, but a mysterious, intangible rustling and whispering was abroad. Surely on such nights in past centuries, my whimsical imagination told me, naked witches on magic broomsticks had flown across the valley, pursued by jeering demoniac familiars.

I came to the cliffs and was somewhat disquieted to note that the illusive moonlight lent them a subtle appearance I had not noticed before – in the weird light they appeared less like natural cliffs and more like the ruins of Cyclopean and Titan-reared battlements jutting from the mountain-slope.

Shaking off this hallucination with difficulty I came upon the plateau and hesitated a moment before I plunged into the brooding darkness of the woods. A sort of breathless tenseness hung over the shadows, like an unseen monster holding its breath lest it scare away its prey. I shook off the sensation – a natural one, considering the eeriness of the place and its evil reputation – and made my way through the wood, experiencing a most unpleasant sensation that I was being followed, and halting once, sure that something clammy and unstable had brushed against my face in the darkness.

I came out into the glade and saw the tall monolith rearing its gaunt height above the sward. At the edge of the woods on the side toward the cliffs was a stone which formed a sort of natural seat. I sat down, reflecting that it was probably while there that the mad poet, Justin Geoffrey, had written his fantastic *People of the Monolith*. Mine host thought that it was the Stone which had caused Geoffrey's insanity, but the seeds of madness had been sown in the poet's brain long before he ever came to Stregoicavar.

A glance at my watch showed that the hour of midnight was close at hand. I leaned back, waiting whatever ghostly demonstration might appear. A thin night wind started up among the branches of the firs, with an uncanny suggestion of faint, unseen pipes whispering an eerie and evil tune. The monotony of the sound and my steady gazing at the monolith produced a sort of self-hypnosis upon me; I grew drowsy. I fought this feeling, but sleep stole on me in spite of myself; the monolith seemed to sway and dance, strangely distorted to my gaze, and then I slept.

I opened my eyes and sought to rise, but lay still, as if an icy hand gripped me helpless. Cold terror stole over me; the glade was no longer deserted. It was thronged by a silent crowd of strange people, and my distended eyes took in strange barbaric details of costume which my reason told me were archaic and forgotten even in this backward land. Surely, I thought, these are villagers who have come here to hold some fantastic conclave – but another glance told me that these people were not the folk of Stregoicavar. They were a shorter, more squat race, whose brows were lower, whose faces were broader and duller. Some had Slavic or Magyar features, but those features were degraded as from a mixture of some baser, alien strain I could not classify. Many wore the hides of wild beasts, and their whole appearance, both men and women, was one of sensual brutishness. They terrified and repelled me, but they gave me no heed. They formed in a vast half-circle in front of the monolith and began a sort of chant, flinging their arms in unison and weaving their bodies rhythmically from the waist upward. All eyes were fixed on the top of the Stone which they seemed to be invoking. But the strangest of all was the dimness of their voices; not fifty yards from me hundreds of men and women were unmistakably lifting their voices in a wild chant, yet those voices came to me as a faint indistinguishable murmur as if from across vast leagues of space – or time.

Before the monolith stood a sort of brazier from which a vile, nauseous yellow smoke billowed upward, curling curiously in a swaying spiral around the black shaft, like a vast unstable snake.

On one side of this brazier lay two figures – a young girl, stark naked and bound hand and foot, and an infant, apparently only a few months old. On the other side of the brazier squatted a hideous old hag with a queer sort of black drum on her lap; this drum she beat with slow, light blows of her open palms, but I could not hear the sound.

The rhythm of the swaying bodies grew faster, and into the space between the people and the monolith sprang a naked young woman, her eyes blazing, her long black hair flying loose. Spinning dizzily on her toes, she whirled across the open space and fell prostrate before the Stone, where she lay motionless. The next instant a fantastic figure followed her – a man from whose waist hung a goatskin, and whose features were entirely hidden by a sort of mask made from a huge wolf's head, so that he looked like a monstrous, nightmare being, horribly compounded of elements both human and bestial. In his hand he held a bunch of long fir switches bound together at the larger ends, and the moonlight glinted on a chain of heavy gold looped about his neck.

A smaller chain depending from it suggested a pendant of some sort, but this was missing.

The people tossed their arms violently and seemed to redouble their shouts as this grotesque creature loped across the open space with many a fantastic leap and caper. Coming to the woman who lay before the monolith, he began to lash her with the switches he bore, and she leaped up and spun into the wild steps of the most incredible dance I have ever seen. And her tormentor danced with her, keeping the wild rhythm, matching her every whirl and bound, while incessantly raining cruel blows on her naked body. And at every blow he shouted a single word, over and over, and all the people shouted it back. I could see the working of their lips, and now the faint far-off murmur of their voices merged and blended into one distant shout, repeated over and over with slobbering ecstasy. But what that one word was, I could not make out.

In dizzy whirls spun the wild dancers, while the lookers-on, standing still in their tracks, followed the rhythm of their dance with swaying bodies and weaving arms. Madness grew in the eyes of the capering votaress and was reflected in the eyes of the watchers. Wilder and more extravagant grew the whirling frenzy of that mad dance – it became a bestial and obscene thing, while the old hag howled and battered the drum like a crazy woman, and the switches cracked out a devil's tune.

Blood trickled down the dancer's limbs but she seemed not to feel the lashing save as a stimulus for further enormities of outrageous motion; bounding into the midst of the yellow smoke which now spread out tenuous tentacles to embrace both flying figures, she seemed to merge with that foul fog and veil herself with it. Then emerging into plain view, closely followed by the beast-thing that flogged her, she shot into an indescribable, explosive burst of dynamic mad motion, and on the very crest of that mad wave, she dropped suddenly to the sward, quivering and panting as if completely overcome by her frenzied exertions. The lashing continued with unabated violence and intensity and she began to wriggle toward the monolith on her belly. The priest – or such I will call him – followed, lashing her unprotected body with all the power of his arm as she writhed along, leaving a heavy track of blood on the trampled earth. She reached the monolith, and gasping and panting, flung both arms about it and covered the cold stone with fierce hot kisses, as in frenzied and unholy adoration.

The fantastic priest bounded high in the air, flinging away the red-dabbled switches, and the worshippers, howling and foaming at the mouths, turned on each other with tooth and nail, rending one another's garments and flesh in a blind passion of bestiality. The priest swept up the infant with a long arm, and shouting again that Name, whirled the wailing babe high in the air and dashed its brains out against the monolith, leaving a ghastly stain on the black surface: Cold with horror I saw him rip the tiny body open with his bare brutish fingers and fling handfuls of blood on the shaft, then toss the red and torn shape into the brazier, extinguishing flame and smoke in a crimson rain, while the maddened brutes behind him howled over and over the Name. Then suddenly they all fell prostrate, writhing like snakes, while the priest flung wide his gory hands as in triumph: I opened my mouth to scream my horror and loathing, but only a dry rattle sounded; a huge monstrous toad-like thing squatted on the top of the monolith!

I saw its bloated, repulsive and unstable outline against the moon-light, and set in what would have been the face of a natural creature, its huge, blinking eyes which reflected all the lust, abysmal greed, obscene cruelty and monstrous evil that has stalked the sons of men since their ancestors moved blind and hairless in the tree-tops. In those grisly eyes were mirrored all the unholy things and vile secrets that sleep in the cities under the sea, and that skulk from the light of day in the blackness of primordial caverns. And so that ghastly thing that the unhallowed ritual and sadism and blood had evoked from the silence of the hills, leered and blinked down on its bestial worshippers, who grovelled in abhorrent abasement before it.

Now the beast-masked priest lifted the bound and weakly writhing girl in his brutish hands and held her up toward that horror on the monolith. And as that monstrosity sucked in its breath, lustfully and slobberingly, something snapped in my brain and I fell into a merciful faint.

I opened my eyes on a still white dawn. All the events of the night rushed back on me and I sprang up, then stared about me in amazement. The monolith brooded gaunt and silent above the sward which waved, green and untrampled, in the morning breeze. A few quick strides took me across the glade; here had the dancers leaped and bounded until the ground should have been trampled bare; and here had the votaress wriggled her painful way to the Stone, streaming blood on the earth. But no drop of crimson showed on the uncrushed sward. I looked, shudderingly, at the side of the monolith against which the bestial priest had brained the stolen baby – but no dark stain nor grisly clot showed there.

A dream! It had been a wild nightmare . . . or else . . . I shrugged my shoulders. What vivid clarity for a dream! I returned quietly to the village and entered the inn without being seen. And there I sat meditating over the strange events of the night. More and more was I prone to discard the dream-theory. That what I had seen was illusion and without material substance, was evident. But I believed that I had looked on the mirrored shadow of a deed perpetrated in ghastly actuality in bygone days. But how was I to know? What proof to show that my vision had been a gathering of foul spectres rather than a nightmare originating in my brain?

As if for answer a name flashed into my mind – Selim Bahadur! According to legend this man, who had been a soldier as well as a scribe, had commanded that part of Suleiman's army which had devastated Stregoicavar. It seemed logical enough; and if so, he had gone straight from the blotted-out countryside to the bloody field of Schomvaal, and his doom. I sprang up with a sudden shout – that manuscript which was taken from the Turk's body, and which Count Boris shuddered over – might it not contain some narration of what the conquering Turks found in Stregoicavar? What else could have shaken the iron nerves of the Polish adventurer? And since the bones of the Count had never been recovered, what more certain than that the lacquered case, with its mysterious contents, still lay hidden beneath the ruins that covered Boris Vladinoff? I began packing my bag with fierce haste.

Three days later found me ensconced in a little village a few miles from the old battlefield, and when the moon rose I was working with savage intensity on the great pile of crumbling stone that crowned the hill. It was back-breaking toil – looking back now I cannot see how I accomplished it. I laboured without a pause from moonrise to dawn. As the sun was coming up I tore aside the last tangle of stones and looked on all that was mortal of Count Boris Vladinoff – only a few, pitiful fragments of crumbling bone – and among them, crushed out of all original shape, lay a case whose lacquered surface had kept it from complete decay through the centuries.

I seized it with frenzied eagerness, and back in my tavern chamber I opened the case and found the parchment comparatively intact; and there was something else in the case – a small squat object wrapped in silk. I was wild to plumb the secrets of those yellowed pages, but weariness forbade me. Since leaving Stregoicavar I had hardly slept at all, and the terrific exertions of the previous night combined to overcome me. In spite of myself I was forced to stretch myself on my bed, nor did I awake until sundown.

I snatched a hasty supper, and then in the light of a flickering candle, read the near-Turkish characters that covered the parchment. It was difficult work, for I am not deeply versed in the language and the archaic style of the narrative baffled me. But as I toiled through it a word or a phrase here and there leaped at me and a dimly growing horror shook me in its grip. I bent my energies fiercely to the task, and as the tale grew clearer and took more tangible form my blood chilled in my veins, my hair stood up and my tongue clove to my mouth.

At last when grey dawn was stealing through the latticed window, I laid down the manuscript and took up and unwrapped the thing in the bit of silk. Staring at it with haggard eyes I knew the truth of the matter was clinched, even had it been possible to doubt the veracity of that terrible manuscript.

And I replaced both obscene things in the case, nor did I rest or sleep or eat until that case containing them had been weighted with stones and flung into the deepest current of the Danube which, God grant, carried them back into the Hell from which they came.

It was no dream I dreamed on Midsummer Midnight in the hills above Stregoicavar. Well for Justin Geoffrey that he tarried there only in the sunlight and went his way, for had he gazed upon that ghastly conclave, his mad brain would have snapped before it did. How my own reason held, I do not know.

No . . . it was no dream – I gazed upon a foul rout of votaries long dead, come up from Hell to worship as of old; ghosts that bowed before a ghost. For Hell has long claimed their hideous god.

By what foul alchemy or godless sorcery the Gates of Hell are opened on that one eerie night I do not know, but mine own eyes have seen. And I know I looked on no living thing that night, for the manuscript written in the careful hand of Selim Bahadur narrated at length what he and his raiders found in the valley of Stregoicavar; and I read, set down in detail, the blasphemous obscenities that torture wrung from the lips of screaming worshippers; and I read, too, of the lost, grim black cavern high in the hills where the horrified Turks hemmed a monstrous, bloated, wallowing toad-like being and slew it with flame and ancient steel blessed in old times by

Muhammad, and with incantations that were old when Arabia was young. And even staunch old Selim's hand shook as he recorded the cataclysmic, earth-shaking death-howls of the monstrosity, which died not alone; for half-score of his slayers perished with him, in ways that Selim would not or could not describe.

And that squat idol carved of gold and wrapped in silk was an image of himself, and Selim tore it from the golden chain that looped the neck of the slain high priest of the mask.

Well that the Turks swept out that foul valley with torch and clean steel! Such sights as those brooding mountains have looked on belong to the darkness and abysses of lost aeons. No – it is not fear of the toad-thing that makes me shudder in the night. He is made fast in Hell with his nauseous horde, freed only for an hour on the most weird night of the year, as I have seen. And of his worshippers, none remains.

But it is the realisation that such things once crouched beastlike above the souls of men which brings cold sweat to my brow; and I fear to peer again into the leaves of Von Junzt's abomination. For now I understand his repeated phrase of keys! Aye! Keys to Outer Doors – links with an abhorrent past and – who knows? – of abhorrent spheres of the present. And I understand why the tavern-keeper's nightmare-haunted nephew saw in his dream, the Black Stone like a spire on a Cyclopean black castle. If men ever excavate among those mountains they may find incredible things below those masking slopes. For the cave wherein the Turks trapped the thing was not truly a cavern, and I shudder to contemplate the gigantic gulf of aeons which must stretch between this age and the time when the earth shook herself and reared up, like a wave, those blue mountains that, rising, enveloped unthinkable things. May no man ever seek to uproot that ghastly spire men call the Black Stone!

A Key! Aye, it is a Key, symbol of a forgotten horror. That horror has faded into the limbo from which it crawled, loathsomely, in the black dawn of the earth. But what of the other fiendish possibilities hinted at by Von Junzt – what of the monstrous hand which strangled out his life? Since reading what Selim Bahadur wrote, I can no longer doubt anything in the Black Book. Man was not always master of the earth – and is he now? What nameless shapes may even now lurk in the dark places of the world?

The Thing on the Roof

They lumber through the night
With their elephantine tread;
I shudder in affright
As I cower in my bed.
They lift colossal wings
On the high gable roofs
Which tremble to the trample
Of their mastodonic hoofs.

JUSTIN GEOFFREY
Out of the Old Land

Let me begin by saying that I was surprised when Tussmann called on me. We had never been close friends; the man's mercenary instincts repelled me; and since our bitter controversy of three years before, when he attempted to discredit my *Evidences of Nahua Culture in Yucatan*, which was the result of years of careful research, our relations had been anything but cordial. However, I received him and found his manner hasty and abrupt, but rather abstracted, as if his dislike for me had been thrust aside in some driving passion that had hold of him.

His errand was quickly stated. He wished my aid in obtaining a volume of the first edition of Von Junzt's *Nameless Cults* – the edition known as the Black Book, not from its colour, but because of its dark contents. He might almost as well have asked me for the original Greek translation of the *Necronomicon*. Though since my return from Yucatan I had devoted practically all my time to my avocation of book collecting, I had not stumbled on to any hint that the book in the Düsseldorf edition was still in existence.

A word as to this rare work. Its extreme ambiguity in spots, coupled with its incredible subject-matter, has caused it long to be regarded as the ravings of a maniac, and the author was damned with the brand of insanity. But the fact remains that many of his assertions are unanswerable, and that he spent the full forty-five years of his life prying into strange places and discovering secret and abysmal things. Not a great many volumes were printed in the first edition and many of these were burned by their frightened owners when Von Junzt was found strangled in a mysterious manner, in his barred and bolted chamber one night in 1840, six months after he had returned from a mysterious journey to Mongolia.

Five years later a London printer, one Bridewall, pirated the work, and issued a cheap translation for sensational effect, full of grotesque woodcuts, and riddled with misspellings, faulty translations and the usual errors of a cheap and unscholarly printing. This still further discredited the original work, and publishers and public forgot about the book until 1909 when the Golden Goblin Press of New York brought out an edition.

Their production was so carefully expurgated that fully a fourth of the original matter was cut out; the book was handsomely bound and decorated with the exquisite and weirdly imaginative illustrations of Diego Vasquez. The edition was intended for popular consumption but the artistic instinct of the publishers defeated that end, since the cost of issuing the book was so great that they were forced to cite it at a prohibitive price.

I was explaining all this to Tussmann when he interrupted brusquely to say that he was not utterly ignorant in such matters. One of the Golden Goblin books ornamented his library, he said, and it was in it that he found a certain line which aroused his interest. If I could procure him a copy of the original 1839 edition, he would make it worth my while; knowing, he added, that it would be useless to offer me money, he would, instead, in return for my trouble on his behalf, make a full retraction of his former accusations in regard to my Yucatan researches, and offer a complete apology in *The Scientific News*.

I will admit that I was astounded at this, and realised that if the matter meant so much to Tussmann that he was willing to make such concessions, it must indeed be of the utmost importance. I answered that I considered that I had sufficiently refuted his charges in the eyes of the world and had no desire to put him in a humiliating position, but that I would make the utmost efforts to procure him what he wanted.

He thanked me abruptly and took his leave, saying rather vaguely that he hoped to find a complete exposition of something in the Black Book which had evidently been slighted in the later edition.

I set to work, writing letters to friends, colleagues and book dealers all over the world, and soon discovered that I had assumed a task of no small magnitude. Three months elapsed before my efforts were crowned with success, but at last, through the aid of Professor James Clement of Richmond, Virginia, I was able to obtain what I wished.

I notified Tussmann and he came to London by the next train. His eyes burned avidly as he gazed at the thick, dusty volume with its heavy leather covers and rusty iron hasps, and his fingers quivered with eagerness as he thumbed the time-yellowed pages.

And when he cried out fiercely and smashed his clenched fist down on the table I knew that he had found what he hunted.

'Listen!' he commanded, and he read to me a passage that spoke of an old, old temple in a Honduras jungle where a strange god was worshipped by an ancient tribe which became extinct before the coming of the Spaniards. And Tussmann read aloud of the mummy that had been, in life, the last high priest of that vanished people, and which now lay in a chamber hewn in the solid rock of the cliff against which the temple was built. About that mummy's withered neck was a copper chain, and on that chain a great red jewel carved in the form of a toad. This jewel was a key, Von Junzt went on to say, to the treasure of the temple which lay hidden in a subterranean crypt far below the temple's altar.

Tussmann's eyes blazed.

'I have seen that temple! I have stood before the altar. I have seen the sealed-up entrance of the chamber in which, the natives say, lies the mummy of the priest. It is a very curious temple, no more like the ruins of the prehistoric Indians than it is like the buildings of the modern Latin-Americans. The Indians in the vicinity disclaim any former connection with the place; they say that the people who built that temple were a different race from themselves, and were there when their own ancestors came into the country. I believe it to be a remnant of some long-vanished civilisation which began to decay thousands of years before the Spaniards came.

'I would have liked to have broken into the sealed-up chamber, but I had neither the time nor the tools for the task. I was hurrying to the coast, having been wounded by an accidental gunshot in the foot, and I stumbled on to the place purely by chance.

'I have been planning to have another look at it, but circumstances have prevented – now I intend to let nothing stand in my way! By chance I came upon a passage in the Golden Goblin edition of this book, describing the temple. But that was all; the mummy was only briefly mentioned. Interested, I obtained one of Bridewall's translations but ran up against a blank wall of baffling blunders. By some

irritating mischance the translator had even mistaken the location of
the Temple of the Toad, as Von Junzt calls it, and has it in Guate-
mala instead of Honduras. The general description is faulty, the
jewel is mentioned and the fact that it is a "key". But a key to what,
Bridewall's book does not state. I now felt that I was on the track of a
real discovery, unless Von Junzt was, as many maintain, a madman.
But that the man was actually in Honduras at one time is well
attested, and no one could so vividly describe the temple – as he does
in the Black Book – unless he had seen it himself. How he learned of
the jewel is more than I can say. The Indians who told me of the
mummy said nothing of any jewel. I can only believe that Von Junzt
found his way into the sealed crypt somehow – the man had uncanny
ways of learning hidden things.

'To the best of my knowledge only one other white man has
seen the Temple of the Toad besides Von Junzt and myself – the
Spanish traveller Juan Gonzales, who made a partial exploration of
that country in 1793. He mentioned, briefly, a curious fane that
differed from most Indian ruins, and spoke sceptically of a legend
current among the natives that there was "something unusual"
hidden under the temple. I feel certain that he was referring to the
Temple of the Toad.

'Tomorrow I sail for Central America. Keep the book; I have no
more use for it. This time I am going fully prepared and I intend to
find what is hidden in that temple, if I have to demolish it. It can be
nothing less than a great store of gold! The Spaniards missed it,
somehow. When they arrived in Central America, the Temple of the
Toad was deserted; they were searching for living Indians from
whom torture could wring gold, not for mummies of lost peoples.
But I mean to have that treasure.'

So saying Tussman took his departure. I sat down and opened the
book at the place where he had left off reading, and I sat until
midnight, wrapt in Von Junzt's curious, wild and at times utterly
vague expoundings. And I found pertaining to the Temple of the
Toad certain things which disquieted me so much that the next
morning I attempted to get in touch with Tussmann, only to find
that he had already sailed.

Several months passed and then I received a letter from Tussmann, asking me to come and spend a few days with him at his estate
in Sussex; he also requested me to bring the Black Book with me.

I arrived at Tussmann's rather isolated estate just after nightfall.
He lived in almost feudal state, his great ivy-grown house and broad

lawns surrounded by high stone walls. As I went up the hedge-bordered way from the gate to the house, I noted that the place had not been well kept in its master's absence. Weeds grew rank among the trees, almost choking out the grass. Among some unkempt bushes over against the outer wall, I heard what appeared to be a horse or an ox blundering and lumbering about. I distinctly heard the clink of its hoof on a stone.

A servant who eyed me suspiciously admitted me and I found Tussmann pacing to and fro in his study like a caged lion. His giant frame was leaner, harder than when I had last seen him; his face was bronzed by a tropic sun. There were more and harsher lines in his strong face and his eyes burned more intensely than ever. A smouldering, baffled anger seemed to underlie his manner.

'Well, Tussmann,' I greeted him, 'what success? Did you find the gold?'

'I found not an ounce of gold,' he growled. 'The whole thing was a hoax – well, not all of it. I broke into the sealed chamber and found the mummy . . .'

'And the jewel?' I exclaimed.

He drew something from his pocket and handed it to me.

I gazed curiously at the thing I held. It was a great jewel, clear and transparent as crystal, but of a sinister crimson, carved, as Von Junzt had declared, in the shape of a toad. I shuddered involuntarily; the image was peculiarly repulsive. I turned my attention to the heavy and curiously wrought copper chain which supported it.

'What are these characters carved on the chain?' I asked curiously.

'I cannot say,' Tussmann replied. 'I had thought perhaps you might know. I find a faint resemblance between them and certain partly defaced hieroglyphics on a monolith known as the Black Stone in the mountains of Hungary. I have been unable to decipher them.'

'Tell me of your trip,' I urged, and over our whisky-and-sodas he began, as if with a strange reluctance.

'I found the temple again with no great difficulty, though it lies in a lonely and little-frequented region. The temple is built against a sheer stone cliff in a deserted valley unknown to maps and explorers. I would not endeavour to make an estimate of its antiquity, but it is built of a sort of unusually hard basalt, such as I have never seen anywhere else, and its extreme weathering suggests incredible age.

'Most of the columns which form its façade are in ruins, thrusting up shattered stumps from worn bases, like the scattered and broken teeth of some grinning hag. The outer walls are crumbling, but the inner walls and the columns which support such of the roof as remains intact, seem good for another thousand years, as well as the walls of the inner chamber.

'The main chamber is a large circular affair with a floor composed of great squares of stone. In the centre stands the altar, merely a huge, round, curiously carved block of the same material. Directly behind the altar, in the solid stone cliff which forms the rear wall of the chamber, is the sealed and hewn-out chamber wherein lay the mummy of the temple's last priest.

'I broke into the crypt with not too much difficulty and found the mummy exactly as is stated in the Black Book. Though it was in a remarkable state of preservation, I was unable to classify it. The withered features and general contour of the skull suggested certain peoples of Lower Egypt, and I feel certain that the priest was a member of a race more akin to the Caucasian than the Indian. Beyond this, I can not make any positive statement.

'But the jewel was there, the chain looped about the dried-up neck.'

From this point Tussmann's narrative became so vague that I had some difficulty in following him and wondered if the tropic sun had affected his mind. He had opened a hidden door in the altar somehow with the jewel – just how, he did not plainly say, and it struck me that he did not clearly understand himself the action of the jewel-key. But the opening of the secret door had had a bad effect on the hardy rogues in his employ. They had refused point-blank to follow him through that gaping black opening which had appeared so mysteriously when the gem was touched to the altar.

Tussmann entered alone with his pistol and electric torch, finding a narrow stone stair that wound down into the bowels of the earth, apparently. He followed this and presently came into a broad corridor, in the blackness of which his tiny beam of light was almost engulfed. As he told this he spoke with strange annoyance of a toad which hopped ahead of him, just beyond the circle of light, all the time he was below ground.

Making his way along dank tunnels and stairways that were wells of solid blackness, he at last came to a heavy door fantastically carved, which he felt must be the crypt wherein was secreted the gold of the ancient worshippers. He pressed the toad-jewel against it at several places and finally the door gaped wide.

'And the treasure?' I broke in eagerly.

He laughed in savage self-mockery.

'There was no gold there, no precious gems – nothing . . . ' – he hesitated – 'nothing that I could bring away.'

Again his tale lapsed into vagueness. I gathered that he had left the temple rather hurriedly without searching any further for the supposed treasure. He had intended bringing the mummy away with him, he said, to present to some museum, but when he came up out of the pits, it could not be found and he believed that his men, in superstitious aversion to having such a companion on their road to the coast, had thrown it into some well or cavern.

'And so,' he concluded, 'I am in England again no richer than when I left.'

'You have the jewel,' I reminded him. 'Surely it is valuable.'

He eyed it without favour, but with a sort of fierce avidness almost obsessional.

'Would you say that it is a ruby?' he asked.

I shook my head. 'I am unable to classify it.'

'And I. But let me see the book.'

He slowly turned the heavy pages, his lips moving as he read. Sometimes he shook his head as if puzzled, and I noticed him dwell long over a certain line.

'This man dipped so deeply into forbidden things,' said he, 'I can not wonder that his fate was so strange and mysterious. He must have had some foreboding of his end – here he warns men not to disturb sleeping things.'

Tussmann seemed lost in thought for some moments.

'Aye, sleeping things,' he muttered, 'that seem dead, but only lie waiting for some blind fool to awake them . . . I should have read further in the Black Book – and I should have shut the door when I left the crypt . . . but I have the key and I'll keep it in spite of Hell.'

He roused himself from his reveries and was about to speak when he stopped short. From somewhere upstairs had come a peculiar sound.

'What was that?' he glared at me. I shook my head and he ran to the door and shouted for a servant. The man entered a few moments later and he was rather pale.

'You were upstairs?' growled Tussmann.

'Yes, sir.'

'Did you hear anything?' asked Tussmann harshly and in a manner almost threatening and accusing.

'I did, sir,' the man answered with a puzzled look on his face.

'What did you hear?' The question was fairly snarled.

'Well, sir,' the man laughed apologetically, 'you'll say I'm a bit off, I fear, but to tell you the truth, sir, it sounded like a horse stamping around on the roof!'

A blaze of absolute madness leaped into Tussmann's eyes.

'You fool!' he screamed. 'Get out of here!' The man shrank back in amazement and Tussmann snatched up the gleaming toad-carved jewel.

'I've been a fool!' he raved. 'I didn't read far enough – and I should have shut the door – but by heaven, the key is mine and I'll keep it in spite of man or devil.'

And with these strange words he turned and fled upstairs. A moment later his door slammed heavily and a servant, knocking timidly, brought forth only a blasphemous order to retire and a luridly worded threat to shoot anyone who tried to obtain entrance into the room.

Had it not been so late I would have left the house, for I was certain that Tussmann was stark mad. As it was, I retired to the room a frightened servant showed me, but I did not go to bed. I opened the pages of the Black Book at the place where Tussmann had been reading.

This much was evident, unless the man was utterly insane: he had stumbled upon something unexpected in the Temple of the Toad. Something unnatural about the opening of the altar door had frightened his men, and in the subterranean crypt Tussmann had found *something* that he had not thought to find. And I believed that he had been followed from Central America, and that the reason for his persecution was the jewel he called the Key.

Seeking some clue in Von Junzt's volume, I read again of the Temple of the Toad, of the strange pre-Indian people who worshipped there, and of the huge, tittering, tentacled, hoofed monstrosity that they worshipped.

Tussmann had said that he had not read far enough when he had first seen the book. Puzzling over this cryptic phrase I came upon the line he had pored over – marked by his thumb nail. It seemed to me to be another of Von Junzt's many ambiguities, for it merely stated that a temple's god was the temple's treasure. Then the dark implication of the hint struck me and cold sweat beaded my forehead.

The Key to the Treasure! And the temple's treasure was the temple's god! And sleeping Things might awaken on the opening of their prison door! I sprang up, unnerved by the intolerable suggestion, and at that moment something crashed in the stillness and the death-scream of a human being burst upon my ears.

In an instant I was out of the room, and as I dashed up the stairs I heard sounds that have made me doubt my sanity ever since. At Tussmann's door I halted, essaying with shaking hand to turn the knob. The door was locked, and as I hesitated I heard from within a hideous high-pitched tittering and then the disgusting squashy sound as if a great, jelly-like bulk was being forced through the window. The sound ceased and I could have sworn I heard a faint swish of gigantic wings. Then silence.

Gathering my shattered nerves, I broke down the door. A foul and overpowering stench billowed out like a yellow mist. Gasping in nausea I entered. The room was in ruins, but nothing was missing except that crimson toad-carved jewel Tussmann called the Key, and that was never found. A foul, unspeakable slime smeared the window-sill, and in the centre of the room lay Tussmann, his head crushed and flattened; and on the red ruin of skull and face, the plain print of an enormous hoof.

The Horror from the Mound

Steve Brill did not believe in ghosts or demons. Juan Lopez did. But neither the caution of the one nor the sturdy scepticism of the other was shield against the horror that fell upon them – the horror forgotten by men for more than three hundred years – a screaming fear monstrously resurrected from the black lost ages.

Yet as Steve Brill sat on his sagging stoop that last evening, his thoughts were as far from uncanny menaces as the thoughts of man can be. His ruminations were bitter but materialistic. He surveyed his farmland and he swore. Brill was tall, rangy and tough as boot-leather – true son of the iron-bodied pioneers who wrenched West Texas from the wilderness. He was browned by the sun and strong as a longhorned steer. His lean legs and the boots on them showed his cowboy instincts, and now he cursed himself that he had ever climbed off the hurricane deck of his crank-eyed mustang and turned to farming. He was no farmer, the young puncher admitted profanely.

Yet his failure had not all been his fault. Plentiful rain in the winter – so rare in West Texas – had given promise of good crops. But as usual, things had happened. A late blizzard had destroyed all the budding fruit. The grain which had looked so promising was ripped to shreds and battered into the ground by terrific hailstorms just as it was turning yellow. A period of intense dryness, followed by another hailstorm, finished the corn.

Then the cotton, which had somehow struggled through, fell before a swarm of grasshoppers which stripped Brill's field almost overnight. So Brill sat and swore that he would not renew his lease – he gave fervent thanks that he did not own the land on which he had wasted his sweat, and that there were still broad rolling ranges to the West where a strong young man could make his living riding and roping.

Now as Brill sat glumly, he was aware of the approaching form of his nearest neighbour, Juan Lopez, a taciturn old Mexican who lived in a hut just out of sight over the hill across the creek, and grubbed for a living. At present he was clearing a strip of land on an adjoining farm, and in returning to his hut he crossed a corner of Brill's pasture.

Brill idly watched him climb through the barbed-wire fence and trudge along the path he had worn in the short dry grass. He had been working at his present job for over a month now, chopping down tough gnarly mesquite trees and digging up their incredibly long roots, and Brill knew that he always followed the same path home. And watching, Brill noted him swerving far aside, seemingly to avoid a low rounded hillock which jutted above the level of the pasture. Lopez went far around this knoll and Brill remembered that the old Mexican always circled it at a distance. And another thing came into Brill's idle mind – Lopez always increased his gait when he was passing the knoll, and he always managed to get by it before sundown – yet Mexican labourers generally worked from the first light of dawn to the last glint of twilight, especially at these grubbing jobs, when they were paid by the acre and not by the day. Brill's curiosity was aroused.

He rose, and sauntering down the slight slope on the crown of which his shack sat, hailed the plodding Mexican.

'Hey, Lopez, wait a minute.'

Lopez halted; looked about, and remained motionless but unenthusiastic as the white man approached.

'Lopez,' said Brill lazily, 'it ain't none of my business, but I just wanted to ask you – how come you always go so far around that old Indian mound?'

'No Babe,' grunted Lopez shortly.

'You're a liar,' responded Brill genially. 'You savvy all right; you speak English as good as me. What's the matter – you think that mound's ha'nted or somethin'!'

Brill could speak Spanish himself and read it, too, but like most Anglo-Saxons he much preferred to speak his own language.

Lopez shrugged his shoulders.

'It is not a good place, no *bueno*,' he muttered, avoiding Brill's eyes. 'Let hidden things rest.'

'I reckon you're scared of ghosts,' Brill bantered. 'Shucks, if that is an Indian mound, them Indians been dead so long their ghosts 'ud be plumb wore out by now.'

Brill knew that the illiterate Mexicans looked with superstitious aversion on the mounds that are found here and there through the south-west – relics of a past and forgotten age, containing the mouldering bones of chiefs and warriors of a lost race.

'Best not to disturb what is hidden in the earth,' grunted Lopez.

'Bosh,' said Brill. 'Me and some boys busted into one of them mounds over in the Palo Pinto country and dug up pieces of a skeleton with some beads and flint arrowheads and the like. I kept some of the teeth a long time till I lost 'em, and I ain't never been ha'nted.'

'Indians?' snorted Lopez unexpectedly. 'Who spoke of Indians? There have been more than Indians in this country. In the old times strange things happened here. I have heard the tales of my people, handed down from generation to generation. And my people were here long before yours, Señor Brill.'

'Yeah, you're right,' admitted Steve. 'First white men in this country was Spaniards, of course. Coronado passed along not very far from here, I hear tell, and Hernando de Estrada's expedition came through here-away back yonder – I dunno how long ago.'

'In 1545,' said Lopez. 'They pitched camp yonder where your corral stands now.'

Brill turned to glance at his rail-fenced corral, inhabited now by his saddlehorse, a pair of workhorses and a scrawny cow.

'How come you know so much about it?' he asked curiously.

'One of my ancestors marched with de Estrada,' answered Lopez. 'A soldier, Porfirio Lopez; he told his son of that expedition, and he told his son, and so down the family line to me, who have no son to whom I can tell the tale.'

'I didn't know you were so well connected,' said Brill. 'Maybe you know somethin' about the gold de Estrada was supposed to have hid around here, somewhere.'

'There was no gold,' growled Lopez. 'De Estrada's soldiers bore only their arms, and they fought their way through hostile country – many left their bones along the trail. Later – many years later – a mule train from Santa Fe was attacked not many miles from here by Comanches and they hid their gold and escaped; so the legends got mixed up. But even their gold is not there now, because gringo buffalo-hunters found it and dug it up.'

Brill nodded abstractedly, hardly heeding. Of all the continent of North America there is no section so haunted by tales of lost or hidden treasure as is the Southwest. Uncounted wealth passed back and forth over the hills and plains of Texas and New Mexico in the old days when Spain owned the gold and silver mines of the New

World and controlled the rich fur trade of the West, and echoes of that wealth linger on in tales of golden caches. Some such vagrant dream, born of failure and pressing poverty, rose in Brill's mind.

Aloud he spoke: 'Well, anyway, I got nothin' else to do and I believe I'll dig into that old mound and see what I can find.'

The effect of that simple statement on Lopez was nothing short of shocking. He recoiled and his swarthy brown face went ashy; his black eyes flared and he threw up his arms in a gesture of intense expostulation.

'Dios, no!' he cried. 'Don't do that, Señor Brill! There is a curse . . . my grandfather told me . . . '

'Told you what?' asked Brill.

Lopez lapsed into sullen silence.

'I cannot speak,' he muttered. 'I am sworn to silence. Only to an eldest son could I open my heart. But believe me when I say better had you cut your throat than break into that accursed mound.'

'Well,' said Brill, impatient of Mexican superstitions, 'if it's so bad, why don't you tell me about it? Gimme a logical reason for not bustin' into it.'

'I cannot speak!' cried the Mexican desperately. 'I know! – but I swore to silence on the Holy Crucifix, just as every man of my family has sworn. It is a thing so dark, it is to risk damnation even to speak of it! Were I to tell you, I would blast the soul from your body. But I have sworn – and I have no son, so my lips are sealed forever.'

'Aw, well,' said Brill sarcastically, 'why don't you write it out?'

Lopez started, stared, and to Steve's surprise, caught at the suggestion.

'I will! *Dios* be thanked the good priest taught me to write when I was a child. My oath said nothing of writing. I only swore not to speak. I will write out the whole thing for you, if you will swear not to speak of it afterward, and to destroy the paper as soon as you have read it.'

'Sure,' said Brill, to humour him, and the old Mexican seemed much relieved.

'*Bueno*! I will go at once and write. Tomorrow as I go to work I will bring you the paper and you will understand why no one must open that accursed mound!'

And Lopez hurried along his homeward path, his stooped shoulders swaying with the effort of his unwonted haste. Steve grinned after him, shrugged his shoulders and turned back toward his own shack. Then he halted, gazing back at the low rounded mound with its grass-grown sides. It must be an Indian tomb, he decided, what with its symmetry and its similarity to other Indian mounds he had seen. He scowled as he tried to figure out the seeming connection between the mysterious knoll and the martial ancestor of Juan Lopez.

Brill gazed after the receding figure of the old Mexican. A shallow valley, cut by a half-dry creek, bordered with trees and underbrush, lay between Brill's pasture and the low sloping hill beyond which lay Lopez's shack. Among the trees along the creek bank the old Mexican was disappearing. And Brill came to a sudden decision.

Hurrying up the slight slope, he took a pick and a shovel from the tool shed built on to the back of his shack. The sun had not yet set and Brill believed he could open the mound deep enough to determine its nature before dark. If not, he could work by lantern light. Steve, like most of his breed, lived mostly by impulse, and his present urge was to tear into that mysterious hillock and find what, if anything, was concealed therein. The thought of treasure came again to his mind, piqued by the evasive attitude of Lopez.

What if, after all, that grassy heap of brown earth hid riches – virgin ore from forgotten mines, or the minted coinage of old Spain? Was it not possible that the musketeers of de Estrada had themselves reared that pile above a treasure they could not bear away, moulding it in the likeness of an Indian mound to fool seekers? Did old Lopez know that? It would not be strange if, knowing of treasure there, the old Mexican refrained from disturbing it. Ridden with grisly superstitious fears, he might well live out a life of barren toil rather than risk the wrath of lurking ghosts or devils – for the Mexicans say that hidden gold is always accursed, and surely there was supposed to be some especial doom resting on this mound. Well, Brill meditated, Latin-Indian devils had no terrors for the Anglo-Saxon, tormented by the demons of drought and storm and crop failure.

Steve set to work with the savage energy characteristic of his breed. The task was no light one; the soil, baked by the fierce sun, was iron-hard, and mixed with rocks and pebbles. Brill sweated profusely and grunted with his efforts, but the fire of the treasure-hunter was on him. He shook the sweat out of his eyes and drove in the pick with mighty strokes that ripped and crumbled the close-packed dirt.

The sun went down, and in the long dreamy summer twilight he worked on, almost oblivious of time or space. He began to be convinced that the mound was a genuine Indian tomb, as he found traces of charcoal in the soil. The ancient people which reared these sepulchres had kept fires burning upon them for days, at some point in the building. All the mounds Steve had ever opened had contained a solid stratum of charcoal a short distance below the surface: But the charcoal traces he found now were scattered about through the soil.

His idea of a Spanish-built treasure trove faded, but he persisted. Who knows? Perhaps that strange folk men now called Mound-Builders had treasure of their own which they laid away with the dead.

Then Steve yelped in exultation as his pick rang on a bit of metal. He snatched it up and held it close to his eyes, straining in the waning light. It was caked and corroded with rust, worn almost paper-thin, but he knew it for what it was – a spur, unmistakably Spanish with its long cruel points. And he halted, completely bewildered. No Spaniard ever reared this mound, with its undeniable marks of aboriginal workmanship. Yet how came that relic of Spanish caballeros hidden deep in the packed soil?

Brill shook his head and set to work again. He knew that in the centre of the mound, if it were indeed an aboriginal tomb, he would find a narrow chamber built of heavy stones, containing the bones of the chief for whom the mound had been reared and the victims sacrificed above it. And in the gathering darkness he felt his pick strike heavily against something granite-like and unyielding. Examination, by sense of feel as well as by sight, proved it to be a solid block of stone, roughly hewn. Doubtless it formed one of the ends of the death-chamber. Useless to try to shatter it. Brill chipped and pecked about it, scraping the dirt and pebbles away from the corners until he felt that wrenching it out would be but a matter of sinking the pick-point underneath and levering it out.

But now he was suddenly aware that darkness had come on. In the young moon objects were dim and shadowy. His mustang nickered in the corral whence came the comfortable crunch of tired beasts' jaws on corn. A whippoorwill called eerily from the dark shadows of the narrow winding creek. Brill straightened reluctantly. Better get a lantern and continue his explorations by its light.

He felt in his pocket with some idea of wrenching out the stone and exploring the cavity by the aid of matches. Then he stiffened. Was it imagination that he heard a faint sinister rustling, which seemed to come from behind the blocking stone? Snakes! Doubtless they had holes somewhere about the base of the mound and there might be a dozen big diamond-backed rattlers coiled up in that cave-like interior waiting for him to put his hand among them.

He shivered slightly at the thought and backed away out of the excavation he had made.

It wouldn't do to go poking about blindly into holes. And for the past few minutes, he realised, he had been aware of a faint foul odour exuding from interstices about the blocking stone – though he admitted that the smell suggested reptiles no more than it did any other menacing scent. It had a charnel-house reek about it – gases formed in the chamber of death, no doubt, and dangerous to the living.

Steve laid down his pick and returned to the house, impatient of the necessary delay. Entering the dark building, he struck a match and located his kerosene lantern hanging on its nail on the wall. Shaking it, he satisfied himself that it was nearly full of coal oil, and lighted it. Then he fared forth again, for his eagerness would not allow him to pause long enough for a bite of food. The mere opening of the mound intrigued him, as it must always intrigue a man of imagination, and the discovery of the Spanish spur had whetted his curiosity.

He hurried from his shack, the swinging lantern casting long distorted shadows ahead of him and behind. He chuckled as he visualised Lopez's thoughts and actions when he learned, on the morrow, that the forbidden mound had been pried into. A good thing he opened it that evening, Brill reflected; Lopez might even have tried to prevent him meddling with it, had he known.

In the dreamy hush of the summer night, Brill reached the mound – lifted his lantern – swore bewilderedly. The lantern revealed his excavations, his tools lying carelessly where he had dropped them – and a black gaping aperture! The great blocking stone lay in the bottom of the excavation he had made, as if thrust carelessly aside. Warily he thrust the lantern forward and peered into the small cave-like chamber, expecting to see he knew not what. Nothing met his eyes except the bare rock sides of a long narrow cell, large enough to receive a man's body, which had apparently been built up of roughly hewn square-cut stones, cunningly and strongly joined together.

'Lopez!' exclaimed Steve furiously. 'The dirty coyote! He's been watchin' me work . . . and when I went after the lantern, he snuck up and pried the rock out and grabbed whatever was in there, I reckon. Blast his greasy hide, I'll fix him!'

Savagely he extinguished the lantern and glared across the shallow, brush-grown valley. And as he looked he stiffened. Over the corner of the hill, on the other side of which the shack of Lopez stood, a shadow moved. The slender moon was setting, the light dim and the play of the shadows baffling. But Steve's eyes were sharpened by the sun and winds of the wastelands, and he knew that it was some two-legged creature that was disappearing over the low shoulder of the mesquite-grown hill.

'Beatin' it to his shack,' snarled Brill. 'He's shore got somethin' or he wouldn't be travellin' at that speed.'

Brill swallowed, wondering why a peculiar trembling had suddenly taken hold of him. What was there unusual about a thieving old greaser running home with his loot? Brill tried to drown the feeling that there was something peculiar about the gait of the dim shadow, which had seemed to move at a sort of slinking lope. There must have been need for swiftness when stocky old Juan Lopez elected to travel at such a strange pace.

'Whatever he found is as much mine as his,' swore Brill, trying to get his mind off the abnormal aspect of the figure's flight. 'I got this land leased and I done all the work diggin'. A curse, heck! No wonder he told me that stuff. Wanted me to leave it alone so he could get it hisself. It's a wonder he ain't dug it up long before this.'

Brill, as he meditated thus, was striding down the gentle slope of the pasture which led down to the creek bed. He passed into the shadows of the trees and dense underbrush and walked across the dry creek bed, noting absently that neither whippoorwill nor hoot-owl called in the darkness. There was a waiting, listening tenseness in the night that he did not like. The shadows in the creek bed seemed too thick, too breathless. He wished he had not blown out the lantern, which he still carried, and was glad he had brought the pick, gripped like a battle-axe in his right hand. He had an impulse to whistle, just to break the silence, then swore and dismissed the thought. Yet he was glad when he clambered up the low opposite bank and emerged into the starlight.

He walked up the slope and onto the hill, and looked down on the mesquite flat wherein stood Lopez's squalid hut. A light showed at the one window.

'Packin' his things for a getaway, I reckon,' grunted Steve. 'Oh, what the – '

He staggered as from a physical impact as a frightful scream knifed the stillness. He wanted to clap his hands over his ears to shut out the horror of that cry, which rose unbearably and then broke in an abhorrent gurgle.

'Good God!' Steve felt the cold sweat spring out upon him. 'Lopez – or somebody – '

Even as he gasped the words he was running down the hill as fast as his long legs could carry him. Some unspeakable horror was taking place in that lonely hut, but he was going to investigate if it meant facing the Devil himself. He tightened his grip on his pick-handle as he ran. Wandering prowlers, murdering old Lopez for the loot he had taken from the mound, Steve thought, and forgot his wrath. It would go hard for anyone he found molesting the old scoundrel, thief though he might be.

He hit the flat, running hard. And then the light in the hut went out and Steve staggered in full flight, bringing up against a mesquite tree with an impact that jolted a grunt out of him and tore his hands on the thorns. Rebounding with a sobbed curse, he rushed for the shack, nerving himself for what he might see – his hair still standing on end at what he had already seen.

Brill tried the one door of the hut and found it bolted. He shouted to Lopez and received no answer. Yet utter silence did not reign. From within came a curious muffled worrying sound that ceased as Brill swung his pick crashing against the door. The flimsy portal splintered and Brill leaped into the dark hut, eyes blazing, pick swung high for a desperate onslaught. But no sound ruffled the grisly silence, and in the darkness nothing stirred, though Brill's chaotic imagination peopled the shadowed corners of the hut with shapes of horror.

With a hand damp with perspiration he found a match and struck it. Besides himself only Lopez occupied the hut – old Lopez, stark dead on the dirt floor, arms spread wide like a crucifix, mouth sagging open in a semblance of idiocy, eyes wide and staring with a horror Brill found intolerable. The one window gaped open, showing the method of the slayer's exit – possibly his entrance as well. Brill went to that window and gazed out warily. He saw only the sloping hillside on one hand and the mesquite flat on the other. He started – was that a hint of movement among the stunted shadows of the mesquites and chaparral – or had he but imagined he glimpsed a dim loping figure among the trees?

He turned back, as the match burned down to his fingers. He lit the old coal-oil lamp on the rude table, cursing as he burned his hand. The globe of the lamp was very hot, as if it had been burning for hours.

Reluctantly he turned to the corpse on the floor. Whatever sort of death had come to Lopez, it had been horrible, but Brill, gingerly examining the dead man, found no wound . . . no mark of knife or bludgeon on him. Wait. There was a thin smear of blood on Brill's questing hand. Searching, he found the source . . . three or four tiny punctures in Lopez's throat, from which blood had oozed sluggishly. At first he thought they had been inflicted with a stiletto – a thin round edgeless dagger – then he shook his head. He had seen stiletto wounds – he had the scar of one on his own body. These wounds more resembled the bite of some animal . . . they looked like the marks of pointed fangs.

Yet Brill did not believe they were deep enough to have caused death, nor had much blood flowed from them. A belief, abhorrent with grisly speculations, rose up in the dark corners of his mind – that Lopez had died of fright and that the wounds had been inflicted either simultaneously . . . with his death, or an instant afterward.

And Steve noticed something else; scrawled about on the floor lay a number of dingy leaves of paper, scrawled in the old Mexican's crude hand – he would write of the curse of the mound, he had said. There were the sheets on which he had written, there was the stump of a pencil on the floor, there was the hot lamp globe, all mute witnesses that the old Mexican had been seated at the rough-hewn table writing for hours. Then it was not he who opened the mound chamber and stole the contents . . . but who was it, in God's name? And who or what was it that Brill had glimpsed loping over the shoulder of the hill?

Well, there was but one thing to do – saddle his mustang and ride the ten miles to Coyote Wells, the nearest town, and inform the sheriff of the murder.

Brill gathered up the papers. The last was crumpled in the old man's clutching hand and Brill secured it with some difficulty. Then as he turned to extinguish the light, he hesitated, and cursed himself for the crawling fear that lurked at the back of his mind – fear of the shadowy thing he had seen cross the window just before the light was extinguished in the hut. The long arm of the murderer, he thought, reaching for the lamp to put it out, no doubt. What had there been abnormal or inhuman about that vision, distorted though it must have been in the dim lamplight and shadow? As a man strives to remember the details of a nightmare dream, Steve tried to define in his mind some clear reason that would explain why that flying glimpse had unnerved him to the extent of blundering headlong into a tree, and why the mere vague remembrance of it now caused cold sweat to break out on him.

Cursing himself to keep up his courage, he lighted his lantern, blew out the lamp on the rough table, and resolutely set forth, grasping his pick like a weapon. After all, why should certain seemingly abnormal aspects about a sordid murder upset him? Such crimes were abhorrent, but common enough, especially among Mexicans, who cherished unguessed feuds.

Then as he stepped into the silent star-flecked night he brought up short. From across the creek sounded the sudden soul-shaking scream of a horse in deadly terror . . . then a mad drumming of hoofs that receded in the distance. And Brill swore in rage and dismay. Had a monster cat slain old Lopez? Then why was not the victim marked with the scars of fierce hooked talons? And who extinguished the light in the hut?

As he wondered, Brill was running swiftly toward the dark creek. Not lightly does a cowpuncher regard the stampeding of his stock. As he passed into the darkness of the brush along the dry creek, Brill found his tongue strangely dry. He kept swallowing, and he held the lantern high. It made but faint impression in the gloom, but seemed to accentuate the blackness of the crowding shadows. For some strange reason, the thought entered Brill's chaotic mind that though the land was new to the Anglo-Saxon, it was in reality very old. That broken and desecrated tomb was mute evidence that the land was ancient to man, and suddenly the night and the hills and the shadows bore on Brill with a sense of hideous antiquity. Here had generations of men lived and died before Brill's ancestors ever heard of the land. In the night, in the shadows of this very creek, men had no doubt given up their ghosts in grisly ways. With these reflections Brill hurried through the shadows of the thick trees.

He breathed deeply in relief when he emerged from the trees on his own side. Hurrying up the gentle slope to the railed corral, he held up his lantern, investigating. The corral was empty; not even the placid cow was in sight. And the bars were down. That pointed to human agency, and the affair took on a newly sinister aspect. Someone did not intend that Brill should ride to Coyote Wells that night. It meant that the murderer intended making his getaway and wanted a good start on the law, or else – Brill grinned wryly. Far away across a mesquite flat he believed he could still catch the faint and faraway noise of running horses. What in God's name had given them such a fright? A cold finger of fear played shudderingly on Brill's spine.

Steve headed for the house. He did not enter boldly. He crept clear around the shack, peering shudderingly into the dark windows, listening with painful intensity for some sound to betray the presence of the lurking killer. At last he ventured to open the door and step in. He threw the door back against the wall to find if anyone were hiding behind it, lifted the lantern high and stepped in, heart pounding, pick gripped fiercely, his feelings a mixture of fear and red rage. But no hidden assassin leaped upon him, and a wary exploration of the shack revealed nothing.

With a sigh of relief Brill locked the doors, made fast the windows and lighted his old coal-oil lamp. The thought of old Lopez lying, a glassy-eyed corpse alone in the hut across the creek, made him wince and shiver, but he did not intend to start for town on foot in the night.

He drew from its hiding-place his reliable old Colt .45, spun the blue-steel cylinder, and grinned mirthlessly. Maybe the killer did not intend to leave any witnesses to his crime alive. Well, let him come! He – or they – would find a young cowpuncher with a six-shooter less easy prey than an old unarmed Mexican. And that reminded Brill of the papers he had brought from the hut. Taking care that he was not in line with a window through which a sudden bullet might come, he settled himself to read, with one ear alert for stealthy sounds.

And as he read the crude laborious script, a slow cold horror grew in his soul. It was a tale of fear that the old Mexican had scrawled – a tale handed down from generation – a tale of ancient times.

And Brill read of the wanderings of the caballero Hernando de Estrada and his armoured pikemen, who dared the deserts of the Southwest when all was strange and unknown. There were some forty-odd soldiers, servants, and masters at the beginning, the manuscript ran. There was the captain, de Estrada, and the priest, and young Juan Zavilla, and Don Santiago de Valdez – a mysterious nobleman who had been taken off a helplessly floating ship in the Caribbean Sea – all the others of the crew and passengers had died of plague, he had said, and he had cast their bodies overboard. So de Estrada had taken him aboard the ship that was bearing the expedition from Spain, and de Valdez joined them in their explorations.

Brill read something of their wanderings, told in the crude style of old Lopez, as the old Mexican's ancestors had handed down the tale for over three hundred years. The bare written words dimly reflected the terrific hardships the explorers bad encountered – drought, thirst, floods, the desert sandstorms, the spears of hostile redskins. But it was of another peril that old Lopez told – a grisly lurking horror that fell upon the lonely caravan wandering through the immensity of the wild. Man by man they fell and no man knew the slayer. Fear and black suspicion ate at the heart of the expedition like a canker, and their leader knew not where to turn. This they all knew: among them was a fiend in human form.

Men began to draw apart from each other, to scatter along the line of march, and this mutual suspicion, that sought security in solitude, made it easier for the fiend. The skeleton of the expedition staggered through the wilderness, lost, dazed and helpless, and still the unseen horror hung on their flanks, dragging down the stragglers, preying on drowsing sentries and sleeping men. And on the throat of each was found the wounds of pointed fangs that bled the victim white; so that the living knew with what manner of evil they had to deal. Men reeled through the wild, calling on the saints, or blaspheming in their terror, fighting frenziedly against sleep, until they fell with exhaustion and sleep stole on them with horror and death.

Suspicion centred on a cannibal slave from Calabar. And they put him in chains. But young Juan Zavilla went the way of the rest, and then the priest was taken. But the priest fought off his fiendish assailant and lived long enough to gasp the demon's name to de Estrada. And Brill, shuddering and wide-eyed, read:

. . . and now it was evident to de Estrada that the good priest had spoken the truth, and the slayer was Don Santiago de Valdez, who was a vampire, an undead fiend, subsisting on the blood of the living. And de Estrada called to mind a certain foul nobleman who had lurked, in the mountains of Castile since the days of the Moors, feeding off the blood of helpless victims which lent him a ghastly immortality. This nobleman had been driven forth; none knew where he had fled but it was evident that he and Don Santiago were the same man: He had fled Spain by ship, and de Estrada knew that the people of that ship had died, not by plague as the fiend had represented, but by the fangs of the vampire.

De Estrada and the black man and the few soldiers who still lived went searching for him and found him stretched in bestial sleep in a clump of chaparral; full gorged he was with human blood from his last victim. Now it is well known that a vampire, like a great serpent, when well gorged, falls into a deep sleep and may be taken without peril. But de Estrada was at a loss as to how to dispose of the monster, for how may the dead be slain? For a vampire is a man who has died long ago, yet is quick with a certain foul unlife.

The men urged that the caballero drive a stake through the fiend's heart and cut off his head, uttering the holy words that would crumble the long-dead body into dust, but the priest was dead and de Estrada feared that in the act the monster might waken.

So . . . they took Don Santiago, lifting him softly, and bore him to an old Indian mound near by. This they opened, taking forth the bones they found there, and they placed the vampire within and sealed up the mound. Him grant until Judgment Day.

It is a place accursed, and I wish I had starved elsewhere before I came into this part of the country seeking work – for I have known of the land and the creek and the mound with its terrible secret, ever since childhood; so you see, Señor Brill, why you must not open the mound and wake the fiend . . .

There the manuscript ended with an erratic scratch of the pencil that tore the crumpled leaf.

Brill rose, his heart pounding wildly, his face bloodless, his tongue cleaving to his palate. He gagged and found words.

'That's why the spur was in the mound – one of them Spaniards dropped it while they was diggin' – and I mighta knowed it's been dug into before, the way the charcoal was scattered out – but, good God – '

Aghast he shrank from the black visions – an undead monster stirring in the gloom of his tomb, thrusting from within to push aside the stone loosened by the pick of ignorance – a shadowy shape loping over the hill toward a light that betokened a human prey – a frightful long arm that crossed a dim-lighted window . . .

'It's madness!' he gasped. 'Lopez was plumb loco! They ain't no such things as vampires! If they is, why didn't he get me first, instead of Lopez – unless he was scoutin' around, makin' sure of everything before he pounced? Aw, hell! It's all a pipe-dream – '

The words froze in his throat. At the window a face glared and gibbered soundlessly at him. Two icy eyes pierced his very soul. A shriek burst from his throat and that ghastly visage vanished. But the very air was permeated by the foul scent that had hung about the ancient mound. And now the door creaked . . . bent slowly inward. Brill backed up against the wall, his gun shaking in his hand: It did not occur to him to fire through the door; in his chaotic brain he had but one thought, that only that thin portal of wood separated him from some horror born out of the womb of night and gloom and the black past. His eyes were distended as he saw the door give, as he heard the staples of the bolt groan.

The door burst inward. Brill did not scream. His tongue was frozen to the roof of his mouth. His fear-glazed eyes took in the tall, vulture-like form . . . the icy eyes, the long black fingernails . . . the mouldering garb, hideously ancient . . . the long spurred boot, the slouch hat with its crumbling feather . . . the flowing cloak that was falling to slow shreds. Framed in the black doorway crouched that abhorrent shape out of the past, and Brill's brain reeled. A savage cold radiated from the figure . . . the scent of mouldering clay and charnel-house refuse. And then the undead came at the living like a swooping vulture.

Brill fired point-blank and saw a shred of rotten cloth fly from the Thing's breast. The vampire reeled beneath the impact of the heavy ball, then righted himself and came on with frightful speed. Brill reeled back against the wall with a choking cry, the gun falling from his nerveless hand. The black legends were true, then – human weapons were powerless – for may a man kill one already dead for long centuries, as mortals die?

Then the clawlike hands at his throat roused the young cow-puncher to a frenzy of madness. As his pioneer ancestors fought hand to hand against brain-shattering odds, Steve Brill fought the cold dead crawling thing that sought his life and his soul.

Of that ghastly battle Brill never remembered much. It was a blind chaos in which he screamed beast-like, tore and slugged and ham-mered, where long black nails like the talons of a panther tore at him, and pointed teeth snapped again and again at his throat. Rolling and tumbling about the room, both half enveloped by the musty folds of that ancient rotting cloak, they smote and tore at each other among the ruins of the shattered furniture, and the fury of the vampire was not more terrible than the fear-crazed desperation of his victim.

They crashed headlong, into the table, knocking it down upon its side, and the coal oil lamp splintered on the floor, spraying the walls with sudden flames. Brill felt the bite of the burning oil that spattered him, but in the red frenzy of the fight he gave no heed. The black talons were tearing at him, the inhuman eyes burning icily into his soul; between his frantic fingers the withered flesh of the monster was hard as dry wood. And wave after wave of blind madness swept over Steve Brill. Like a man battling a nightmare he screamed and smote, while all about them the fire leaped up and caught at the walls and roof.

Through darting jets and licking tongues of flames they reeled and rolled like a demon and a mortal warring on the fire-lanced floors of hell. And in the growing tumult of the flames, Brill gathered himself for one last volcanic burst of frenzied strength. Breaking away and staggering up, gasping and bloody, he lunged blindly at the foul shape and caught it in a grip not even the vampire could break. And whirling his fiendish assailant bodily on high, he dashed him down across the uptilted edge of the fallen table as a man might break a stick of wood across his knee. Something cracked like a snapping branch and the vampire fell from Brill's grasp to writhe in a strange broken posture on the burning floor. Yet it was not dead, for its flaming eyes still burned on Brill with a ghastly hunger, and it strove to crawl toward him with its broken spine, as a dying snake crawls.

Brill, reeling and gasping, shook the blood from his eyes, and staggered blindly through the broken door. And as a man runs from the portals of hell, he ran stumblingly through the mesquite and chaparral until he fell from utter exhaustion. Looking back he saw the flames of the burning house and thanked God that it would burn until the very bones of Don Santiago de Valdez were utterly consumed and destroyed from the knowledge of men.

People of the Dark

I came to Dagon's Cave to kill Richard Brent. I went down the dusky avenues made by the towering trees, and my mood well matched the primitive grimness of the scene.

The approach to Dagon's Cave is always dark, for the mighty branches and thick leaves shut out the sun, and now the sombreness of my own soul made the shadows seem more ominous and gloomy than was natural.

Not far away I heard the slow wash of the waves against the tall cliffs, but the sea itself was out of sight, masked by the dense oak forest. The darkness and the stark gloom of my surroundings gripped my shadowed soul as I passed beneath the ancient branches . . . as I came out into a narrow glade and saw the mouth of the ancient cavern before me. I paused, scanning the cavern's exterior and the dim reaches of the silent oaks.

The man I hated had not come before me! I was in time to carry out my grim intent. For a moment my resolution faltered, then like a wave there surged over me the fragrance of Eleanor Bland, a vision of wavy golden hair and deep grey eyes, changing and mystic as the sea. I clenched my hands until the knuckles showed white, and instinctively touched the wicked snub-nosed revolver whose weight sagged my coat pocket.

But for Richard Brent, I felt certain I had already won this woman, desire for whom made my waking hours a torment and my sleep a torture. Whom did she love? She would not say; I did not believe she knew. Let one of us go away, I thought, and she would turn to the other. And I was going to simplify matters for her . . . and for myself. By chance I had overheard my blonde English rival remark that he intended coming to lonely Dagon's Cave on an idle exploring outing . . . alone.

I am not by nature criminal. I was born and raised in a hard country, and have lived most of my life on the raw edges of the world, where a man took what he wanted, if he could, and mercy was a virtue little known. But it was a torment that racked me day and night that sent me out to take the life of Richard Brent. I have lived hard, and violently, perhaps. When love overtook me, it also was fierce and violent. Perhaps I was not wholly sane, what with my love for Eleanor Bland and my hatred for Richard Brent. Under any other circumstances, I would have been glad to call him friend – a fine, rangy, upstanding young fellow, clear-eyed and strong. But he stood in the way of my desire and he must die.

I stepped into the dimness of the cavern and halted. I had never before visited Dagon's Cave, yet a vague sense of misplaced familiarity troubled me as I gazed on the high arching roof, the even stone walls and the dusty floor. I shrugged my shoulders, unable to place the elusive feeling; doubtless it was evoked by a similarity to caverns in the mountain country of the American Southwest where I was born and spent my childhood.

And yet I knew that I had never seen a cave like this one, whose regular aspect gave rise to myths that it was not a natural cavern, but had been hewn from the solid rock ages ago by the tiny hands of the mysterious Little People, the prehistoric beings of British legend. The whole countryside thereabouts was a haunt for ancient folk lore.

The country folk were predominantly Celtic; here the Saxon invaders had never prevailed, and the legends reached back, in that long-settled countryside, further than anywhere else in England – back beyond the coming of the Saxons, aye, and incredibly beyond that distant age, beyond the coming of the Romans, to those unbelievably ancient days when the native Britons warred with black-haired Irish pirates.

The Little People, of course, had their part in the lore. Legend said that this cavern was one of their last strongholds against the conquering Celts, and hinted at lost tunnels, long fallen in or blocked up, connecting the cave with a network of subterranean corridors which honeycombed the hills. With these chance meditations vying idly in my mind with grimmer speculations, I passed through the outer chamber of the cavern and entered a narrow tunnel which, I knew by former descriptions, connected with a larger room.

It was dark in the tunnel, but not too dark for me to make out the vague, half-defaced outlines of mysterious etchings on the stone walls. I ventured to switch on my electric torch and examine them more closely. Even in their dimness I was repelled by their abnormal and revolting character. Surely no men cast in human mould as we know it, scratched those grotesque obscenities.

The Little People . . . I wondered if those anthropologists were correct in their theory of a squat Mongoloid aboriginal race, so low in the scale of evolution as to be scarcely human, yet possessing a distinct, though repulsive, culture of their own. They had vanished before the invading races, theory said, forming the base of all Aryan legends of trolls, elves, dwarfs and witches. Living in caves from the start, these aborigines had retreated farther and farther into the caverns of the hills before the conquerors, vanishing at last entirely, though folklore fancy pictures their descendants still dwelling in the lost chasms far beneath the hills, loathsome survivors of an outworn age.

I snapped off the torch and passed through the tunnel, to come out into a sort of doorway which seemed entirely too symmetrical to have been the work of nature. I was looking into a vast dim cavern, at a somewhat lower level than the outer chamber, and again I shuddered with a strange alien sense of familiarity. A short flight of steps led down from the tunnel to the floor of the cavern . . . tiny steps, too small for normal human feet, carved into the solid stone. Their edges were greatly worn away, as if by ages of use. I started the descent . . . my foot slipped suddenly. I instinctively knew what was coming – it was all in part with that strange feeling of familiarity – but I could not catch myself. I fell headlong down the steps and struck the stone floor with a crash that blotted out my senses . . .

Slowly, consciousness returned to me, with a throbbing of my head and a sensation of bewilderment. I lifted a hand to my head and found it caked with blood. I had received a blow, or had taken a fall, but so completely had my wits been knocked out of me that my mind was an absolute blank. Where I was, who I was, I did not know. I looked about, blinking in the dim light, and saw that I was in a wide, dusty cavern. I stood at the foot of a short flight of steps which led upward into some kind of tunnel. I ran my hand dazedly through my square-cut black mane, and my eyes wandered over my massive naked limbs and powerful torso. I was clad, I noticed absently, in a sort of loincloth, from the girdle of which swung an empty scabbard, and leathern sandals were on my feet.

Then I saw an object lying at my feet, and stooped and took it up. It was a heavy iron sword, whose broad blade was darkly stained. My fingers fitted instinctively about its hilt with the familiarity of long usage. Then suddenly I remembered and laughed to think that a fall on his head should render me, Conan of the reavers, so completely daft. Aye, it all came back to me now. It had been a raid on the Britons, on whose coasts we continually swooped with torch and sword, from the island called Eireann. That day we of the black-haired Gael had swept suddenly down on a coastal village in our long, low ships and in the hurricane of battle which followed, the Britons had at last given up the stubborn contest and retreated, warriors, women and bairns, into the deep shadows of the oak forests, whither we seldom dared follow.

But I had followed, for there was a girl of my foes whom I desired with a burning passion, a lithe, slim young creature with wavy golden hair and deep grey eyes, changing and mystic as the sea. Her name was Tamera . . . well I knew it, for there was trade between the races as well as war, and I had been in the villages of the Britons as a peaceful visitor, in times of rare truce.

I saw her white half-clad body flickering among the trees as she ran with the swiftness of a doe, and I followed, panting with fierce eagerness. Under the dark shadows of the gnarled oaks she fled, with me in close pursuit, while far away behind us died out the shouts of slaughter and the clashing of swords. Then we ran in silence, save for her quick laboured panting, and I was so close behind her as we emerged into a narrow glade before a sombre-mouthed cavern, that I caught her flying golden tresses with one mighty hand. She sank down with a despairing wail, and even so, a shout echoed her cry and I wheeled quickly to face a rangy young Briton who sprang from among the trees, the light of desperation in his eyes.

'Vertorix!' the girl wailed, her voice breaking in a sob, and fiercer rage welled up in me, for I knew the lad was her lover.

'Run for the forest, Tamera!' he shouted, and leaped at me as a panther leaps, his bronze axe whirling like a flashing wheel about his head. And then sounded the clangour of strife and the hard-drawn panting of combat.

The Briton was as tall as I, but he was lithe where I was massive. The advantage of sheer muscular power was mine, and soon he was on the defensive, striving desperately to parry my heavy strokes with his axe. Hammering on his guard like a smith on an anvil, I pressed him relentlessly, driving him irresistibly before me. His chest heaved, his breath came in laboured gasps, his blood dripped from scalp, chest and thigh where my whistling blade had cut the skin, and all but gone home. As I redoubled my strokes and he bent and swayed beneath them like a sapling in a storm, I heard the girl cry: 'Vertorix! Vertorix! the cave! Into the cave!'

I saw his face pale with a fear greater than that induced by my hacking sword.

'Not there!' he gasped. 'Better a clean death! In Il-marenin's name, girl, run into the forest and save yourself!'

'I will not leave you!' she cried. 'The cave! It is our one chance!'

I saw her flash past us like a flying wisp of white and vanish in the cavern, and with a despairing cry, the youth launched a wild desperate stroke that nigh cleft my skull. As I staggered beneath the blow I had barely parried, he sprang away, leaped into the cavern after the girl and vanished in the gloom.

With a maddened yell that invoked all my grim Gaelic gods, I sprang recklessly after them, not reckoning if the Briton lurked beside the entrance to brain me as I rushed in. But a quick glance showed the chamber empty and a wisp of white disappearing through a dark doorway in the back wall.

I raced across the cavern and came to a sudden halt as an axe licked out of the gloom of the entrance and whistled perilously close to my black-maned head. I gave back suddenly. Now the advantage was with Vertorix, who stood in the narrow mouth of the corridor where I could hardly come at him without exposing myself to the devastating stroke of his axe.

I was near frothing with fury and the sight of a slim white form among the deep shadows behind the warrior drove me into a frenzy. I attacked savagely but warily, thrusting venomously at my foe, and drawing back from his strokes. I wished to draw him out into a wide lunge, avoid it and run him through before he could recover his balance. In the open I could have beat him down by sheer power and heavy blows, but here I could only use the point and that at a disadvantage; I always preferred the edge. But I was stubborn; if I could not come at him with a finishing stroke, neither could he or the girl escape me while I kept him hemmed in the tunnel.

It must have been the realisation of this fact that prompted the girl's action, for she said something to Vertorix about looking for a way leading out, and though he cried out fiercely forbidding her to venture away into the darkness, she turned and ran swiftly down the tunnel to vanish in the dimness. My wrath rose appallingly and I nearly got my head split in my eagerness to bring down my foe before she found a means for their escape.

Then the cavern echoed with a terrible scream and Vertorix cried out like a man death-stricken, his face ashy in the gloom. He whirled, as if he had forgotten me and my sword, and raced down the tunnel like a madman, shrieking Tamera's name. From far away, as if from the bowels of the earth, I seemed to hear her answering cry, mingled with a strange sibilant clamour that electrified me with nameless but instinctive horror. Then silence fell, broken only by Vertorix's frenzied cries, receding farther and farther into the earth.

Recovering myself I sprang into the tunnel and raced after the Briton as recklessly as he had run after the girl. And to give me my due, red-handed reaver though I was, cutting down my rival from behind was less in my mind than discovering what dread thing had Tamera in its clutches.

As I ran along I noted absently that the sides of the tunnel were scrawled with monstrous pictures, and realised suddenly and creepily that this must be the dread Cavern of the Children of the Night, tales of which had crossed the narrow sea to resound horrifically in the ears of the Gaels. Terror of me must have ridden Tamera hard to have driven her into the cavern shunned by her people, where, it was said, lurked the survivors of that grisly race which inhabited the land before the coming of the Picts and Britons, and which had fled before them into the unknown caverns of the hills.

Ahead of me the tunnel opened into a wide chamber, and I saw the white form of Vertorix glimmer momentarily in the semi-darkness and vanish in what appeared to be the entrance of a corridor opposite the mouth of the tunnel I had just traversed. Instantly there sounded a short, fierce shout and the crash of a hard-driven blow, mixed with the hysterical screams of a girl and a medley of serpent-like hissing that made my hair bristle. And at that instant I shot out of the tunnel, running at full speed, and realised too late the floor of the cavern lay several feet below the level of the tunnel. My flying feet missed the tiny steps and I crashed terrifically on the solid stone floor.

Now as I stood in the semi-darkness, rubbing my aching head, all this came back to me, and I stared fearsomely across the vast chamber at that black cryptic corridor into which Tamera and her lover had disappeared, and over which silence lay like a pall. Gripping my sword, I warily crossed the great still cavern and peered into the corridor. Only a denser darkness met my eyes. I entered, striving to pierce the gloom, and as my foot slipped on a wide wet smear on the stone floor, the raw acrid scent of fresh-spilled blood met my nostrils. Someone or something had died there, either the young Briton or his unknown attacker.

I stood there uncertainly, all the supernatural fears that are the heritage of the Gael rising in my primitive soul. I could turn and stride out of these accursed mazes, into the clear sunlight and down to the clean blue sea where my comrades, no doubt, impatiently awaited me after the routing of the Britons. Why should I risk my life among these grisly rat dens? I was eaten with curiosity to know what manner of beings haunted the cavern, and who were called the Children of the Night by the Britons, but it was my love for the yellow-haired girl which drove me down that dark tunnel . . . and love her I did, in my way, and would have been kind to her, had I carried her away to my island haunt.

I walked softly along the corridor, blade ready. What sort of creatures the Children of the Night were, I had no idea, but the tales of the Britons had lent them a distinctly inhuman nature.

The darkness closed around me as I advanced, until I was moving in utter blackness. My groping left hand encountered a strangely carven doorway, and at that instant something hissed like a viper beside me and slashed fiercely at my thigh. I struck back savagely and felt my blind stroke crunch home, and something fell at my feet and died. What thing I had slain in the dark I could not know, but it must have been at least partly human because the shallow gash in my thigh had been made with a blade of some sort, and not by fangs or talons. And I sweated with horror, for the gods know, the hissing voice of the Thing had resembled no human tongue I had ever heard.

And now in the darkness ahead of me I heard the sound repeated, mingled with horrible slitherings, as if numbers of reptilian creatures were approaching. I stepped quickly into the entrance my groping hand had discovered and came near repeating my headlong fall, for instead of letting into another level corridor, the entrance gave on to a flight of dwarfish steps on which I floundered wildly.

Recovering my balance I went on cautiously, groping along the sides of the shaft for support. I seemed to be descending into the very bowels of the earth, but I dared not turn back. Suddenly, far below me, I glimpsed a faint eerie light. I went on, perforce, and came to a spot where the shaft opened into another great vaulted chamber; and I shrank back, aghast.

In the centre of the chamber stood a grim, black altar; it had been rubbed all over with a sort of phosphorus, so that it glowed dully, lending a semi-illumination to the shadowy cavern. Towering behind it on a pedestal of human skulls, lay a cryptic black object, carven with mysterious hieroglyphics. The Black Stone! The ancient, ancient Stone before which, the Britons said, the Children of the Night bowed in gruesome worship, and whose origin was lost in the black mists of a hideously distant past. Once, legend said, it had stood in that grim circle of monoliths called Stonehenge, before its votaries had been driven like chaff before the bows of the Picts.

But I gave it but a passing, shuddering glance. Two figures lay, bound with rawhide thongs, on the glowing black altar. One was Tamera; the other was Vertorix, bloodstained and dishevelled. His bronze axe, crusted with clotted blood, lay near the altar. And before the glowing stone squatted Horror.

Though I had never seen one of those ghoulish aborigines, I knew this thing for what it was, and shuddered. It was a man of a sort, but so low in the stage of life that its distorted humanness was more horrible than its bestiality.

Erect, it could not have been five feet in height. Its body was scrawny and deformed, its head disproportionately large. Lank snaky hair fell over a square inhuman face with flabby writhing lips that bared yellow fangs, flat spreading nostrils and great yellow slant eyes. I knew the creature must be able to see in the dark as well as a cat. Centuries of skulking in dim caverns had lent the race terrible and inhuman attributes. But the most repellent feature was its skin: scaly, yellow and mottled, like the hide of a serpent. A loincloth made of a real snake's skin girt its lean loins, and its taloned hands gripped a short stone-tipped spear and a sinister-looking mallet of polished flint.

So intently was it gloating over its captives, it evidently had not heard my stealthy descent. As I hesitated in the shadows of the shaft, far above me I heard a soft sinister rustling that chilled the blood in my veins. The Children were creeping down the shaft behind me, and I was trapped. I saw other entrances opening on the chamber, and I acted, realising that an alliance with Vertorix was our only hope. Enemies though we were, we were men, cast in the same mould, trapped in the lair of these indescribable monstrosities.

As I stepped from the shaft, the horror beside the altar jerked up his head and glared full at me. And as he sprang up, I leaped and he crumpled, blood spurting, as my heavy sword split his reptilian heart. But even as he died, he gave tongue in an abhorrent shriek which was echoed far up the shaft. In desperate haste I cut Vertorix's bonds and dragged him to his feet. And I turned to Tamera, who in that dire extremity did not shrink from me, but looked up at me with pleading, terror-dilated eyes. Vertorix wasted no time in words, realising chance had made allies of us. He snatched up his axe as I freed the girl.

'We can't go up the shaft,' he explained swiftly; 'we'll have the whole pack upon us quickly. They caught Tamera as she sought for an exit, and overpowered me by sheer numbers when I followed. They dragged us hither and all but that carrion scattered – bearing word of the sacrifice through all their burrows, I doubt not. Il-marenin alone knows how many of my people, stolen in the night, have died on that altar. We must take our chance in one of these tunnels – all lead to Hell! Follow me!'

Seizing Tamera's hand he ran fleetly into the nearest tunnel and I followed. A glance back into the chamber before a turn in the corridor blotted it from view showed a revolting horde streaming out of the shaft. The tunnel slanted steeply upward, and suddenly ahead of us we saw a bar of grey light. But the next instant our cries of hope changed to curses of bitter disappointment. There was daylight, aye, drifting in through a cleft in the vaulted roof, but far, far above our reach. Behind us the pack gave tongue exultingly. And I halted.

'Save yourselves if you can,' I growled. 'Here I make my stand. They can see in the dark and I cannot. Here at least I can see them. Go!'

But Vertorix halted also. 'Little use to be hunted like rats to our doom. There is no escape. Let us meet our fate like men.'

Tamera cried out, wringing her hands, but she clung to her lover.

'Stand behind me with the girl,' I grunted. 'When I fall, dash out her brains with your axe lest they take her alive again. Then sell your own life as high as you may, for there is none to avenge us.'

His keen eyes met mine squarely.

'We worship different gods, reaver,' he said, 'but all gods love brave men. Mayhap we shall meet again, beyond the Dark.'

'Hail and farewell, Briton!' I growled, and our right hands gripped like steel.

'Hail and farewell, Gael!'

And I wheeled as a hideous horde swept up the tunnel and burst into the dim light, a flying nightmare of streaming snaky hair, foam-flecked lips and glaring eyes. Thundering my war-cry I sprang to meet them and my heavy sword sang and a head spun grinning from its shoulder on an arching fountain of blood. They came upon me like a wave and the fighting madness of my race was upon me. I fought as a maddened beast fights and at every stroke I clove through flesh and bone, and blood spattered in a crimson rain.

Then as they surged in and I went down beneath the sheer weight of their numbers, a fierce yell cut the din and Vertorix's axe sang above me, splattering blood and brains like water. The press slackened and I staggered up, trampling the writhing bodies beneath my feet.

'A stair behind us!' the Briton was screaming. 'Half-hidden in an angle of the wall! It must lead to daylight! Up it, in the name of Il-marenin!'

So we fell back, fighting our way inch by inch. The vermin fought like blood-hungry devils, clambering over the bodies of the slain to screech and hack. Both of us were streaming blood at every step when we reached the mouth of the shaft, into which Tamera had preceded us.

Screaming like very fiends the Children surged in to drag us down. The shaft was not as light as had been the corridor, and it grew darker as we climbed, but our foes could only come at us from in front. By the gods, we slaughtered them till the stair was littered with mangled corpses and the Children frothed like mad wolves! Then suddenly they abandoned the fray and raced back down the steps.

'What portends this?' gasped Vertorix, shaking the bloody sweat from his eyes.

'Up the shaft, quick!' I panted. 'They mean to mount some other stair and come at us from above!'

So we raced up those accursed steps, slipping and stumbling, and as we fled past a black tunnel that opened into the shaft, far down it we heard a frightful howling. An instant later we emerged from the shaft into a winding corridor, dimly illumined by a vague grey light filtering in from above, and somewhere in the bowels of the earth I seemed to hear the thunder of rushing water. We started down the corridor and as we did so, a heavy weight smashed on my shoulders, knocking me headlong, and a mallet crashed again and again on my head, sending dull red flashes of agony across my brain. With a volcanic wrench I dragged my attacker off and under me, and tore out his throat with my naked fingers. And his fangs met in my arm in his death-bite.

Reeling up, I saw that Tamera and Vertorix had passed out of sight. I had been somewhat behind them, and they had run on, knowing nothing of the fiend which had leaped on my shoulders. Doubtless they thought I was still close on their heels. A dozen steps I took, then halted. The corridor branched and I knew not which way my companions had taken. At blind venture I turned into the left-hand branch, and staggered on in the semi-darkness. I was weak from fatigue and loss of blood, dizzy and sick from the blows I had received. Only the thought of Tamera kept me doggedly on my feet. Now distinctly I heard the sound of an unseen torrent.

That I was not far underground was evident by the dim light which filtered in from somewhere above, and I momentarily expected to come upon another stair. But when I did, I halted in black despair; instead of up, it led down. Somewhere far behind me I heard faintly the howls of the pack, and I went down, plunging into utter darkness. At last I struck a level and went along blindly. I had given up all hope of escape, and only hoped to find Tamera – if she and her lover had not found a way of escape – and die with her. The thunder of rushing water was above my head now, and the tunnel was slimy and dank. Drops of moisture fell on my head and I knew I was passing under the river.

Then I blundered again upon steps cut in the stone, and these led upward. I scrambled up as fast as my stiffening wounds would allow – and I had taken punishment enough to have killed an ordinary man. Up I went and up, and suddenly daylight burst on me through a cleft in the solid rock. I stepped into the blaze of the sun. I was standing on a ledge high above the rushing waters of a river which raced at awesome speed between towering cliffs. The ledge on which I stood was close to the top of the cliff; safety was within arm's length. But I hesitated and such was my love for the golden-haired girl that I was ready to retrace my steps through those black tunnels on the mad hope of finding her. Then I started.

Across the river I saw another cleft in the cliff-wall which fronted me, with a ledge similar to that on which I stood, but longer. In olden times, I doubt not, some sort of primitive bridge connected the two ledges . . . possibly before the tunnel was dug beneath the riverbed. Now as I watched, two figures emerged upon that other ledge – one gashed, dust-stained, limping, gripping a bloodstained axe; the other slim, white and girlish.

Vertorix and Tamera! They had taken the other branch of the corridor at the fork and had evidently followed the windings of the tunnel to emerge as I had done, except that I had taken the left turn and passed clear under the river. And now I saw that they were in a trap. On that side the cliffs rose half a hundred feet higher than on my side of the river, and so sheer a spider could scarce have scaled them. There were only two ways of escape from the ledge: back through the fiend-haunted tunnels, or straight down to the river which raved far beneath.

I saw Vertorix look up the sheer cliffs and then down, and shake his head in despair. Tamara put her arms about his neck, and though I could not hear their voices for the rush of the river, I saw them smile, and then they went together to the edge of the ledge. And out of the cleft swarmed a loathsome mob, as foul reptiles writhe up out of the darkness, and they stood blinking in the sunlight like the night-things they were. I gripped my sword-hilt in the agony of my help-lessness until the blood trickled from under my fingernails. Why had not the pack followed me instead of my companions?

The Children hesitated an instant as the two Britons faced them, then with a laugh Vertorix hurled his axe far out into the rushing river, and turning, caught Tamara in a last embrace. Together they sprang far out, and still locked in each other's arms, hurtled down-ward, struck the madly foaming water that seemed to leap up to meet them, and vanished. And the wild river swept on like a blind, insens-ate monster, thundering along the echoing cliffs.

A moment I stood frozen, then like a man in a dream I turned, caught the edge of the cliff above me and wearily drew myself up and over, and stood on my feet above the cliffs, hearing like a dim dream the roar of the river far beneath.

I reeled up, dazedly clutching my throbbing head, on which dried blood was clotted. I glared wildly about me. I had clambered the cliffs – no, by the thunder of Crom, I was still in the cavern! I reached for my sword . . .

The mists faded and I stared about dizzily, orienting myself with space and time. I stood at the foot of the steps down which I had fallen. I who had been Conan the reaver, was John O'Brien. Was all that grotesque interlude a dream? Could a mere dream appear so vivid? Even in dreams, we often know we are dreaming, but Conan the reaver had no cognisance of any other existence. More, he remembered his own past life as a living man remembers, though in the waking mind of John O'Brien that memory faded into dust and mist. But the adventures of Conan in the Cavern of the Children stood clear-etched in the mind of John O'Brien.

I glanced across the dim chamber toward the entrance of the tunnel into which Vertorix had followed the girl. But I looked in vain, seeing only the bare blank wall of the cavern. I crossed the chamber, switched on my electric torch – miraculously unbroken in my fall – and felt along the wall.

Ha! I started, as from an electric shock! Exactly where the entrance should have been, my fingers detected a difference in material, a section which was rougher than the rest of the wall. I was convinced that it was of comparatively modern workmanship; the tunnel had been walled up.

I thrust against it, exerting all my strength, and it seemed to me that the section was about to give. I drew back, and taking a deep breath, launched my full weight against it, backed by all the power of my giant muscles. The brittle, decaying wall gave way with a shattering crash and I catapulted through in a shower of stones and falling masonry.

I scrambled up, a sharp cry escaping me. I stood in a tunnel, and I could not mistake the feeling of similarity this time. Here Vertorix had first fallen foul of the Children, as they dragged Tamera away, and here where I now stood the floor had been awash with blood.

I walked down the corridor like a man in a trance. Soon I should come to the doorway on the left . . . aye, there it was, the strangely carven portal, at the mouth of which I had slain the unseen being which reared up in the dark beside me. I shivered momentarily. Could it be possible that remnants of that foul race still lurked hideously in these remote caverns?

I turned into the doorway and my light shone down a long, slanting shaft, with tiny steps cut into the solid stone. Down these had Conan the reaver gone groping and down them went I, John O'Brien, with memories of that other life filling my brain with vague phantasms. No light glimmered ahead of me but I came into the great dim chamber I had known of yore, and I shuddered as I saw the grim black altar etched in the gleam of my torch. Now no bound figures writhed there, no crouching horror gloated before it. Nor did the pyramid of skulls support the Black Stone before which unknown races had bowed before Egypt was born out of time's dawn. Only a littered heap of dust lay strewn where the skulls had upheld the hellish thing. No, that had been no dream: I was John O'Brien, but I had been Conan of the reavers in that other life, and that grim interlude a brief episode of reality which I had relived.

I entered the tunnel down which we had fled, shining a beam of light ahead, and saw the bar of grey light drifting down from above . . . just as in that other, lost age. Here the Briton and I, Conan, had turned at bay. I turned my eyes from the ancient cleft high up in the vaulted roof, and looked for the stair. There it was, half-concealed by an angle in the wall.

I mounted, remembering how hurriedly Vertorix and I had gone up so many ages before, with the horde hissing and frothing at our heels. I found myself tense with dread as I approached the dark, gaping entrance through which the pack had sought to cut us off. I had snapped off the light when I came into the dim-lit corridor below, and now I glanced into the well of blackness which opened on the stair. And with a cry I started back, nearly losing my footing on the worn steps. Sweating in the semi-darkness I switched on the light and directed its beam into the cryptic opening, revolver in hand.

I saw only the bare rounded sides of a small shaftlike tunnel and I laughed nervously. My imagination was running riot; I could have sworn that hideous yellow eyes glared terribly at me from the darkness, and that a crawling something had scuttered away down the tunnel. I was foolish to let these imaginings upset me. The Children had long vanished from these caverns; a nameless and abhorrent race closer to the serpent than the man, they had centuries ago faded back into the oblivion from which they had crawled in the black dawn ages of the Earth.

I came out of the shaft into the winding corridor, which, as I remembered of old, was lighter. Here from the shadows a lurking thing had leaped on my back while my companions ran on, un-knowing. What a brute of a man Conan had been, to keep going after receiving such savage wounds! Aye, in that age all men were iron.

I came to the place where the tunnel forked and as before I took the left-hand branch and came to the shaft that led down. Down this I went, listening for the roar of the river, but not hearing it. Again the darkness shut in about the shaft, so I was forced to have recourse to my electric torch again, lest I lose my footing and plunge to my death. Oh, I, John O'Brien, am not nearly so sure-footed as was I, Conan the reaver; no, nor as tigerishly powerful and quick, either.

I soon struck the dank lower level and felt again the dampness that denoted my position under the riverbed, but still I could not hear the rush of the water. And indeed I knew that whatever mighty river had rushed roaring to the sea in those ancient times, there was no such body of water among the hills today. I halted, flashing my light about. I was in a vast tunnel, not very high of roof, but broad. Other smaller tunnels branched off from it and I wondered at the network which apparently honeycombed the hills.

I cannot describe the grim, gloomy effect of those dark, low-roofed corridors far below the earth. Over all hung an overpowering sense of unspeakable antiquity. Why had the little people carved out these mysterious crypts, and in which black age? Were these caverns their last refuge from the onrushing tides of humanity, or their castles since time immemorial? I shook my head in bewilderment; the bestiality of the Children I had seen, yet somehow they had been able to carve these tunnels and chambers that might balk modern engineers. Even supposing they had but completed a task begun by nature, still it was a stupendous work for a race of dwarfish aborigines.

Then I realised with a start that I was spending more time in these gloomy tunnels than I cared for, and began to hunt for the steps by which Conan had ascended. I found them and, following them up, breathed again deeply in relief as the sudden glow of daylight filled the shaft. I came out upon the ledge, now worn away until it was little more than a bump on the face of the cliff. And I saw the great river, which had roared like a prisoned monster between the sheer walls of its narrow canyon, had dwindled away with the passing aeons until it was no more than a tiny stream, far beneath me, trickling soundlessly among the stones on its way to the sea.

Aye, the surface of the earth changes; the rivers swell or shrink, the mountains heave and topple, the lakes dry up, the continents alter; but under the earth the work of lost, mysterious hands slumbers untouched by the sweep of Time. Their work, aye, but what of the hands that reared that work? Did they, too, lurk beneath the bosoms of the hills?

How long I stood there, lost in dim speculations, I do not know, but suddenly, glancing across at the other ledge, crumbling and weathered, I shrank back into the entrance behind me. Two figures came out upon the ledge and I gasped to see that they were Richard Brent and Eleanor Bland. Now I remembered why I had come to the cavern and my hand instinctively sought the revolver in my pocket. They did not see me. But I could see them, and hear them plainly, too, since no roaring river now thundered between the ledges.

'By gad, Eleanor,' Brent was saying, 'I'm glad you decided to come with me. Who would have guessed there was anything to those old tales about hidden tunnels leading from the cavern? I wonder how that section of wall came to collapse? I thought I heard a crash just as we entered the outer cave. Do you suppose some beggar was in the cavern ahead of us, and broke it in?'

'I don't know,' she answered. 'I remember – oh, I don't know. It almost seems as if I'd been here before, or dreamed I had. I seem to faintly remember, like a far-off nightmare, running, running, running endlessly through these dark corridors with hideous creatures on my heels . . . '

'Was I there?' jokingly asked Brent.

'Yes, and John, too,' she answered. 'But you were not Richard Brent, and John was not John O'Brien. No, and I was not Eleanor Bland, either. Oh, it's so dim and far-off I can't describe it at all. It's hazy and misty and terrible.'

'I understand, a little,' he said unexpectedly. 'Ever since we came to the place where the wall had fallen and revealed the old tunnel, I've had a sense of familiarity with the place. There was horror and danger and battle . . . and love, too.'

He stepped nearer the edge to look down in the gorge, and Eleanor cried out sharply and suddenly, seizing him in a convulsive grasp.

'Don't, Richard, don't! Hold me, oh, hold me tight!'

He caught her in his arms. 'Why, Eleanor, dear, what's the matter?'

'Nothing,' she faltered, but she clung closer to him and I saw she was trembling. 'Just a strange feeling . . . rushing dizziness and fright, just as if I were falling from a great height. Don't go near the edge, Dick; it scares me.'

'I won't, dear,' he answered, drawing her closer to him, and continuing hesitantly: 'Eleanor, there's something I've wanted to ask you for a long time . . . well, I haven't the knack of putting things in an elegant way. I love you, Eleanor; always have. You know that. But if you don't love me, I'll take myself off and won't annoy you any more. Only please tell me one way or another, for I can't stand it any longer. Is it I or the American?'

'You, Dick,' she answered, hiding her face on his shoulder. 'It's always been you, though I didn't know it. I think a great deal of John O'Brien. I didn't know which of you I really loved. But today as we came through those terrible tunnels and climbed those fearful stairs, and just now, when I thought for some strange reason we were falling from the ledge, I realised it was you I loved – that I always loved you, through more lives than this one. Always!'

Their lips met and I saw her golden head cradled on his shoulder. My lips were dry, my heart cold, yet my soul was at peace. They belonged to each other. Aeons ago they lived and loved, and because of that love they suffered and died. And I, Conan, had driven them to that doom.

I saw them turn toward the cleft, their arms about each other, then I heard Tamera – I mean Eleanor – shriek. I saw them both recoil. And out of the cleft a horror came writhing, a loathsome, brain-shattering thing that blinked in the clean sunlight. Aye, I knew it of old – vestige of a forgotten age, it came writhing its horrid shape up out of the darkness of the Earth and the lost past to claim its own.

What three thousand years of retrogression can do to a race hideous in the beginning, I saw, and shuddered. And instinctively I knew that in all the world it was the only one of its kind, a monster that had lived on. God alone knows how many centuries, wallowing in the slime of its dank subterranean lairs. Before the Children had vanished, the race must have lost all human semblance, living as they did the life of the reptile.

This thing was more like a giant serpent than anything else, but it had aborted legs and snaky arms with hooked talons. It crawled on its belly, writhing back mottled lips to bare needle-like fangs, which I felt must drip with venom. It hissed as it reared up its ghastly head on a horribly long neck, while its yellow slanted eyes glittered with all the horror that is spawned in the black lairs under the earth.

I knew those eyes had blazed at me from the dark tunnel opening on the stair. For some reason the creature had fled from me, possibly because it feared my light, and it stood to reason that it was the only one remaining in the caverns, else I had been set upon in the darkness. But for it, the tunnels could be traversed in safety.

Now the reptilian thing writhed toward the humans trapped on the ledge. Brent had thrust Eleanor behind him and stood, face ashy, to guard her as best he could. And I gave thanks silently that I, John O'Brien, could pay the debt I, Conan the reaver, owed these lovers since long ago.

The monster reared up and Brent, with cold courage, sprang to meet it with his naked hands. Taking quick aim, I fired once. The shot echoed like the crack of doom between the towering cliffs, and the Horror, with a hideously human scream, staggered wildly, swayed and pitched headlong, knotting and writhing like a wounded python, to tumble from the sloping ledge and fall plummetlike to the rocks far below.

The Cairn on the Headland

And the next instant this great red loon was shaking me like a dog shaking a rat. 'Where is Meve MacDonnal?' he was screaming. By the saints, it's a grisly thing to hear a madman in a lonely place at midnight screaming the name of a woman dead three hundred years.

THE LONGSHOREMAN'S TALE

'This is the cairn you seek,' I said, laying my hand gingerly on one of the rough stones which composed the strangely symmetrical heap.

An avid interest burned in Ortali's dark eyes. His gaze swept the landscape and came back to rest on the great pile of massive weather-worn boulders.

'What a wild, weird, desolate place!' he said. 'Who would have thought to find such a spot in this vicinity? Except for the smoke rising yonder, one would scarcely dream that beyond that headland lies a great city! Here there is scarcely even a fisherman's hut within sight.'

'The people shun the cairn as they have shunned it for centuries,' I replied.

'Why?'

'You've asked me that before,' I replied impatiently. 'I can only answer that they now avoid by habit what their ancestors avoided through knowledge.'

'Knowledge!' he laughed derisively. 'Superstition!'

I looked at him sombrely with unveiled hate. Two men could scarcely have been of more opposite types. He was slender, self-possessed, unmistakably Latin with his dark eyes and sophisticated air. I am massive, clumsy and bearlike, with cold blue eyes and tousled red hair. We were countrymen in that we were born in the same land; but the homelands of our ancestors were as far apart as South from North.

'Nordic superstition,' he repeated. 'I cannot imagine a Latin people allowing such a mystery as this to go unexplored all these years. The Latins are too practical, too prosaic, if you will. Are you sure of the date of this pile?'

'I find no mention of it in any manuscript prior to 1014 A.D.,' I growled, 'and I've read all such manuscripts extant, in the original. MacLiag, King Brian Boru's poet, speaks of the rearing of the cairn immediately after the battle, and there can be little doubt that this is the pile referred to. It is mentioned briefly in the later chronicles of the Four Masters, also in the Book of Leinster, compiled in the late 1150s, and again in the Book of Lecan, compiled by the Mac-Firbis about 1416. All connect it with the battle of Clontarf, without mentioning why it was built.'

'Well, what is the mystery about it?' he queried. 'What more natural than that the defeated Norsemen should rear a cairn above the body of some great chief who had fallen in the battle?'

'In the first place,' I answered, 'there is a mystery concerning the existence of it. The building of cairns above the dead was a Norse, not an Irish, custom. Yet according to the chroniclers, it was not Norsemen who reared this heap. How could they have built it immediately after the battle, in which they had been cut to pieces and driven in headlong flight through the gates of Dublin? Their chieftains lay where they had fallen and the ravens picked their bones. It was Irish hands that heaped these stones.'

'Well, was that so strange?' persisted Ortali. 'In old times the Irish heaped up stones before they went into battle, each man putting a stone in place; after the battle the living removed their stones, leaving in that manner a simple tally of the slain for any who wished to count the remaining stones.'

I shook my head.

'That was in more ancient times; not in the battle of Clontarf. In the first place, there were more than twenty thousand warriors, and four thousand fell here; this cairn is not large enough to have served as a tally of the men killed in battle. And it is too symmetrically built. Hardly a stone has fallen away in all these centuries. No, it was reared to cover something.'

'Nordic superstitions!' the man sneered again.

'Aye, superstitions if you will!' Fired by his scorn, I exclaimed so savagely that he involuntarily stepped back, his hand slipping inside his coat. 'We of North Europe had gods and demons before which the pallid mythologies of the South fade to childishness. At a time when your ancestors were lolling on silken cushions among the crumbling marble pillars of a decaying civilisation, my ancestors were building their own civilisation in hardships and gigantic battles against foes human and inhuman.

'Here on this very plain the Dark Ages came to an end and the light of a new era dawned on the world of hate and anarchy. Here, as even you know, in the year 1014, Brian Boru and his Dalcassian axe-wielders broke the power of the heathen Norsemen forever – those grim anarchistic plunderers who had held back the progress of civilisation for centuries.'

'It was more than a struggle between Gael and Dane for the crown of Ireland. It was a war between the White Christ and Odin, between Christian and pagan. It was the last stand of the heathen . . . of the people of the old, grim ways. For three hundred years the world had writhed beneath the heel of the Viking, and here on Clontarf that scourge was lifted forever.

'Then, as now, the importance of that battle was underestimated by polite Latin and Latinised writers and historians. The polished sophisticates of the civilised cities of the South were not interested in the battles of barbarians in the remote north-western corner of the world – a place and peoples of whose very names they were only vaguely aware. They only knew that suddenly the terrible raids of the sea kings ceased to sweep along their coasts, and in another century the wild age of plunder and slaughter had almost been forgotten – all because a rude, half-civilised people who scantily covered their naked-ness with wolf hides rose up against the conquerors.'

'Here was Ragnarok, the fall of the gods! Here in very truth Odin fell, for his religion was given its death-blow. He was last of all the heathen gods to stand before Christianity, and it looked for a time as if his children might prevail and plunge the world back into darkness and savagery. Before Clontarf, legends say, he often appeared on earth to his worshippers, dimly seen in the smoke of the sacrifices where naked human victims died screaming, or riding the wind-torn clouds, his wild locks flying in the gale, or, apparelled like a Norse warrior, dealing thunderous blows in the forefront of nameless battles. But after Clontarf he was seen no more; his worshippers called on him in vain with wild chants and grim sacrifices. They lost faith in him, who had failed them in their wildest hour; his altars crumbled, his priests turned grey and died, and men turned to his conqueror, the White Christ. The reign of blood and iron was forgotten; the age of the red-handed sea kings passed. The rising sun, slowly, dimly, lighted the night of the Dark Ages, and men forgot Odin, who came no more on earth.'

'Aye, laugh if you will! But who knows what shapes of horror have-had birth in the darkness, the cold gloom and the whistling black gulfs of the North? In the southern lands the sun shines and flowers bloom; under the soft skies men laugh at demons. But in the North, who can say what elemental spirits of evil dwell in the fierce storms and the darkness? Well may it be that from such fiends of the night men evolved the worship of the grim ones, Odin and Thor, and their terrible kin.'

Ortali was silent for an instant, as if taken aback by my vehemence; then he laughed. 'Well said, my northern philosopher! We will argue these questions another time. I could hardly expect a descendant of Nordic barbarians to escape some trace of the dreams and mysticism of his race. But you cannot expect me to be moved by your imaginings, either. I still believe that this cairn covers no grimmer secret than a Norse chief who fell in the battle – and really your ravings concerning Nordic devils have no bearing on the matter. Will you help me tear into this cairn?'

'No,' I answered shortly.

'A few hours' work will suffice to lay bare whatever it may hide,' he continued as if he had not heard. 'By the way, speaking of superstitions, is there not some wild tale concerning holly connected with this heap?'

'An old legend says that all trees bearing holly were cut down for a league in all directions, for some mysterious reason,' I answered sullenly. 'That's another mystery. Holly was an important part of Norse magic-making. The Four Masters tell of a Norseman – a white-bearded ancient of wild aspect, and apparently a priest of Odin, who was slain by the natives while attempting to lay a branch of holly on the cairn, a year after the battle.'

'Well,' he laughed, 'I have procured a sprig of holly – see? – and shall wear it in my lapel; perhaps it will protect me against your Nordic devils. I feel more certain than ever that the cairn covers a sea king – and they were always laid to rest with all their riches: golden cups and jewel-set sword hilts and silver corselets. I feel that this cairn holds wealth, wealth over which clumsy-footed Irish peasants have been stumbling for centuries, living in want and dying in hunger. Bah! We shall return here at midnight, when we may be fairly certain that we will not be interrupted . . . and you will aid me at the excavations.'

The last sentence was rapped out in a tone that sent a red surge of blood-lust through my brain. Ortali turned and began examining the cairn as he spoke, and almost involuntarily my hand reached out stealthily and closed on a wicked bit of jagged stone that had become detached from one of the boulders. In that instant I was a potential murderer if ever one walked the earth. One blow, quick, silent and savage, and I would be free forever from a slavery bitter as my Celtic ancestors knew beneath the heels of the Vikings.

As if sensing my thoughts, Ortali wheeled to face me. I quickly slipped the stone into my pocket, not knowing whether he noted the action. But he must have seen the red killing instinct burning in my eyes, for again he recoiled and again his hand sought the hidden revolver.

But he only said: 'I've changed my mind. We will not uncover the cairn tonight. Tomorrow night, perhaps. We may be spied upon. Just now I am going back to the hotel.'

I made no reply, but turned my back upon him and stalked moodily away in the direction of the shore. He started up the slope of the headland beyond which lay the city, and when I turned to look at him, he was just crossing the ridge, etched, clearly against the hazy sky. If hate could kill, he would have dropped dead. I saw him in a red-tinged haze, and the pulses in my temples throbbed like hammers.

I turned back toward the shore, and stopped suddenly. Engrossed with my own dark thoughts, I had approached within a few feet of a woman before seeing her. She was tall and strongly made, with a strong stern face, deeply lined and weather-worn as the hills. She was dressed in a manner strange to me, but I thought little of it, knowing the curious styles of clothing worn by certain backward types of our people.

'What would you be doing at the cairn?' she asked in a deep, powerful voice. I looked at her in surprise; she spoke in Gaelic, which was not strange of itself, but the Gaelic she used I had supposed was extinct as a spoken language: it was the Gaelic of scholars, pure, and with a distinctly archaic flavour. A woman from some secluded hill country, I thought, where the people still spoke the unadulterated tongue of their ancestors.

'We were speculating on its mystery,' I answered in the same tongue, hesitantly, however, for though skilled in the more modern form taught in the schools, to match her use of the language was a strain on my knowledge of it. She shook her head slowly.' I like not the dark man who was with you,' she said sombrely. 'Who are you?'

'I'm an American, though born and raised here,' I answered. 'My name is James O'Brien.'

A strange light gleamed in her cold eyes.

'O'Brien . . . You are of my clan. I was born an O'Brien. I married a man of the MacDonnals, but my heart was ever with the folk of my blood.'

'You live hereabouts?' I queried, my mind on her unusual accent.

'Aye, I lived here upon a time,' she answered, 'but I have been far away for a long time. All is changed – changed. I would not have returned, but I was drawn back by a call you would not understand. Tell me, would you open the cairn?'

I started and gazed at her closely, deciding that she had somehow overheard our conversation.

'It is not mine to say,' I answered bitterly. 'Ortali, my companion . . . he will doubtless open it and I am constrained to aid him. Of my own will I would not molest it.'

Her cold eyes bored into my soul.

'Fools rush blind to their doom,' she said sombrely. 'What does this man know of the mysteries of this ancient land? Deeds have been done here whereof the world re-echoed. Yonder, in the long ago, when Tomar's Wood rose dark and rustling against the plain of Contarf, and the Danish walls of Dublin loomed south of the river Liffey, the ravens fed on the slain and the setting sun lighted lakes of crimson. There King Brian, your ancestor and mine, broke the spears of the North. From all lands they came, and from the isles of the sea; they came in gleaming mail and their horned helmets cast long shadows across the land. Their dragon-prows thronged the waves and the sound of their oars was as the beat of a storm.

'On yonder plain the heroes fell like ripe wheat before the reaper. There fell Jarl Sigurd of the Orkneys, and Brodir of Man, last of the sea kings, and all their chiefs. There fell, too, Prince Murrough and his son, Turlogh, and many chieftains of the Gael, and King Brian Boru himself, Erin's mightiest monarch.'

'True!' My imagination was always fired by the epic tales of the land of my birth. 'Blood of mine was spilled here, and, though I have passed the best part of my life in a far land, there are ties of blood to bind my soul to this shore.'

She nodded slowly, and from beneath her robes drew forth something that sparkled dully in the setting sun.

'Take this,' she said. 'As a token of blood tie, I give it to you. I feel the weird of strange and monstrous happenings but this will keep you safe from evil and the people of the night. Beyond reckoning of man, it is holy.'

I took it, wonderingly. It was a crucifix of curiously-worked gold, set with tiny jewels. The workmanship was extremely archaic and unmistakably Celtic. And vaguely within me stirred a memory of a long-lost relic described by forgotten monks in dim manuscripts.

'Great heavens!' I exclaimed. 'This is . . . this must be . . . this can be nothing less than the lost crucifix of Saint Brandon the Blessed!'

'Aye.' She inclined her grim head. 'Saint Brandon's cross, fashioned by the hands of the holy man long ago, before the Norse barbarians made Erin a red hell . . . in the days when a golden peace and holiness ruled the land.'

'But, woman!' I exclaimed wildly. 'I cannot accept this as a gift from you! You cannot know its value! Its intrinsic worth alone is equal to a fortune; as a relic it is priceless – '

'Enough!' Her deep voice struck me suddenly silent. 'Have done with such talk, which is sacrilege. The cross of Saint Brandon is beyond price. It was never stained with gold; only as a free gift has it ever changed hands. I give it to you to shield you against the powers of evil. Say no more.'

'But it has been lost for three hundred years!' I exclaimed. 'How – I – here . . . '

'A holy man gave it to me long ago,' she answered. 'I hid it in my bosom . . . long it lay in my bosom. But now I give it to you; I have come from a far country to give it to you, for there are monstrous happenings in the wind, and it is sword and shield against the people of the night. An ancient evil stirs in its prison, which blind bands of folly may break open; but stronger than any evil is the cross of Saint Brandon, which has gathered power and strength through the long, long ages since that forgotten evil fell to the earth.'

'But who are you?' I exclaimed.

'I am Meve MacDonnal,' she answered.

Then, turning without a word, she strode away in the deepening twilight while I stood bewildered and watched her cross the headland and pass from sight, turning inland as she topped the ridge. Then I, too, shaking myself like a man waking from a dream, went slowly up the slope and across the headland. When I crossed the ridge it was as if I had passed out of one world into another: behind me lay the wilderness and desolation of a weird medieval age; before me pulsed the lights and the roar of modern Dublin. Only one archaic touch was lent to the scene before me: some distance inland loomed the straggling and broken lines of an ancient graveyard, long deserted and grown up in weeds, barely discernible in the dusk. As I looked I saw a tall figure moving ghostily among the crumbling tombs, and I shook my head bewilderedly. Surely Meve MacDonnal was touched with madness, living in the past, like one seeking to stir to flame the ashes of dead yesterday. I set out toward where, in the near distance, began the straggling window-gleams that grew into the swarming ocean of lights that was Dublin.

Back at the suburban hotel where Ortali and I had our rooms, I did not speak to him of the cross the woman had given me. In that, at least, he should not share. I intended keeping it until she requested its return, which I felt sure she would do. Now as I recalled her appearance, the strangeness of her costume returned to me, with one item which had impressed itself on my subconscious mind at the time, but which I had not consciously realised. Meve MacDonnal had been wearing sandals of a type not worn in Ireland for centuries. Well, it was perhaps natural that with her retrospective nature she should imitate the apparel of the past ages which seemed to claim all her thoughts.

I turned the cross reverently in my hands. There was no doubt that it was the very cross for which antiquarians had searched so long in vain, and at last in despair had denied the existence of. The priestly scholar, Michael O'Rourke, in a treatise written about 1690, described the relic at length, chronicled its history exhaustively, and maintained that it was last heard of in the possession of Bishop Liam O'Brien, who, dying in 1955, gave it into the keeping of a kinswoman; but who this woman was, it was never known, and O'Rourke maintained that she kept her possession of the cross a secret, and that it was laid away with her in her tomb.

At another time my elation at discovering the relic would have been extreme, but, at the time, my mind was too filled with hate and smouldering fury. Replacing the cross in my pocket, I fell moodily to reviewing my connections with Ortali, connections which puzzled my friends, but which were simple enough.

Some years before I had been connected with a certain large university in a humble way. One of the professors with whom I worked – a man named Reynolds – was of intolerably overbearing disposition toward those whom he considered his inferiors. I was a poverty-ridden student striving for life in a system which makes the very existence of a scholar precarious. I bore Professor Reynolds' abuse as well as I could, but one day we clashed.

The reason does not matter; it was trivial enough in itself. Because I dared reply to his insults, Reynolds struck me and I knocked him senseless.

That very day he caused my dismissal from the university. Facing not only an abrupt termination of my work and studies, but actual starvation, I was reduced to desperation, and I went to Reynolds' study late that night intending to thrash him within an inch of his life. I found him alone in his study, but the moment I entered, he sprang up and rushed at me like a wild beast, with a dagger he used for a paperweight. I did not strike him; I did not even touch him. As I stepped aside to avoid his rush, a small rug slipped beneath his charging feet: he fell headlong, and, to my horror, in his fall the dagger in his hand was driven into his heart. He died instantly. I was at once aware of my position, I was known to have quarrelled, and even exchanged blows with the man. I had every reason to hate him. If I were found in the study with the dead man, no jury in the world would believe that I had not murdered him. I hurriedly left by the way I had come, thinking that I had been unobserved. But Ortali, the dead man's secretary, had seen me. Returning from a dance, he had observed me entering the premises, and, following me, had seen the whole affair through the window. But this I did not know until later.

The body was found by the professor's housekeeper, and naturally there was a great stir. Suspicion pointed to me, but lack of evidence kept me from being indicted, and this same lack of evidence brought about a verdict of suicide. All this time Ortali had kept quiet. Now he came to me and disclosed what he knew. He knew, of course, that I had not killed Reynolds, but he could prove that I was in the study when the professor met his death, and I knew Ortali was capable of carrying out his threat of swearing that he had seen me murder Reynolds in cold blood. And thus began a systematic blackmail.

I venture to say that a stranger blackmail was never levied. I had no money then; Ortali was gambling on my future, for he was assured of my abilities. He advanced me money, and, by clever wire-pulling, got me an appointment in a large college. Then he sat back to reap the benefits of his scheming, and he reaped full fold of the seed he sowed. In my line I became eminently successful. I soon commanded an enormous salary in my regular work, and I received rich prizes and awards for researches of various difficult natures, and of these Ortali took the lion's share . . . in money at least. I seemed to have the Midas touch. Yet of the wine of my success I tasted only the dregs.

I scarcely had a cent to my name. The money that had flowed through my hands had gone to enrich my slaver, unknown to the world. A man of remarkable gifts, he could have gone to the heights in any line, but for a queer streak in him, which, coupled with an inordinately avaricious nature, made him a parasite, a blood-sucking leech.

This trip to Dublin had been in the nature of a vacation for me. I was worn out with study and labour. But he had somehow heard of Grimmin's Cairn, as it was called, and, like a vulture that scents dead flesh, he conceived himself on the track of hidden gold. A golden wine cup would have been, to him, sufficient reward for the labour of tearing into the pile, and reason enough for desecrating or even destroying the ancient landmark. He was a swine whose only god was gold.

Well, I thought grimly, as I disrobed the bed, all things end, both good and bad. Such a life as I had lived was unbearable. Ortali had dangled the gallows before my eyes until it had lost its terrors. I had staggered beneath the load I carried because of my love for my work. But all human endurance has its limits. My hands turned to iron as I thought of Ortali, working beside me at midnight at the lonely cairn. One stroke, with such a stone as I had caught up that day, and my agony would be ended. That life and hopes and career and ambition would be ended as well, could not be helped. Ah, what a sorry, sorry end to all my high dreams! When a rope and the long drop through the black trap should cut short an honourable career and a useful life! And all because of a human vampire who feasted his rotten lust on my soul, and drove me to murder and ruin.

But I knew my fate was written in the iron books of doom. Sooner or later I would turn on Ortali and kill him, be the consequences what they might. And I reached the end of my road. Continual torture had rendered me, I believe, partly insane. I knew that at Grimmin's Cairn, when we toiled at midnight, Ortali's life would end beneath my hands, and my own life be cast away.

Something fell out of my pocket and I picked it up. It was the piece of sharp stone I had caught up off the cairn. Looking at it moodily, I wondered what strange hands had touched it in old times, and what grim secret it helped to hide on the bare headland of Grimmin. I switched out the light and lay in the darkness, the stone still in my hand, forgotten, occupied with my own dark broodings. And I glided gradually into deep slumber.

At first I was aware that I was dreaming, as people often are. All was dim and vague, and connected in some strange way, I realised, with the bit of stone still grasped in my sleeping hand. Gigantic, chaotic scenes and landscapes and events shifted before me, like clouds that rolled and tumbled before a gale. Slowly these settled and crystallised into one distinct landscape, familiar and yet wildly strange. I saw a broad bare plain, fringed by the grey sea on one side, and a dark, rustling forest on the other; this plain was cut by a winding river, and beyond this river I saw a city . . . such a city as my waking eyes had never seen: bare, stark, massive, with the grim architecture of an earlier, wilder age. On the plain I saw, as in a mist, a mighty battle. Serried ranks rolled backward and forward, steel flashed like a sunlit sea, and men fell like ripe wheat beneath the blades. I saw men in wolfskins, wild and shock-headed, wielding dripping axes, and tall men in horned helmets, and glittering mail, whose eyes were cold and blue as the sea. And I saw myself.

Yes, in my dream I saw and recognised, in a semidetached way, myself. I was tall and rangily powerful; I was shockheaded and naked but for a wolf-hide girt about my loins. I ran among the ranks yelling and smiting with a red axe, and blood ran down my flanks from wounds I scarcely felt. My eyes were cold blue and my shaggy hair and beard were red.

Now for an instant I was cognisant of my dual personality, aware that I was at once the wild man who ran and smote with the gory axe, and the man who slumbered and dreamed across the centuries. But this sensation quickly faded. I was no longer aware of any personality other than that of the barbarian who ran and smote. James O'Brien had no existence; I was Red Cumal, kern of Brian Boru, and my axe was dripping with the blood of my foes.

The roar of conflict was dying away, though here and there struggling clumps of warriors still dotted the plain. Down along the river, half-naked tribesmen, waist-deep in reddening water, tore and slashed with helmeted warriors whose mail could not save them from the stroke of the Dalcassian axe. Across the river a bloody, disorderly horde was staggering through the gates of Dublin.

The sun was sinking low toward the horizon. All day I had fought beside the chiefs. I had seen Jarl Sigurd fall beneath Prince Murrough's sword. I had seen Murrough himself die in the moment of victory, by the hand of a grim mailed giant whose name none knew. I had seen, in the flight of the enemy, Brodir and King Brian fall together at the door of the great king's tent.

Aye, it had been a feasting of ravens, a red flood of slaughter, and I knew that no more would the dragon-prowed fleets sweep from the blue North with torch and destruction. Far and wide the Vikings lay in their glittering mail, as the ripe wheat lies after the reaping. Among them lay thousands of bodies clad in the wolf hides of the tribes, but the dead of the Northern people far outnumbered the dead of Erin. I was weary and sick of the stench of raw blood. I had glutted my soul with slaughter; now I sought plunder. And I found it on the corpse of a richly-clad Norse chief which lay close to the seashore. I tore off the silver-scaled corselet, the horned helmet. They fitted as if made for me, and I swaggered among the dead, calling on my wild comrades to admire my appearance, though the harness felt strange to me, for the Gaels scorned armour and fought half-naked.

In my search for loot I had wandered far out on the plain, away from the river, but still the mail-clad bodies lay thickly strewn, for the bursting of the ranks had scattered fugitives and pursuers all over the countryside, from the dark waving Wood of Tomar to the river and the seashore. And on the seaward slope of Drumna's headland, out of sight of the city and the plain of Clontarf, I came suddenly upon a dying warrior. He was tall and massive, clad in grey mail. He lay partly in the folds of a great dark cloak, and his sword lay broken near his mighty right hand. His horned helmet had fallen from his head and his elf-locks blew in the wind that swept out of the west.

Where one eye should have been was an empty socket, and the other eye glittered cold and grim as the North Sea, though it was glazing with approach of death. Blood oozed from a rent in his corselet. I approached him warily, a strange cold fear, that I could not understand, gripping me. Axe ready to dash out his brains, I bent over him, and recognised him as the chief who had slain Prince Murrough, and who had mown down the warriors of the Gael like a harvest.. Wherever he had fought, the Norsemen had prevailed, but in all other parts of the field, the Gaels had been irresistible.

And now he spoke to me in Norse and I understood, for had I not toiled as slave among the sea people for long bitter years?

'The Christians have overcome,' he gasped in a voice whose timbre, though low-pitched, sent a curious shiver of fear through me; there was in it an undertone as of icy waves sweeping along a Northern shore, as of freezing winds whispering among the pine trees. 'Doom and shadows stalk on Asgaard and here has fallen Ragnarok. I could not be in all parts of the field at once, and now I am wounded unto death. A spear – a spear with a cross carved in the blade; no other weapon could wound me.'

I realised that the chief, seeing mistily my red beard and the Norse armour I wore, supposed me to be one of his own race. But crawling horror surged darkly in the depths of my soul.

'White Christ, thou hast not yet conquered,' he muttered deliriously. 'Lift me up, man, and let me speak to you.'

Now for some reason I complied, and, as I lifted him to a sitting posture, I shuddered and my flesh crawled at the feel of him, for his flesh was like ivory . . . smoother and harder than is natural for human flesh, and colder than even a dying man should be.

'I die as men die;' he muttered. 'Fool, to assume the attributes of mankind, even though it was to aid the people who deify me. The gods are immortal, but flesh can perish, even when it clothes a god. Haste and bring a sprig of the magic plant – even holly – and lay it on my bosom. Aye, though it be no larger than a dagger point, it will free me from this fleshy prison I put on when I came to war with men with their own weapons. And I will shake off this flesh and stalk once more among the thundering clouds. Woe, then, to all men who bend not the knee to me! Haste; I will await your coming.'

His lion-like head fell back, and feeling shudderingly under his corselet, I could distinguish no heartbeat. He was dead, as men die, but I knew that locked in that semblance of a human body, there but slumbered the spirit of a fiend of the frost and darkness.

Aye, I knew him: Odin, the Grey Man, the One-eyed, the god of the North who had taken the form of a warrior to fight for his people. Assuming the form of a human, he was subject to many of the limitations of humanity. All men knew this of the gods, who often walked the earth in the guise of men. Odin, clothed in human semblance, could be wounded by certain weapons, and even slain, but a touch of the mysterious holly would rouse him in grisly resurrection. This task he had set me, not knowing me for an enemy; in human form he could only use human faculties, and these had been impaired by onstriding death.

My hair stood up and my flesh crawled. I tore from my body the Norse armour, and fought a wild panic that prompted me to run blind and screaming with terror across the plain. Nauseated with fear, I gathered boulders and heaped them for a rude couch, and on it, shaking with horror, I lifted the body of the Norse god. And as the sun set and the stars came silently out, I was working with fierce energy, piling huge rocks above the corpse. Other tribesmen came up and I told them of what I was sealing up . . . I hoped forever. And they, shivering with horror, fell to aiding me. No sprig of magic holly should be laid on Odin's terrible bosom. Beneath these rude stones the Northern demon should slumber until the thunder of Judgment Day, forgotten by the world which had once cried out beneath his iron heel. Yet not wholly forgotten, for, as we laboured, one of my comrades said: 'This shall be no longer Drumna's Headland, but the Headland of the Grey Man.'

That phrase established a connection between my dream-self and my sleeping-self. I started up from sleep exclaiming: 'Grey Man's Headland!'

I looked about dazedly, the furnishings of the room, faintly lighted by the starlight in the windows, seeming strange and unfamiliar until I slowly oriented myself with time and space.

'Grey Man's Headland,' I repeated, 'Grey Man – Graymin – Grimmin – Grimmin's Headland! Great God, the thing under the cairn!'

Shaken, I sprang up, and realised that I still gripped the piece of stone from the cairn. It is well known that inanimate objects retain psychic associations. A round stone from the plain of Jericho has been placed in the land of a hypnotised medium, and she has at once reconstructed in her mind the battle and siege of the city, and the shattering fall of the walls. I did not doubt that this bit of stone had acted as a magnet to drag my modern mind through the mists of the centuries into a life I had known before.

I was more shaken than I can describe, for the whole fantastic affair fitted in too well with certain formless vague sensations concerning the cairn which had already lingered at the back of my mind, to be dismissed as an unusually vivid dream. I felt the need of a glass of wine, and remembered that Ortali always had wine in his room. I hurriedly donned my clothes, opened my door, crossed the corridor and was about to knock at Ortali's door, when I noticed that it was partly open, as if someone had neglected to close it carefully. I entered, switching on a light. The room was empty.

I realised what had occurred. Ortali mistrusted me; he feared to risk himself alone with me in a lonely spot at midnight. He had postponed the visit to the cairn merely to trick me, to give himself a chance to slip away alone.

My hatred for Ortali was for the moment completely submerged by a wild panic of horror at the thought of what the opening of the cairn might result in. For I did not doubt the authenticity of my dream. It was no dream; it was a fragmentary bit of memory, in which I had relived that other life of mine. Grey Man's Headland . . . Grimmin's Headland, and under those rough stones that grisly corpse in its semblance of humanity. I could not hope that, imbued with the imperishable essence of an elemental spirit, that corpse had crumbled to dust in the ages.

Of my race out of the city and across those semi-desolate reaches, I remember little. The night was a cloak of horror through which peered red stars like the gloating eyes of uncanny beasts, and my footfalls echoed hollowly so that repeatedly I thought some monster loped at my heels.

The straggling lights fell away behind me and I entered the region of mystery and horror. No wonder that progress had passed to the right and to the left of this spot, leaving it untouched, a blind back-eddy given over to goblin-dreams and nightmare memories. Well that so few suspected its very existence.

Dimly I saw the headland, but fear gripped me and held me aloof. I had a vague, incoherent idea of finding the ancient woman, Meve MacDonnal. She was grown old in the mysteries and traditions of the mysterious land. She could aid me, if indeed the blind fool Ortali loosed on the world the forgotten demon men once worshipped in the North.

A figure loomed suddenly in the starlight and I caromed against him, almost upsetting him. A stammering voice in a thick brogue protested with the petulance of intoxication. It was a burly long-shoreman returning to his cottage, no doubt, from some late revel in a tavern. I seized him and shook him, my eyes glaring wildly in the starlight.

'I am looking for Meve MacDonnal! Do you know her? Tell me, you fool! Do you know old Meve MacDonnal?'

It was as if my words sobered him as suddenly as a dash of icy water in his face. In the starlight I saw his face glimmer whitely and a catch of fear was at his throat. He sought to cross himself with an uncertain hand.

'Meve MacDonnal! Are ye mad? What would ye be doin' with her?'

'Tell me!' I shrieked, shaking him savagely. 'Where is Meve Mac-Donnal?'

'There!' he gasped, pointing with a shaking hand, where dimly in the night something loomed against the shadows. 'In the name of the holy saints, begone, by ye madman or devil, and rave an honest man alone! There, there ye'll find Meve MacDonnal . . . where they laid her, full three hundred years ago!'

Half heeding his words, I flung him aside with a fierce exclam-ation, and, as I raced across the weed-grown plain, I heard the sound of his lumbering flight. Half blind with panic, I came to the low structure the man had pointed out. And floundering deep in weeds, my feet sinking into the musty mould, I realised with a shock that I was in the ancient graveyard on the inland side of Grimmin's Headland, into which I had seen Meve MacDonnal disappear the evening before. I was close by the door of the largest tomb, and with an eerie premonition I leaned close, seeking to make out the deeply carven inscription. And partly by the dim light of the stars and partly by the touch of my tracing fingers, I made out the words and figures, in the half-forgotten Gaelic of three centuries ago:

Meve MacDonnal 1556–1640

With a cry of horror, I recoiled and, snatching out the crucifix she had given me, made to hurl it into the darkness . . . but it was as if an invisible hand caught my wrist. Madness and insanity . . . but I could not doubt: Meve MacDonnal had come to me from the tomb wherein she had rested for three hundred years to give me the ancient, ancient relic entrusted to her so long ago by her priestly kin. The memory of her words came to me, and the memory of Ortali and the Grey Man. From a lesser horror I turned squarely to a greater, and ran swiftly toward the headland which loomed dimly against the stars toward the sea.

As I crossed the ridge I saw, in the starlight, the cairn, and the figure that toiled gnome-like above it. Ortali, with his accustomed, almost superhuman energy, had dislodged many of the boulders; and as I approached, shaking with horrified anticipation, I saw him tear aside the last layer, and I heard his savage cry of triumph that froze me in my tracks some yards behind him, looking down from the slope. An unholy radiance rose from the cairn, and I saw, in the north, the aurora come up suddenly with terrible beauty, paling the starlight. All about the cairn pulsed a weird light, turning the rough stones to a cold shimmering silver, and in this glow I saw Ortali, all heedless, cast aside his pick and lean gloatingly over the aperture he had made – and I saw there the helmeted head, reposing on the couch of stones where I, Red Cumal, had placed it so long ago. I saw the inhuman terror and beauty of that awesome carven face, in which was neither human weakness, pity nor mercy. I saw the soul-freezing glitter of the one eye, which stared wide open in a fearful semblance of life. All up and down the tall mailed figure shimmered and sparkled cold darts and gleams of icy light, like the northern lights that blazed in the shuddering skies. Aye, the Grey Man lay as I had left him more than nine hundred years before, without trace of rust or rot or decay.

And now as Ortali leaned forward to examine his find, a gasping cry broke from his lips . . . for the sprig of holly, worn in his lapel in defiance of 'Nordic superstition', slipped from its place, and in the weird glow I plainly saw it fall upon the mighty mailed breast of the figure, where it blazed suddenly with a brightness too dazzling for human eyes. My cry was echoed by Ortali. The figure moved; the mighty limbs flexed, tumbling the shining stones aside. A new gleam lighted the terrible eye, and a tide of life flooded and animated the carven features.

Out of the cairn he rose, and the northern lights played terribly about him. And the Grey Man changed and altered in horrific trans-mutation. The human features faded like a fading mask; the armour fell from his body and crumbled to dust as it fell; and the fiendish spirit of ice and frost and darkness that the sons of the North deified as Odin, stood nakedly and terribly, in the stars. About his grisly head played lightnings and the shuddering gleams of the aurora. His tower-ing anthropomorphic form was dark as shadow and gleaming as ice; his horrible crest reared colossally against the vaulting arch of the sky.

Ortali cowered, screaming wordlessly, as the taloned, malformed hands reached for him. In the shadowy, indescribable features of the Thing, there was no tinge of gratitude toward the man who had released it – only a demoniac gloating and a demoniac hate for all the sons of men. I saw the shadowy arms shoot out and strike. I heard Ortali scream once – a single, unbearable screech that broke short at the shrillest pitch. A single instant a blinding blue glare burst about him, lighting his convulsed features and his upward-rolling eyes; then his body was dashed earthward as by an electric shock, so savagely that I distinctly heard the splintering of his bones. But Ortali was dead before he touched the ground – dead, shrivelled and blackened, exactly like a man blasted by a thunderbolt, to which cause, indeed, men later ascribed his death.

The slavering monster that had slain him lumbered now toward me, shadowy, tentacle-like arms outspread, the pale starlight making a luminous pool of his great inhuman eye, his frightful talons drip-ping with I know not what elemental forces to blast the bodies and souls of men.

But I flinched not, and in that instant I feared him not, neither the horror of his countenance nor the threat of his thunderbolt dooms. For in a blinding white flame had come to me the realisation of why Meve MacDonnal had come from her tomb to bring me the ancient cross which had lain in her bosom for three hundred years, gathering unto itself unseen forces of good and light, which war forever against the shapes of lunacy and shadow.

As I plucked from my garments the ancient cross, I felt the play of gigantic unseen forces in the air about me. I was but a pawn in the game – merely the hand that held the relic of holiness, that was the symbol of the powers opposed forever against the fiends of darkness. As I held it high, from it shot a single shaft of white light, unbearably pure, unbearably white, as if all the awesome forces of Light were combined in the symbol and loosed in one concentrated arrow of wrath against the monster of darkness. And with a hideous shriek the demon reeled back, shrivelling before my eyes. Then, with a great rush of vulture-like wings, he soared into the stars, dwindling among the play of the flaming fires and the lights of the haunted skies, fleeing back into the dark limbo which gave him birth, God only knows how many grisly aeons ago.

Black Talons

Joel Brill slapped shut the book he had been scanning, and gave vent to his dissatisfaction in language more appropriate for the deck of a whaling ship than for the library of the exclusive Corinthian Club. Buckley, seated in an alcove nearby, grinned quietly. Buckley looked more like a college professor than a detective, and perhaps it was less because of a studious nature than a desire to play the part he looked, that caused him to loaf around the library of the Corinthian.

'It must be something unusual to drag you out of your lair at this time of the day,' he remarked. 'This is the first time I ever saw you in the evening. I thought you spent your evenings secluded in your rooms, poring over musty tomes in the interests of that museum you're connected with.'

'I do, ordinarily.' Brill looked as little like a scientist as Buckley looked like a dick. He was squarely built, with thick shoulders and the jaw and fists of a prizefighter; low-browed, with a mane of tousled black hair contrasting with his cold blue eyes.

'You've been shoving your nose into books here since six o'clock,' asserted Buckley.

'I've been trying to get some information for the directors of the museum,' answered Brill. 'Look!' He pointed an accusing finger at the rows of lavishly bound volumes. 'Books till it would sicken a dog – and not a blasted one can tell me the reason for a certain ceremonial dance practised by a certain tribe on the West African Coast.'

'A lot of the members have knocked around a bit,' suggested Buckley. 'Why not ask them?'

'I'm going to.' Brill took down a phone from its hook.

'There's John Galt . . . ' began Buckley.

'Too hard to locate. He flits about like a mosquito with the St Vitus. I'll try Jim Reynolds.' He twirled the dial.

'Thought you'd done some exploring in the tropics yourself,' remarked Buckley.

'Not worthy of the name. I hung around that God-forsaken hell-hole of the West African Coast for a few months until I came down with malaria – Hello!'

A suave voice, too perfectly accented, came along the wire.

'Oh, is that you, Yut Wuen? I want to speak to Mr Reynolds.'

Polite surprise tinged the meticulous tone.

'Why, Mr Reynolds went out in response to your call an hour ago, Mr Brill.'

'What's that?' demanded Brill. 'Went where?'

'Why, surely you remember, Mr Brill.' A faint uneasiness seemed to edge the Chinaman's voice. 'At about nine o'clock you called, and I answered the phone. You said you wished to speak to Mr Reynolds. Mr Reynolds talked to you, then told me to have his car brought around to the side entrance. He said that you had requested him to meet you at the cottage on White Lake shore.'

'Nonsense!' exclaimed Brill. 'This is the first time I've phoned Reynolds for weeks! You've mistaken somebody else for me.'

There was no reply, but a polite stubbornness seemed to flow over the wire. Brill replaced the phone and turned to Buckley, who was leaning forward with aroused interest.

'Something fishy here,' scowled Brill. 'Yut Wuen, Jim's Chinese servant, said *I* called, an hour ago, and Jim went out to meet me. Buckley, you've been here all evening. *Did* I call up anybody? I'm so infernally absent-minded –'

'No, you didn't,' emphatically answered the detective. 'I've been sitting right here close to the phone ever since six o'clock. Nobody's used it. And you haven't left the library during that time. I'm so accustomed to spying on people, I do it unconsciously.'

'Well, say,' said Brill, uneasily, 'suppose you and I drive over to White Lake. If this is a joke, Jim may be over there waiting for me to show up.'

As the city lights fell behind them, and houses gave way to clumps of trees and bushes, velvet black in the star-light, Buckley said: 'Do you think Yut Wuen made a mistake?'

'What else could it be?' answered Brill, irritably.

'Somebody might have been playing a joke, as you suggested. Why should anybody impersonate you to Reynolds?'

'How should I know? But I'm about the only acquaintance he'd bestir himself for, at this time of night. He's reserved, suspicious of people. Hasn't many friends. I happen to be one of the few.'

'Something of a traveller, isn't he?'

'There's no corner of the world with which he isn't familiar.'

'How'd he make his money?' Bucklcy asked, abruptly.

'I've never asked him. But he has plenty of it.'

The clumps on each side of the road grew denser, and scattered pinpoints of light that marked isolated farm houses faded out behind them. The road tilted gradually as they climbed higher and higher into the wild hill region which, an hour's drive from the city, locked the broad crystalline sheet of silver that men called White Lake. Now ahead of them a glint shivered among the trees, and topping a wooded crest, they saw the lake spread out below them, reflecting the stars in myriad flecks of silver. The road meandered along the curving shore.

'Where's Reynolds' lodge?' inquired Buckley.

Brill pointed. 'See that thick clump of shadows, within a few yards of the water's edge? It's the only cottage on this side of the lake. The others are three or four miles away. None of them occupied, this time of the year. There's a car drawn up in front of the cottage.'

'No light in the shack,' grunted Buckley, pulling up beside the long low roadster that stood before the narrow stoop. The building reared dark and silent before them, blocked against the rippling silver sheen behind it.

'Hey, Jim!' called Brill. 'Jim Reynolds!'

No answer. Only a vague echo shuddering down from the blackly wooded hills.

'Devil of a place at night,' muttered Buckley, peering at the dense shadows that bordered the lake. 'We might be a thousand miles from civilisation.'

Brill slid out of the car. 'Reynolds must be here . . . unless he's gone for a midnight boat ride.'

Their steps echoed loudly and emptily on the tiny stoop. Brill banged the door and shouted. Somewhere back in the woods a night bird lifted a drowsy note. There was no other answer.

Buckley shook the door. It was locked from the inside.

'I don't like this,' he growled. 'Car in front of the cottage . . . door locked on the inside . . . nobody answering it. I believe I'll break the door in – '

'No need.' Brill fumbled in his pocket. 'I'll use my key.'

'How comes it you have a key to Reynolds' shack?' demanded Buckley.

'It was his own idea. I spent some time with him up here last summer, and he insisted on giving me a key, so I could use the

cottage any time I wanted to. Turn on your flash, will you? I can't
find the lock. All right, I've got it. Hey, Jim! Are you here?'

Buckley's flash played over chairs and card tables, coming to rest
on a closed door in the opposite wall. They entered and Buckley
heard Brill fumbling about with an arm elevated. A faint click followed and Brill swore.

'The juice is off. There's a line running out from town to supply
the cottage owners with electricity, but it must be dead. As long as
we're in here, let's go through the house. Reynolds may be sleeping
somewhere . . . '

He broke off with a sharp intake of breath. Buckley had opened the
door that led to the bedroom. His flash played on the interior . . . on
a broken chair, a smashed table . . . a crumpled shape that lay in the
midst of a dark widening pool.

'Good God, it's Reynolds!'

Buckley's gun glinted in his hand as he played the flash around the
room, sifting the shadows for lurking shapes of menace; it rested on a
bolted rear door; rested longer on an open window, the screen of
which hung in tatters.

'We've got to have more light,' he grunted. 'Where's the switch?
Maybe a fuse has blown.'

'Outside, near that window.' Stumblingly Brill led the way out of
the house and around to the window. Buckley flashed his light,
grunted.

'The switch has been pulled!' He pushed it back in place, and light
flooded the cottage. The light streaming through the windows
seemed to emphasise the blackness of the whispering woods around
them. Buckley glared into the shadows, seemed to shiver. Brill had
not spoken; he shook as with ague.

Back in the house they bent over the man who lay in the middle of
the red-splashed floor.

Jim Reynolds had been a stocky, strongly built man of middle age.
His skin was brown and weather-beaten, hinting of tropic suns. His
features were masked with blood; his head lolled back, disclosing an
awful wound beneath his chin.

'His throat's been cut!' stammered Brill. Buckley shook his head.

'Not cut – torn. Good God, it looks like a big cat had ripped him.'

The whole throat had literally been torn out; muscles, arteries,
windpipe and the great jugular vein had been severed; the bones of
the vertebrae showed beneath.

'He's so bloody I wouldn't have recognised him,' muttered the detective. 'How did you know him so quickly? The instant we saw him, you cried out that it was Reynolds.'

'I recognised his garments and his build,' answered the other. 'But what in God's name killed him?'

Buckley straightened and looked about. 'Where does that door lead to?'

'To the kitchen; but it's locked on this side.'

'And the outer door of the front room was locked on the inside,' muttered Buckley. 'Doesn't take a genius to see how the murderer got in . . . and he – or *it* – went out the same way.'

'What do you mean, *it*?'

'Does that look like the work of a human being?' Buckley pointed to the dead man's mangled throat. Brill winced.

'I've seen boys mauled by the big cats on the West Coast – '

'And whatever tore Reynolds' gullet out, tore that window screen. It wasn't cut with a knife.'

'Do you suppose a panther from the hills . . . ' began Brill.

'A panther smart enough to throw the electric switch before he slid through the window?' scoffed Buckley.

'We don't know the killer threw the switch.'

'Was Reynolds fooling around in the dark, then? No; when I pushed the switch back in place, the light came on in here. That shows it had been on; the button hadn't been pushed back. Whoever killed Reynolds had a reason for wanting to work in the dark. Maybe this was it!' The detective indicated, with a square-shod toe, a stubby chunk of blue steel that lay not far from the body.

'From what I hear about Reynolds, he was quick enough on the trigger.' Buckley slipped on a glove, carefully lifted the revolver, and scanned the chamber. His gaze, roving about the room again, halted at the window, and with a single long stride, he reached it and bent over the sill.

'One shot's been fired from this gun. The bullet's in the window sill. At least, one bullet is, and it's logical to suppose it's the one from the empty chamber of Reynolds' gun. Here's the way I reconstruct the crime: *something* sneaked up to the shack, threw the switch, and came busting through the window. Reynolds shot once in the dark and missed, and then the killer got in his work. I'll take this gun to headquarters; don't expect to find any fingerprints except Reynolds', however. We'll examine the light switch, too, though maybe my dumb pawing erased any fingerprints that might have been there. Say, it's a good thing you have an iron-clad alibi.'

Brill started violently. 'What the Hell do you mean?'

'Why, there's the Chinaman to swear you called Reynolds to his death.'

'Why the devil should I do such a thing?' hotly demanded the scientist.

'Well,' answered Buckley, 'I know you were in the library of the club all evening. That's an unshakable alibi . . . I suppose.'

Brill was tired as he locked the door of his garage and turned toward the house, which rose dark and silent among the trees. He found himself wishing that his sister, with whom he was staying, had not left town for the weekend with her husband and children. Dark empty houses were vaguely repellent to him after the happenings of the night before.

He sighed wearily as he trudged toward the house, under the dense shadows of the trees that lined the driveway. It had been a morbid and harrying day. Tag ends of thoughts and worries flitted through his mind. Uneasily he remembered Buckley's cryptic remark: 'Either Yut Wuen is lying about that telephone call, or . . . ' The detective had left the sentence unfinished, casting a glance at Brill that was as inscrutable as his speech. Nobody believed the Chinaman was deliberately lying. His devotion to his master was well known – a devotion shared by the other servants of the dead man. Police suspicion had failed to connect them in any way with the crime. Apparently none of them had left Reynolds' town house during the day or the night of the murder. Nor had the murder-cottage given up any clues. No tracks had been found on the hard earth, no fingerprints on the gun other than the dead man's, nor any except Buckley's on the light switch. If Buckley had had any luck in trying to trace the mysterious phone call, he had not divulged anything.

Brill remembered, with a twinge of nervousness, the way in which they had looked at him, those inscrutable Orientals. Their features had been immobile, but in their dark eyes had gleamed suspicion and a threat. He had seen it in the eyes of Yut Wuen; of Ali, the Egyptian, a lean, sinewy statue of bronze; of Jugra Singh, the tall, broad-shouldered, turbaned Sikh. They had not spoken their thoughts, but their eyes had followed him, hot and burning, like beasts of prey.

Brill turned from the meandering driveway to cut across the lawn. As he passed under the black shadow of the trees, something sudden, clinging and smothering, enveloped his head, and steely arms locked fiercely about him. His reaction was as instinctive and violent as that of a trapped leopard. He exploded into a galvanised burst of frantic action, a bucking heave that tore the stifling cloak from his head, and freed his arms from the arms that pinioned him. But another pair of arms hung like grim Fate to his legs, and figures surged in on him from the darkness. He could not tell the nature of his assailants; they were like denser, moving shadows in the blackness.

Staggering, fighting for balance, he lashed out blindly, felt the jolt of a solid hit shoot up his arm, and saw one of the shadows sway and pitch backward. His other arm was caught in a savage grasp and twisted up behind his back so violently that he felt as if the tendons were being ripped from their roots. Hot breath hissed in his ear, and bending his head forward, he jerked it backward again with all the power of his thick neck muscles. He felt the back of his skull crash into something softer – a man's face. There was a groan, and the crippling grip on his imprisoned arm relaxed. With a desperate wrench he tore away, but the arms that clung to his legs tripped him. He pitched headlong, spreading his arms to break his fall, and even before his fingers touched the ground, something exploded in his brain, showering a suddenly starless night of blackness with red sparks that were engulfed abruptly in formless oblivion.

Joel Brill's first conscious thought was that he was being tossed about in an open boat on a stormy sea. Then as his dazed mind cleared, be realised that he was lying in an automobile which was speeding along an uneven road. His head throbbed; he was bound hand and foot, and blanketed in some kind of a cloak. He could see nothing, could hear nothing but the purr of the racing motor. Bewilderment clouded his mind as be sought for a clue to the identity of the kidnappers. Then a sudden suspicion brought out the cold sweat on his skin.

The car lurched to a halt. Powerful hands lifted him, cloak and all, and he felt himself being carried over a short stretch of level ground, and apparently up a step or so. A key grated in a lock, a door rasped on its hinges. Those carrying him advanced; there was a click, and light shone through the folds of the cloth over Brill's head. He felt himself being lowered onto what felt like a bed. Then the cloth was ripped away, and he blinked in the glare of the light. A cold premonitory shudder passed over him.

He was lying on the bed in the room in which James Reynolds had died. And about him stood, arms folded, three grim and silent shapes: Yut Wuen, Ali the Egyptian, and Jugra Singh. There was dried blood on the Chinaman's yellow face, and his lip was cut. A dark blue bruise showed on Jugra Singh's jaw.

'The *sahib* awakes,' said the Sikh, in his perfect English.

'What the devil's the idea, Jugra?' demanded Brill, trying to struggle to a sitting posture. 'What do you mean by this? Take these ropes off me – ' His voice trailed away, a shaky resonance of futility as he read the meaning in the hot dark eyes that regarded him.

'In this room our master met his doom,' said Ali.

'*You* called him forth,' said Yut Wuen.

'But I didn't!' raged Brill, jerking wildly at the cords which cut into his flesh. 'Damn it, I knew nothing about it!'

'Your voice came over the wire and our master followed it to his death,' said Jugra Singh.

A panic of helplessness swept over Joel Brill. He felt like a man beating at an insurmountable wall – the wall of inexorable Oriental fatalism, of conviction unchangeable. If even Buckley believed that somehow he, Joel Brill, was connected with Reynolds' death, how was he to convince these immutable Orientals? He fought down an impulse to hysteria.

'The detective, Buckley, was with me all evening,' he said, in a voice unnatural from his efforts at control. 'He has told you that he did not see me touch a phone; nor did I leave his sight. I could not have killed my friend, your master, because while he was being killed, I was either in the library of the Corinthian Club, or driving from there with Buckley.'

'How it was done, we do not know,' answered the Sikh, tranquilly. 'The ways of the *sahibs* are beyond us. But we *know* that somehow, in some manner, you caused our master's death. And we have brought you here to expiate your crime.'

'You mean to murder me?' demanded Brill, his flesh crawling.

'If a *sahib* judge sentenced you, and a *sahib* hangman dropped you through a black trap, white men would call it execution. So it is execution we work upon you, not murder.'

Brill opened his mouth, then closed it, realising the utter futility of argument. The whole affair was like a fantastic nightmare from which he would presently awaken.

Ali came forward with something, the sight of which shook Brill with a nameless foreboding. It was a wire cage, in which a great gaunt rat squealed and bit at the wires. Yut Wuen laid upon a card table a copper bowl, furnished with a slot on each side of the rim, to one of which was made fast a long leather strap. Brill turned suddenly sick.

'These are the tools of execution, *sahib*,' said Jugra Singh, sombrely. 'That bowl shall be laid on your naked belly, the strap drawn about your body and made fast so that the bowl shall not slip. Inside the bowl the rat will be imprisoned. He is ravenous with hunger, wild with fear and rage. For a while he will only run about the bowl, treading on your flesh. But with irons hot from the fire, we shall gradually heat the bowl, until, driven by pain, the rat begins to gnaw his way *out*. He can not gnaw through copper; he can gnaw through flesh . . . through flesh and muscles and intestines and bones, *sahib*.'

Brill wet his lips three times before he found voice to speak.

'You'll hang for this!' he gasped, in a voice he did not himself recognise.

'If it be the will of Allah,' assented Ali calmly. 'This is your fate; what ours is, no man can say. It is the will of Allah that you die with a rat in your bowels. If it is Allah's will, we shall die on the gallows. Only Allah knows.'

Brill made no reply. Some vestige of pride still remained to him. He set his jaw hard, feeling that if he opened his mouth to speak, to reason, to argue, he would collapse into shameful shrieks and entreaties.

Ali set the cage with its grisly occupant on the table beside the copper bowl – without warning the light went out.

In the darkness Brill's heart began to pound suffocatingly. The Orientals stood still, patiently, expecting the light to come on again. But Brill instinctively felt that the stage was set for some drama darker and more hideous than that which menaced him. Silence reigned; somewhere off in the woods a night bird lifted a drowsy note. There was a faint scratching sound, somewhere . . .

'The electric torch,' muttered a ghostly voice which Brill recognised as Jugra Singh's. 'I laid it on the card table. Wait!'

He heard the Sikh fumbling in the dark; but he was watching the window, a square of dim, star-flecked sky blocked out of blackness. And as Brill watched, he saw something dark and bulky rear up in that square. Etched against the stars he saw a misshapen head, vague monstrous shoulders.

A scream sounded from inside the room, the crash of a wildly thrown missile. On the instant there was a scrambling sound, and the object blotted out the square of starlight, then vanished from it. *It was inside the room.*

Brill, lying frozen in his cords, heard all Hell and bedlam break loose in that dark room. Screams, shouts, strident cries of agony mingled with the smashing of furniture, the impact of blows, and a hideous, worrying, tearing sound that made Brill's flesh crawl. Once the battling pack staggered past the window, but Brill made out only a dim writhing of limbs, the pale glint of steel, and the terrible blaze of a pair of eyes he knew belonged to none of his three captors.

Somewhere a man was moaning horribly, his gasps growing weaker and weaker. There was a last convulsion of movement, the groaning impact of a heavy body; then the starlight in the window was for an instant blotted out again, and silence reigned once more in the cottage on the lake shore; silence broken only by the death gasps in the dark, and the laboured panting of a wounded man.

Brill heard someone stumbling and floundering in the darkness, and it was from this one that the racking panting was emanating. A circle of light flashed on, and in it Brill saw the blood-smeared face of Jugra Singh.

The light wandered erratically away, dancing crazily about the walls. Brill heard the Sikh blundering across the room, moving like a drunken man, or like one wounded unto death. The flash shone full in the scientist's face, blinding him. Fingers tugged awkwardly at his cords, a knife edge was dragged across them, slicing skin as well as hemp.

Jugra Singh sank to the floor. The flash thumped beside him and went out. Brill groped for him, found his shoulder. The cloth was soaked with what Brill knew was blood.

'You spoke truth, *sahib*,' the Sikh whispered. 'How the call came in the likeness of your voice, I do not know. But I know, now, what slew Reynolds, *sahib*. After all these years . . . but they never forget, though the broad sea lies between. Beware! The fiend may return. The gold – the gold was cursed . . . I told Reynolds, *sahib* . . . had he heeded me, he – '

A sudden welling of blood drowned the labouring voice. Under Brill's hand the great body stiffened and twisted in a brief convulsion, then went limp.

Groping on the floor, the scientist failed to find the flashlight. He groped along the wall, found the switch and flooded the cottage with light.

Turning back into the room, a stifled cry escaped his lips.

Jugra Singh lay slumped near the bed; huddled in a corner was Yut Wuen, his yellow hands, palms upturned, limp on the floor at his sides; Ali sprawled face down in the middle of the room. All three were dead. Throats, breasts and bellies were slashed to ribbons; their garments were in strips, and among the rags hung bloody tatters of flesh. Yut Wuen had been disembowelled, and the gaping wounds of the others were like those of sheep after a mountain lion has ranged through the fold.

A blackjack still stuck in Yut Wuen's belt. Ali's dead hand clutched a knife, but it was unstained. Death had struck them before they could use their weapons. But on the floor near Jugra Singh lay a great curved dagger, and it was red to the hilt. Bloody stains led across the floor and up over the window sill. Brill found the flash, snapped it on, and leaned out the window, playing the white beam on the ground outside. Dark, irregular splotches showed, leading off toward the dense woods.

With the flash in one hand and the Sikh's knife in the other, Brill followed those stains. At the edge of the trees he came upon a track, and the short hairs lifted on his scalp. A foot, planted in a pool of blood, had limned its imprint in crimson on the hard loam. And the foot, bare and splay, was that of a human.

That print upset vague theories of a feline or anthropoid killer, stirred nebulous thoughts at the back of his mind – dim and awful race memories of semi-human ghouls, of werewolves who walked like men and slew like beasts.

A low groan brought him to a halt, his flesh crawling. Under the black trees in the silence, that sound was pregnant with grisly probabilities. Gripping the knife firmly, he flashed the beam ahead of him. The thin light wavered, then focused on a black heap that was not part of the forest.

Brill bent over the figure and stood transfixed, transported back across the years and across the world to another wilder, grimmer woodland.

It was a naked black man that lay at his feet, his glassy eyes reflecting the waning light. His legs were short, bowed and gnarled, his arms long, his shoulders abnormally broad, his shaven head set plump between them without visible neck. That head was hideously malformed; the forehead projected almost into a peek, while the back of the skull was unnaturally flattened. White paint banded face, shoulders and breast. But it was at the creature's fingers which Brill looked longest. At first glance they seemed monstrously deformed. Then he saw that those hands were furnished with long curving steel hooks, sharp-pointed, and keen-edged on the concave side. To each finger one of these barbarous weapons was made fast, and those fingers, like the hooks clotted and smeared with blood, twitched exactly as the talons of a leopard twitch.

A light step brought him round. His dimming light played on a tall figure, and Brill mumbled: 'John Galt!' in no great surprise. He was so numbed by bewilderment that the strangeness of the man's presence did not occur to him.

'What in God's name is this?' demanded the tall explorer, taking the light from Brill's hand and directing it on the mangled shape. 'What in Heaven's name is that?'

'A nightmare from Africa!' Brill found his tongue at last, and speech came in a rush. 'An Egbo! A leopard man! I learned of them when I was on the West Coast. He belongs to a native cult which worships the leopard. They take a male infant and subject his head to pressure, to make it deformed; and he is brought up to believe that the spirit of a leopard inhabits his body. He does the bidding of the cult's head, which mainly consists of executing the enemies of the cult. He is, in effect, a human leopard!'

'What's he doing here?' demanded Galt, in seeming incredulity.

'God knows. But he must have been the thing that killed Reynolds. He killed Reynolds' three servants tonight . . . would have killed me, too, I suppose, but Jugra Singh wounded him, and he evidently dragged himself away like a wild beast to die in the jungle – '

Galt seemed curiously uninterested in Brill's stammering narrative.

'Sure he's dead?' he muttered, bending closer to flash the light into the hideous face. The illumination was dim; the battery was swiftly burning out.

As Brill was about to speak, the painted face was briefly convulsed. The glazed eyes gleamed as with a last surge of life. A clawed hand stirred, lifted feebly up toward Galt. A few gutturals seeped through the blubbery lips; the fingers writhed weakly, slipped from the iron talons, which the man lifted, as if trying to hand them to Galt. Then he shuddered, sank back and lay still. He had been stabbed under the heart, and only a beast-like vitality had carried him so far.

Galt straightened and faced Brill, turning the light on him. A beat of silence cut between them, in which the atmosphere was electric with tension.

'You understand the Ekoi dialect?' It was more an assertion than a question.

Brill's heart was pounding, a new bewilderment vying with a rising wrath. 'Yes,' he answered shortly.

'What did that fool say?' softly asked Galt.

Brill set his teeth and stubbornly took the plunge reason cried out against. 'He said,' he replied between his teeth, ' "Master, take my tools to the tribe, and tell them of our vengeance; they will give you what I promised you." '

Even as he ground out the words, his powerful body crouched, his nerves taut for the grapple. But before he could move, the black muzzle of an automatic trained on his belly.

'Too bad you had to understand that deathbed confession, Brill,' said Galt, coolly. 'I don't want to kill you. I've kept blood off *my* hands so far through this affair. Listen, you're a poor man, like most scientists – how'd you consider cutting in on a fortune? Wouldn't that be preferable to getting a slug through your guts and being planted alongside those yellow-bellied stiffs down in Reynolds's shack for them to get the blame?'

'No man wants to die,' answered Brill, his gaze fixed on the light in Galt's hand – the glow which was rapidly turning redder and dimmer.

'Good!' snapped Galt. 'I'll give you the lowdown. Reynolds got his money in the Kameroons – stole gold from the Ekoi, which they had stored in the ju-ju hut; he killed a priest of the Egbo cult in getting away. Jugra Singh was with him. But they didn't get all the gold. And after that the Ekoi took good care to guard it so nobody could steal what was left.

'I knew this fellow, Guja, when I was in Africa. I was after the Ekoi gold then, but I never had a chance to locate it. I met Guja a few months ago, again. He'd been exiled from his tribe for some crime, had wandered to the Coast and been picked up with some more natives who were brought to America for exhibition in the World's Fair.

'Guja was mad to get back to his people, and he spilled the whole story of the gold. Told me that if he could kill Reynolds, his tribe would forgive him. He knew that Reynolds was somewhere in America, but he was helpless as a child to find him. I offered to arrange his meeting with the gold-thief, if Guja would agree to give me some of the gold his tribe hoarded.

'He swore by the skull of the great leopard. I brought him secretly into these hills, and hid him up yonder in a shack the existence of which nobody suspects. It took me a wretched time to teach him just what he was to do. Night after night I went through the thing with him, until he learned the procedure: to watch in the hills until he saw a light flash in Reynolds' shack. Then steal down there, jerk the switch – and kill. These leopard men can see like cats at night.

'I called Reynolds up myself; it wasn't hard to imitate your voice. I used to do impersonations in vaudeville. While Guja was tearing the life out of Reynolds, I was dining at a well-known night club, in full sight of all.

'I came here tonight to smuggle him out of the country. But his blood-lust must have betrayed him. When he saw the light flash on in the cottage again, it must have started a train of associations that led him once more to the cottage, to kill whoever he found there. I saw the tag-end of the business – saw him stagger away from the shack, and then you follow him.

'Now then, I've shot the works. Nobody knows I'm mixed up in this business, but you. Will you keep your mouth shut and take a share of the Ekoi gold?'

The glow went out. In the sudden darkness, Brill, his pent-up feelings exploding at last, yelled: 'Damn you, no! You murdering dog!' and sprang aside. The pistol cracked, an orange jet sliced the darkness, and the bullet fanned Brill's ear as he threw the heavy knife blindly. He heard it rattle futilely through the bushes, and stood frozen with the realisation that he had lost his desperate gamble.

But even as he braced himself against the tearing impact of the bullet he expected, a sudden beam drilled the blackness, illuminating the convulsed features of John Galt.

'Don't move, Galt; I've got the drop on you.'

It was the voice of Buckley. With a snarl, Galt took as desperate a chance as Brill had taken. He wheeled toward the source of the light, snapping down his automatic. But even as he did so, the detective's .45 crashed, and outlined against the brief glare, Galt swayed and fell like a tall tree struck by lightning.

'Dead?' asked the scientist, mechanically.

'Bullet tore through his forearm and smashed his shoulder,' grunted Buckley. 'Just knocked out temporarily. He'll live to decorate the gallows.'

'You – you heard – ?' Brill stuttered.

'Everything. I was just coming around the bend of the lake shore and saw a light in Reynolds' cottage, then your flash bobbing among the trees. I came sneaking through the bushes just in time to hear you give your translation of the dying words. I've been prowling around this lake all night.'

'You suspected Galt all the time?'

The detective grinned wryly.

'I ought to say yes, and establish myself as a super sleuth. But the fact is, I suspected *you* all the time. That's why I came up here to-night – trying to figure out your connection with the murder. That alibi of yours was so iron-clad it looked phoney to me. I had a sneaking suspicion that I'd bumped into a master-mind trying to put over the "perfect crime". I apologise! I've been reading too many detective stories lately!'

Fangs of Gold

'This is the only trail into the swamp, mister.' Steve Harrison's guide pointed a long finger down the narrow path which wound in and out among the live-oaks and cypresses. Harrison shrugged his massive shoulders. The surroundings were not inviting, with the long shadows of the late afternoon sun reaching dusky fingers into the dim recesses among the moss-hung trees.

'You ought to wait till mornin',' opined the guide, a tall lanky man in cowhide boots and sagging overall. 'It's gittin' late, and we don't want to git catched in the swamp after night.'

'I can't wait, Rogers,' answered the detective. 'The man I'm after might get clean away by morning.'

'He'll have to come out by this path,' answered Rogers as they swung along. 'Ain't no other way in or out. If he tries to push through to high ground on the other side, he'll shore fall into a bottomless bog, or git et by a 'gator. There's lots of them. I reckon he ain't much used to swamps?'

'I don't suppose he ever saw one before. He's city-bred.'

'Then he won't das't leave the beaten path,' confidently predicted Rogers.

'On the other hand, he might, not realising the danger,' grunted Harrison.

'What'd you say he done?' pursued Rogers, directing a jet of tobacco juice at a beetle crawling through the dark loam.

'Knocked an old Chinaman in the head with a meat-cleaver and stole his life-time savings . . . ten thousand dollars, in bills of a thousand each. The old man left a little granddaughter who'll be penniless if this money isn't recovered. That's one reason I want to get this rat before he loses himself in a bog. I want to recover that money, for the kid.'

'And you figure the Chinaman seen goin' down this path a few days ago was him?'

'Couldn't be anybody else,' snapped Harrison. 'We've hounded him half way across the continent, cut him off from the borders and the ports. We were closing in on him when he slipped through, somehow. This was about the only place left for him to hide. I've chased him too far to delay now. If he drowns in the swamp, we'll probably never find him, and the money will be lost, too. The man he murdered was a fine, honest old Chinaman. This fellow, Woon Shang, is bad all the way through.'

'He'll run into some bad folks down here,' ruminated Rogers. 'These came here fifty or sixty years back – refugees from Haiti, or somewhere. You know we ain't far from the coast. They keep to theirselves, and they don't like strangers. *What's that*?'

They were just rounding a bend in the path, and something lay on the ground ahead of them – something black, and dabbled with red, that groaned and moved feebly.

'He's been knifed,' exclaimed Rogers.

It took no expert to deduce that. They bent over him and Rogers voiced profane recognition. 'Why, I know this feller! He ain't no swamp rat. He's Joe Corley. Joe! Joe Corley!'

The wounded man groaned and rolled up his glassy eyes; his skin was ashy with the nearness of approaching death.

'Who stabbed you, Joe?' demanded Rogers.

'De Swamp Cat!' The gasp was scarcely audible. Rogers swore and looked fearfully about him, as if expecting something to spring on them from the trees. 'I wuz tryin' to git outside.'

'What for?' demanded Rogers. 'Didn't you know you'd git jailed if they catched you?'

'Ruther go to de jail-house dan git mixed up . . . in de devilment . . . dey's cookin' up . . . in de swamp.' The voice sank lower as speech grew more difficult.

'What you mean, Joe?' uneasily demanded Rogers.

'Voodoo,' muttered Corley. 'Took dat Chinaman 'stead uh me . . . didn't want me to git away, though . . . then John Bartholomew – uuuugh!'

A trickle of blood started from the corner of his thick lips, he stiffened in brief convulsion and then lay still.

'He's dead!' whispered Rogers, staring down the swamp path with dilated eyes.

'He spoke of a Chinaman,' said Harrison. 'That clinches it that we're on the right trail. Have to leave him here for the time being. Nothing we can do for him now. Let's get going.'

'You aim to go on, after this?' exclaimed Rogers.

'Why not?'

'Mr Harrison,' said Rogers solemnly, 'you offered me a good wage to guide you into this here swamp. But I'm tellin' you fair there ain't enough money to make me go in there now, with night comin' on.'

'But why?' protested Harrison. 'Just because this man got into a fight – '

'It's more 'n just that,' declared Rogers decisively. 'He knowed he'd git jailed on the outside, but he was goin' anyway; that means somethin' had scared the livin' daylights out of him. You heard him say it was the Swamp Cat that got him?'

'Well?'

'Well, the Swamp Cat lives in the swamp. It's been so long since any folks claimed they seen him, I'd begun to believe he was just a myth told to scare people away from the swamp. But this shows he ain't. He killed Joe Corley. He'll kill us if he catches us in the dark. Why, by golly, he may be watchin' us right now!' This thought so disturbed Rogers that he drew a big six-shooter with an enormous length of barrel, and peered about, masticating his quid with a rapidity that showed his mental perturbation.

'Who's the other follow he named, John Bartholomew?' inquired Harrison.

'Don't know. Never heard of him. Come on, let's shove out of here. We'll git some boys and come back after Joe's body.'

'I'm going on,' growled Harrison, rising and dusting his hands.

Rogers stared. 'Man, you're plumb crazy! You'll git lost – '

'Not if I keep to the path.'

'Well, then, the Swamp Cat'll git you, or them 'gators will – '

'I'll take my chance,' answered Harrison brusque ly. 'Woon Shang's somewhere in this swamp. If he manages to get out before I get my hands on him, he may get clean away. I'm going after him.'

'But if you'll wait we'll raise a posse and go after him first thing in the mornin',' urged Rogers.

Harrison did not attempt to explain to the man his almost obsessional preference for working alone. With no further comment he turned and strode off down the narrow path. Rogers yelled after him: 'You're crazy as Hell! If you git as far as Celia Pompoloi's hut, you better stay there tonight! She's the big boss. It's the first cabin you come to. I'm goin' back to town and git a posse, and tomorrow mornin' we'll . . . ' The words became unintelligible among the dense growth as Harrison rounded a turn that shut off the sight of the other man.

As the detective strode along he saw that blood was smeared on the rotting leaves, and there were marks as if something heavy had been dragged over the trail. Joe Corley had obviously crawled for some distance after being attacked. Harrison visualised him dragging himself along on his belly like a crippled snake. The man must have had intense vitality to have gotten so far with a mortal wound in his back. And his fear must have been desperate to so drive him.

Harrison could no longer see the sun, but he knew it was hanging low. The shadows were gathering, and he was plunging deeper and deeper into the swamp. He began to glimpse patches of scummy ooze among the trees, and the path grew more tortuous as it wound to avoid these slimy puddles. Harrison plunged on without pausing. The dense growth might lend concealment to a desperate fugitive, but it was not in the woods, but among the scattered cabins of the swamp dwellers that he expected to find the man he hunted. The city-bred Chinaman, fearful of solitude and unable to fend for himself, would seek the company of men.

The detective wheeled suddenly. About him, in the dusk, the swamp was waking. Insects lifted strident voices, wings of bats or owls beat the air, and bullfrogs boomed from the lily pads. But he had heard a sound that was not of these things. It was a stealthy movement among the trees that marched in solid ranks beside the trail. Harrison drew his .45 and waited. Nothing happened. But in primitive solitudes a man's instincts are whetted. The detective felt that he was being watched by unseen eyes; he could almost sense the intensity of their glare. Was it the Chinaman, after all?

A bush beside the trail moved, without a wind to stir it. Harrison sprang through the curtain of creeper-hung cypresses, gun ready, snarling a command. His feet sank in slimy ooze, he stumbled in rotting vegetation and felt the dangling strands of moss slap against his face. There was nothing behind the bush, but he could have sworn that he saw a shadowy form move and vanish among the trees a short distance away. As he hesitated, he glanced down and saw a distinct mark in the loam. He bent closer; it was the print of a great, bare, splay foot. Moisture was oozing into the depression. A man *had* been standing behind that bush.

With a shrug Harrison stepped back into the trail. That was not the footprint of Woon Shang, and the detective was not looking for anybody else. It was natural that one of the swamp dwellers would spy on a stranger. The detective sent a hail into the gathering darkness, to assure the unseen watcher of his friendly intentions.

There was no reply. Harrison turned and strode on down the trail, not feeling entirely at ease, as he heard, from time to time, a faint snapping of twigs and other sounds that seemed to indicate some-one moving along a course paralleling the path. It was not soothing to know that he was being followed by some unseen and possibly hostile being.

It was so dark now that he kept the path more by feel than by sight. About him sounded weird cries of strange birds or animals, and from time to time a deep grunting reverberation that puzzled him until he recognised it as the bellow of a bull alligator. He wondered if the scaly brutes ever crawled up on the trail, and how the fellow that was shadowing him out there in the darkness managed to avoid them. With the thought another twig snapped, much closer to the trail than before. Harrison swore softly, trying to peer into the Stygian gloom under the moss-festooned branches. The fellow was closing in on him with the growing darkness.

There was a sinister implication about the thing that made Harri-son's flesh creep a bit. This reptile-haunted swamp-trail was no place for a fight . . . for it seemed probable that the unknown stalker was the killer of Joe Corley. Harrison was meditating on the matter when a light glimmered through the trees ahead of him. Quickening his steps he came abruptly out of the darkness into a grey twilight.

He had reached an expanse of solid ground, where the thinning trees let in the last grey light of the outer dusk. They made a black wall with waving fringes all about a small clearing, and through their boles, on one side, Harrison caught a glimmer of inky water. In the clearing stood a cabin of rough-hewn logs, and through a tiny win-dow shone the light of an oil lamp.

As Harrison emerged from among the growth he glanced back, but saw no movement among the ferns, heard no sound of pursuit. The path, dimly marked on the higher ground, ran past the cabin and vanished in the further gloom. This cabin must be the abode of that Celia Pompoloi Rogers had mentioned. Harrison strode to the sagging stoop and rapped on the handmade door.

Inside there was movement, and the door swung open. Harrison was not prepared for the figure that confronted him. He had ex-pected to see a bare-footed slattern; instead he saw a tall, rangily powerful man, neatly dressed, whose regular features and light skin portrayed his mixed blood.

'Good evening, sir.' The accent hinted of education above the average.

'Name's Harrison,' said the detective abruptly, displaying his badge. 'I'm after a crook that ran in here — a Chinese murderer, named Woon Shang. Know anything about him?'

'Yes, sir,' the man replied promptly. 'That man went past my cabin three days ago.'

'Where is he now?' demanded Harrison.

The other spread his hands in a curiously Latin gesture.

'I can not say. I have little intercourse with the other people who live in the swamp, but it is my belief that he is hiding among them somewhere. I have not seen him pass my cabin going back up the path.'

'Can you guide me to these other cabins?'

'Gladly, sir; by daylight.'

'I'd like to go tonight,' growled Harrison.

'That's impossible, sir,' the other protested. 'It would be most dangerous. You ran a great risk in coming this far alone. The other cabins are further back in the swamp. We do not leave our huts at night; there are many things in the swamp which are dangerous to human beings.'

'The Swamp Cat, for instance?' grunted Harrison.

The man cast him a quick glance of interrogation.

'He killed a man named Joe Corley a few hours ago,' said the detective. 'I found Corley on the trail. And if I'm not mistaken, that same lunatic has been following me for the past half hour.'

The mulatto evinced considerable disquiet and glanced across the clearing into the shadows.

'Come in,' he urged. 'If the Swamp Cat is prowling tonight, no man is safe out of doors. Come in and spend the night with me, and at dawn I will guide you to all the cabins in the swamp.'

Harrison saw no better plan. After all, it was absurd to go blundering about in the night, in an unknown marsh. He realised that he had made a mistake in coming in by himself, in the dusk; but working alone had become a habit with him, and he was tinged with a strong leaven of recklessness. Following a tip he had arrived at the little town on the edge of the swamplands in the mid-afternoon, and plunged on into the woods without hesitation. Now he doubted the wisdom of the move.

'Is this Celia Pompoloi's cabin?' he asked.

'It was,' the mulatto replied. 'She has been dead for three weeks. I live here alone. My name is John Bartholomew.'

Harrison's head snapped up and he eyed the other with new

interest. John Bartholomew; Joe Corley had muttered that name just before he died.

'Did you know Joe Corley?' he demanded.

'Slightly; he came into the swamp to hide from the law. He was a rather low-grade sort of human, though naturally I am sorry to hear of his death.'

'What's a man of your intelligence and education doing in this jungle?' the detective asked bluntly.

Bartholomew smiled rather wryly. 'We can not always choose our environments, Mr Harrison. The waste places of the world provide retreat for others than criminals. Some come to the swamps like your Chinaman, fleeing from the law. Others come to forget bitter disappointments forced upon them by circumstances.'

Harrison glanced about the cabin while Bartholomew was putting a stout bar in place across the door. It had but two rooms, one behind the other, connected by a strongly built door. The slab floor was clean, the room scantily furnished; a table, benches, a bunk built against the wall, all hand-made. There was a fireplace, over which hung primitive cooking utensils, and a cloth-covered cupboard.

'Would you like some fried bacon and corn pone?' asked Bartholomew. 'Or perhaps a cup of coffee? I do not have much to offer you, but – '

'No, thanks, I ate a big meal just before I started into the swamp. Just tell me something about these people.'

'As I said, I have little intercourse with them,' answered Bartholomew. 'They are clannish and suspicious, and keep much to themselves. Their fathers came here from Haiti, following one of the bloody revolutions which have cursed that unfortunate island in the past. They have curious customs. Have you heard of the worship of Voodoo?'

Harrison nodded.

'These people are Voodooists. I know that they have mysterious conclaves back in the swamps. I have heard drums booming in the night, and seen the glow of fires through the trees. I have sometimes felt a little uneasy for my safety at such times. Such people are capable of bloody extremes, when their primitive natures are maddened by the bestial rites of the Voodoo. No one ever comes here unless he is a fugitive from the law. The swamp people carry on their worship without interference.

'Celia Pompoloi, who once occupied this very hut, was a woman of considerable intelligence and some education; she was the one swamp dweller who ever went "outside", as they call the outer world, and attended school. Yet, to my actual knowledge, she was the priestess of the cult and presided over their rituals. It is my belief that she met her fate at last during one of those saturnalias. Her body was found in the marshes, so badly mangled by the alligators that it was recognisable only by her garments.'

'What about the Swamp Cat?' asked Harrison.

'A maniac, living like a wild beast in the marshes, only sporadically violent; but at those times a thing of horror.'

'Would he kill the Chinaman if he had a chance?'

'He would kill anyone when his fit is on him. You said the Chinaman was a murderer?'

'Murderer and thief,' grunted Harrison. 'Stole ten grand from the man he killed.'

Bartholomew looked up as with renewed interest, started to speak, then evidently changed his mind.

Harrison rose, yawning. 'Think I'll hit the hay,' he announced.

Bartholomew took up the lamp and led his guest into the back room, which was of the same size as the other, but whose furnishings consisted only of a bunk and a bench.

'I have but the one lamp, sir,' said Bartholomew. 'I shall leave it with you.'

'Don't bother,' grunted Harrison, having a secret distrust of oil lamps, resultant from experiencing an explosion of one in his boyhood. 'I'm like a cat in the dark. I don't need it.'

With many apologies for the rough accommodations and wishes for a good night's sleep, Bartholomew bowed himself out, and the door closed. Harrison, through force of habit, studied the room. A little starlight came in through the one small window, which he noticed was furnished with heavy wooden bars. There was no door other than the one by which he had entered. He lay down on the bunk fully dressed, without even removing his shoes, and pondered rather glumly. He was beset by fears that Woon Shang might escape him, after all. Suppose the Chinaman slipped out by the way he had come in? True, local officers were watching at the edge of the swampland, but Woon Shang might avoid them in the night. And what if there *was* another way out, known only to the swamp people? And if Bartholomew was as little acquainted with his neighbours as he said, what assurance was there that the mulatto would be able to guide him to the Chinaman's hiding place? These and other doubts assailed him while he lay and listened to the soft sounds of his host's retiring, and saw the thin line of light under the door vanish as the lamp was blown out. At last Harrison consigned his doubts to the devil, and fell asleep.

Chapter 2. *Murder tracks*

It was a noise at the windows, a stealthy twisting and wrenching at the bars, that awakened him. He woke quickly, with all his faculties alert, as was his habit. Something bulked in the window, something dark and round, with gleaming spots in it. He realised with a start that it was a human head he saw, with the faint starlight shining on rolling eyes and bared teeth. Without shifting his body, the detective stealthily reached for his gun; lying as he was in the darkness of the bunk, the man watching him could scarcely have seen the movement. But the head vanished, as if warned by some instinct.

Harrison sat up on his bunk, scowling, resisting the natural impulse to rush to the window and look out. That might be exactly what the man outside was wanting. There was something deadly about this business; the fellow had evidently been trying to get in. Was it the same creature that had followed him through the swamp? A sudden thought struck him. What was more likely than that the Chinaman had set a man to watch for a possible pursuer? Harrison cursed himself for not having thought of it before.

He struck a match, cupped it in his hand, and looked at his watch. It was scarcely ten o'clock. The night was still young. He scowled abstractedly at the rough wall behind the bunk, minutely illuminated in the flare of the match, and suddenly his breath hissed between his teeth. The match burned down to his fingers and went out. He struck another and leaned to the wall. Thrust in a chink between the logs was a knife, and its wicked curved blade was grimly smeared and clotted. The implication sent a shiver down Harrison's spine. The blood might be that of an animal . . . but who would butcher a calf or a hog in that room? Why had not the blade been cleansed? It was as if it had been hastily concealed, after striking a murderous blow.

He took it down and looked at it closely. The blood was dried and blackened as if at least many hours had elapsed since it had been let. The weapon was no ordinary butcher's knife . . . Harrison stiffened. *It was a Chinese dagger*. The match went out and Harrison did what the average man would have done. He leaned over the edge of the bunk, the only thing in the room that would conceal an object of any size, and lifted the cloth that hung to the floor. He did not actually expect to find the corpse of Woon Shang beneath it. He merely acted through instinct. Nor did he find a corpse. His hand, groping in the dark, encountered only the uneven floor and rough logs; then his fingers felt something else . . . something at once compact and yielding, wedged between the logs as the knife had been.

He drew it forth; it felt like a flat package of crisp paper, bound with oiled silk. Cupping a match in his hand, he tore it open. Ten worn bills met his gaze; on each bill was the numerals of $1,000. He crushed the match out and sat in the dark, mental pictures tumbling rapidly across his consciousness.

So John Bartholomew had lied. Doubtless he had taken in the Chinaman as he had taken in Harrison. The detective visualised a dim form bending in the darkness above a sleeping figure in that same bunk . . . a murderous stroke with the victim's own knife.

He growled inarticulately, with the chagrin of the cheated man-hunter, certain that Woon Shang's body was rotting in some slimy marsh. At least he had the money. Careless of Bartholomew to hide it there. But was it? It was only by an accidental chain of circumstances that he had found it . . .

He stiffened again. Under the door he saw a thin pencil of light. Had Bartholomew not yet gone to bed? But he remembered the blowing out of the lamp. Harrison rose and glided noiselessly to the thick door. When he reached it he heard a low mumble of voices in the outer room. The speakers moved nearer, stood directly before the door. He strained his ears and recognised the crisp accents of John Bartholomew. 'Don't bungle the job,' the mulatto was mutter-ing. 'Get him before he has a chance to use his gun. He doesn't suspect anything. I just remember that I left the Chinaman's knife in the crack over the bunk. But the detective will never see it, in the dark. He had to come butting in here, this particular night. We can't let him see what he'd see if he lived through this night.'

'We do de job quick and clean, mastah,' murmured another voice, with a guttural accent different from any Harrison had ever heard, and impossible to reproduce.

'All right; we haven't anything to fear from Joe Corley. The Swamp Cat carried out my instructions.'

'Dat Swamp Cat prowlin' 'round outside right now,' muttered another man. 'Ah don't like him. Why can't he do dis job?'

'He obeys my orders, but he can't be trusted too far. But we can't stand here talking like this. The detective will wake up and get suspicious. Throw open that door and rush him. Knife him in his bunk . . .'

Harrison always believed that the best defence was a strong offensive. There was but one way out of this jam. He took it without hesitation. He hurled a massive shoulder against the door, knocking it open, and sprang into the outer room, gun levelled, and barked: 'Hands up, damn you!'

There were five men in that room: Bartholomew, holding the lamp and shading it with his left hand, and four others, four lean, rangy giants in nondescript garments, with sinister features. Each man of the four had a knife in his hand.

They recoiled with yells of dismay as Harrison crashed upon them. Automatically their hands went up and their knives clattered on the floor.

'Back up against that wall!' snapped Harrison.

They obeyed dumbly, rendered incapable of action by the shock of surprise. Harrison knew that it was John Bartholomew, more than these hulking butchers, that he had to fear.

'Set that lamp on the table,' he snapped. 'Line up there with them – ha!'

Bartholomew had stooped to lower the lamp to the table . . . then quick as a cat he threw it crashing to the floor, ducking behind the table with the same motion. Harrison's gun crashed almost simultaneously, but even in the bedlam darkness that followed, the detective knew he had missed. Whirling, he leaped through the outer door. Inside the dark cabin he would have no chance against the knives. As Harrison raced across the clearing he heard Bartholomew's furious voice yelling commands. He rounded the cabin and darted toward the trees on the other side. He had no intention of fleeing until he was run down from behind. He was seeking a place where he could turn at bay and shoot it out with a little advantage on his side. The moon was just coming up above the trees, emphasising rather than illuminating the shadows.

He reached the shadows before they rounded the hut, and glancing back through the bushes, saw them running about the clearing like hunting dogs seek a spoor, howling in primitive blood-lust and disappointment. The growing moonlight glittered on the long knives in their hands.

He drew back further among the trees, finding the ground more solid underfoot than he had expected. Then he came suddenly upon the marshy edge of a stretch of black water. Something grunted and thrashed amidst it, and two green lamps burned suddenly like jewels on the inky water. He recoiled, well knowing what those twin lights were. And as he did so, he bumped full into something that locked fierce arms like an ape about him.

Harrison ducked and heaved, bowing his powerful back like a great cat, and his assailant tumbled over his head and thumped on the ground, still clutching the detective's coat with the grip of a vice. Harrison lunged backward, ripping the garment down the back, wrenching his arms from the sleeves, in his frenzy to free himself.

The man leaped to his feet on the edge of the pool, snarling like a wild beast. Harrison saw a gaunt half naked man with wild strands of hair caked with mud hanging over a contorted mask of a face, the thick loose lips drooling foam. This indeed, he knew, was the dread Swamp Cat.

Still grasping Harrison's torn coat brainlessly in his left hand, his right swept up with a sheen of sharp steel, and even as he sensed the madman's intention, the detective ducked and fired from the hip. The thrown knife hummed by his ear, and with the crash of the shot the Swamp Cat swayed and pitched backward into the black pool. There was a threshing rush, the waters stormed foamily, there was a glimpse of a blunted, reptilian snout, and the trailing body vanished with it.

Harrison stepped back, sickened, and heard behind him the shouting progress of men through the bushes. His hunters had heard the shot. He drew back into the shadows among a cluster of gum trees, and waited, gun in hand. An instant later they rushed out upon the bank of the pool, John Bartholomew and his dusky knife-fighters.

They ranged the bank, gaping, and then Bartholomew laughed and pointed to a blood-stained piece of cloth that floated soggily on the foam-flecked waters.

'The fool's coat! He must have run right into the pool, and the 'gators got him! I can see them tearing at something, over there among the reeds. Hear those bones crack?' Bartholomew's laugh was fiendish to hear.

'Well,' said the mulatto, 'we don't have to worry about him. If they send anybody in after him, we'll just tell them the truth: that he fell into the water and got grabbed by the 'gators, just like Celia Pompoloi.'

'She wuz a awful sight when us foun' huh body,' muttered one of the swamp Negroes.

'We'll never find that much of him,' prophesied Bartholomew.

'Did he say what de Chinaman done?' asked another of the men.

'Just what the Chinaman said; that he'd murdered a man.'

'Wish he'd uh robbed uh bank,' murmured the swamp dweller plaintively. 'Wish he'd uh brung uh lot uh money in wid him.'

'Well, he didn't,' snapped Bartholomew. 'You saw me search him. Now get back to the others and help them watch him. More men may come looking for him tomorrow, but if they do, they're welcome to all of him they can find!' He laughed with sinister meaning, and then added abruptly: 'Hurry and get out of here. I want to be alone. There are spirits to be communed with before the hour arrives, and dread rites that I must perform alone. Go!'

The others bent their heads in a curious gesture of subservience, and trooped away, in the direction of the clearing. He followed leisurely.

Harrison glared after them, turning what he had heard over in his mind. Some of it was gibberish, but certain things were clear. For one thing, the Chinaman was obviously alive, and imprisoned somewhere. Bartholomew had lied about his own relations with the swamp people; one of them he certainly was not, but he was just as certainly a leader among them. Yet he had lied to them about the money. Harrison remembered the mulatto's expression when he had mentioned it to him. The detective believed that Bartholomew had never seen the money; that Woon Shang, suspicious, had hidden it himself before he was attacked.

As long as they believed him dead, he could conduct his investigations without being harried by pursuit. His shirt was of dark material and did not show in the darkness, and the big detective was trained in stealth by adventures in the haunted dives of Oriental quarters where unseen eyes always watched and ears were forever alert.

When he came to the edge of the trees, he saw the four giants trooping down the trail that led deeper into the swamp. They walked in single file, their heads bent forward, stooping from the waist. Bartholomew was just going into the cabin. Harrison started to follow the disappearing forms, then hesitated. Bartholomew was in his power. He could steal up on the cabin, throw his gun on the mulatto and make him tell where Woon Shang was imprisoned – maybe. Even as he ruminated, Bartholomew came out of the cabin and stood peering about with a strange furtiveness. He held a heavy whip in his hand. Presently he glided across the clearing toward the quarter where the detective crouched. He passed within a few yards of Harrison's covert, and the moonlight illumined his features.

Harrison was astounded at the change in his face, at the sinister vitality and evil strength reflected there.

Harrison altered his plans and stole after him, wishing to know on what errand the man went with such secrecy. It was not difficult. Bartholomew looked neither back nor sideways, but wound a tortuous way among inky pools and clusters of rotting vegetation that looked poisonous, even in the moonlight. Presently the detective crouched low; ahead of the mulatto there was a tiny hut, almost hidden among the trees which trailed Spanish moss over it like a grey veil. Bartholomew looked carefully about him, then drew forth a key and manipulated a large padlock on the door. Harrison was convinced that he had been led to the prison of Woon Shang.

Bartholomew disappeared inside, closing the door. A light gleamed through the chinks of the logs. Then came a mumble of voices, too indistinct for Harrison to tell anything about them; that was followed by the sharp, unmistakable crack of a whip on bare flesh, and a shrill cry of pain. Enlightenment came to Harrison. Bartholomew had come secretly to his prisoner – and for what reason but to make him divulge the hiding-place of the money, of which Harrison had spoken? Obviously Bartholomew had no intentions of sharing that money with his mates.

Harrison began to work his way stealthily toward the cabin, fully intending to burst in and put a stop to that lashing. He would cheerfully have shot down Woon Shang himself, had the occasion arisen, but before he reached the hut, the sounds ceased, the light went out and Bartholomew emerged, wiping the perspiration of exertion from his brow. He locked the door, thrust the key in his pocket, and turned away through the trees, trailing his whip in his hand. Harrison, crouching in the shadows, let him go. It was Woon Shang he was after. Bartholomew could be dealt with later.

When the mulatto had disappeared, Harrison rose and strode to the door of the hut. The absence of guards was rather puzzling, after the conversation he had overheard, but be wasted no time on conjecture. The door was secured by a chain made fast to a big hasp driven deep into a log. He thrust his gun barrel through this hasp, and using it as a lever, pried out the hasp with no great difficulty.

Pulling open the door he peered in; it was too dark to see, but be heard somebody's breath coming in jerky hysterical sobs. He struck a match, looked . . . then glared. The prisoner was there, crouching on the dirt floor. But it was not Woon Shang. It was a woman.

She was a mulatto, young, and handsome in her way. She was clad only in a ragged and scanty chemise, and her hands were bound behind her. From her wrists a long strand of rawhide ran to a heavy staple in the wall. She stared wildly at Harrison, her dark eyes reflecting both hope and terror. There were tear stains on her cheeks.

'Who the devil are you?' demanded the detective.

'Celia Pompoloi!' Her voice was rich and musical despite its hysteria. 'Oh, for God's sake let me go! I can't stand it any more. I'll die; I know I will!'

'I thought you *were* dead,' he grunted.

'John Bartholomew did it!' she exclaimed. 'He persuaded a girl from "outside" into the swamp, and then he killed her and dressed her in my clothes, and threw her into the marsh where the alligators would chew the body till nobody could tell it wasn't me. The people found it and thought it was Celia Pompoloi. He's kept me here for three weeks and tortured me every night.'

'Why?' Harrison found and lighted a candle stump stuck on the wall. Then he stooped and cut the rawhide thongs that bound her hands. She climbed to her feet, chafing her bruised and swollen wrists. In her scanty garb the brutality of the floggings she had received was quite apparent.

'He's a devil!' Her dark eyes flashed murderously; whatever her wrongs, she obviously was no meek sufferer. 'He came here posing as a priest of the Great Serpent. He said he was from Haiti, the lying dog. He's from Santo Domingo, and no more priest than you are. *I* am the proper priestess of the Serpent, and the people obeyed me. That's why he put me out of the way. I'll kill him!'

'But why did he lick you?' asked Harrison.

'Because I wouldn't tell him what he wanted to know,' she muttered sullenly, bending her head and twisting one bare foot behind the other ankle, school-girl fashion. She did not seem to think of refusing to answer his questions.

'He came here to steal the jewel, the Heart of the Great Serpent, which we brought with us from Haiti, long ago. He is no priest. He is an impostor. He proposed that I give the Heart to him and run away from my people with him. When I refused, he tied me in this old hut where none can hear my screams; the swamp people shun it, thinking it's haunted. He said he'd keep beating me until I told him where the Heart was hidden, but I wouldn't tell him – not though he stripped all the flesh from my bones. I alone know that secret, because I am a priestess of the Serpent, and the guardian of its Heart.'

This was Voodoo stuff with a vengeance; her matter-of-fact manner evinced an unshaken belief in her weird cult.

'Do you know anything about Woon Shang?' he demanded.

'John Bartholomew told me of him in his boastings. He came running from the law and Bartholomew promised to hide him. Then he summoned the swamp men, and they seized the Chinaman, though he wounded one of them badly with his knife. They made a prisoner of him . . .'

'Why?'

Celia was in that vengeful mood in which a woman recklessly tells everything, and repeats things she would not otherwise mention.

'Bartholomew came saying he was a priest of old time. That's how he caught the fancy of the people. He promised them an *old* sacrifice, of which there has not been one for thirty years. We have offered the white cock and the red cock to the Great Serpent. But Bartholomew promised them the *goat-without-horns*. He did that to get the Heart into his hands, for only then is it taken from its secret hiding place. He thought to get it into his hands and run away before the sacrifice was made. But when I refused to aid him, it upset his plans. Now he can not get the Heart, but he must go through with the sacrifice anyway. The people are becoming impatient. If he fails them, they will kill him.

'He first chose the "outside" man, Joe Corley, who was hiding in the swamp, for the sacrifice; but when the Chinaman came, Bartholomew decided he would make a better offering. Bartholomew told me tonight that the Chinaman had money, and he was going to make him tell where he hid it, so he would have the money, and the Heart, too, when I finally gave in and told him . . .'

'Wait a minute,' interposed Harrison. 'Let me get this straight. What is it that Bartholomew intends doing with Woon Shang?'

'He will offer him up to the Great Serpent,' she answered, making a conventional gesture of conciliation and adoration as she spoke the dread name.

'A *human* sacrifice?'

'Yes.'

'Well, I'll be damned!' he muttered. 'If I hadn't been raised in the South myself, I'd never believe it. When is this sacrifice to take place?'

'Tonight!'

'Eh, what's that?' He remembered Bartholomew's cryptic instructions to his henchmen. 'The devil! Where does it happen, and what time?'

'Just before dawn; far back in the swamp.'

'I've got to find Woon Shang and stop it!' he exclaimed. 'Where is he imprisoned?'

'At the place of the sacrifice; many men guard him. You'd never find your way there. You'd drown and get eaten by the 'gators. Besides, if you did get there, the people would tear you to pieces.'

'You lead me there and I'll take care of the people,' he snarled. 'You want revenge on Bartholomew. All right; guide me there and I'll see that you get plenty. I've always worked alone,' he ruminated angrily, 'but the swamp country isn't River Street.'

'I'll do it!' Her eyes blazed and her white teeth gleamed in a mask of passion. 'I'll guide you to the place of the Altar. We'll kill him, the dog!'

'How long will it take us to get there?'

'I could go there in an hour, alone. Guiding you, it will take longer. Much longer, the way we must go. You can't travel the road I would take, alone.'

'I can follow you anywhere you walk,' he grunted, slightly nettled. He glanced at his watch, then extinguished the candle. 'Let's get going. Take the shortest route and don't worry about me. I'll keep up.'

She caught his wrist in a fierce grasp and almost jerked him out of the door, quivering with the eagerness of a hunting hound.

'Wait a minute!' A thought struck him. 'If I go back to the cabin and capture Bartholomew – '

'He will not be there; he is well on his way to the Place of the Altar; better that we beat him there.'

Chapter 3. *Voodoo Lair*

As long as he lived Harrison remembered that race through the swamp, as he followed Celia Pompoloi along pathless ways that seemed impossible. Mire caught at his feet, and sometimes black scummy water lapped about his ankles, but Celia's swift sure feet always found solid ground where none seemed possible, or guided him over bogs that quaked menacingly beneath their weight. She sprang lightly from hummock to hummock, or slid between snaky pools of black slime where unseen monsters grunted and wallowed. Harrison floundered after her, sweating, half nauseated with the miasmic reek of the oozy slime that plastered him; but all the bulldog was roused in him, and he was ready to wade through swamps for a week if the man he hunted was at the other end of the loathsome journey. Dank misty clouds had veiled the sky, through which the moon shone fitfully, and Harrison stumbled like a blind man, depending entirely on his guide, whose dusky half-naked body was all but invisible to him at times in the darkness.

Ahead of them he began to hear a rhythmic throbbing, a barbaric pulsing that grew as they advanced. A red glow flickered through the black trees.

'The flames of the sacrifice!' gasped Celia, quickening her pace. 'Hasten!'

Somewhere in his big, weary body Harrison found enough reserve energy to keep up with her. She seemed to run lightly over bogs that engulfed him to the knees. She possessed the swamp dweller's instinct for safe footing. Ahead of them Harrison saw the shine of something that was not mud, and Celia halted at the verge of a stretch of noisome water.

'The Place of the Altar is surrounded by water on all sides but one,' she hissed. 'We are in the very heart of the swamp, deeper than anyone ever goes except on such occasions as these. There are no cabins near. Follow me! I have a bridge none knows of except myself.'

At a point where the sluggish stream narrowed to some fifty feet, a fallen tree spanned it. Celia ran out upon it, balancing herself upright. She swayed across, a slim ghostly figure in the cloudy light. Harrison straddled the log and hitched himself ignominiously along.

He was too weary to trust *his* equilibrium. His feet dangled a foot or so above the black surface, and Celia, waiting impatiently on the further bank as she peered anxiously at the distant glow, cast him a look over her shoulder and cried a sudden urgent warning.

Harrison jerked up his legs just as something bulky and grisly heaved up out of the water with a great splash and an appalling clash of mighty fangs. Harrison fairly flung himself over the last few feet and landed on the further bank in a more demoralised condition than he would have admitted. A criminal in a dark room with a knife was less nerve-shaking than these ghoulish slayers of the dark waters.

The ground was firmer; they were, as Celia said, on a sort of island in the heart of the marshes. The girl threaded her supple way among the cypresses, panting with the intensity of her emotions. Perspiration soaked her; the hand that held Harrison's wrist was wet and slippery.

A few minutes later, when the glow in the trees had grown to an illuminating glare, she halted and slipped to the damp mould, drawing her companion with her. They looked out upon a scene incredible in its primitive starkness.

There was a clearing, free of underbrush, circled by a black wall of cypress. From its outer edge a sort of natural causeway wandered away into the gloom, and over that low ridge ran a trail, beaten by many feet. The trail ended in the clearing, the ultimate end of the path that Harrison had followed into the swamp. On the other side of the clearing there was a glimpse of dusky water, reflecting the firelight.

In a wide horseshoe formation, their backs to the causeway, sat some fifty men, women and children, resembling Celia Pompoloi in complexion. Harrison had not supposed that so many people inhabited the swamp. Their gaze was fixed on an object in the centre of the opening of the human horseshoe. This was a great block of dark wood that had an unfamiliar appearance, as of an altar, brought from afar. There was an intolerable suggestion about that block, and the misshapen, leering figure that rose behind it – a fantastically carven idol, to whose bestial features the flickering firelight lent life and mobility. Harrison intuitively knew that this monstrosity was never carved in America. The people had brought it with them from Haiti, and surely their ancestors had brought it originally from Africa. There was an aura of the Congo about it, the reek of black squalling jungles, and squirming faceless shapes of a night more primeval than this. Harrison was not superstitious, but he felt gooseflesh rise on his limbs. At the back of his consciousness dim racial memories stirred, conjuring up unstable and monstrous images from the dim mists of the primitive, when men worshipped such gods as these.

Before the idol, near the block, sat an old crone, striking a bowl tom-tom with quick staccato strokes of her open hands; it growled and rumbled and muttered. Their voices were low, but they hummed with a note of hysteria.

Harrison looked in vain for John Bartholomew and Woon Shang. He reached out a hand to get his companion's attention. She did not heed him. Her supple figure was tense and quivering as a taut wire under his hand. A sudden change in the chanting, a wild wolfish baying, brought him about again.

Out of the shadows of the trees behind the idol strode John Bartholomew. He was clad only in a loincloth, and it was as if he had doffed his civilised culture with his clothing. His facial expression, his whole bearing, were changed; he was like an image of barbarism incarnate. Harrison stared at the knotted biceps, the ridged body muscles which the firelight displayed. But something else gripped his whole attention. With John Bartholomew came another, unwillingly, at the sight of whom the crowd gave tongue to another bestial yell.

About Bartholomew's mighty left hand was twisted the pigtail of Woon Shang, whom he dragged after him like a fowl to the chopping block. The Chinaman was stark naked, his yellow body gleaming like old ivory in the fire. His hands were bound behind his back, and he was like a child in the grasp of his executioner. Woon Shang was not a large man; beside the great mulatto he seemed slimmer than ever. His hysterical panting came plainly to Harrison in the silence that fell tensely as the shouting ceased. His straining feet tore at the sod as he struggled against the inexorable advance of his captor. In Bartholomew's right hand shone a great razor-edged crescent of steel. The watchers sucked in their breath loudly; in a single stride they had returned to the jungle whence they had crawled; they were mad for the bloody saturnalia their ancestors had known.

In Bartholomew's face Harrison read stark horror and mad determination. He sensed that the mulatto was not enjoying this ghastly primordial drama into which be had been trapped. He also realised that the man must go through with it, and that he would go through with it. It was more than the jewel heart of the serpent-god for which Bartholomew strove now; it was the continued dominance of these wolfish devil-worshippers on which his life depended.

Harrison rose to one knee, drew and cocked his revolver and sighted along the blue barrel. The distance was not great, but the light was illusive. But he felt he must trust to the chance of sending a slug crashing through John Bartholomew's broad breast. If their priest was shot down, panic might seize them. His finger was crooking about the trigger when something was thrown into the fire. Abruptly the flames died down, throwing everything into deep shallow. As suddenly they flared up again, burning with a weird green radiance. The dusky faces looked like those of drowned corpses in the glow.

In the moment of darkness Bartholomew had reached the block. His victim's head was thrust down upon it, and the mulatto stood like a bronze image, his muscular right arm lifted, poising above his head the broad steel crescent. And then, before could strike the blow that would send Woon Shang's head rolling to the misshapen feet of the grinning idol, before Harrison could jerk the trigger, something froze them all in their places.

Into the weird glow moved a figure, so lithely that it seemed to float in the uncertain light rather than move on earthly feet. In the green glow that lent her features the aspect of death, with perspiration dripping from her draggled garment, Celia Pompoloi looked hideously like the corpse of a drowned woman newly risen from a watery grave.

'Celia!'

It was a scream from a score of gaping mouths. Bedlam followed.

'Celia Pompoloi! Oh Gawd, she done come back from de watah! Done come back from Hell!'

'Yes you dogs!' It was a most unghostly scream from Celia. 'It's Celia Pompoloi, come back from Hell to send John Bartholomew there!'

And like a fury she rushed across the green-lit space, a knife she had found somewhere glittering in her hand. Bartholomew, momentarily paralysed by the appearance of his prisoner, came to life. Releasing Woon Shang he stepped aside and swung the heavy beheading knife with all his power. Harrison saw the great muscles leap up under his glossy skin as he struck. But Celia's spring was that of a swamp panther. It carried her inside the circular sweep of the weighted blade, and her knife flashed as it sank to the hilt under John Bartholomew's heart. With a strangled cry he reeled and fell, dragging her down with him as she strove to wrench her blade free.

Abandoning it she rose, panting, her hair standing on end, her eyes starting from her head, her red lips writhing back in a curl of devilish rage. The people shrieked and gave back from her, still evidently in the grip of the delusion that they looked on one risen from the dead.

'Dogs!' she screamed, an incarnation of fury. 'Fools! Swine! Have you lost your reason, to forget all my teachings, and let this dead dog make of you the beasts your fathers were? Oh – !' Glaring about for a weapon she caught up a blazing fire-brand and rushed at them, striking furiously. Men yelped as the flames bit them, and the sparks showered. Howling, cursing, and screaming they broke and fled, a frenzied mob, streaming out across the causeway, with their maddened priestess at their heels, screaming maledictions and smiting with the splintering faggot. They vanished in the darkness, and their clamour came back faintly.

Harrison rose, shaking his head in wonder, and went stiffly up to the dying fire. Bartholomew was dead, staring glassily up at the moon which was breaking through the scattering clouds. Woon

Shang crouched babbling incoherent Chinese as Harrison hauled him to his feet.

'Woon Shang,' said the detective wearily, 'I arrest you for the murder of Li-keh-tsung. I warn you that anything you say will be used against you.'

That formula seemed to invest the episode with some sanity, in contrast to the fantastic horror of the recent events. The Chinaman made no struggle. He seemed dazed, muttering: 'This will break the heart of my honourable father; he had rather see me dead than dishonoured.'

'You ought to have thought of that before,' said Harrison heavily. Through force of habit he cut Woon Shang's cords and reached for his handcuffs before he realised that they had been lost with his coat.

'Oh, well,' he sighed. 'I don't reckon you'll need them. Let's get going.'

Laying a heavy hand on his captive's naked shoulder, Harrison half guided, half pushed him toward the causeway. The detective was dizzy with fatigue, but combined with it was a muddled determination to get his prisoner out of the swamp and into a jail before he stopped. He felt he had no more to fear from the swamp people, but he wanted to get out of that atmosphere of decay and slime in which he seemed to have been wandering for ages. Woon Shang took note of his condition with furtive sidelong glances, as the stark fear died out of the Chinaman's beady black eyes to be replaced by one of craft.

'I have ten thousand dollars,' he began babbling. 'I will give you all of it if you will let me go . . .'

'Oh, shut up!' groaned Harrison wearily, giving him an exasperated shove. Woon Shang stumbled and went to his knees, his bare shoulder slipping from Harrison's grasp. The detective was stooping, fumbling for him when the Chinaman rose with a chunk of wood in his hand, and smote him savagely on the head. Harrison staggered back, almost falling, and Woon Shang, in a last desperate bid for freedom, dashed, not for the neck of land between which himself and Harrison stood, but straight toward the black water that glimmered beyond the fringe of cypresses. Harrison fired mechanically and without aim, but the fugitive kept straight on and hit the dusky water with a long dive.

Woon Shang's bobbing head was scarcely visible in the shadows of the overhanging ferns. Then a wild shriek cut the night; the water threshed and foamed, there was the glimpse of a writhing, horribly contorted yellow body and of a longer, darker shape, and then the blood-streaked waters closed over Woon Shang forever.

Harrison exhaled gustily and sank down on a rotting log.

'Well,' he said wearily, aloud, 'that winds *that* up. It's better this way. Woon's family had rather he died this way than in the chair, and they're decent folks, in spite of him. If this business had come to trial, I'd have had to tell about Celia shoving a knife into that devil Bartholomew, and I'd hate to see her on trial for killing that rat. This way it can be smoothed over. He had it coming to him. And I've got the money that's coming to old Li-keh-tsung's granddaughter. And it's me for the feather beds and fried steaks of civilisation.'

Names in the Black Book

'Three unsolved murders in a week are not so unusual – for River Street,' grunted Steve Harrison, shifting his muscular bulk restlessly in his chair.

His companion lighted a cigarette, and Harrison observed that her slim hand was none too steady. She was exotically beautiful, a dark, supple figure, with the rich colours of purple Eastern nights and crimson dawns in her dusky hair and red lips. But in her dark eyes Harrison glimpsed the shadow of fear. Only once before had he seen fear in those marvellous eyes, and the memory made him vaguely uneasy.

'It's your business to solve murders,' she said.

'Give me a little time. You can't rush things, when you're dealing with the people of the Oriental quarter.'

'You have less time than you think,' she answered cryptically. 'If you do not listen to me, you'll never solve these killings.'

'I'm listening.'

'But you won't believe. You'll say I'm hysterical – seeing ghosts and shying at shadows.'

'Look here, Joan,' he exclaimed impatiently. 'Come to the point. You called me to your apartment and I came because you said you were in deadly danger. But now you're talking riddles about three men who were killed last week. Spill it plain, won't you?'

'Do you remember Erlik Khan?' she asked abruptly.

Involuntarily his hand sought his face, where a thin scar ran from temple to jaw-rim. 'I'm not likely to forget him,' he said. 'A Mongol who called himself Lord of the Dead. His idea was to combine all the Oriental criminal societies in America in one big organisation, with himself at the head. He might have done it, too, if his own men hadn't turned on him.'

'Erlik Khan has returned,' she said.

'What!' His head jerked up and he glared at her incredulously. 'What are you talking about? I saw him die, and so did you!'

'I saw his hood fall apart as Ali ibn Suleyman struck with his keen-edged scimitar,' she answered. 'I saw him roll to the floor and lie still. And then the house went up in flames, and the roof fell in, and only charred bones were ever found among the ashes. Nevertheless, Erlik Khan has returned.'

Harrison did not reply, but sat waiting for further disclosures, sure they would come in an indirect way. Joan La Tour was half Oriental, and partook of many of the characteristics of her subtle kin.

'How did those three men die?' she asked, though he was aware that she knew as well as he.

'Li-crin, the Chinese merchant, fell from his own roof,' he grunted. 'The people on the street heard him scream and then saw him come hurtling down. Might have been an accident . . . but middle-aged Chinese merchants don't go climbing around on roofs at midnight.

'Ibrahim ibn Achmet, the Syrian curio dealer, was bitten by a cobra. That might have been an accident too, only I know somebody dropped the snake on him through his skylight.

'Jacob Kossova, the exporter, was simply knifed in a back alley. Dirty jobs, all of them, and no apparent motive on the surface. But motives are hidden deep, in River Street. When I find the guilty parties I'll uncover the motives.'

'And these murders suggest nothing to you?' exclaimed the girl, tense with suppressed excitement. 'You do not see the link that connects them? You do not grasp the point they all have in common? Listen – all these men were formerly associated in one way or another with Erlik Khan!'

'Well?' he demanded. 'That doesn't mean that the Khan's spook killed them! We found plenty of bones in the ashes of the house, but there were members of his gang in other parts of the city. His gigantic organisation went to pieces, after his death, for lack of a leader, but the survivors were never uncovered. Some of them might be paying off old grudges.'

'Then why did they wait so long to strike? It's been a year since we saw Erlik Khan die. I tell you, the Lord of the Dead himself, alive or dead, has returned and is striking down these men for one reason or another. Perhaps they refuse to do his bidding once more. Five were marked for death. Three have fallen.'

'How do you know that?' said he.

'Look!' From beneath the cushions of the divan on which she sat she drew something, and rising, came and bent beside him while she unfolded it.

It was a square piece of parchment-like substance, black and glossy. On it were written five names, one below the other, in a bold flowing hand . . . and in crimson, like spilled blood. Through the first three names a crimson bar had been drawn. They were the names of Li-chin, Ibrahim ibn Achmet, and Jacob Kossova. Harrison grunted explosively. The last two names, as yet unmarred, were those of Joan La Tour and Stephen Harrison.

'Where did you get this?' he demanded.

'It was shoved under my door last night, while I slept. If all the doors and windows had not been locked, the police would have found it pinned to my corpse this morning.'

'But still I don't see what connection – '

'It is a page from the Black Book of Erlik Khan!' she cried. 'The book of the dead! I have seen it, when I was a subject of his in the old days. There he kept accounts of his enemies, alive and dead. I saw that book, open, the very day of the night Ali ibn Suleyman killed him – a big book with jade-hinged ebony covers and glossy black parchment pages. Those names were not in it then; they have been written in since Erlik Khan died . . . and that is Erlik Khan's handwriting!'

If Harrison was impressed he failed to show it.

'Does he keep his books in English?'

'No, in a Mongolian script. This is for our benefit. And I know we are hopelessly doomed. Erlik Khan never warned his victims unless he was sure of them.'

'Might be a forgery,' grunted the detective.

'No! No man could imitate Erlik Khan's hand. He wrote those names himself. He has come back from the dead! Hell could not hold a devil as black as he!' Joan was losing some of her poise in her fear and excitement. She ground out the half-consumed cigarette and broke the cover of a fresh carton. She drew forth a slim white cylinder and tossed the package on the table. Harrison took it up and absently extracted one for himself.

'Our names are in the Black Book! It is a sentence of death from which there is no appeal!' She struck a match and was lifting it, when Harrison struck the cigarette from her with a startled oath. She fell back on the divan, bewildered at the violence of his action, and he caught up the package and began gingerly to remove the contents.

'Where'd you get these things?'

'Why, down at the corner drug store, I guess,' she stammered. 'That's where I usually – '

'Not these you didn't,' he grunted. 'These fags have been specially treated. I don't know what it is, but I've seen one puff of the stuff knock a man stone dead. Some kind of a hellish Oriental drug mixed with the tobacco. You were out of your apartment while you were phoning me – '

'I was afraid my wire was tapped,' she answered. 'I went to a public booth down the street.'

'And it's my guess somebody entered your apartment while you were gone and switched cigarettes on you. I only got a faint whiff of the stuff when I started to put that fag in my mouth, but it's unmistakable. Smell it yourself. Don't be afraid. It's deadly only when ignited.'

She obeyed, and turned pale.

'I told you! We were the direct cause of Erlik Khan's overthrow! If you hadn't smelt that drug, we'd both be dead now, as he intended!'

'Well,' he grunted, 'it's a cinch somebody's after you, anyway. I still say it can't be Erlik Khan, because nobody could live after the lick on the head I saw Ali ibn Suleyman hand him, and I don't believe in ghosts. But you've got to be protected until I run down whoever is being so free with his poisoned cigarettes.'

'What about yourself? Your name's in his book, too.'

'Never mind me,' Harrison growled pugnaciously. 'I reckon I can take care of myself.' He looked capable enough, with his cold blue eyes, and the muscles bulging in his coat. He had shoulders like a bull.

'This wing's practically isolated from the rest of the building,' he said, 'and you've got the third floor to yourself?'

'Not only the third floor of the wing,' she answered. 'There's no one else on the third floor anywhere in the building at present.'

'That makes it fine!' he exclaimed irritably. 'Somebody could sneak in and cut your throat without disturbing anyone. That's what they'll try, too, when they realise the cigarettes didn't finish you. You'd better move to a hotel.'

'That wouldn't make any difference,' she answered, trembling. Her nerves obviously were in a bad way. 'Erlik Khan would find me, anywhere. In a hotel, with people coming and going all the time, and the rotten locks they have on the doors, with transoms and fire escapes and everything, it would just be that much easier for him.'

'Well, then, I'll plant a bunch of cops around here.'

'That wouldn't do any good, either. Erlik Khan has killed again and again in spite of the police. They do not understand his ways.'

'That's right,' he muttered, uncomfortably aware of a conviction that to summon men from headquarters would surely be signing those men's death warrants, without accomplishing anything else. It was absurd to suppose that the dead Mongol fiend was behind these murderous attacks, yet . . . Harrison's flesh crawled along his spine at the memory of things that had taken place in River Street – things he had never reported, because he did not wish to be thought either a liar or a madman. The dead do not return . . . but what seems absurd on Thirty-ninth Boulevard takes on a different aspect among the haunted labyrinths of the Oriental quarter.

'Stay with me!' Joan's eyes were dilated, and she caught Harrison's arm with hands that shook violently. 'We can defend these rooms! While one sleeps the other can watch! Do not call the police; their blunders would doom us. You have worked in the quarter for years, and are worth more than the whole police force. The mysterious instincts that are a part of my Eastern heritage are alert to danger. I feel peril for us both, near, creeping closer, gliding around us like serpents in the darkness!'

'But I can't stay here,' he scowled worriedly. 'We can't barricade ourselves and wait for them to starve us out. I've got to hit back – find out who's behind all this. The best defence is a good offence. But I can't leave you here unguarded, either. Damn!' He clenched his big fists and shook his head like a baffled bull in his perplexity.

'There is one man in the city besides yourself I could trust,' she said suddenly. 'One worth more than all the police. With him guarding me I could sleep safely.'

'Who is he?'

'Khoda Khan.'

'That fellow? Why, I thought he'd skipped months ago.'

'No; he's been hiding in Levant Street.'

'But he's a confounded killer himself!'

'No, he isn't; not according to his standards, which means as much to him as yours do to you. He's an Afghan who was raised in a code of blood-feud and vengeance. He's as honourable according to his creed of life as you or I. And he's my friend. He'd die for me.'

'I reckon that means you've been hiding him from the law,' said Harrison with a searching glance which she did not seek to evade. He made no further comment. River Street is not South Park Avenue. Harrison's own methods were not always orthodox, but they generally got results.

'Can you reach him?' he asked abruptly. She nodded.

'All right. Call him and tell him to beat it up here. Tell him he won't be molested by the police, and after the brawl's over, he can go back into hiding. But after that it's open season if I catch him. Use your phone. Wire may be tapped, but we'll have to take the chance. I'll go downstairs and use the booth in the office. Lock the door, and don't open it to anybody until I get back.'

When the bolts clicked behind him, Harrison turned down the corridor toward the stairs. The apartment house boasted no elevator. He watched all sides warily as he went. A peculiarity of architecture had, indeed, practically isolated that wing. The wall opposite Joan's doors was blank. The only way to reach the other suites on that floor was to descend the stair and ascend another on the other side of the building.

As he reached the stair he swore softly; his heel had crunched a small vial on the first step. With some vague suspicion of a planted poison trap he stooped and gingerly investigated the splintered bits and the spilled contents. There was a small pool of colourless liquid which gave off a pungent, musky odour, but there seemed nothing lethal about it.

'Some damned Oriental perfume Joan dropped, I reckon,' he decided. He descended the twisting stair without further delay and was presently in the booth in the office which opened on the street; a sleepy clerk dozed behind the desk.

Harrison got the chief of police on the wire and began abruptly.

'Say, Hoolihan, you remember that Afghan, Khoda Khan, who knifed a Chinaman about three months ago? Yes, that's the one. Well, listen: I'm using him on a job for a while, so tell your men to lay off, if they see him. Pass the word along *pronto*. Yes, I know it's very irregular; so's the job I hold down. In this case it's the choice of using a fugitive from the law, or seeing a law-abiding citizen murdered. Never mind what it's all about. This is my job, and I've got to handle it my own way. All right; thanks.'

He hung up the receiver, thought vigorously for a few minutes, and then dialled another number that was definitely not related to the police station. In place of the chief's booming voice there sounded at the other end of the wire a squeaky whine framed in the argot of the underworld.

'Listen, Johnny,' said Harrison with his customary abruptness, 'you told me you thought you had a lead on the Kossova murder. What about it?'

'It wasn't no lie, boss!' The voice at the other end trembled with excitement. 'I got a tip, and it's big! – *big*! I can't spill it over the phone, and I don't dare stir out. But if you'll meet me at Shan Yang's hop joint, I'll give you the dope. It'll knock you loose from your props, believe me it will!'

'I'll be there in an hour,' promised the detective. He left the booth and glanced briefly out into the street. It was a misty night, as so many River Street nights are. Traffic was only a dim echo from some distant, busier section. Drifting fog dimmed the street lamps, shrouding the forms of occasional passers-by. The stage was set for murder; it only awaited the appearance of the actors in the dark drama.

Harrison mounted the stairs again. They wound up out of the office and up into the third-storey wing without opening upon the second floor at all. The architecture, like much of it in or near the Oriental section, was rather unusual. People of the quarter were notoriously fond of privacy, and even apartment houses were built with this passion in mind. His feet made no sound on the thickly carpeted stairs, though a slight crunching at the top step reminded him of the broken vial again momentarily. He had stepped on the splinters.

He knocked at the locked door, answered Joan's tense challenge and was admitted. He found the girl more self-possessed.

'I talked with Khoda Khan. He's on his way here now. I warned him that the wire might be tapped – that our enemies might know as soon as I called him, and try to stop him on his way here.'

'Good,' grunted the detective. 'While I'm waiting for him I'll have a look at your suite.'

There were four rooms: drawing room in front, with a large bedroom behind it, and behind that two smaller rooms, the maid's bedroom and the bathroom. The maid was not there, because Joan had sent her away at the first intimation of danger threatening. The corridor ran parallel with the suite, and the drawing room, large bedroom and bathroom opened upon it. That made three doors to consider. The drawing room had one big east window, overlooking the street, and one on the south. The big bedroom had one south window, and the maid's room one south and one west window. The bathroom had one window, a small one in the west wall, overlooking a small court bounded by a tangle of alleys and board-fenced backyards.

'Three outside doors and six windows to be watched, and this the top storey,' muttered the detective. 'I still think I ought to get some cops here.' But he spoke without conviction. He was investigating the bathroom when Joan called him cautiously from the drawing room, telling him that she thought she had heard a faint scratching outside the door. Gun in hand he opened the bathroom door and peered out into the corridor. It was empty. No shape of horror stood before the drawing room door. He closed the door, called reassuringly to the girl, and completed his inspection, grunting approval. Joan La Tour was a daughter of the Oriental quarter. Long ago she had provided against secret enemies as far as special locks and bolts could provide. The windows were guarded with heavy iron-braced shutters, and there was no trapdoor, dumb waiter nor skylight anywhere in the suite.

'Looks like you're ready for a siege,' he commented.

'I am. I have canned goods laid away to last for weeks. With Khoda Khan I can hold the fort indefinitely. If things get too hot for you, you'd better come back here yourself . . . if you can. It's safer than the police station – unless they burn the house down.'

A soft rap on the door brought them both around.

'Who is it?' called Joan warily.

'I, Khoda Khan, *sahiba*,' came the answer in a low-pitched, but strong and resonant voice. Joan sighed deeply and unlocked the door. A tall figure bowed with a stately gesture and entered.

Khoda Khan was taller than Harrison, and though he lacked something of the American's sheer bulk, his shoulders were equally broad, and his garments could not conceal the hard lines of his limbs, the tigerish suppleness of his motions. His garb was a curious combination of costume, which is common in River Street. He wore a turban which well set off his hawk nose and black beard, and a long silk coat hung nearly to his knees. His trousers were conventional, but a silk sash girdled his lean waist, and his foot-gear was Turkish slippers.

In any costume it would have been equally evident that there was something wild and untameable about the man. His eyes blazed as no civilised man's ever did, and his sinews were like coiled springs under his coat. Harrison felt much as he would have felt if a panther had padded into the room, for the moment placid but ready at an instant's notice to go flying into flaming-eyed, red-taloned action.

'I thought you'd left the country,' he said.

The Afghan smiled, a glimmer of white amidst the dark tangle of his beard.

'Nay, *sahib*. That son of a dog I knifed did not die.'

'You're lucky he didn't,' commented Harrison. 'If you kill him you'll hang, sure.'

'*Inshallah*,' agreed Khoda Khan cheerfully. 'But it was a matter of izzat – *honour*. The dog fed me swine's flesh. But no matter. The *memsahib* called me and I came.'

'All right. As long as she needs your protection the police won't arrest you. But when the matter's finished, things stand as they were. I'll give you time to hide again, if you wish, and then I'll try to catch you as I have in the past. Or if you want to surrender and stand trial, I'll promise you as much leniency as possible.'

'You speak fairly,' answered Khoda Khan. 'I will protect the *memsahib*, and when our enemies are dead, you and I will begin our feud anew.'

'Do you know anything about these murders?'

'Nay, *sahib*. The *memsahib* called me, saying Mongol dogs threatened her. I came swiftly, over the roofs, lest they seek to ambush me. None molested me. But here is something I found outside the door.'

He opened his hand and exhibited a bit of silk, evidently torn from his sash. On it lay a crushed object that Harrison did not recognise. But Joan recoiled with a low cry.

'God! A black scorpion of Assam!'

'Aye – whose sting is death. I saw it running up and down before the door, seeking entrance. Another man might have stepped upon it without seeing it, but I was on my guard, for I smelled the Flower of Death as I came up the stairs. I saw the thing at the door and crushed it before it could sting me.'

'What do you mean by the Flower of Death?' demanded Harrison.

'It grows in the jungles where these vermin abide. Its scent attracts them as wine draws a drunkard. A trail of the juice had somehow been laid to this door. Had the door been opened before I slew it, it would have darted in and struck whoever happened to be in its way.'

Harrison swore under his breath, remembering the faint scratching noise Joan had heard outside the door.

'I get it now! They put a bottle of that juice on the stairs where it was sure to be stepped on. I did step on it, and broke it, and got the liquid on my shoe. Then I tracked down the stairs, leaving the scent wherever I stepped. Came back upstairs, stepped in the stuff again and tracked it on through the door. Then somebody downstairs turned that scorpion loose – the devil!! That means they've been in this house since I was downstairs! – may be hiding somewhere here now! But somebody had to come into the office to put the scorpion on the trail – I'll ask the clerk – '

'He sleeps like the dead,' said Khoda Khan. 'He did not waken when I entered and mounted the stairs. What matters if the house is full of Mongols? These doors are strong, and I am alert!' From beneath his coat he drew the terrible Khyber knife – a yard long, with an edge like a razor. 'I have slain *men* with this,' he announced, grinning like a bearded mountain devil. 'Pathans, Indians, a Russian or so. These Mongols are dogs on whom the good steel will be shamed.'

'Well,' grunted Harrison. 'I've got an appointment that's overdue now. I feel queer walking out and leaving you two to fight these devils alone. But there'll be no safety for us until I've smashed this gang at its root, and that's what I'm out to do.'

'They'll kill you as you leave the building,' said Joan with conviction.

'Well, I've got to risk it. If you're attacked call the police anyway, and call me, at Shan Yang's joint. I'll come back here some time before dawn. But I'm hoping the tip I expect to get will enable me to hit straight at whoever's after us.'

He went down the hallway with an eerie feeling of being watched, and scanned the stairs as if he expected to see it swarming with black scorpions, and he shied wide of the broken glass on the step. He had an uncomfortable sensation of duty ignored, in spite of himself, though he knew that his two companions did not want the police, and that in dealing with the East it is better to heed the advice of the East.

The clerk still sagged behind his desk. Harrison shook him without avail. The man was not asleep; he was drugged. But his heartbeat was regular, and the detective believed he was in no danger. Anyway, Harrison had no more time to waste. If he kept Johnny Kleck waiting too long, the fellow might become panicky and bolt, to hide in some rat-run for weeks.

He went into the street, where the lamps gleamed luridly through the drifting river mist, half expecting a knife to be thrown at him, or to find a cobra coiled on the seat of his automobile. But he found nothing his suspicion anticipated, even though he lifted the hood and the rumble-seat to see if a bomb had been planted. Satisfying himself at last, he climbed in, and the girl watching him through the slits of a third-storey shutter sighed relievedly to see him roar away unmolested.

Khoda Khan had gone through the rooms, giving approval in his beard of the locks, and having extinguished the lights in the other chambers he returned to the drawing room, where he turned out all lights except one small desk lamp. It shed a pool of light in the centre of the room, leaving the rest in shadowy vagueness.

'Darkness baffles rogues as well as honest men,' he said sagely, 'and I see like a cat in the dark.'

He sat cross-legged near the door that let into the bedroom, which he left partly open. He merged with the shadows so that all of him Joan could make out with any distinctness was his turban and the glimmer of his eyes as he turned his head.

'We will remain in this room, *sahiba*,' he said. 'Having failed with poison and reptile, it is certain that men will next be sent. Lie down on that divan and sleep, if you can. I will keep watch.'

Joan obeyed, but she did not sleep. Her nerves seemed to thrum with tautness. The silence of the house oppressed her, and the few noises of the street made her start.

Khoda Khan sat motionless as a statue, imbued with the savage patience and immobility of the hills that bred him. Grown to manhood on the raw barbaric edge of the world, where survival depended on personal ability, his senses were whetted keener than is possible for civilised men. Even Harrison's trained faculties were blunt in comparison. Khoda Khan could still smell the faint aroma of the Flower of Death, mingled with the acrid odour of the crushed scorpion. He heard and identified every sound in or outside the house – knew which were natural, and which were not.

He heard the sounds on the roof long before his warning hiss brought Joan upright on the divan. The Afghan's eyes glowed like phosphorus in the shadows and his teeth glimmered dimly in a savage grin. Joan looked at him inquiringly. Her civilised ears heard nothing. But he heard and with his ears followed the sounds accurately and located the place where they halted. Joan heard something then, a faint scratching somewhere in the building, but she did not identify it – as Khoda Khan did – as the forcing of the shutters on the bathroom window.

With a quick reassuring gesture to her, Khoda Khan rose and melted like a slinking leopard into the darkness of the bedroom. She took up a blunt-nosed automatic, with no great conviction of reliance upon it, and groped on the table for a bottle of wine, feeling an intense need of stimulants. She was shaking in every limb and cold sweat was gathering on her flesh. She remembered the cigarettes, but the unbroken seal on the bottle reassured her. Even the wisest have their thoughtless moments. It was not until she had begun to drink that the peculiar flavour made her realise that the man who had shifted the cigarettes might just as easily have taken a bottle of wine and left another in its place, a facsimile that included an unbroken seal. She fell back on the divan, gagging.

Khoda Khan wasted no time, because he heard other sounds, out in the hall. His ears told him, as he crouched by the bathroom door, that the shutters had been forced – done almost in silence – and now the window was being jemmied. Then he heard something stealthy and bulky drop into the room. Then it was that he threw open the door and charged in like a typhoon, his long knife held low.

Enough light filtered into the room from outside to limn a powerful, crouching figure, with dim snarling yellow features. The intruder yelped explosively, started a motion – and then the long Khyber knife, driven by an arm nerved to the fury of the Himalayas, ripped him open from groin to breastbone.

Khoda Khan did not pause. He knew there was only one man in the room, but through the open window he saw a thick rope dangling from above. He sprang forward, grasped it with both hands and heaved backward like a bull. The men on the roof holding it released it to keep from being jerked headlong over the edge, and he tumbled backward, sprawling over the corpse, the loose rope in his hands. He yelped exultantly, then sprang up and glided to the door that opened into the corridor. Unless they had another rope, which was unlikely, the men on the roof were temporarily out of the fight.

He flung open the door and ducked deeply. A hatchet cut a great chip out of the jamb, and he stabbed upward once, then sprang over a writhing body into the corridor, jerking a big pistol from its hidden scabbard.

The bright light of the corridor did not blind him. He saw a second hatchet-man crouching by the bedroom door, and a man in the silk robes of a mandarin working at the lock of the drawing room door. He was between them and the stairs. As they wheeled toward him he shot the hatchet-man in the belly. An automatic spat in the hand of the mandarin, and Khoda Khan felt the wind of the bullet. The next instant his own gun roared again and the Manchu staggered, the pistol flying from a hand that was suddenly a dripping red pulp. Then he whipped a long knife from his robes with his left hand and came along the corridor like a hurricane, his eyes glaring and his silk garments whipping about him.

Khoda Khan shot him through the head and the mandarin fell so near his feet that the long knife stuck into the floor and quivered a matter of inches from the Afghan's slipper.

But Khoda Khan paused only long enough to pass his knife through the hatchet-man he had shot in the belly – for his fighting ethics were those of the savage Hills – and then he turned and ran back into the bathroom. He fired a shot through the window, though the men on the roof were making [no] further demonstration, and then ran through the bedroom, snapping on lights as he went.

'I have slain the dogs, *sahiba*!' he exclaimed. 'By Allah, they have tasted lead and steel! Others are on the roof but they are helpless for the moment. But men will come to investigate the shots, that being the custom of the *sahibs*, so it is expedient that we decide on our further actions, and the proper lies to tell – Allah!'

Joan La Tour stood bolt upright, clutching the back of the divan. Her face was the colour of marble, and the expression was rigid too, like a mask of horror carved in stone. Her dilated eyes blazed like weird black fire.

'Allah shield us against Shaitan the Damned!' ejaculated Khoda Khan, making a sign with his fingers that antedated Islam by some thousands of years. 'What has happened to you, *sahiba*?'

He moved toward her, to be met by a scream that sent him cowering back, cold sweat starting out on his flesh.

'Keep back!' she cried in a voice he did not recognise. 'You are a demon! You are all demons! I see you! I hear your cloven feet padding in the night! I see your eyes blazing from the shadows! Keep your taloned hands from me! *Aie*!' Foam flecked her lips as she screamed blasphemies in English and Arabic that made Khoda Khan's hair stand stiffly on end.

'*Sahiba*!' he begged, trembling like a leaf. 'I am no demon! I am Khoda Khan! I – ' His outstretched hand touched her, and with an awful shriek she turned and darted for the door, tearing at the bolts. He sprang to stop her, but in her frenzy she was even quicker than he. She whipped the door open, eluded his grasping hand and flew down the corridor, deaf to his anguished yells.

When Harrison left Joan's house, he drove straight to Shan Yang's dive, which, in the heart of River Street, masqueraded as a low-grade drinking joint. It was late. Only a few derelicts huddled about the bar, and he noticed that the barman was a Chinaman that he had never seen before. He stared impassively at Harrison, but jerked a thumb toward the back door, masked by dingy curtains, when the detective asked abruptly: 'Johnny Kleck here?'

Harrison passed through the door, traversed a short dimly-lighted hallway and rapped authoritatively on the door at the other end. In the silence he heard rats scampering. A steel disk in the centre of the door shifted and a slanted black eye glittered in the opening.

'Open the door, Shan Yang,' ordered Harrison impatiently, and the eye was withdrawn, accompanied by the rattling of bolts and chains.

He pushed open the door and entered the room whose illumination was scarcely better than that of the corridor. It was a large, dingy, drab affair, lined with bunks. Fires sputtered in braziers, and Shan Yang was making his way to his accustomed seat behind a low counter near the wall. Harrison spent but a single casual glance on the familiar figure, the well-known dingy silk jacket worked in gilt dragons. Then he strode across the room to a door in the wall opposite the counter to which Shan Yang was making his way. This was an opium joint and Harrison knew it – knew those figures in the bunks were sleeping the sleep of the smoke. Why he had not raided it, as he had raided and destroyed other opium-dens, only Harrison could have said. But law-enforcement on River Street is not the orthodox routine it is on Baskerville Avenue, for instance. Harrison's reasons were those of expediency and necessity. Sometimes certain conventions have to be sacrificed for the sake of more important gains – especially when the law-enforcement of a whole district (and in the Oriental quarter) rests on one's shoulders.

A characteristic smell pervaded the dense atmosphere, in spite of the reek of dope and unwashed bodies – the dank odour of the river, which hangs over the River Street dives or wells up from their floors like the black intangible spirit of the quarter itself. Shan Yang's dive, like many others, was built on the very bank of the river. The back room projected out over the water on rotting piles, at which the black river lapped hungrily.

Harrison opened the door, entered and pushed it to behind him, his lips framing a greeting that was never uttered. He stood dumbly, glaring.

He was in a small dingy room, bare except for a crude table and some chairs. An oil lamp on the table cast a smoky light. And in that light he saw Johnny Kleck. The man stood bolt upright against the far wall, his arms spread like a crucifix, rigid, his eyes glassy and staring, his mean, ratty features twisted in a frozen grin. He did not speak, and Harrison's gaze, travelling down him, halted with a shock. Johnny's feet did not touch the floor by several inches . . .

Harrison's big blue pistol jumped into his hand. Johnny Kleck was dead; that grin was a contortion of horror and agony. He was crucified to the wall by skewer-like dagger blades through his wrists and ankles, his ears spiked to the wall to keep his head upright. But that was not what had killed him. The bosom of Johnny's shirt was charred, and there was a round, blackened hole.

Feeling suddenly sick the detective wheeled, opened the door and stepped back into the larger room. The light seemed dimmer, the smoke thicker than ever. No mumblings came from the bunks; the fires in the braziers burned blue, with weird sputterings. Shan Yang crouched behind the counter. His shoulders moved as if he were tallying beads on an abacus.

'Shan Yang!' the detective's voice grated harshly in the murky silence. 'Who's been in that room tonight besides Johnny Kleck?'

The man behind the counter straightened and looked full at him, and Harrison felt his skin crawl. Above the gilt-worked jacket an unfamiliar face returned his gaze. That was no Shan Yang; it was a man he had never seen – it was a Mongol. He started and stared about him as the men in the bunks rose with supple ease. They were not Chinese; they were Mongols to a man, and their eyes were not clouded by drugs.

With a curse Harrison sprang toward the outer door and with a rush they were on him. His gun crashed and a man staggered in mid-stride. Then the lights went out, the braziers were overturned, and in the Stygian blackness hard bodies caromed against the detective. Long-nailed fingers clawed at his throat, thick arms locked about his waist and legs. Somewhere a sibilant voice was hissing orders.

Harrison's mauling left worked like a piston, crushing flesh and bone; his right wielded the gun barrel like a club. He forged toward the unseen door blindly, dragging his assailants by sheer strength. He seemed to be wading through a solid mass, as if the darkness had turned to bone and muscle about him. A knife licked through his coat, stinging his skin, and then he gasped as a silk cord looped about his neck, shutting off his wind, sinking deeper and deeper into the straining flesh. Blindly he jammed the muzzle against the nearest body and pulled the trigger. At the muffled concussion something fell away from him and the strangling agony lessened. Gasping for breath he groped and tore the cord away – then he was borne down under a rush of heavy bodies and something smashed savagely against his head. The darkness exploded in a shower of sparks that were instantly quenched in Stygian blackness.

The smell of the river was in Steve Harrison's nostrils as he regained his addled senses, river-scent mingled with the odour of stale blood. The blood, he realised, when he had enough sense to realise anything, was clotted on his own scalp. His head swam and he tried to raise a hand to it, thereby discovering that he was bound hand and foot with cords that cut into the flesh. A candle was dazzling his eyes, and for a while he could see nothing else. Then things began to assume their proper proportions, and objects grew out of nothing and became identifiable.

He was lying on a bare floor of new, unpainted wood, in a large square chamber, the walls of which were of stone, without paint or plaster. The ceiling was likewise of stone, with heavy, bare beams, and there was an open trap-door almost directly above him, through which, in spite of the candle, he got a glimpse of stars. Fresh air flowed through that trap, bearing with it the river-smell stronger than ever. The chamber was bare of furniture, the candle stuck in a niche in the wall. Harrison swore, wondering if he was delirious. This was like an experience in a dream, with everything unreal and distorted.

He tried to struggle to a sitting position, but that made his head swim, so that he lay back and swore fervently. He yelled wrathfully, and a face peered down at him through the trap. He cursed the face and it mocked him and was withdrawn. The noise of the door softly opening checked Harrison's profanity and he wriggled around to glare at the intruder.

And he glared in silence, feeling an icy prickling up and down his spine. Once before he had lain bound and helpless, staring up at a tall black-robed figure whose yellow eyes glimmered from the shadow of a dusky hood. But that man was dead; Harrison had seen him cut down by the scimitar of a maddened Druse.

'Erlik Khan!' The words were forced out of him. He licked lips suddenly dry.

'*Aie!*' It was the same ghostly, hollow voice that had chilled him in the old days. 'Erlik Khan, the Lord of the Dead.'

'Are you a man or a ghost?' demanded Harrison.

'I live.'

'But I saw Ali ibn Suleyman kill you!' exclaimed the detective. 'He slashed you across the head with a heavy sword that was sharp as a razor. He was a stronger man than I am. He struck with the full power of his arm. Your hood fell in two pieces – '

'And I fell like a dead man in my own blood,' finished Erlik Khan. 'But the steel cap I wore – as I wear now – under my hood, saved my life as it has more than once. The terrible stroke cracked it across the top and cut my scalp, fracturing my skull and causing concussion of the brain. But I lived, and some of my faithful followers, who escaped the sword of the Druse, carried me down through the subterranean tunnels which led from my house, and so I escaped the burning building. But I lay like a dead man for weeks, and it was not until a very wise man was brought from Mongolia that I recovered my senses, and sanity.

'But now I am ready to take up my work where I left off, though I must rebuild much. Many of my former followers had forgotten my authority. Some required to be taught anew who was master.'

'And you've been teaching them,' grunted Harrison, recovering his pugnacious composure.

'True. Some examples had to be made. One man fell from a roof, a snake bit another, yet another ran into knives in a dark alley. Then there was another matter. Joan La Tour betrayed me in the old days. She knows too many secrets. She had to die. So that she might taste agony in anticipation, I sent her a page from my book of the dead.'

'Your devils killed Kleck,' accused Harrison.

'Of course. All wires leading from the girl's apartment house are tapped. I myself heard your conversation with Kleck. That is why you were not attacked when you left the building. I saw that you were playing into my hands. I sent my men to take possession of Shan Yang's dive. He had no more use for his jacket, presently, so one donned it to deceive you. Kleck had somehow learned of my return; these stool pigeons are clever. But he had time to regret. A man dies hard with a white-hot point of iron bored through his breast.'

Harrison said nothing and presently the Mongol continued.

'I wrote your name in my book because I recognised you as my most dangerous opponent. It was because of you that Ali ibn Suleyman turned against me.

'I am rebuilding my empire again, but more solidly. First I shall consolidate River Street, and create a political machine to rule the city. The men in office now do not suspect my existence. If all were to die, it would not be hard to find others to fill their places . . . men who are not indifferent to the clink of gold.'

'You're mad,' growled Harrison. 'Control a whole city government from a dive in River Street?'

'It has been done,' answered the Mongol tranquilly. 'I will strike like a cobra from the dark. Only the men who obey my agent will live. He will be a figurehead whom men will think the real power, while I remain unseen. You might have been he, if you had a little more intelligence.'

He took a bulky object from under his arm, a thick book with glossy black covers . . . ebony with green jade hinges. He riffled the night-hued pages and Harrison saw they were covered with crimson characters.

'My book of the dead,' said Erlik Khan. 'Many names have been crossed out. Many more have been added since I recovered my sanity. Some of them would interest you; they include names of the mayor, the chief of police, district attorney, a number of aldermen.'

'That lick must have addled your brains permanently,' snarled Harrison. 'Do you think you can substitute a whole city government and get away with it?'

'I can and will. These men will die in various ways, and men of my own choice will succeed them in office. Within a year I will hold this city in the palm of my hand, and there will be none to interfere with me.'

Lying staring up at the bizarre figure, whose features were, as always, shadowed beyond recognition by the hood, Harrison's flesh crawled with the conviction that the Mongol was indeed mad. His crimson dreams, always ghastly, were too grotesque and incredible for the visions of a wholly sane man. Yet he was dangerous as a maddened cobra. His monstrous plot must ultimately fail, yet he held the lives of many men in his hand. And Harrison lay bound and helpless before him. The detective cursed in fury.

'Always the man of violence,' mocked Erlik Khan, with the suggestion of scorn in his voice. 'Barbarian! who lays his trust in guns and blades, who would check the stride of imperial power with blows of the naked fists! Brainless arm striking blind blows! Well, you have struck your last. Smell the river damp that creeps in through the ceiling? Soon it shall enfold you utterly and your dreams and aspirations will be one with the mist of the river.'

'Where are we?' demanded Harrison.

'On an island below the city, where the marshes begin. Once there were warehouses here, and a factory, but they were abandoned as the city grew in the other direction, and have been crumbling into ruin for twenty years. I purchased the entire island through one of my agents, and am rebuilding to suit my own purposes an old stone mansion which stood here before the factory was built. None notices, because my own henchmen are the workmen, and no one ever comes to this marshy island. The house is invisible from the river, hidden as it is among the tangle of old rotting warehouses. You came here in a motorboat which was anchored beneath the rotting wharves behind Shan Yang's dive. Another boat will presently fetch my men who were sent to dispose of Joan La Tour.'

'They may not find that so easy,' commented the detective.

'Never fear. I know she summoned that hairy wolf, Khoda Khan, to her aid, and it's true that my men failed to slay him before he reached her. But I suppose it was a false sense of trust that caused you to make your appointment with Kleck. I rather expected you to remain with the foolish girl and try to protect her in your way.'

Somewhere below them a gong sounded. Erlik Khan did not start, but there was a surprise in the lift of his head. He closed the black book.

'I have wasted enough time on you,' he said. 'Once before I bade you farewell in one of my dungeons. Then the fanaticism of a crazy Druse saved you. This time there will be no upset of my plans. The only men in this house know no law but my will. I go, but you will not be lonely. Soon one will come to you.'

And with a low, chilling laugh the phantom-like figure moved through the door and disappeared. Outside a lock clicked, and then there was stillness.

The silence was broken suddenly by a muffled scream. It came from somewhere below and was repeated half a dozen times. Harrison shuddered. No one who has ever visited an insane asylum could fail to recognise that sound. It was the shrieking of a mad woman. After these cries the silence seemed even more stifling and menacing.

Harrison swore to quiet his feelings, and again the velvet-capped head leered down at him through the trap.

'Grin, you yellow-bellied ape!' roared Harrison, tugging at his cords until the veins stood out on his temples. 'If I could break these damned ropes I'd knock that grin around where your pigtail ought to be, you – ' The head vanished from the trap and there came a sound like the blow of a butcher's cleaver.

Then another face was poked into the trap – a wild, bearded face, with blazing, bloodshot eyes, and surmounted by a dishevelled turban.

'*Sahib*!' hissed the apparition.

'Khoda Khan!' ejaculated the detective, galvanised. 'What the devil are you doing here?'

'Softly!' muttered the Afghan. 'Let not the accursed ones hear!'

He tossed the loose end of a rope ladder down through the trap and came down in a rush, his bare feet making no sound as he hit the floor. He held his long knife in his teeth, and blood dripped from the point.

Squatting beside the detective he cut him free with reckless slashes that threatened to slice flesh as well as hemp. The Afghan was quivering with half-controlled passion. His teeth gleamed like a wolf's fangs amidst the tangle of his beard.

Harrison sat up, chafing his swollen wrists.

'Where's Joan? Quick, man, where is she?'

'Here! In this accursed den!'

'But – '

'That was she screaming a few minutes ago,' broke in the Afghan, and Harrison's flesh crawled with a vague monstrous premonition.

'But that was a mad woman!' he almost whispered.

'The *sahiba* is mad,' said Khoda Khan sombrely. 'Hearken, *sahib*, and then judge if the fault is altogether mine.

'After you left, the accursed ones let down a man from the roof on a rope. Him I knifed, and I slew three more who sought to force the doors. But when I returned to the *sahiba*, she knew me not. She fled from me into the street, and other devils must have been lurking nearby, because as she ran shrieking along the sidewalk, a big automobile loomed out of the fog and an arm dragged her into the car, from under my very fingers. I saw his accursed face by the light of a street lamp.

'Knowing she were better dead by a bullet than in their hands, I emptied my pistol after the car, but it fled like Shaitan the Damned from the face of Allah, and if I hit anyone in it, I know not. Then as I rent my garments and cursed the day of my birth – for I could not pursue it on foot – Allah willed that another automobile should appear. It was driven by a young man in evening clothes, returning from a revel, no doubt, and being cursed with curiosity he slowed down near the curb to observe my grief.

'So, praising Allah, I sprang in beside him and placing my knife point against his ribs bade him go with speed, and he obeyed in great fear. The car of the damned ones was out of sight, but presently I glimpsed it again, and exhorted the youth to greater speed, so the machine seemed to fly like the steed of the Prophet. So, presently I saw the car halt at the river bank. I made the youth halt likewise, and he sprang out and fled in the other direction in terror.

'I ran through the darkness, hot for the blood of the accursed ones, but before I could reach the bank I saw four Mongols leave the car, carrying the *memsahib* who was bound and gagged, and they entered a motorboat and headed out into the river toward an island which lay on the breast of the water like a dark cloud.

'I cast up and down on the shore like a madman, and was about to leap in and swim, though the distance was great, when I came upon a boat chained to a pile, but one driven by oars. I gave praise to Allah and cut the chain with my knife – see the nick in the edge? – and rowed after the accursed ones with great speed.

'They were far ahead of me, but Allah willed it that their engine should sputter and cease when they had almost reached the island. So I took heart, hearing them cursing in their heathen tongue, and hoped to draw alongside and slay them all before they were aware of me. They saw me not in the darkness, nor heard my oars because of their own noises, but before I could reach them the accursed engine began again. So they reached a wharf on the marshy shore ahead of me, but they lingered to make the boat fast, so I was not too far behind them as they bore the *memsahib* through the shadows of the crumbling shacks which stood all about.

'Then I was hot to overtake and slay them, but before I could come up with them they had reached the door of a great stone house – this one, *sahib* – set in a tangle of rotting buildings. A steel fence surrounded it, with razor-edged spearheads set along the top, but by Allah! that could not hinder a *lifter* of the Khyber! I went over it without so much as tearing my garments. Inside was a second wall of stone, but it stood in ruins.

'I crouched in the shadows near the house and saw that the windows were heavily barred and the doors strong. Moreover, the lower part of the house is full of armed men. So I climbed a corner of the wall, and it was not easy, but presently I reached the roof which at that part is flat, with a parapet. I expected a watcher, and so there was, but he was too busy taunting his captive to see or hear me until my knife sent him to Hell. Here is his dagger; he bore no gun.'

Harrison mechanically took the wicked, lean-bladed poniard.

'But what caused Joan to go mad?'

'*Sahib*, there was a broken wine bottle on the floor, and a goblet. I had no time to investigate it, but I know that wine must have been poisoned with the juice of the fruit called the black pomegranate. She cannot have drunk much, or she would have died frothing and champing like a mad dog. But only a little will rob one of sanity. It grows in the jungles of Indo-China, and white men say it is a lie. But it is no lie; thrice I have seen men die after having drunk its juice, and more than once I have seen men, and women too, turn mad because of it. I have travelled in that hellish country where it grows.'

'God!' Harrison's foundations were shaken by nausea. Then his big hands clenched into chunks of iron and baleful fire glimmered in his savage blue eyes. The weakness of horror and revulsion was followed by cold fury, dangerous as the blood-hunger of a timber wolf.

'She may be already dead,' he muttered thickly. 'But dead or alive we'll send Erlik Khan to Hell. Try that door.'

It was of heavy teak, braced with bronze straps.

'It is locked,' muttered the Afghan. 'We will burst it.'

He was about to launch his shoulder against it when he stopped short, the long Khyber knife jumping into his fist like a beam of light.

'Someone approaches!' he whispered, and a second later Harrison's duller ears caught a cat-like tread.

Instantly he acted. He shoved the Afghan behind the door and sat down quickly in the centre of the room, wrapped a piece of rope about his ankles and then lay full length, his arms behind and under him. He was lying on the other pieces of severed cord, concealing them, and to the casual glance he resembled a man lying bound hand and foot. The Afghan understood and grinned hugely.

Harrison worked with the celerity of trained mind and muscles that eliminates fumbling delay and bungling. He accomplished his purpose in a matter of seconds and without undue noise. A key grated in the lock as he settled himself, and then the door swung open. A giant Mongol stood limned in the opening. His head was shaven, his square features passionless as the face of a copper idol. In one hand he carried a curiously shaped ebony block, in the other a mace such as was borne by the horsemen of Genghis Khan – a straight-hafted iron bludgeon with a round head covered with steel points, and a knob on the other end to keep the hand from slipping.

He did not see Khoda Khan because when he threw back the door, the Afghan was hidden behind it. Khoda Khan did not stab him as he entered because the Afghan could not see into the outer corridor, and had no way of knowing how many men were following the first.

But the Mongol was alone, and he did not bother to shut the door. He went straight to the man lying on the floor, scowling slightly to see the rope ladder hanging down through the trap, as if it was not usual to leave it that way, but he did not show any suspicion or call to the man on the roof.

He did not examine Harrison's cords. The detective presented the appearance the Mongol had expected, and this fact blunted his faculties as anything taken for granted is likely to do. As he bent down, over his shoulder Harrison saw Khoda Khan glide from behind the door as silently as a panther.

Leaning his mace against his leg, spiked head on the floor, the Mongol grasped Harrison's shirt bosom with one hand, lifted his head and shoulders clear of the floor, while he shoved the block under his head. Like twin striking snakes the detective's hands whipped from behind him and locked on the Mongol's bull throat.

There was no cry; instantly the Mongol's eyes distended and his lips parted in a grin of strangulation. With a terrific heave he reared upright, dragging Harrison with him, but not breaking his hold, and the weight of the big American pulled them both down again. Both hands tore frantically at Harrison's iron wrists; then the giant stiffened convulsively and brief agony reddened his black eyes. Khoda Khan had driven his knife between the Mongol's shoulders so that the point cut through the silk over the man's breastbone.

Harrison caught up the mace, grunting with savage satisfaction. It was a weapon more suited to his temperament than the dagger Khoda Khan had given him. No need to ask its use; if he had been bound and alone when the executioner entered, his brains would now have been clotting its spiked ball and the hollowed ebon block which so nicely accommodated a human head. Erlik Khan's executions varied along the whole gamut from the exquisitely subtle to the crudely bestial.

'The door's open,' said Harrison. 'Let's go!'

There were no keys on the body. Harrison doubted if the key in the door would fit any other in the building, but he locked the door and pocketed the key, hoping that would prevent the body from being soon discovered.

They emerged into a dim-lit corridor which presented the same unfinished appearance as the room they had just left. At the other end stairs wound down into shadowy gloom, and they descended warily, Harrison feeling along the wall to guide his steps. Khoda Khan seemed to see like a cat in the dark; he went down silently and surely. But it was Harrison who discovered the door. His hand, moving along the convex surface, felt the smooth stone give way to wood – a short narrow panel, through which a man could just squeeze. When the wall was covered with tapestry – as he knew it would be when Erlik Khan completed his house – it would be sufficiently hidden for a secret entrance.

Khoda Khan, behind him, was growing impatient at the delay, when somewhere below them both heard a noise simultaneously. It might have been a man ascending the winding stairs and it might not, but Harrison acted instinctively. He pushed and the door opened inward on noiseless oiled springs. A groping foot discovered narrow steps inside. With a whispered word to the Afghan he stepped through and Khoda Khan followed. He pulled the door shut again and they stood in total blackness with a curving wall on either hand. Harrison struck a match and a narrow stair was revealed, winding down.

'This place must be built like a castle,' Harrison muttered, wondering at the thickness of the walls. The match went out and they groped down in darkness too thick for even the Afghan to pierce. And suddenly both halted in their tracks. Harrison estimated that they had reached the level of the second floor, and through the inner wall came the mutter of voices. Harrison groped for another door, or a peep-hole for spying, but he found nothing of the sort. But straining his ear close to the stone, he began to understand what was being said beyond the wall, and a long-drawn hiss between clenched teeth told him that Khoda Khan likewise understood.

The first voice was Erlik Khan's; there was no mistaking that hollow reverberance. It was answered by a piteous, incoherent whimpering that brought sweat suddenly out on Harrison's flesh.

'No,' the Mongol was saying. 'I have come back, not from Hell as your barbarian superstitions suggest, but from a refuge unknown to your stupid police. I was saved from death by the steel cap I always wear beneath my coif. You are at a loss as to how you got here?'

'I don't understand!' It was the voice of Joan La Tour, half-hysterical, but undeniably sane. 'I remember opening a bottle of wine, and as soon as I drank I knew it was drugged. Then everything faded out . . . I don't remember anything except great black walls, and awful shapes skulking in the darkness. I ran through gigantic shadowy halls for a thousand years – '

'They were hallucinations of madness, of the juice of the black pomegranate,' answered Erlik Khan. Khoda Khan was muttering

blasphemously in his beard until Harrison admonished him to silence
with a fierce dig of his elbow. 'If you had drunk more you would have
died like a rabid dog. As it was, you went insane. But I knew the
antidote – possessed the drug that restored your sanity.'

'Why?' the girl whimpered bewilderedly.

'Because I did not wish you to die like a candle blown out in the
dark, my beautiful white orchid. I wish you to be fully sane so as to
taste to the last dregs the shame and agony of death, subtle and
prolonged. For the exquisite, an exquisite death. For the coarse-
fibered, the death of an ox, such as I have decreed for your friend
Harrison.'

'That will be more easily decreed than executed,' she retorted with
a flash of spirit.

'It is already accomplished,' the Mongol asserted imperturbably.
'The executioner has gone to him, and by this time Mr Harrison's
head resembles a crushed egg.'

'Oh, God!' At the sick grief and pain in that moan Harrison winced
and fought a frantic desire to shout out denial and reassurance.

Then she remembered something else to torture her.

'Khoda Khan! What have you done with Khoda Khan?'

The Afghan's fingers clamped like iron on Harrison's arm at the
sound of his name.

'When my men brought you away they did not take time to deal
with him,' replied the Mongol. 'They had not expected to take you
alive, and when fate cast you into their hands, they came away in
haste. He matters little. True, he killed four of my best men, but that
was merely the deed of a wolf. He has no mentality. He and the
detective are much alike – mere masses of brawn, brainless, helpless
against intellect like mine. Presently I shall attend to him. His corpse
shall be thrown on a dung-heap with a dead pig.'

'Allah!' Harrison felt Khoda Khan trembling with fury. 'Liar! I will
feed his yellow guts to the rats!'

Only Harrison's grip on his arm kept the maddened Moslem from
attacking the stone wall in an effort to burst through to his enemy.
The detective was running his hand over the surface, seeking a door,
but only blank stone rewarded him. Erlik Khan had not had time to
provide his unfinished house with as many secrets as his rat-runs
usually possessed.

They heard the Mongol clap his hands authoritatively, and they
sensed the entrance of men into the room. Staccato commands followed in Mongolian, there was a sharp cry of pain or fear, and then

silence followed the soft closing of a door. Though they could not see, both men knew instinctively that the chamber on the other side of the wall was empty. Harrison almost strangled with a panic of helpless rage. He was penned in these infernal walls and Joan La Tour was being borne away to some abominable doom.

'*Wallah!*' the Afghan was raving. 'They have taken her away to slay her! Her life and our *izzat* is at stake! By the Prophet's beard and my feet! I will burn this accursed house! I will slake the fire with Mongol blood! In Allah's name, *sahib*, let us do something!'

'Come on!' snarled Harrison. 'There must be another door somewhere!'

Recklessly they plunged down the winding stair, and about the time they had reached the first floor level, Harrison's groping hand felt a door. Even as he found the catch, it moved under his fingers. Their noise must have been heard through the wall, for the panel opened, and a shaven head was poked in, framed in the square of light. The Mongol blinked in the darkness, and Harrison brought the mace down on his head, experiencing a vengeful satisfaction as he felt the skull give way beneath the iron spikes. The man fell face down in the narrow opening and Harrison sprang over his body into the outer room before he took time to learn if there were others. But the chamber was untenanted. It was thickly carpeted, the walls hung with black velvet tapestries. The doors were of bronze-bound teak, with gilt-worked arches. Khoda Khan presented an incongruous contrast, bare-footed, with draggled turban and red-smeared knife.

But Harrison did not pause to philosophise. Ignorant as he was of the house, one way was as good as another. He chose a door at random and flung it open, revealing a wide corridor carpeted and tapestried like the chamber. At the other end, through wide satin curtains that hung from roof to floor, a file of men was just disappearing – tall, black-silk clad Mongols, heads bent sombrely, like a train of dusky ghosts. They did not look back.

'Follow them!' snapped Harrison. 'They must be headed for the execution –'

Khoda Khan was already sweeping down the corridor like a vengeful whirlwind. The thick carpet deadened their footfalls, so even Harrison's big shoes made no noise. There was a distinct feeling of unreality, running silently down that fantastic hall – it was like a dream in which natural laws are suspended. Even in that moment Harrison had time to reflect that this whole night had been like a nightmare, its violence and bloodshed like an evil dream. Erlik Khan had loosed the forces of chaos and insanity; murder had gone mad, and its frenzy was imparted to all actions and men caught in its maelstrom.

Khoda Khan would have burst headlong through the curtains – he was already drawing breath for a yell, and lifting his knife – if Harrison had not seized him. The Afghan's sinews were like cords under the detective's hands, and Harrison doubted his own ability to restrain him forcibly, but a vestige of sanity remained to the hillman.

Pushing him back, Harrison gazed between the curtains. There was a great double-valved door there, but it was partly open, and he looked into the room beyond. Khoda Khan's beard was jammed hard against his neck as the Afghan glared over his shoulder.

It was a large chamber, hung like the others with black velvet on which golden dragons writhed. There were thick rugs, and lanterns hanging from the ivory-inlaid ceiling cast a red glow that made for illusion. Black-robed men ranged along the wall might have been shadows but for their glittering eyes.

On a throne-like chair of ebony sat a grim figure, motionless as an image except when its loose robes stirred in the faintly moving air. Harrison felt the short hairs prickle at the back of his neck, just as a dog's hackles rise at the sight of an enemy. Khoda Khan muttered some incoherent blasphemy.

The Mongol's throne was set against a side wall. No one stood near him as he sat in solitary magnificence, like an idol brooding on human doom. In the centre of the room stood what looked uncomfortably like a sacrificial altar – a curiously carved block of stone that might have come out of the heart of the Gobi. On that stone lay Joan La Tour, white as a marble statue, her arms outstretched like a crucifix, her hands and feet extending over the edges of the block. Her dilated eyes stared upward as one lost to hope, aware of doom and eager only for death to put an end to agony. The physical torture had not yet begun, but a gaunt half-naked brute squatted on his haunches at the end of the altar, heating the point of a bronze rod in a dish full of glowing coals.

'Damn!' It was half curse, half sob of fury bursting from Harrison's lips. Then he was hurled aside and Khoda Khan burst into the room like a flying dervish, bristling beard, blazing eyes, knife and all. Erlik Khan came erect with a startled guttural as the Afghan came tearing down the room like a headlong hurricane of destruction. The torturer sprang up just in time to meet the yard-long knife lashing down, and it split his skull down through the teeth.

'*Aie!*' It was a howl from a score of Mongol throats.

'*Allaho akabar!*' yelled Khoda Khan, whirling the red knife about his head. He threw himself on the altar, slashing at Joan's bonds with a frenzy that threatened to dismember the girl.

Then from all sides the black-robed figures swarmed in, not noticing in their confusion that the Afghan had been followed by another grim figure who came with less abandon but with equal ferocity.

They were aware of Harrison only when he dealt a prodigious sweep of his mace, right and left, bowling men over like ten-pins, and reached the altar through the gap made in the bewildered throng. Khoda Khan had freed the girl and he wheeled, spitting like a cat, his bared teeth gleaming and each hair of his beard stiffly on end.

'*Allah!*' he yelled, spat in the faces of the oncoming Mongols, crouched as if to spring into the midst of them, then whirled and rushed headlong at the ebony throne.

The speed and unexpectedness of the move were stunning. With a choked cry Erlik Khan fired and missed at point-blank range – and then the breath burst from Khoda Khan in an ear-splitting yell as his knife plunged into the Mongol's breast and the point sprang a hand's breadth out of his black-clad back.

The impetus of his rush unchecked, Khoda Khan hurtled into the falling figure, crashing it back onto the ebony throne which splintered under the impact of the two heavy bodies. Bounding up, wrenching his dripping knife free, Khoda Khan whirled it high and howled like a wolf.

'*Ya Allah!* Wearer of steel caps! Carry the taste of my knife in your guts to Hell with you!'

There was a long hissing intake of breath as the Mongols stared wide-eyed at the black-robed, red-smeared figure crumpled grotesquely among the ruins of the broken throne; and in the instant that they stood like frozen men, Harrison caught up Joan and ran for the nearest door, bellowing: 'Khoda Khan! This way! Quick!'

With a howl and a whickering of blades the Mongols were at his heels. Fear of steel in his back winged Harrison's big feet, and Khoda Khan ran slantingly across the room to meet him at the door.

'Haste, *sahib!* Down the corridor! I will cover your retreat!'

'No! Take Joan and run!' Harrison literally threw her into the Afghan's arms and wheeled back in the doorway, lifting the mace. He was as berserk in his own way as was Khoda Khan, frantic with the madness that sometimes inspired men in the midst of combat.

The Mongols came on as if they, too, were blood-mad. They jammed the door with square snarling faces and squat silk-clad bodies before he could slam it shut. Knives licked at him, and gripping the mace with both hands he wielded it like a flail, working awful havoc among the shapes that strove in the doorway, wedged by the pressure from behind. The lights, the upturned snarling faces that dissolved in crimson ruin beneath his flailing, all swam in a red mist. He was not aware of his individual identity. He was only a man with a club, transported back fifty thousand years, a hairy-breasted, red-eyed primitive, wholly possessed in the crimson instinct for slaughter.

He felt like howling his incoherent exultation with each swing of his bludgeon that crushed skulls and spattered blood into his face. He did not feel the knives that found him, hardly realising it when the men facing him gave back, daunted at the havoc he was wreaking. He did not close the door then; it was blocked and choked by a ghastly mass of crushed and red-dripping flesh.

He found himself running down the corridor, his breath coming in great gulping gasps, following some dim instinct of preservation or realisation of duty that made itself heard amidst the red dizzy urge to grip his foes and strike, strike, strike, until he was himself engulfed in the crimson waves of death. In such moments the passion to die – die fighting – is almost equal to the will to live.

In a daze, staggering, bumping into walls and caroming off them, he reached the further end of the corridor where Khoda Khan was struggling with a lock. Joan was standing now, though she reeled on her feet, and seemed on the point of collapse. The mob was coming down the long corridor full cry behind them. Drunkenly Harrison thrust Khoda Khan aside and whirling the blood-fouled mace around his head, struck a stupendous blow that shattered the lock, burst the bolts out of their sockets and caved in the heavy panels as if they had been cardboard. The next instant they were through and Khoda Khan slammed the ruins of the door which sagged on its hinges, but somehow held together. There were heavy metal brackets on each jamb, and Khoda Khan found and dropped an iron bar in place just as the mob surged against it.

Through the shattered panels they howled and thrust their knives, but Harrison knew until they hewed away enough wood to enable them to reach in and dislodge it, the bar across the door would hold the splintered barrier in place. Recovering some of his wits, and feeling rather sick, he herded his companions ahead of him with desperate haste. He noticed, briefly, that he was stabbed in the calf, thigh, arm and shoulder. Blood soaked his ribboned shirt and ran down his limbs in streams. The Mongols were hacking at the door, snarling like jackals over carrion.

The apertures were widening, and through then he saw other Mongols running down the corridor with rifles; just as he wondered why they did not shoot through the door, then saw the reason. They were in a chamber which had been converted into a magazine. Cartridge cases were piled high along the wall, and there was at least one box of dynamite. But he looked in vain for rifles or pistols. Evidently they were stored in another part of the building.

Khoda Khan was jerking bolts on an opposite door, but he paused to glare about and yelping 'Allah!' he pounced on an open case, snatched something out – wheeled, yelled a curse and threw back his arm, but Harrison grabbed his wrist.

'Don't throw that, you idiot! You'll blow us all to Hell! They're afraid to shoot into this room, but they'll have that door down in a second or so, and finish us with their knives. Help Joan!'

It was a hand grenade Khoda Khan had found – the only one in an otherwise empty case, as a glance assured Harrison. The detective threw the door open, slammed it shut behind them as they plunged out into the starlight, Joan reeling, half carried by the Afghan. They seemed to have emerged at the back of the house. They ran across an open space, hunted creatures looking for a refuge. There was a crumbling stone wall, about breast-high to a man, and they ran through a wide gap in it, only to halt, a groan bursting from Harrison's lips. Thirty steps behind the ruined wall rose the steel fence of which Khoda Khan had spoken, a barrier ten feet high, topped with keen points. The door crashed open behind them and a gun spat venomously. They were in a trap. If they tried to climb the fence the Mongols had but to pick them off like monkeys shot off a ladder.

'Down behind the wall!' snarled Harrison, forcing Joan behind an uncrumbled section of the stone barrier. 'We'll make 'em pay for it, before they take us!'

The door was crowded with snarling faces, now leering in triumph. There were rifles in the hands of a dozen. They knew their victims had no firearms, and could not escape, and they themselves could use rifles without fear. Bullets began to splatter on the stone, then with a long-drawn yell Khoda Khan bounded to the top of the wall, ripping out the pin of the hand grenade with his teeth.

'*La illaha illulah; Muhammad rassoul ullah*!' he yelled, and hurled the bomb – not at the group which howled and ducked, but over their heads, into the magazine!

The next instant a rending crash tore the guts out of the night and a blinding blaze of fire ripped the darkness apart. In that glare Harrison had a glimpse of Khoda Khan, etched against the flame, hurtling backward, arms out-thrown . . . then there was utter blackness in which roared the thunder of the fall of the house of Erlik Khan as the shattered walls buckled, the beams splintered, the roof fell in and storey after storey came crashing down on the crumpled foundations.

How long Harrison lay like dead he never knew, blinded, deafened and paralysed; covered by falling debris. His first realisation was that there was something soft under him, something that writhed and whimpered. He had a vague feeling he ought not to hurt this soft something, so he began to shove the broken stones and mortar off him. His arm seemed dead, but eventually he excavated himself and staggered up, looking like a scarecrow in his rags. He groped among the rubble, grasped the girl and pulled her up.

'Joan!' His own voice seemed to come to him from a great distance; he had to shout to make her hear him. Their eardrums had been almost split by the concussion.

'Are you hurt?' He ran his one good hand over her to make sure.

'I don't think so,' she faltered dazedly. 'What – what happened?'

'Khoda Khan's bomb exploded the dynamite. The house fell in on the Mongols. We were sheltered by that wall; that's all that saved us.'

The wall was a shattered heap of broken stone, half covered by rubble – a waste of shattered masonry with broken beams thrust up through the litter, and shards of walls reeling drunkenly. Harrison fingered his broken arm and tried to think, his head swimming.

'Where is Khoda Khan?' cried Joan, seeming finally to shake off her daze.

'I'll look for him.' Harrison dreaded what he expected to find. 'He was blown off the wall like a straw in a wind.'

Stumbling over broken stones and bits of timber, he found the Afghan huddled grotesquely against the steel fence. His fumbling fingers told him of broken bones – but the man was still breathing. Joan came stumbling toward him, to fall beside Khoda Khan and flutter her quick fingers over him, sobbing hysterically.

'If we could get him medical attention he'll live. Listen!' She caught Harrison's arm with galvanised fingers; but he had heard it too – the sputter of a motor that was probably a police launch, coming to investigate the explosion.

Joan was tearing her scanty garments to pieces to staunch the blood that seeped from the Afghan's wounds, when miraculously Khoda Khan's pulped lips moved. Harrison, bending close, caught fragments of words: 'The curse of Allah – swine's flesh – my *izzat*.'

'You needn't worry about your *izzat*,' grunted Harrison, glancing at the ruins which hid the mangled figures that had been Mongolian terrorists. 'After this night's work you'll not go to jail.'

The Haunter of the Ring

As I entered John Kirowan's study I was too much engrossed in my own thoughts to notice, at first, the haggard appearance of his visitor, a big, handsome young fellow well known to me.

'Hello, Kirowan,' I greeted. 'Hello, Gordon. Haven't seen you for quite a while. How's Evelyn?' And before he could answer, still on the crest of the enthusiasm which had brought me there, I exclaimed: 'Look here, you fellows, I've got something that will make you stare! I got it from that robber Ahmed Mektub, and I paid high for it, but it's worth it. Look!' From under my coat I drew the jewel-hilted Afghan dagger which had fascinated me as a collector of rare weapons.

Kirowan, familiar with my passion, showed only polite interest, but the effect on Gordon was shocking.

With a strangled cry he sprang up and backward, knocking the chair clattering to the floor. Fists clenched and countenance livid he faced me, crying: 'Keep back! Get away from me, or – '

I was frozen in my tracks.

'What in the – ' I began bewilderedly, when Gordon, with another amazing change of attitude, dropped into a chair and sank his head in his hands. I saw his heavy shoulders quiver. I stared helplessly from him to Kirowan, who seemed equally dumbfounded.

'Is he drunk?' I asked.

Kirowan shook his head, and filling a brandy glass, offered it to the man. Gordon looked up with haggard eyes, seized the drink and gulped it down like a man half famished. Then he straightened up and looked at us shamefacedly.

'I'm sorry I went off my handle, O'Donnel,' he said. 'It was the unexpected shock of you drawing that knife.'

'Well,' I retorted, with some disgust, 'I suppose you thought I was going to stab you with it!'

'Yes, I did!' Then, at the utterly blank expression on my face, he added: 'Oh, I didn't actually think that; at least, I didn't reach that conclusion by any process of reasoning. It was just the blind primitive instinct of a hunted man, against whom anyone's hand may be turned.'

His strange words and the despairing way he said them sent a queer shiver of nameless apprehension down my spine.

'What are you talking about?' I demanded uneasily. 'Hunted? For what? You never committed a crime in your life.'

'Not in this life, perhaps,' he muttered.

'What do you mean?'

'What if retribution for a black crime committed in a previous life were hounding me?' he muttered.

'That's nonsense,' I snorted.

'Oh, is it?' he exclaimed, stung. 'Did you ever hear of my great-grandfather, Sir Richard Gordon of Argyle?'

'Sure; but what's that got to do with – '

'You've seen his portrait: doesn't it resemble me?'

'Well, yes,' I admitted, 'except that your expression is frank and wholesome whereas his is crafty and cruel.'

'He murdered his wife,' answered Gordon. 'Suppose the theory of reincarnation were true? Why shouldn't a man suffer in one life for a crime committed in another?'

'You mean you think you are the reincarnation of your great-grandfather? Of all the fantastic – well, since he killed his wife, I suppose you'll be expecting Evelyn to murder you!' This last was delivered in searing sarcasm, as I thought of the sweet, gentle girl Gordon had married. His answer stunned me.

'My wife,' he said slowly, 'has tried to kill me three times in the past week.'

There was no reply to that. I glanced helplessly at John Kirowan. He sat in his customary position, chin resting on his strong, slim hands; his white face was immobile, but his dark eyes gleamed with interest. In the silence I heard a clock ticking like a death-watch.

'Tell us the full story, Gordon,' suggested Kirowan, and his calm, even voice was like a knife that cut a strangling, relieving the unreal tension.

'You know we've been married less than a year,' Gordon began, plunging into the tale as though he were bursting for utterance; his words stumbled and tripped over one another. 'All couples have spats, of course, but we've never had any real quarrels. Evelyn is the best-natured girl in the world.'

'The first thing out of the ordinary occurred about a week ago. We had driven up in the mountains, left the car, and were wandering around picking wild flowers. At last we came to a steep slope, some thirty feet in height, and Evelyn called my attention to the flowers which grew thickly at the foot. I was looking over the edge and wondering if I could climb down without tearing my clothes to ribbons, when I felt a violent shove from behind that toppled me over.

'If it had been a sheer cliff, I'd have broken my neck. As it was, I went tumbling down, rolling and sliding, and brought up at the bottom scratched and bruised, with my garments in rags. I looked up and saw Evelyn staring down, apparently frightened half out of her wits.'

'Oh Jim!' she cried. 'Are you hurt? How came you to fall?'

'It was on the tip of my tongue to tell her that there was such a thing as carrying a joke too far, but these words checked me. I decided that she must have stumbled against me unintentionally, and actually didn't know it was she who precipitated me down the slope.'

'So I laughed it off, and went home. She made a great fuss over me, insisted on swabbing my scratches with iodine, and lectured me for my carelessness! I hadn't the heart to tell her it was her fault.'

'But four days later, the next thing happened. I was walking along our driveway, when I saw her coming up it in the automobile. I stepped out on the grass to let her by, as there isn't any curb along the driveway. She was smiling as she approached me, and slowed down the car, as if to speak to me. Then, just before she reached me, a most horrible change came over her expression. Without warning the car leaped at me like a living thing as she drove her foot down on the accelerator. Only a frantic leap backward saved me from being ground under the wheels. The car shot across the lawn and crashed into a tree. I ran to it and found Evelyn dazed and hysterical, but unhurt. She babbled of losing control of the machine.'

'I carried her into the house and sent for Doctor Donnelly. He found nothing seriously wrong with her, and attributed her dazed condition to fright and shock. Within half an hour she regained her normal senses, but she's refused to touch the wheel since. Strange to say, she seemed less frightened on her own account than on mine. She seemed vaguely to know that she'd nearly run me down, and grew hysterical again when she spoke of it. Yet she seemed to take it for granted that I knew the machine had got out of her control. But I distinctly saw her wrench the wheel around, and I know she deliberately tried to hit me – why, God alone knows.'

'Still I refused to let my mind follow the channel it was getting into. Evelyn had never given any evidence of any psychological weakness or "nerves"; she's always been a level-headed girl, whole-some and natural. But I began to think she was subject to crazy impulses. Most of us have felt the impulse to leap from tall buildings. And sometimes a person feels a blind, childish and utterly reason-less urge to harm someone. We pick up a pistol, and the thought suddenly enters our mind how easy it would be to send our friend, who sits smiling and unaware, into eternity with a touch of the trigger. Of course we don't do it, but the impulse is there. So I thought perhaps some lack of mental discipline made Evelyn sus-ceptible to these unguided impulses, and unable to control them.'

'Nonsense,' I broke in. 'I've known her since she was a baby. If she has any such trait, she's developed it since she married you.'

It was an unfortunate remark. Gordon caught it up with a des-pairing gleam in his eyes. 'That's just it – since she married me! It's a curse – a black, ghastly curse, crawling like a serpent out of the past! I tell you, I was Richard Gordon and she – she was Lady Elizabeth, his murdered wife!' His voice sank to a blood-freezing whisper.

I shuddered; it is an awful thing to look upon the ruin of a keen clean brain, and such I was certain that I surveyed in James Gordon. Why or how, or by what grisly chance it had come about I could not say, but I was certain the man was mad.

'You spoke of three attempts.' It was John Kirowan's voice again, calm and stable amid the gathering webs of horror and unreality.

'Look here!' Gordon lifted, his arm, drew back the sleeve and dis-played a bandage, the cryptic significance of which was intolerable.

'I came into the bathroom this morning looking for my razor,' he said. 'I found Evelyn just on the point of using my best shaving implement for some feminine purpose – to cut out a pattern, or something. Like many women she can't seem to realise the differ-ence between a razor and a butcher-knife or a pair of shears.

'I was a bit irritated, and I said: "Evelyn, how many times have I told you not to use my razors for such things? Bring it here; I'll give you my pocket-knife."

' "I – I – I'm sorry, Jim," she said. "I didn't know it would hurt the razor. Here it is." '

'She was advancing, holding the open razor toward me. I reached for it – then something warned me. It was the same look in her eyes, just as I had seen it the day she nearly ran over me. That was all that saved my life, for I instinctively threw up my hand just as she slashed at my throat with all her power. The blade gashed my arm as you see, before I caught her wrist. For an instant she fought me like a wild thing; her slender body was taut as steel beneath my hands. Then she went limp and the look in her eyes was replaced by a strange dazed expression. The razor slipped out of her fingers.

'I let go of her and she stood swaying as if about to faint. I went to the lavatory – my wound was bleeding in a beastly fashion – and the next thing I heard her cry out, and she was hovering over me.

' "Jim!" she cried. "How did you cut yourself so terribly?" '

Gordon shook his head and sighed heavily. 'I guess I was a bit out of my head. My self-control snapped.

' "Don't keep up this pretence, Evelyn," I said. "God knows what's got into you, but you know as well as I that you've tried to kill me three times in the past week."

'She recoiled as if I'd struck her, catching at her breast and staring at me as if at a ghost. She didn't say a word – and just what I said I don't remember. But when I finished I left her standing there white and still as a marble statue. I got my arm bandaged at a drugstore, and then came over here, not knowing what else to do.

'Kirowan, O'Donnel – it's damnable! Either my wife is subject to fits of insanity – ' He choked on the word. 'No, I can't believe it. Ordinarily her eyes are too clear and level – too utterly sane. But every time she has an opportunity to harm me, she seems to become a temporary maniac.'

He beat his fists together in his impotence and agony.

'But it isn't insanity! I used to work in a psychopathic ward, and I've seen every form of mental unbalance. My wife is not insane!'

'Then what – ' I began, but he turned haggard eyes on me.

'Only one alternative remains,' he answered. 'It is the old curse – from the days when I walked the earth with a heart as black as hell's darkest pits, and did evil in the sight of man and of God. She knows, in fleeting snatches of memory. People have glimpsed forbidden things in momentary liftings of the veil which bars life from life. She was Elizabeth Douglas, the ill-fated bride of Richard Gordon, whom he murdered in jealous frenzy, and the vengeance is hers. I shall die by her hands, as it was meant to be. And she – ' he bowed his head in his hands.

'Just a moment.' It was Kirowan again. 'You have mentioned a strange look in your wife's eyes. What sort of a look? Was it of maniacal frenzy?'

Gordon shook his head. 'It was an utter blankness. All the life and intelligence simply vanished, leaving her eyes dark wells of emptiness.'

Kirowan nodded, and asked a seemingly irrelevant question. 'Have you any enemies?'

'Not that I know of.'

'You forget Joseph Roelocke,' I said. 'I can't imagine that elegant sophisticate going to the trouble of doing you actual harm, but I have an idea that if he could discomfort you without any physical effort on his part, he'd do it with a right good will.'

Kirowan turned on me an eye that had suddenly become piercing. 'And who is this Joseph Roelocke?'

'A young exquisite who came into Evelyn's life and nearly rushed her off her feet for a while. But in the end she came back to her first love – Gordon here. Roelocke took it pretty hard. For all his suaveness there's a streak of violence and passion in the man that might have cropped out but for his infernal indolence and blasé indifference.'

'Oh, there's nothing to be said against Roelocke,' interrupted Gordon impatiently. 'He must know that Evelyn never really loved him. He merely fascinated her temporarily with his romantic Latin air.'

'Not exactly Latin, Jim,' I protested. 'Roelocke does look foreign, but it isn't Latin. It's almost Oriental.'

'Well, what has Roelocke to do with this matter?' Gordon snarled with the irascibility of frayed nerves. 'He's been as friendly as a man could be since Evelyn and I were married. In fact, only a week ago he sent her a ring which he said was a peace-offering and a belated wedding gift; said that after all, her jilting him was a greater misfortune for her than it was for him – the conceited jackass!'

'A ring?' Kirowan had suddenly come to life; it was as if something hard and steely had been sounded in him. 'What sort of a ring?'

'Oh, a fantastic thing – copper, made like a scaly snake coiled three times, with its tail in its mouth and yellow jewels for eyes. I gather he picked it up somewhere in Hungary.'

'He has travelled a great deal in Hungary?'

Gordon looked surprised at this questioning but answered: 'Why, apparently the man's travelled everywhere. I put him down as the pampered son of a millionaire. He never did any work, so far as I know.'

'He's a great student,' I put in. 'I've been up to his apartment several times, and I never saw such a collection of books – '

Gordon leaped to his feet with an oath, 'Are we all crazy?' he cried. 'I came up here hoping to get some help and you fellows fall to talking of Joseph Roelocke. I'll go to Doctor Donnelly – '

'Wait!' Kirowan stretched out a detaining hand. 'If you don't mind, we'll go over to your house. I'd like to talk to your wife.'

Gordon dumbly acquiesced. Harried and haunted by grisly forebodings, he knew not which way to turn, and welcomed anything that promised aid.

We drove over in his car, and scarcely a word was spoken on the way. Gordon was sunk in moody ruminations, and Kirowan had withdrawn himself into some strange aloof domain of thought beyond my ken. He sat like a statue, his dark vital eyes staring into space, not blankly, but as one who looks with understanding into some far realm.

Though I counted the man as my best friend, I knew but little of his past. He had come into my life as abruptly and unannounced as Joseph Roelocke had come into the life of Evelyn Ash. I had met him at the Wanderer's Club, which is composed of the drift of the world, travellers, eccentrics, and all manner of men whose paths lie outside the beaten tracks of life. I had been attracted to him, and intrigued by his strange powers and deep knowledge. I vaguely knew that he was the black sheep younger son of a titled Irish family, and that he had walked many strange ways. Gordon's mention of Hungary struck a chord in my memory; one phase of his life Kirowan had once let drop fragmentarily. I only knew that he had once suffered a bitter grief and a savage wrong, and that it had been in Hungary. But the nature of the episode I did not know.

At Gordon's house Evelyn met us calmly, showing inner agitation only by the over-restraint of her manner. I saw the beseeching look she stole at her husband. She was a slender, soft-spoken girl, whose dark eyes were always vibrant and alight with emotion. That child try to murder her adored husband? The idea was monstrous. Again I was convinced that James Gordon himself was deranged.

Following Kirowan's lead, we made a pretence of small talk, as if we had casually dropped in, but I felt that Evelyn was not deceived. Our conversation rang false and hollow, and presently Kirowan said: 'Mrs Gordon, that is a remarkable ring you are wearing. Do you mind if I look at it?'

'I'll have to give you my hand,' she laughed. 'I've been trying to get it off today, and it won't come off.'

She held out her slim white hand for Kirowan's inspection, and his face was immobile as he looked at the metal snake that coiled about her slim finger. He did not touch it. I myself was aware of an unaccountable repulsion. There was something almost obscene about that dull copperish reptile wound about the girl's white finger.

'It's evil-looking, isn't it?' She involuntarily shivered. 'At first I liked it, but now I can hardly bear to look at it. If I can get it off I intend to return it to Joseph – Mr Roelocke.'

Kirowan was about to make some reply, when the doorbell rang. Gordon jumped as if shot, and Evelyn rose quickly.

'I'll answer it, Jim – I know who it is.'

She returned an instant later with two more mutual friends, those inseparable cronies, Doctor Donnelly, whose burly body, jovial manner and booming voice were combined with as keen a brain as any in the profession, and Bill Bain, elderly, lean, wiry, acidly witty. Both were old friends of the Ash family. Doctor Donnelly had ushered Evelyn into the world, and Bain was always Uncle Bill to her.

'Howdy, Jim! Howdy, Mr Kirowan!' roared Donnelly. 'Hey, O'Donnel, have you got any firearms with you? Last time you nearly blew my head off showing me an old flintlock pistol that wasn't supposed to be loaded!'

'Doctor Donnelly!'

We all turned. Evelyn was standing beside a wide table, holding it as if for support. Her face was white. Our badinage ceased instantly. A sudden tension was in the air.

'Doctor Donnelly,' she repeated, holding her voice steady by an effort, 'I sent for you and Uncle Bill – for the same reason for which I know Jim has brought Mr Kirowan and Michael. There is a matter Jim and I can no longer deal with alone. There is something between us – something black and ghastly and terrible.'

'What are you talking about, girl?' All the levity was gone from Donnelly's great voice.

'My husband – ' She choked, then went blindly on: 'My husband has accused me of trying to murder him.'

The silence that fell was broken by Bain's sudden and energetic rise. His eyes blazed and his fists quivered.

'You young pup!' he shouted at Gordon. 'I'll knock the living daylights – '

'Sit down, Bill!' Donnelly's huge hand crushed his smaller companion back into his chair. 'No use goin' off half cocked. Go ahead, honey.'

'We need help. We can not carry this thing alone.' A shadow crossed her comely face. 'This morning Jim's arm was badly cut. He said I did it. I don't know. I was handing him the razor. Then I must have fainted. At least, everything faded away. When I came to myself he was washing his arm in the lavatory – and – and he accused me of trying to kill him.'

'Why, the young fool!' barked the belligerent Bain. 'Hasn't he sense enough to know that if you did cut him, it was an accident?'

'Shut up, won't you?' snorted Donnelly. 'Honey, did you say you fainted? That isn't like you.'

'I've been having fainting spells,' she answered. 'The first time was when we were in the mountains and Jim fell down a cliff. We were standing on the edge . . . then everything went black, and when my sight cleared, he was rolling down the slope.' She shuddered at the recollection.

'Then when I lost control of the car and it crashed into the tree. You remember – Jim called you over.'

Doctor Donnelly nodded his head ponderously.

'I don't remember you ever having fainting spells before.'

'But Jim says I pushed him over the cliff!' she cried hysterically. 'He says I tried to run him down in the car! He says I purposely slashed him with the razor!'

Doctor Donnelly turned perplexedly, toward the wretched Gordon.

'How about it, son?'

'God help me,' Gordon burst out in agony; 'it's true!'

'Why, you lying hound!' It was Bain who gave tongue, leaping again to his feet. 'If you want a divorce, why don't you get it in a decent way, instead of resorting to these despicable tactics – '

'Damn you!' roared Gordon, lunging up, and losing control of himself completely. 'If you say that I'll tear your jugular out!'

Evelyn screamed; Donnelly grabbed Bain ponderously and banged him back into his chair with no overly gentle touch, and Kirowan laid a hand lightly on Gordon's shoulder. The man seemed to crumple into himself. He sank back into his chair and held out his hands gropingly toward his wife.

'Evelyn,' he said, his voice thick with labouring emotion, 'you know I love you. I feel like a dog. But God help me, it's true. If we go on this way, I'll be a dead man, and you – '

'Don't say it!' she screamed. 'I know you wouldn't lie to me, Jim. If you say I tried to kill you, I know I did. But I swear, Jim, I didn't do it consciously. Oh, I must be going mad! That's why my dreams have been so wild and terrifying lately – '

'Of what have you dreamed, Mrs Gordon?' asked Kirowan gently.

She pressed her hands to her temples and stared dully at him, as if only half comprehending.

'A black thing,' she muttered. 'A horrible faceless black thing that mews and mumbles and paws over me with apish hands. I dream of it every night. And in the daytime I try to kill the only man I ever loved. I'm going mad! Maybe I'm already crazy and don't know it.'

'Calm yourself, honey.' To Doctor Donnelly, with all his science, it was only another case of feminine hysteria. His matter-of-fact voice seemed to soothe her, and she sighed and drew a weary hand through her damp locks.

'We'll talk this all over, and everything's goin' to be okay,' he said, drawing a thick cigar from his vest pocket. 'Gimme a match, honey.'

She began mechanically to feel about the table, and just as mechanically Gordon said: 'There are matches in the drawer, Evelyn.'

She opened the drawer and began groping in it, when suddenly, as if struck by recollection and intuition, Gordon sprang up, white-faced, and shouted: 'No, no! Don't open that drawer – don't – '

Even as he voiced that urgent cry, she stiffened, as if at the feel of something in the drawer. Her change of expression held us all frozen, even Kirowan. The vital intelligence vanished from her eyes like a blown-out flame, and into them came the look Gordon had described as blank. The term was descriptive. Her beautiful eyes were dark wells of emptiness, as if the soul had been withdrawn from behind them.

Her hand came out of the drawer holding a pistol, and she fired point-blank. Gordon reeled with a groan and went down, blood starting from his head. For a flashing instant she looked down stupidly at the smoking gun in her hand, like one suddenly waking from a nightmare. Then her wild scream of agony smote our ears.

'Oh God, I've killed him! Jim! Jim!'

She reached him before any of us, throwing herself on her knees and cradling his bloody head in her arms, while she sobbed in an unbearable passion of horror and anguish. The emptiness was gone from her eyes; they were alive and dilated with grief and terror.

I was making toward my prostrate friend with Donnelly and Bain, but Kirowan caught my arm. His face was no longer immobile; his eyes glittered with a controlled savagery.

'Leave him to them!' he snarled. 'We are hunters, not healers! Lead me to the house of Joseph Roelocke!'

I did not question him. We drove there in Gordon's car.

I had the wheel, and something about the grim face of my companion caused me to hurl the machine recklessly through the traffic. I had the sensation of being part of a tragic drama which was hurtling with headlong speed toward a terrible climax.

I wrenched the car to a grinding halt at the curb before the building where Roelocke lived in a bizarre apartment high above the city. The very elevator that shot us skyward seemed imbued with something of Kirowan's driving urge for haste. I pointed out Roelocke's door, and he cast it open without knocking and shouldered his way in. I was close at his heels.

Roelocke, in a dressing-gown of Chinese silk worked with dragons, was lounging on a divan, puffing quickly at a cigarette. He sat up, overturning a wine-glass which stood with a half-filled bottle at his elbow.

Before Kirowan could speak, I burst out with our news. 'James Gordon has been shot!'

He sprang to his feet. 'Shot? When? When did she kill him?'

'She?' I glared in bewilderment. 'How did you know – '

With a steely hand Kirowan thrust me aside, and as the men faced each other, I saw recognition flare up in Roelocke's face. They made a strong contrast: Kirowan, tall, pale with some white-hot passion; Roelocke, slim, darkly handsome, with the saracenic arch of his slim brows above his black eyes. I realised that whatever else occurred, it lay between those two men. They were not strangers; I could sense like a tangible thing the hate that lay between them.

'John Kirowan!' softly whispered Roelocke.

'You remember me, Yosef Vrolok!' Only an iron control kept Kirowan's voice steady. The other merely stared at him without speaking.

'Years ago,' said Kirowan more deliberately, 'when we delved in the dark mysteries together in Budapest, I saw whither you were drifting. I drew back; I would not descend to the foul depths of forbidden occultism and diabolism to which you sank. And because I would not, you despised me, and you robbed me of the only woman I ever loved; you turned her against me by means of your vile arts, and then you degraded and debauched her, sank her into your own foul slime. I had killed you with my hands then, Yosef Vrolok – vampire by nature as well as by name that you are – but your arts protected you from physical vengeance. But you have trapped yourself at last!'

Kirowan's voice rose in fierce exultation. All his cultured restraint had been swept away from him, leaving a primitive, elemental man, raging and gloating over a hated foe.

'You sought the destruction of James Gordon and his wife, because she unwittingly escaped your snare; you – '

Roelocke shrugged his shoulders and laughed. 'You are mad. I have not seen the Gordons for weeks. Why blame me for their family troubles?'

Kirowan snarled. 'Liar as always. What did you say just now when O'Donnel told you Gordon had been shot? "When did she kill him?" You were expecting to hear that the girl had killed her husband. Your psychic powers had told you that a climax was close at hand. You were nervously awaiting news of the success of your devilish scheme.

'But I did not need a slip of your tongue to recognise your handiwork. I knew as soon as I saw the ring on Evelyn Gordon's finger; the ring she could not remove; the ancient and accursed ring of Thoth-amon, handed down by foul cults of sorcerers since the days of forgotten Stygia, I knew that ring was yours, and I knew by what ghastly rites you came to possess it. And I knew its power. Once she put it on her finger, in her innocence and ignorance, she was in your power. By your black magic you summoned the black elemental spirit, the haunter of the ring, out of the gulfs of Night and the ages. Here in your accursed chamber you performed unspeakable rituals to drive Evelyn Gordon's soul from her body, and to cause that body to be possessed by that godless sprite from outside the human universe.

'She was too clean and wholesome, her love for her husband too strong, for the fiend to gain complete and permanent possession of her body; only for brief instants could it drive her own spirit into the void and animate her form. But that was enough for your purpose. But you have brought ruin upon yourself by your vengeance!'

Kirowan's voice rose to a feline screech.

'What was the price demanded by the fiend you drew from the Pits? Ha, you blench! Yosef Vrolok is not the only man to have learned forbidden secrets! After I left Hungary, a broken man, I took up again the study of the black arts, to trap you, you cringing serpent! I explored the ruins of Zimbabwe, the lost mountains of inner Mongolia, and the forgotten jungle islands of the southern seas. I learned what sickened my soul so that I forswore occultism for ever, but I learned of the black spirit that deals death by the hand of a beloved one, and is controlled by a master of magic.

'But, Yosef Vrolok, you are not an adept! You have not the power to control the fiend you have invoked. And you have sold your soul!'

The Hungarian tore at his collar as if it were a strangling noose. His face had changed, as if a mask had dropped away; he looked much older.

'You lie!' he panted. 'I did not promise him my soul – '

'I do not lie!' Kirowan's shriek was shocking in its wild exultation. 'I know the price a man must pay for calling forth the nameless shape that roams the gulfs of Darkness. Look! There in the corner behind you! A nameless, sightless thing is laughing – is mocking you! It has fulfilled its bargain, and it has come for you, Yosef Vrolok!'

'No! No!' shrieked Vrolok, tearing his limp collar away from his sweating throat. His composure had crumpled, and his demoralisation was sickening to see. 'I tell you it was not my soul . . . I promised it a soul, but not my soul – he must take the soul of the girl, or of James Gordon.'

'Fool!' roared Kirowan. 'Do you think he could take the souls of innocence? That he would not know they were beyond his reach? The girl and the youth he could kill; their souls were not his to take or yours to give. But your black soul is not beyond his reach, and he will have his wage. Look! He is materialising behind you! He is growing out of thin air!'

Was it the hypnosis inspired by Kirowan's burning words that caused me to shudder and grow cold, to feel an icy chill that was not of earth pervade the room? Was it a trick of light and shadow that seemed to produce the effect of a black anthropomorphic shadow on the wall behind the Hungarian? No, by heaven! It grew, it swelled – Vrolok had not turned. He stared at Kirowan with eyes starting from his head, hair standing stiffly on his scalp, sweat dripping from his livid face.

Kirowan's cry started shudders down my spine.

'Look behind you, fool! I see him! He has come! He is here! His grisly mouth gapes in awful laughter! His misshapen paws reach for you!'

And then at last Vrolok wheeled, with an awful shriek, throwing his arms above his head in a gesture of wild despair. And for one brain-shattering instant he was blotted out by a great black shadow . . . Kirowan grasped my arm and we fled from that accursed chamber, blind with horror.

The same paper which bore a brief item telling of James Gordon having suffered a slight scalp-wound by the accidental discharge of a pistol in his home, headlined the sudden death of Joseph Roelocke, wealthy and eccentric clubman, in his sumptuous apartments – apparently from heart-failure.

I read it at breakfast, while I drank cup after cup of black coffee, from a hand that was not too steady, even after the lapse of a night.

Across the table from me Kirowan likewise seemed to lack appetite. He brooded, as if he roamed again through bygone years.

'Gordon's fantastic theory of reincarnation was wild enough,' I said at last. 'But the actual facts were still more incredible. Tell me, Kirowan, was that last scene the result of hypnosis? Was it the power of your words that made me seem to see a black horror grow out of the air and rip Yosef Vrolok's soul from his living body?'

He shook his head. 'No human hypnotism would strike that black-hearted devil dead on the floor. No; there are beings outside the ken of common humanity, foul shapes of transcosmic evil. Such a one it was with which Vrolok dealt.'

'But how could it claim his soul?' I persisted. 'If indeed such an awful bargain had been struck, it had not fulfilled its part, for James Gordon was not dead, but merely knocked senseless.'

'Vrolok did not know it,' answered Kirowan. 'He thought that Gordon was dead, and I convinced him that he himself had been trapped, and was doomed. In his demoralisation he fell easy prey to the thing he called forth. It, of course, was always watching for a moment of weakness on his part. The powers of Darkness never deal fairly with human beings; he who traffics with them is always cheated in the end.'

'It's a mad nightmare,' I muttered. 'But it seems to me, then, that you as much as anything else brought about Vrolok's death.'

'It is gratifying to think so,' Kirowan answered. 'Evelyn Gordon is safe now; and it is a small repayment for what he did to another girl, years ago, and in a far country.'

Graveyard Rats

Chapter 1. *The head from the grave*

Saul Wilkinson awoke suddenly, and lay in the darkness with beads of cold sweat on his hands and face. He shuddered at the memory of the dream from which he had awakened.

But horrible dreams were nothing uncommon. Grisly nightmares had haunted his sleep since early childhood. It was another fear that clutched his heart with icy fingers – fear of the sound that had roused him. It had been a furtive step – hands fumbling in the dark.

And now a small scurrying sounded in the room – a rat running back and forth across the floor.

He groped under his pillow with trembling fingers. The house was still, but imagination peopled its darkness with shapes of horror. But it was not all imagination. A faint stir of air told him the door that gave on the broad hallway was open. He knew he had closed that door before he went to bed. And he knew it was not one of his brothers who had come so subtly to his room.

In that fear-tense, hate-haunted household, no man came by night to his brother's room without first making himself known.

This was especially the case since an old feud had claimed the eldest brother four days since – John Wilkinson, shot down in the streets of the little hill-country town by Joel Middleton, who had escaped into the post oak grown hills, swearing still greater vengeance against the Wilkinsons.

All this flashed through Saul's mind as he drew the revolver from under his pillow.

As he slid out of bed, the creak of the springs brought his heart into his throat, and he crouched there for a moment, holding his breath and straining his eyes into the darkness.

Richard was sleeping upstairs, and so was Harrison, the city detective Peter had brought out to hunt down Joel Middleton. Peter's room was on the ground floor, but in another wing. A yell for help might awaken all three, but it would also bring a hail of lead at him, if Joel Middleton were crouching over there in the blackness.

Saul knew this was his fight, and must be fought out alone, in the darkness he had always feared and hated. And all the time sounded that light, scampering patter of tiny feet, racing up and down, up and down . . .

Crouching against the wall, cursing the pounding of his heart, Saul fought to steady his quivering nerves. He was backed against the wall which formed the partition between his room and the hall.

The windows were faint grey squares in the blackness, and he could dimly make out objects of furniture in all except one side of the room. Joel Middleton must be over there, crouching by the old fireplace, which was invisible in the darkness.

But why was he waiting? And why was that accursed rat racing up and down before the fireplace, as if in a frenzy of fear and greed? Just so Saul had seen rats race up and down the floor of the meat-house, frantic to get at flesh suspended out of reach.

Noiselessly, Saul moved along the wall toward the door. If a man was in the room, he would presently be lined between himself and a window. But as he glided along the wall like a night-shirted ghost, no ominous bulk grew out of the darkness. He reached the door and closed it soundlessly, wincing at his nearness to the unrelieved blackness of the hall outside.

But nothing happened. The only sounds were the wild beating of his heart, the loud ticking of the old clock on the mantelpiece, the maddening patter of the unseen rat. Saul clenched his teeth against the shrieking of his tortured nerves. Even in his growing terror he found time to wonder frantically why that rat ran up and down before the fireplace.

The tension became unbearable. The open door proved that Middleton, or someone – or *something* – had come into that room. Why would Middleton come save to kill? But why in God's name had he not struck already? What was he waiting for?

Saul's nerve snapped suddenly. The darkness was strangling him and those pattering rat-feet were red-hot hammers on his crumbling brain. He must have light, even though that light brought hot lead ripping through him.

In stumbling haste he groped to the mantelpiece, fumbling for the lamp. And he cried out – a choked, horrible croak that could not have carried beyond his room. For his hand, groping in the dark on the mantel, had touched the hair on a human scalp!

A furious squeal sounded in the darkness at his feet and a sharp pain pierced his ankle as the rat attacked him, as if he were an intruder seeking to rob it of some coveted object.

But Saul was hardly aware of the rodent as he kicked it away and reeled back, his brain a whirling turmoil. Matches and candles were on the table, and to it he lurched, his hands sweeping the dark and finding what he wanted.

He lighted a candle and turned, gun lifted in a shaking hand. There was no living man in the room except himself. But his distended eyes focused themselves on the mantelpiece . . . and the object on it.

He stood frozen, his brain at first refusing to register what his eyes revealed. Then he croaked inhumanly and the gun crashed on the hearth as it slipped through his numb fingers.

John Wilkinson was dead, with a bullet through his heart. It had been three days since Saul had seen his body nailed into the crude coffin and lowered into the grave in the old Wilkinson family graveyard. For three days the hard clay soil had baked in the hot sun above the coffined form of John Wilkinson.

Yet from the mantel John Wilkinson's face leered at him . . . white and cold and dead.

It was no nightmare, no dream of madness. There on the mantelpiece rested John Wilkinson's severed head.

And before the fireplace, up and down, up and down, scampered a creature with red eyes, that squeaked and squealed . . . a great grey rat, maddened by its failure to reach the flesh its ghoulish hunger craved.

Saul Wilkinson began to laugh – horrible, soul-shaking shrieks that mingled with the squealing of the grey ghoul. Saul's body rocked to and fro, and the laughter turned to insane weeping, that gave way in turn to hideous screams that echoed through the old house and brought the sleepers out of their sleep.

They were the screams of a madman. The horror of what he had seen had blasted Saul Wilkinson's reason like a blown-out candle flame.

Chapter 2. *Madman's hate*

It was those screams which roused Steve Harrison, sleeping in an upstairs chamber. Before he was fully awake he was on his way down the unlighted stairs, pistol in one hand and flashlight in the other.

Down in the hallway he saw light streaming from under a closed door, and made for it. But another was before him. Just as Harrison reached the landing, he saw a figure rushing across the hall, and flashed his beam on it.

It was Peter Wilkinson, tall and gaunt, with a poker in his hand. He yelled something incoherent, threw open the door and rushed in.

Harrison heard him exclaim: 'Saul! What's the matter? What are you looking at – ' Then a terrible cry: '*My God!*'

The poker clanged on the floor, and then the screams of the maniac rose to a crescendo of fury.

It was at this instant that Harrison reached the door and took in the scene with one startled glance. He saw two men in nightshirts grappling in the candlelight, while from the mantel a cold, dead, white face looked blindly down on them, and a grey rat ran in mad circles about their feet.

Into that scene of horror and madness Harrison propelled his powerful, thick-set body. Peter Wilkinson was in sore straits. He had dropped his poker and now, with blood streaming from a wound in his head, he was vainly striving to tear Saul's lean fingers from his throat.

The glare in Saul's eyes told Harrison the man was mad. Crooking one massive arm about the maniac's neck, he tore him loose from his victim with an exertion of sheer strength that not even the abnormal energy of insanity could resist.

The madman's stringy muscles were like steel wires under the detective's hands, and Saul twisted about in his grasp, his teeth snapping, beastlike, for Harrison's bull-throat. The detective shoved the clawing, frothing fury away from him and smashed a fist to the madman's jaw. Saul crashed to the floor and lay still, eyes glazed and limbs quivering.

Peter reeled back against a table, purple-faced and gagging.

'Get cords, quick!' snapped Harrison, heaving the limp figure off the floor and letting it slump into a great arm-chair. 'Tear that sheet in strips. We've got to tie him up before he comes to. Hell's fire!'

The rat had made a ravening attack on the senseless man's bare feet. Harrison kicked it away, but it squeaked furiously and came charging back with ghoulish persistence. Harrison crushed it under his foot, cutting short its maddened squeal.

Peter, gasping convulsively, thrust into the detective's hands the strips he had torn from the sheet, and Harrison bound the limp limbs with professional efficiency. In the midst of his task he looked up to see Richard, the youngest brother, standing in the doorway, his face like chalk.

'Richard!' choked Peter. 'Look! My God! John's head!'

'I see!' Richard licked his lips. 'But why are you tying up Saul?'

'He's crazy,' snapped Harrison. 'Get me some whiskey, will you?'

As Richard reached for a bottle on a curtained shelf, booted feet hit the porch outside, and a voice yelled: 'Hey, there! Dick! What's wrong?'

'That's our neighbour, Jim Allison,' muttered Peter.

He stepped to the door opposite the one that opened into the hall and turned the key in the ancient lock. That door opened upon a side porch. A tousle-headed man with his pants pulled on over his night-shirt came blundering in.

'What's the matter?' he demanded. 'I heard somebody hollerin', and run over quick as I could. What you doin' to Saul – good God Almighty!'

He had seen the head on the mantel, and his face went ashen.

'Go get the marshal, Jim!' croaked Peter. 'This is Joel Middleton's work!'

Allison hurried out, stumbling as he peered back over his shoulder in morbid fascination.

Harrison had managed to spill some liquor between Saul's livid lips. He handed the bottle to Peter and stepped to the mantel. He touched the grisly object, shivering slightly as he did so. His eyes narrowed suddenly.

'You think Middleton dug up your brother's grave and cut off his head?' he asked.

'Who else?' Peter stared blankly at him.

'Saul's mad. Madmen do strange things. Maybe Saul did this.'

'No! No!' exclaimed Peter, shuddering. 'Saul hasn't left the house all day. John's grave was undisturbed this morning, when I stopped by the old graveyard on my way to the farm. Saul was sane when he went to bed. It was seeing John's head that drove him mad. Joel Middleton has been here, to take this horrible revenge!' He sprang up suddenly, shrilling, 'My God, he may still be hiding in the house somewhere!'

'We'll search it,' snapped Harrison. 'Richard, you stay here with Saul. You might come with me, Peter.'

In the hall outside the detective directed a beam of light on the heavy front door. The key was turned in the massive lock. He turned and strode down the hall, asking: 'Which door is farthest from any sleeping chamber?'

'The back kitchen door!' Peter answered, and led the way. A few moments later they were standing before it. It stood partly open, framing a crack of starlit sky.

'He must have come and gone this way,' muttered Harrison. 'You're sure this door was locked?'

'I locked all outer doors myself,' asserted Peter. 'Look at those scratches on the outer side! And there's the key lying on the floor inside.'

'Old-fashioned lock,' grunted Harrison. 'A man could work the key out with a wire from the outer side and force the lock easily. And this is the logical lock to force, because the noise of breaking it wouldn't likely be heard by anybody in the house.'

He stepped out onto the deep back porch. The broad back yard was without trees or brushes, separated by a barbed-wire fence from a pasture-lot, which ran to a wood-lot thickly grown with post oaks, part of the woods which hemmed in the village of Lost Knob on all sides.

Peter stared toward that woodland, a low, black rampart in the faint starlight, and he shivered.

'He's out there, somewhere!' he whispered. 'I never suspected he'd dare strike at us in our own house. I brought you here to hunt him down. I never thought we'd need you to protect us!'

Without replying, Harrison stepped down into the yard. Peter cringed back from the starlight, and remained crouching at the edge of the porch.

Harrison crossed the narrow pasture and paused at the ancient rail fence which separated it from the woods. They were black as only post oak thickets can be.

No rustle of leaves, no scrape of branches betrayed a lurking presence. If Joel Middleton had been there, he must have already sought refuge in the rugged hills that surrounded Lost Knob.

Harrison turned back toward the house. He had arrived at Lost Knob late the preceding evening. It was now somewhat past midnight. But the grisly news was spreading, even in the dead of night.

The Wilkinson house stood at the western edge of the town, and the Allison house was the only one within a hundred yards of it. But Harrison saw lights springing up in distant windows.

Peter stood on the porch, head out-thrust on his long, buzzard-like neck.

'Find anything?' he called anxiously.

'Tracks wouldn't show on this hard-baked ground,' grunted the detective. 'Just what did you see when you ran into Saul's room?'

'Saul standing before the mantelboard, screaming with his mouth wide open,' answered Peter. 'When I saw – what he saw, I must have cried out and dropped the poker. Then Saul leaped on me like a wild beast.'

'Was his door locked?'

'Closed, but not locked. The lock got broken accidentally a few days ago.'

'One more question: has Middleton ever been in this house before?'

'Not to my knowledge,' replied Peter grimly. 'Our families have hated each other for twenty-five years. Joel's the last of his name.'

Harrison re-entered the house. Allison had returned with the marshal, McVey, a tall, taciturn man who plainly resented the detective's presence. Men were gathering on the side porch and in the yard. They talked in low mutters, except for Jim Allison, who was vociferous in his indignation.

'This finishes Joel Middleton!' he proclaimed loudly. 'Some folks sided with him when he killed John. I wonder what they think now? Diggin' up a dead man and cuttin' his head off! I reckon folks won't wait for no jury to tell 'em what to do with Joel Middleton!'

'Better catch him before you start lynchin' him,' grunted McVey. 'Peter, I'm takin' Saul to the county seat.'

Peter nodded mutely. Saul was recovering consciousness, but the mad glaze of his eyes was unaltered. Harrison spoke: 'Suppose we go to the Wilkinson graveyard and see what we can find? We might be able to track Middleton from there.'

'They brought you in here to do the job they didn't think I was good enough to do,' snarled McVey. 'All right. Go ahead and do it – alone. I'm takin' Saul to the county seat.'

With the aid of his deputies he lifted the bound maniac and strode out. Neither Peter nor Richard offered to accompany him. A tall, gangling man stepped from among his fellows and awkwardly addressed Harrison: 'What the marshal does is his own business, but all of us here are ready to help all we can, if you want to git a posse together and comb the country.'

'Thanks, no.' Harrison was unintentionally abrupt. 'You can help me by all clearing out, right now. I'll work this thing out alone, in my own way, as the marshal suggested.'

The men moved off at once, silent and resentful, and Jim Allison followed them, after a moment's hesitation. When all had gone, Harrison closed the door and turned to Peter.

'Will you take me to the graveyard?'

Peter shuddered. 'Isn't it a terrible risk? Middleton has shown he'll stop at nothing.'

'Why should he?' Richard laughed savagely. His mouth was bitter, his eyes alive with harsh mockery, and lines of suffering were carven deep in his face.

'We never stopped hounding him,' said he. 'John cheated him out of his last bit of land – that's why Middleton killed him. For which you were devoutly thankful!'

'You're talking wild!' exclaimed Peter.

Richard laughed bitterly. 'You old hypocrite! We're all beasts of prey, we Wilkinsons – like this thing!' He kicked the dead rat viciously. 'We all hated each other. You're glad Saul's crazy! You're glad John's dead. Only me left now, and I have a heart disease. Oh, stare if you like! I'm no fool. I've seen you poring over Aaron's lines in *Titus Andronicus*:

> Oft have I digg'd up dead men from their graves,
> And set them upright at their dear friends' doors!

'You're mad yourself!' Peter sprang up, livid.

'Oh, am I?' Richard had lashed himself almost into a frenzy. 'What proof have we that you didn't cut off John's head? You knew Saul was a neurotic, that a shock like that might drive him mad! And you visited the graveyard yesterday!'

Peter's contorted face was a mask of fury. Then, with an effort of iron control, he relaxed and said quietly: 'You are over-wrought, Richard.'

'Saul and John hated you,' snarled Richard. 'I know why. It was because you wouldn't agree to leasing our farm on Wild River to that oil company. But for your stubbornness we might all be wealthy.'

'You know why I wouldn't lease,' snapped Peter. 'Drilling there would ruin the agricultural value of the land – certain profit, not a risky gamble like oil.'

'So you say,' sneered Richard. 'But suppose that's just a smoke screen? Suppose you dream of being the sole, surviving heir, and becoming an oil millionaire all by yourself, with no brothers to share . . .'

Harrison broke in: 'Are we going the chew the rag all night?'

'No!' Peter turned his back on his brother. 'I'll take you to the graveyard. I'd rather face Joel Middleton in the night than listen to the ravings of this lunatic any longer.'

'I'm not going,' snarled Richard. 'Out there in the black night there's too many chances for you to remove the remaining heir. I'll go and stay the rest of the night with Jim Allison.'

He opened the door and vanished in the darkness.

Peter picked up the head and wrapped it in a cloth, shivering lightly as he did so.

'Did you notice how well preserved the face is?' he muttered. 'One would think that after three days – Come on. I'll take it and put it back in the grave where it belongs.'

'I'll kick this dead rat outdoors,' Harrison began, turning – and then stopped short. 'The damned thing's gone!'

Peter Wilkinson paled as his eyes swept the empty floor.

'It was there!' he whispered. 'It was dead. You smashed it! It couldn't come to life and run away.'

'We'll, what about it?' Harrison did not mean to waste time on this minor mystery.

Peter's eyes gleamed wearily in the candlelight.

'It was a graveyard rat!' he whispered. 'I never saw one in an inhabited house, in town, before! The Indians used to tell strange tales about them! They said they were not beasts at all, but evil, cannibal demons, into which entered the spirits of wicked, dead men at whose corpses they gnawed!'

'Hell's fire!' Harrison snorted, blowing out the candle. But his flesh crawled. After all, a dead rat could not crawl away by itself.

Chapter 3. *The feathered shadow*

Clouds had rolled across the stars. The air was hot and stifling. The narrow, rutty road that wound westward into the hills was atrocious. But Peter Wilkinson piloted his ancient Model T Ford skilfully, and the village was quickly lost to sight behind them. They passed no more houses. On each side the dense post oak thickets crowded close to the barbed-wire fences.

Peter broke the silence suddenly: 'How did that rat come into our house? They overrun the woods along the creeks, and swarm in every country graveyard in the hills. But I never saw one in the village before. It must have followed Joel Middleton when he brought the head – '

A lurch and a monotonous bumping brought a curse from Harrison. The car came to a stop with a grind of brakes.

'Flat,' muttered Peter. 'Won't take me long to change tyres. You watch the woods. Joel Middleton might be hiding anywhere.'

That seemed good advice. While Peter wrestled with rusty metal and stubborn rubber, Harrison stood between him and the nearest clump of trees, with his hand on his revolver. The night wind blew fitfully through the leaves, and once he thought he caught the gleam of tiny eyes among the stems.

'That's got it,' announced Peter at last, turning to let down the jack. 'We've wasted enough time.'

'*Listen*!' Harrison started, tensed. Off to the west had sounded a sudden scream of pain or fear. Then there came the impact of racing feet on the hard ground, the crackling of brush, as if someone fled blindly through the bushes within a few hundred yards of the road. In an instant Harrison was over the fence and running toward the sounds.

'Help! Help!' it was the voice of dire terror. 'Almighty God! Help!'

'This way!' yelled Harrison, bursting into an open flat. The unseen fugitive evidently altered his course in response, for the heavy footfalls grew louder, and then there rang out a terrible shriek, and a figure staggered from the bushes on the opposite side of the glade and fell headlong.

The dim starlight showed a vague writhing shape, with a darker figure on its back. Harrison caught the glint of steel, heard the sound of a blow. He threw up his gun and fired at a venture. At the crack of the shot, the darker figure rolled free, leaped up and vanished in the bushes. Harrison ran on, a queer chill crawling along his spine because of what he had seen in the flash of the shot.

He crouched at the edge of the bushes and peered into them. The shadowy figure had come and gone, leaving no trace except the man who lay groaning in the glade.

Harrison bent over him, snapping on his flashlight. He was an old man, a wild, unkempt figure with matted white hair and beard. That beard was stained with red now, and blood oozed from a deep stab in his back.

'Who did this?' demanded Harrison, seeing that it was useless to try to stanch the flow of blood. The old man was dying. 'Joel Middleton?'

'It couldn't have been!' Peter had followed the detective. 'That's old Joash Sullivan, a friend of Joel's. He's half crazy, but I've suspected that he's been keeping in touch with Joel and giving his tips – '

'Joel Middleton,' muttered the old man. 'I'd been to find him, to tell the news about John's head – '

'Where's Joel hiding?' demanded the detective.

Sullivan choked on a flow of blood, spat and shook his head.

'You'll never learn from me!' He directed his eyes on Peter with the eerie glare of the dying. 'Are you taking your brother's head back to his grave, Peter Wilkinson? Be careful you don't find your own grave before this night's done! Evil on all your name! The devil owns your souls and the graveyard rats'll eat your flesh! The ghost of the dead walks the night!'

'What do you mean?' demanded Harrison. 'Who stabbed you?'

'A dead man!' Sullivan was going fast. 'As I come back from meetin' Joel Middleton I met him. Wolf Hunter, the Tonkawa chief your grandpap murdered so long ago, Peter Wilkinson! He chased me and knifed me. I saw him plain, in the starlight – naked in his loin-clout and feathers and paint, just as I saw him when I was a child, before your grandpap killed him!

'Wolf Hunter took your brother's head from the grave!' Sullivan's voice was a ghastly whisper. 'He's come back from Hell to fulfil the curse he laid on your grandpa when your grandpap shot him in the back, to get the land his tribe claimed. Beware! His ghost walks the night! The graveyard rats are his servants. The graveyard rats . . . '

Blood burst from his white-bearded lips and he sank back, dead.

Harrison rose sombrely.

'Let him lie. We'll pick up his body as we go back to town. We're going on to the graveyard.'

'Dare we?' Peter's face was white. 'A human I do not fear, not even Joel Middleton, but a ghost . . . '

'Don't be a fool!' snorted Harrison. 'Didn't you say the old man was half crazy?'

'But what if Joel Middleton is hiding somewhere near . . . '

'I'll take care of him!' Harrison had an invincible confidence in his own fighting ability. What he did not tell Peter, as they returned to the car, was that he had had a glimpse of the slayer in the flash of his shot. The memory of that glimpse still had the short hair prickling at the base of his skull.

That figure had been naked but for a loin-cloth and moccasins and a headdress of feathers.

'Who was Wolf Hunter?' he demanded as they drove on.

'A Tonkawa chief,' muttered Peter. 'He befriended my grand-father and was later murdered by him, just as Joash said. They say his bones lie in the old graveyard to this day.'

Peter lapsed into silence, seemingly a prey of morbid broodings.

Some four miles from town the road wound past a dim clearing. That was the Wilkinson graveyard. A rusty barbed-wire fence surr-ounded a cluster of graves whose white headstones leaned at crazy angles. Weeds grew thick, straggling over the low mounds.

The post oaks crowded close on all sides, and the road wound through them, past the sagging gate. Across the tops of the trees, nearly half a mile to the west, there was visible a shapeless bulk which Harrison knew was the roof of a house.

'The old Wilkinson farmhouse,' Peter answered in reply to his question. 'I was born there, and so were my brothers. Nobody's lived in it since we moved to town, ten years ago.'

Peter's nerves were taut. He glanced fearfully at the black woods around him, and his hands trembled as he lighted a lantern he took from the car. He winced as he picked up the round cloth-wrapped object that lay on the back seat; perhaps he was visualising the cold, white, stony face that cloth concealed.

As he climbed over the low gate and led the way between the weed-grown mounds he muttered: 'We're fools. If Joel Middleton's laying out there in the woods he could pick us both off easy as shooting rabbits.'

Harrison did not reply, and a moment later Peter halted and shone the light on a mound which was bare of weeds. The surface was tumbled and disturbed, and Peter exclaimed: 'Look! I expected to find an open grave. Why do you suppose he took the trouble of filling it again?'

'We'll see,' grunted Harrison. 'Are you game to open that grave?'

'I've seen my brother's head,' answered Peter grimly. 'I think I'm man enough to look on his headless body without fainting. There are tools in the tool-shed in the corner of the fence. I'll get them.'

Returning presently with pick and shovel, he set the lighted lan-tern on the ground, and the cloth-wrapped head near it. Peter was pale, and sweat stood on his brow in thick drops. The lantern cast their shadows, grotesquely distorted, across the weed-grown graves. The air was oppressive. There was an occasional dull flicker of lightning along the dusky horizons.

'What's that?' Harrison paused, pick lifted. All about them sounded rustlings and scurryings among the weeds. Beyond the circle of lantern light clusters of tiny red beads glittered at him.

'Rats!' Peter hurled a stone and the beads vanished, though the rustlings grew louder. 'They swarm in this graveyard. I believe they'd devour a living man, if they caught him helpless. Begone, you servants of Satan!'

Harrison took the shovel and began scooping out mounds of loose dirt.

'Ought not to be hard work,' he grunted. 'If he dug it out today or early tonight, it'll be loose all the way down . . .'

He stopped short, with his shovel jammed hard against the dirt, and a prickling in the short hairs at the nape of his neck. In the tense silence he heard the graveyard rats running through the grass.

'What's the matter?' A new pallor greyed Peter's face.

'I've hit solid ground,' said Harrison slowly. 'In three days, this clayey soil bakes hard as a brick. But if Middleton or anybody else had opened this grave and refilled it today, the soil would be loose all the way down. It's not. Below the first few inches it's packed and baked hard! The top has been scratched, but the grave has never been opened since it was first filled, three days ago!'

Peter staggered with an inhuman cry.

'Then it's true!' he screamed. 'Wolf Hunter *has* come back! He reached up from Hell and took John's head without opening the grave! He sent his familiar devil into our house in the form of a rat! A ghost-rat that could not be killed! Hands off, curse you!'

For Harrison had caught at him, growling: 'Pull yourself together, Peter!'

But Peter struck his arm aside and tore free. He turned and ran – not toward the car parked outside the graveyard, but toward the opposite fence. He scrambled across the rusty wires with a ripping of cloth and vanished in the woods, heedless of Harrison's shouts.

'Hell!' Harrison pulled up, and swore fervently. Where but in the black-hill country could such things happen? Angrily he picked up the tools and tore into the close-packed clay, baked by a blazing sun into almost iron hardness.

Sweat rolled from him in streams, and he grunted and swore, but persevered with all the power of his massive muscles. He meant to prove or disprove a suspicion growing in his mind – a suspicion that the body of John Wilkinson had never been placed in that grave.

The lightning flashed oftener and closer, and a low mutter of thunder began in the west. An occasional gust of wind made the lantern flicker, and as the mound beside the grave grew higher, and the man digging there sank lower and lower in the earth, the rustling in the grass grew louder and the red beads began to glint in the weeds. Harrison heard the eerie gnashings of tiny teeth all about him, and swore at the memory of grisly legends about the graveyard rats.

The grave was not deep. No Wilkinson would waste much labour on the dead. At last the rude coffin lay uncovered before him. With the point of the pick he pried up one corner of the lid, and held the lantern close. A startled oath escaped his lips. The coffin was not empty. It held a huddled, headless figure.

Harrison climbed out of the grave, his mind racing, fitting together pieces of the puzzle. The stray bits snapped into place, forming a pattern, dim and yet incomplete, but taking shape. He looked for the cloth-wrapped head, and got a frightful shock.

The head was gone!

For an instant Harrison felt cold sweat clammy on his hands. Then he heard a clamorous squeaking, the gnashing of tiny fangs.

He caught up the lantern and shone the light about. In its reflection he saw a white blotch on the grass near a straggling clump of bushes that had invaded the clearing. It was the cloth in which the head had been wrapped. Beyond that a black, squirming mound heaved and tumbled with nauseous life.

With an oath of horror he leaped forward, striking and kicking. The graveyard rats abandoned the head with rasping squeaks, scattering before him like darting black shadows. And Harrison shuddered. It was no face that stared up at him in the lantern light, but a white, grinning skull, to which clung only shreds of gnawed flesh.

While the detective burrowed into John Wilkinson's grave, the graveyard rats had torn the flesh from John Wilkinson's head.

Harrison stooped and picked up the hideous thing, now triply hideous. He wrapped it in the cloth, and as he straightened, something like fright took hold of him.

He was ringed in on all sides by a solid circle of gleaming red sparks that shone from the grass. Held back by their fear, the graveyard rats surrounded him, squealing their hate.

They gave back before him as he turned toward the grave, and he did not see the dark figure that slunk from the bushes behind him. The thunder boomed out, drowning even the squeaking of the rats, but he heard the swift footfall behind him an instant before the blow was struck.

He whirled, drawing his gun, and dropping his head, but just as he whirled, something like a louder clap of thunder exploded in his head, with a shower of sparks before his eyes.

As he reeled backward he fired blindly, and cried out as the flash showed him a horrific, half-naked, painted, feathered figure, crouching with a tomahawk uplifted – the open grave was behind Harrison as he fell.

Down into the grave he toppled, and his head struck the edge of the coffin with a sickening impact. His powerful body went limp; and like darting shadows, from every side raced the graveyard rats, hurling themselves into the grave in a frenzy of hunger and blood-lust.

Chapter 4. *Rats in Hell*

It seemed to Harrison's stunned brain that he lay in blackness on the darkened floors of Hell, a blackness lit by darts of flame from the eternal fires. The triumphant shrieking of demons was in his ears as they stabbed him with red-hot skewers.

He saw them, now – dancing monstrosities with pointed noses, twitching ears, red eyes and gleaming teeth – a sharp pain knifed through his flesh.

And suddenly the mists cleared. He lay, not on the floor of Hell, but on a coffin in the bottom of a grave; the fires were lightning flashes from the black sky; and the demons were rats that swarmed over him, slashing with razor-sharp teeth.

Harrison yelled and heaved convulsively, and at his movement the rats gave back in alarm. But they did not leave the grave; they massed solidly along the walls, their eyes glittering redly.

Harrison knew he could have been senseless only a few seconds. Otherwise, these grey ghouls would have already stripped the living flesh from his bones . . . as they had ripped the dead flesh from the head of the man on whose coffin he lay.

Already his body was stinging in a score of places, and his clothing was damp with his own blood.

Cursing, he started to rise – and a chill of panic shot through him! Falling, his left arm had been jammed into the partly-open coffin, and the weight of his body on the lid clamped his hand fast. Harrison fought down a mad wave of terror.

He would not withdraw his hand unless he could lift his body from the coffin lid . . . and the imprisonment of his hand held him prostrate there.

Trapped!

In a murdered man's grave, his hand locked in the coffin of a headless corpse, with a thousand grey ghoul-rats ready to tear the flesh from his living frame!

As if sensing his helplessness, the rats swarmed upon him. Harrison fought for his life, like a man in a nightmare. He kicked, he yelled, he cursed, he smote them with the heavy six-shooter he still clutched in his hand.

Their fangs tore at him, ripping cloth and flesh, their acrid scent nauseated him; they almost covered him with their squirming, writhing bodies. He beat them back, smashed and crushed them with blows of his six-shooter barrel.

The living cannibals fell on their dead brothers. In desperation he twisted half-over and jammed the muzzle of his gun against the coffin lid.

At the flash of fire and the deafening report, the rats scurried in all directions.

Again and again, he pulled the trigger until the gun was empty. The heavy slugs crashed through the lid, splitting off a great sliver from the edge. Harrison drew his bruised hand from the aperture.

Gagging and shaking, he clambered out of the grave and rose groggily to his feet. Blood was clotted in his hair from the gash the ghostly hatchet had made in his scalp, and blood trickled from a score of tooth-wounds in his flesh. Lightning played constantly, but the lantern was still shining. But it was not on the ground.

It seemed to be suspended in mid-air . . . and then he was aware that it was held in the hand of a man – a tall man in a black slicker, whose eyes burned dangerously under his broad hat-brim. In his other hand a black pistol muzzle menaced the detective's midriff.

'You must be that damn' low-country law Pete Wilkinson brung up here to run me down!' growled this man.

'Then you're Joel Middleton!' grunted Harrison.

'Sure I am!' snarled the outlaw. 'Where's Pete, the old devil?'

'He got scared and ran off.'

'Crazy, like Saul, maybe,' sneered Middleton. 'Well, you tell him I been savin' a slug for his ugly mug a long time. And one for Dick, too.'

'Why did you come here?' demanded Harrison.

'I heard shootin'. I got here just as you was climbin' out of the grave. What's the matter with you? Who was it that broke your head?'

'I don't know his name,' answered Harrison, caressing his aching head.

'Well, it don't make no difference to me. But I want to tell you that I didn't cut John's head off. I killed him because he needed it.' The outlaw swore and spat. 'But I didn't do that other!'

'I know you didn't,' Harrison answered.

'Eh?' The outlaw was obviously startled.

'Do you know which rooms the Wilkinsons sleep in, in their house in town?'

'Naw,' snorted Middleton. 'Never was in their house in my life.'

'I thought not. Whoever put John's head on Saul's mantel knew. The back kitchen door was the only one where the lock could have been forced without waking somebody up. The lock on Saul's door was broken. You couldn't have known those things. It looked like an inside job from the start. The lock was forced to make it look like an outside job.

'Richard spilled some stuff that cinched my belief that it was Peter. I decided to bring him out to the graveyard and see if his nerve would stand up under an accusation across his brother's open coffin. But I hit hard-packed soil and knew the grave hadn't been opened. It gave me a turn and I blurted out what I'd found. But it's simple, after all.

'Peter wanted to get rid of his brothers. When you killed John, that suggested a way to dispose of Saul. John's body stood in its coffin in the Wilkinsons' parlour until it was placed in the grave the next day. No death watch was kept. It was easy for Peter to go into the parlour while his brothers slept, pry up the coffin lid and cut off John's head. He put it on ice somewhere to preserve it. When I touched it I found it was nearly frozen.

'No one knew what had happened, because the coffin was not opened again. John was an atheist, and there was the briefest sort of ceremony. The coffin was not opened for his friends to take a last look, as is the usual custom. Then tonight the head was placed in Saul's room. It drove him raving mad.

'I don't know why Peter waited until tonight, or why he called me into the case. He must be partly insane himself. I don't think he meant to kill me when we drove out here tonight. But when he discovered I knew the grave hadn't been opened tonight, he saw the game was up. I ought to have been smart enough to keep my mouth shut, but I was so sure that Peter had opened the grave to get the head, that when I found it *hadn't* been opened, I spoke involuntarily, without stopping to think of the other alternative. Peter pretended a panic and ran off. Later he sent back his partner to kill me.'

'Who's he?' demanded Middleton.

'How should I know? Some fellow who looks like an Indian!'

'That old yarn about a Tonkawa ghost has went to your brain!' scoffed Middleton.

'I didn't say it was a ghost,' said Harrison, nettled. 'It was real enough to kill your friend Joash Sullivan!'

'What?' yelled Middleton. 'Joash killed? Who done it?'

'The Tonkawa ghost, whoever he is. The body is lying about a mile back, beside the road, amongst the thickets, if you don't believe me.'

Middleton ripped out a terrible oath.

'By God, I'll kill somebody for that! Stay where you are! I ain't goin' to shoot no unarmed man, but if you try to run me down I'll kill you sure as Hell. So keep off my trail. I'm goin', and don't you try to follow me!'

The next instant Middleton had dashed the lantern to the ground where it went out with a clatter of breaking glass.

Harrison blinked in the sudden darkness that followed, and the next lightning flash showed him standing alone in the ancient graveyard.

The outlaw was gone.

Chapter 5. *The Rats Eat*

Cursing, Harrison groped on the ground, lit by the lightning flashes. He found the broken lantern, and he found something else.

Rain drops splashed against his face as he started toward the gate. One instant he stumbled in velvet blackness, the next the tombstones shone white in the dazzling glare. Harrison's head ached frightfully. Only chance and a tough skull had saved his life. The would-be killer must have thought the blow was fatal and fled, taking John Wilkinson's head for what grisly purpose there was no knowing. But the head was gone.

Harrison winced at the thought of the rain filling the open grave, but he had neither the strength nor the inclination to shovel the dirt back in it. To remain in that dark graveyard might well be death. The slayer might return.

Harrison looked back as he climbed the fence. The rain had disturbed the rats; the weeds were alive with scampering, flame-eyed shadows. With a shudder, Harrison made his way to the flivver. He climbed in, found his flashlight and reloaded his revolver.

The rain grew in volume. Soon the rutty road to Lost Knob would be a welter of mud. In his condition he did not feel equal to the task of driving back through the storm over that abominable road. But it could not be long until dawn. The old farmhouse would afford him a refuge until daylight.

The rain came down in sheets, soaking him, dimming the already uncertain lights as he drove along the road, splashing noisily through the mud-puddles. Wind ripped through the post oaks. Once he grunted and batted his eyes. He could have sworn that a flash of lightning had fleetingly revealed a painted, naked, feathered figure gliding among the trees!

The road wound up a thickly wooded eminence, rising close to the bank of a muddy creek. On the summit the old house squatted. Weeds and low bushes straggled from the surrounding woods up to the sagging porch. He parked the car as close to the house as he could get it, and climbed out, struggling with the wind and rain.

He expected to have to blow the lock off the door with his gun, but it opened under his fingers. He stumbled into a musty-smelling room, weirdly lit by the flickering of the lightning through the cracks of the shutters.

His flashlight revealed a rude bunk built against a side wall, a heavy hand-hewn table, a heap of rags in a corner. From this pile of rags black furtive shadows darted in all directions.

Rats! Rats again!

Could he never escape them?

He closed the door and lit the lantern, placing it on the table. The broken chimney caused the flame to dance and flicker, but not enough wind found its way into the room to blow it out. Three doors, leading into the interior of the house, were closed. The floor and walls were pitted with holes gnawed by the rats.

Tiny red eyes glared at him from the apertures.

Harrison sat down on the bunk, flashlight and pistol on his lap. He expected to fight for his life before day broke. Peter Wilkinson was out there in the storm somewhere, with a heart full of murder, and either allied to him or working separately – in either case an enemy to the detective – was that mysterious painted figure.

And that figure was Death, whether living masquerader or Indian ghost. In any event, the shutters would protect him from a shot from the dark, and to get at him his enemies would have to come into the lighted room where he would have an even chance . . . which was all the big detective had ever asked.

To get his mind off the ghoulish red eyes glaring at him from the floor, Harrison brought out the object he had found lying near the broken lantern, where the slayer must have dropped it.

It was a smooth oval of flint, made fast to a handle with rawhide thongs – the Indian tomahawk of an elder generation. And Harrison's eyes narrowed suddenly; there was blood on the flint, and some of it was his own. But on the other point of the oval there was more blood, dark and crusted, with strands of hair lighter than his, clinging to the clotted point.

Joash Sullivan's blood? No. The old man had been knifed. But someone else had died that night. The darkness had hidden another grim deed . . . .

Black shadows were stealing across the floor. The rats were coming back . . . ghoulish shapes, creeping from their holes, converging on the heap of rags in the far corner – a tattered carpet, Harrison now saw, rolled in a long compact heap. Why should the rats leap upon that rag? Why should they race up and down along it, squealing and biting at the fabric?

There was something hideously suggestive about its contour . . . a shape that grew more definite and ghastly as he looked.

The rats scattered, squeaking, as Harrison sprang across the room. He tore away the carpet – and looked down on the corpse of Peter Wilkinson.

The back of the head had been crushed. The white face was twisted in a leer of awful terror.

For an instant Harrison's brain reeled with the ghastly possibilities his discovery summoned up. Then he took a firm grasp on himself, fought off the whispering potency of the dark, howling night, the thrashing wet black woods and the abysmal aura of the ancient hills, and recognised the only sane solution of the riddle.

Sombrely he looked down on the dead man. Peter Wilkinson's fright had been genuine, after all. In his blind panic he had reverted to the habits of his boyhood and fled toward his old home . . . and met death instead of security.

Harrison started convulsively as a weird sound smote his ears above the roar of the storm – the wailing horror of an Indian warwhoop. The killer was upon him!

Harrison sprang to a shuttered window, peered through a crack, waiting for a flash of lightning. When it came he fired through the window at a feathered head he saw peering around a tree close to the car.

In the darkness that followed the flash he crouched, waiting – there came another white glare – he grunted explosively but did not fire. The head was still there, and he got a better look at it. The lightning shone weirdly white upon it.

It was John Wilkinson's fleshless skull, clad in a feathered head-dress and bound in place – and it was the bait of a trap.

Harrison wheeled and sprang toward the lantern on the table. That grisly ruse had been to draw his attention to the front of the house while the killer slunk upon him through the rear of the building! The rats squealed and scattered. Even as Harrison whirled an inner door began to open. He smashed a heavy slug through the panels, heard a groan and the sound of a falling body, and then, just as he reached a hand to extinguish the lantern, the world crashed over his head.

A blinding burst of lightning, a deafening clap of thunder, and the ancient house staggered from gables to foundations! Blue fire crackled from the ceiling and ran down the walls and over the floor. One livid tongue just flicked the detective's shin in passing.

It was like the impact of a sledgehammer. There was an instant of blindness and numb agony, and Harrison found himself sprawling, half-stunned on the floor. The lantern lay extinguished beside the overturned table, but the room was filled with a lurid light.

He realised that a bolt of lightning had struck the house, and that the upper story was ablaze. He hauled himself to his feet, looking for his gun. It lay halfway across the room, and as he started toward it, the bullet-split door swung open. Harrison stopped dead in his tracks.

Through the door limped a man naked but for a loin-cloth and moccasins on his feet. A revolver in his hand menaced the detective. Blood oozing from a wound in his thigh mingled with the paint with which he had smeared himself.

'So it was you who wanted to be the oil millionaire, Richard!' said Harrison.

The other laughed savagely. 'Aye, and I will be! And no cursed brothers to share with – brothers I always hated, damn them! Don't move! You nearly got me when you shot through the door. I'm taking no chances with you! Before I send you to Hell, I'll tell you everything.

'As soon as you and Peter started for the graveyard, I realised my mistake in merely scratching the top of the grave – knew you'd hit hard clay and know the grave hadn't been opened. I knew then I'd have to kill you, as well as Peter. I took the rat you mashed when neither of you were looking, so its disappearance would play on Peter's superstitions.

'I rode to the graveyard through the woods, on a fast horse. The Indian disguise was one I thought up long ago. What with that rotten road, and the flat that delayed you, I got to the graveyard before you and Peter did. On the way, though, I dismounted and stopped to kill that old fool Joash Sullivan. I was afraid he might see and recognise me.

'I was watching when you dug into the grave. When Peter got panicky and ran through the woods I chased him, killed him, and brought his body here to the old house. Then I went back after you. I intended bringing your body here, or rather your bones, after the rats finished you, as I thought they would. Then I heard Joel Middleton coming and had to run for it – I don't care to meet that gun-fighting devil anywhere!

'I was going to burn this house with both your bodies in it. People would think, when they found the bones in the ashes, that Middleton killed you both and burnt the house! And now you play right into my hands by coming here! Lightning has struck the house and it's burning! Oh, the gods fight for me tonight!'

A light of unholy madness played in Richard's eyes, but the pistol muzzle was steady, as Harrison stood clenching his great fists helplessly.

'You'll lie here with that fool Peter!' raved Richard. 'With a bullet through your head, until your bones are burnt to such a crisp that nobody can tell how you died! Joel Middleton will be shot down by some posse without a chance to talk. Saul will rave out his days in a madhouse! And I, who will be safely sleeping in my house in town before sun-up, will live out my allotted years in wealth and honour, never suspected – never . . . '

He was sighting along the black barrel, eyes blazing, teeth bared like the fangs of a wolf between painted lips . . . his finger was curling on the trigger.

Harrison crouched tensely, desperately, poising to hurl himself with bare hands at the killer and try to pit his naked strength against hot lead spitting from that black muzzle – then . . .

The door crashed inward behind him and the lurid glare framed a tall figure in a dripping slicker.

An incoherent yell rang to the roof and the gun in the outlaw's hand roared. Again, and again, and yet again it crashed, filling the room with smoke and thunder, and the painted figure jerked to the impact of the tearing lead.

Through the smoke Harrison saw Richard Wilkinson toppling – but he too was firing as he fell. Flames burst through the ceiling, and by their brighter glare Harrison saw a painted figure writhing on the floor, a taller figure wavering in the doorway. Richard was screaming in agony.

Middleton threw his empty gun at Harrison's feet.

'Heard the shootin' and come,' he croaked. 'Reckon that settles the feud for good!' He toppled, and Harrison caught him in his arms, a lifeless weight.

Richard's screams rose to an unbearable pitch. The rats were swarming from their holes. Blood streaming across the floor had dripped into their holes, maddening them. Now they burst forth in a ravening horde that heeded not cries, or movement, or the devouring flames, but only their own fiendish hunger.

In a grey-black wave they swept over the dead man and the dying man. Peter's white face vanished under that wave. Richard's screaming grew thick and muffled. He writhed, half covered by grey, tearing figures who sucked at his gushing blood, tore at his flesh.

Harrison retreated through the door, carrying the dead outlaw. Joel Middleton, outlaw and killer, yet deserved a better fate than was befalling his slayer.

To save that ghoul, Harrison would not have lifted a finger, had it been in his power.

It was not. The graveyard rats had claimed their own. Out in the yard, Harrison let his burden fall limply. Above the roar of the flames still rose those awful, smothered cries.

Through the blazing doorway he had a glimpse of a horror, a gory figure rearing upright, swaying, enveloped by a hundred clinging, tearing shapes. He glimpsed a face that was not a face at all, but a blind, bloody skull-mask. Then the awful scene was blotted out as the flaming roof fell with a thundering, ear-rending crash.

Sparks showered against the sky, the flames rose as the walls fell in, and Harrison staggered away, dragging the dead man, as a storm-wrapped dawn came haggardly over the oak-clad ridges.

Black Wind Blowing

Chapter 1. *'I take this woman!'*

Emmett Glanton jammed on the brakes of his old Model T and skidded to a squealing stop within a few feet of the apparition that had materialised out of the black, gusty night.

'What the Hell do you mean by jumping in front of my car like that?' he yelled wrathfully, recognising the figure that posed grotesquely in the glare of the headlights. It was Joshua, the lumbering halfwit who worked for old John Bruckman; but Joshua in a mood such as Glanton had never seen before. In the white glare of the lights the fellow's broad brutish face was convulsed; foam flecked his lips and his eyes were red as those of a rabid wolf. He brandished his arms and croaked incoherently. Impressed, Glanton opened the door and stepped out of the car. On his feet he was inches taller than Joshua, but his rangy, broad-shouldered frame did not look impressive compared to the stooped, apish bulk of the halfwit.

There was menace in Joshua's mien. Gone was the dull, apathetic expression he usually wore. He bared his teeth and snarled like a wild beast as he rolled toward Glanton.

'Keep away from me, blast you!' Glanton warned. 'What's the matter with you, anyway?'

'You're goin' over there!' mouthed the halfwit, gesturing vaguely southward. 'Old John called you over the phone. I heered him!'

'Yes, he did,' answered Glanton. 'Asked me to come over as quick as I could. Didn't say why. What about it? You want to ride back with me?'

Joshua jumped up and down and battered his hairy breast like an ape with his splay fists. He gnashed his teeth and howled. Glanton's flesh crawled a little. It was black night, with the wind howling under a black sky, whipping the mesquite. And there in that little spot of light that apish figure cavorted and raved like a witch's familiar summoned up from Hell.

'I don't want to ride with you!' bellowed Joshua. 'You ain't goin' there! I'll kill you if you try to go! I'll twist your head off with my hands!' He spread his great fingers and worked them like the hairy legs of great spiders before Glanton's face. Glanton bristled at the threat.

'What are you raving about?' he demanded. 'I don't know why Bruckman called me, but – '

'I know!' howled Joshua, froth flying from his loose, working lips. 'I listened outside the winder! You can't have her! I want her!'

'Want who?' Glanton was bewildered. This was mystery piled on mystery. Black, howling night, and old John Bruckman's voice shrieking over the party line, edged with frenzy, begging and demanding that his neighbour come to him as quickly as his car could get him there; then the wild drive over the wind-lashed road, and now this lunatic prancing in the glare of the headlights and mouthing bloody threats.

Joshua ignored his question. He seemed to have lost what little sense he had ever had. He was acting like a homicidal maniac. And through the rents in his ragged shirt bulged muscles capable of rending the average man limb from limb.

'I never seen one I wanted before!' he screamed. 'But I want her! Old John don't want her! I heered him say so! If you didn't come maybe he'd give her to me! You go on back home or I'll kill you! I'll twist your head off and feed it to the buzzards! You think I'm just a harmless big fool, I bet!'

Grotesquely his bellowing voice rose to a high-pitched squeal.

'Well, if it'll satisfy you,' said Glanton, watching him warily, 'I've always thought you were dangerous. Bruckman's a fool to keep you on the ranch. I've expected you to go clean crazy and kill him some time.'

'I ain't goin' to kill John,' howled Joshua. 'I'm goin' to kill you. You won't be the first, neither. I killed my brother Jake. He beat me once too often. I beat his head to jelly with a rock and dragged the body down the canyon and throwed it into the pool below the rapids!'

A maniacal glee convulsed his face as he screamed his hideous secret to the night, and his eyes looked like nothing this side of Hell.

'So that's what became of Jake! I always wondered why he disappeared and you came to live with old John. Couldn't stay in your shack in that lonely canyon after you killed him, eh?'

A momentary gleam of fear shot the murk of the maniac's eyes.

'He wouldn't stay in the pool,' muttered Joshua. 'He used to come back and scratch at the winder, with his head all bloody. I'd wake up at night and see him lookin' in at me and gaspin' and gurglin' tryin' to talk through the blood in his throat.

'But you won't come back and ha'nt me!' he shrieked suddenly, beginning to sway from side to side like a bull about to charge. 'I'll spike you down with a stake and weight you down with rocks! I'll – ' In the midst of his tirade he lunged suddenly at Glanton.

Glanton knew that if those huge arms ever locked about him his spine would snap like a stick. But he knew, too, that nine times out of ten a maniac will try to reach his victim's throat with his teeth.

Joshua was no exception.

Reverting completely to the beast, he plunged in with his arms groping vaguely, and his jaws thrust out like a wolf's muzzle, slavering teeth bared in the glare of the headlights. Glanton stepped inside those waving arms and smashed his right fist against the out-jutting jaw with all his power. It would have stretched another man senseless. It stopped the halfwit in his tracks, and blood spurted.

Before he could recover his balance Glanton struck again and again, raining terrific blows to face and head, driving Joshua reeling and staggering before him. It was like beating a bull, but the ceaseless smashes kept the maniac off balance, confused and dazed him, kept him on the defensive.

Glanton was beginning to tire, and he wondered desperately what the end would be. The moment his blows began weakening Joshua would shake off his bewilderment and lunge to the attack again . . .

Abruptly they were out of the range of the car lights, and floundering in darkness. In panic lest the maniac should find his throat in the blackness, Glanton swung blindly and desperately, connected glancingly and felt his man fall away from him.

He stumbled himself and went on all fours, almost pitching down the slope that fell away beneath him. Crouching there he heard the sounds of Joshua's thundering fall down the slant. Glanton knew where he was now, knew that a few yards from the road the ground fell away in a steep slope a hundred feet long. It was not hard to navigate by daylight, but by night a man might take a nasty tumble and hurt himself badly on the broken rocks at the bottom. And Joshua, knocked over the edge by Glanton's last wild haymaker, was taking that tumble.

It might have been an animal falling down the slope, from the grunts and howls that welled up from below, but presently, when the rattle of pebbles and the sounds of a heavy rolling body had ceased, there was silence, and Glanton wondered if the lunatic lay senseless or dead at the bottom of the slope.

He called, but there was no answer. Then a sudden shudder shook him. Joshua might be creeping back up the slope in utter silence, this time maybe with a rock in his hand, such a rock as he had used to batter his brother Jake's head into a crimson pulp . . .

Glanton's eyes were getting accustomed to the darkness and he could make out the vague forms of black ridges, boulders and trees. The devil-begotten wind that shrieked through the trees would drown a stealthy footstep. When a man turns his back on peril it assumes an aspect of thousand-fold horror.

When Glanton started back to the car his flesh crawled cold, and at each step he expected to feel a frightful form land on his back, gnashing and tearing. It was with a gasp of relief that he lunged into the car, eased off the hand-brake, and clattered off down the dim road.

He was leaving Joshua behind him, alive or dead, and such was the grim magic of the gusty dark that at the moment he feared Joshua dead no less than Joshua living.

He heaved another sigh of relief when the red spot that was the light of John Bruckman's house began to glow in the black curtain ahead of him. He disliked Bruckman, but the old skinflint was sane at least, and any sane company was welcome after his experience with a brutish maniac in the black heart of this evil night.

A car stood before Bruckman's gate and Glanton recognised it as the one belonging to Lem Richards, justice of the peace in Skurlock, the little village which lay a few miles south of the Bruckman ranch.

Glanton knocked on the door and Bruckman's voice, with a strange, unnatural quaver in it, shouted: 'Who's there? Speak quick, or I'll shoot through the door!'

'It's me, Glanton!' called the ranchman in a hurry. 'You asked me to come, didn't you?'

Chains rattled, a key grated in the lock, and the door swung inward. The black night seemed to flow in after Glanton with the wind that made the lamp flicker and the shadows dance along the walls, and Bruckman moaned and slammed the door in its ebon face. He jammed bolt and chain with trembling hands.

'Your confounded hired hand tried to kill me on the way over,' Glanton began angrily. 'I've told you that lunatic would go bad some day – '

He stopped short. Two other people were in the room. One was Lem Richards, the justice of the peace, a short, stolid, unimaginative man who sat before the hearth placidly chewing his quid. The other was a girl, and at the sight of her a sort of shock passed over Emmett Glanton, bringing a sudden realisation of his work-hardened hands and hickory shirt and rusty boots. She was like a breath of perfume from the world of tinsel and bright lights and evening gowns that he had almost forgotten in his toil to build up his fortune in this primitive country.

Her supple young figure was set off to its best advantage by the neat but costly dress she wore. Her loveliness dazzled Glanton at first glance; then he looked again and was appalled. For she was white and cold as a statue of marble, and her dilated eyes stared at him as though she had just seen a serpent writhe through the door.

'Oh, excuse me!' he said awkwardly, dragging off his battered Stetson. 'I wouldn't have come busting in here like this if I'd known there was a lady . . . '

'Never mind that!' snapped John Bruckman. He faced Glanton across the table, his face limned in the lamp-light. It was a haggard face, and in the burning eyes Glanton saw fear, murky bestial fear that made the man repulsive. Bruckman spoke hurriedly, the words tumbling over each other, and from time to time he glanced at the big clock on the mantel sullenly ticking off the seconds.

'Glanton, I hold a mortgage on your ranch, and it's due in a few days. Do you think you can meet your payment?'

Glanton felt like cursing the man. Had he called him over that windswept road on a night like this to discuss a mortgage? A glance at the white, tense girl told him something else was behind all this.

'I reckon I can,' he said shortly. 'I'm getting by . . . or would if you'd stay off my back long enough for me to get a start.'

'I'll do that!' Bruckman's hands were shaking as he fumbled in his coat. 'Look here! Here's the mortgage!' He tossed a document on the table. 'And a thousand dollars in cash!' A compact bundle of banknotes plopped down on the table before Glanton's astounded eyes. 'It's all yours – mortgage and money – if you'll do one thing for me!'

'And what's that?'

Bruckman's bony forefinger stabbed at the cringing girl.

'Marry her!'

'What?' Glanton wheeled and stared at her with a new intensity, and she stared wildly back, in evident fright and bewilderment.

'Marry her?' He ran a hand dazedly across his head, vividly aware of the loneliness of the life he had been leading for the past three years.

'What does the young lady think about it?' he asked.

Bruckman snarled impatiently.

'What does it matter what she thinks? She's my niece, my ward. She'll do as I say. She could do worse than marry you. You're no common ridge-runner. You're a gentleman by birth and breeding – '

'Never mind that,' growled Glanton, waving him aside. He stepped toward the girl.

'Are you willing to marry me?' he asked directly.

She looked full into his eyes for a long moment, with a desperate and pitiful intensity in her gaze. She must have read kindness and honesty there, for suddenly, impulsively, she sprang forward and caught his brown hand in both of hers, crying: 'Yes! Yes! *Please* marry me! Marry me and take me away from *him* . . . ' Her gesture toward John Bruckman was one of fear and loathing, but the old man did not heed. He was staring fearfully at the clock again.

He clapped his hands in a spasm of nervousness.

'Quick! Quick! Lem brought the licence, according to my instructions. He'll marry you now – now! Stand over here by the table and join hands.'

Richards rose heavily and lumbered over to the table, fingering his worn book. All this drama and mystery meant nothing to him, except that another couple were to be married.

And so Emmett Glanton found himself standing holding the quivering hand of a girl he had never seen before, while the justice of the peace mumbled the ritual which made them husband and wife. And only then did he learn the girl's name – Joan Zukor.

'Do you, Emmett, take this woman . . . ' droned the monotonous voice.

Glanton gave his reply mechanically, his fingers involuntarily clenching on the slim fingers they grasped. For, pressed briefly against a window, he had seen a face – a white, blood-streaked mask of murder . . . the face of the halfwit Joshua.

The maniac's eyes burned on Glanton with a mad hate, and on the woman at his side with a sickening flame of desire. Then the face was gone and the window framed only the blackness of the night.

None but Glanton had seen the lunatic. Richards, paid by old John, lumbered stolidly forth and the door shut behind him. Glanton and the girl stood looking at each other speechlessly, in sudden self-consciousness, but old John gave them no pause. He glared at the clock again, which showed ten minutes after eleven, jammed the mortgage and the bank notes into Glanton's hand and pushed him and the girl toward the door. Sweat dripped from his livid face, but a sort of wild triumph mingled with his strange fear.

'Get out! Get off my place! Take your wife and go! I wash my hands of her! I am no longer responsible for her! She's your burden! Go – and go quick!'

Chapter 2. *'Tell them . . . in pity's name'*

In a sort of daze Glanton found himself out on the porch with the girl, and from inside came the sound of drawn bolts and hooked chains.

Angrily he took a step toward the door, then noticed the girl shivering beside him, huddling about her a cloak she had snatched as they were evicted.

'Come on, Joan,' he said awkwardly, taking her arm. 'I think your uncle must be crazy. We'd better go.'

He felt her shudder.

'Yes, let us go quickly.'

Richards, characteristically, had left the yard gate unfastened.

It was flapping and banging in the wind which moaned through the junipers. Glanton groped his way toward the sound, sheltering the cowering girl against the gusts that whipped her cloak about her.

He shivered at the thick-set, cone-shaped outlines of the junipers along the walk. Either of them might be hiding the maniac who had glared through the window. The creature was no longer human; he was a beast of prey, ranging the night.

John Bruckman had given Glanton no chance to warn him of the madman. But Glanton decided he would phone back from his ranch house. They could not loiter there in the darkness, with that skulking fiend abroad.

He half expected to find Joshua crouching in the car, but it was empty, and a feeling of relief flooded him as he turned on the lights and their twin beams lanced the dark. The girl beside him sighed too, though she knew nothing of the death that lurked near them. But she sensed the evil of the night, the menace of the crowding blackness. Even such a dim illumination as this was comforting.

Wordless, Glanton started the car and they began the bumping, jolting ride. He was consumed with curiosity, but hesitated to put the question that itched on his tongue. Presently the girl herself spoke.

'You wonder why my uncle sold me like a slave . . . or an animal!'

'Don't say that!' exclaimed Glanton in quick sympathy. 'You need not – '

'Why *shouldn't* you wonder?' she retorted bitterly. 'I can only say – I don't know. He's my only relative, as far as I know. I've seen him only a few times in my life. Ever since I was a small child I've lived in boarding schools and I always understood he was supplying the money that lodged, dressed and educated me. But he seldom wrote; hardly ever visited me.

'I was in a school in Houston when I received a wire from my uncle ordering me to come to him at once. I came on the train to Skurlock, and arrived about nine tonight. Mr Richards met me at the station. He told me that my uncle had phoned and asked him to drive me out to his ranch. He had the licence with him, though I didn't know it at the time.

'When we got here my uncle told me abruptly that I'd have to marry a young man he had sent for. Naturally, I – I was terrified . . . ' She faltered and then laid a timid hand on his arm. 'I was afraid . . . I didn't know what kind of a man it might be.'

'I'll be a good husband to you, girl,' he said awkwardly, and thrilled with pleasure at the sincerity in her tone as she replied: 'I know it. You have kind eyes and gentle hands. Strong, but gentle.'

They were approaching a place where the road had been straightened by a new track, which, instead of swinging wide around the sloping edge of a steep, thicket-grown knoll, crossed a shallow ravine by a crude bridge and ran close by the knob on the opposite side, where it sheered off in a forty-foot cliff.

As the knoll grew dimly out of the windy darkness ahead of them, a grisly premonition rose in Glanton's breast. Joshua, loping through the mesquite like a lobo wolf, could have reached that knob ahead of them. It was the most logical place along the road for an ambush. A man crouching on the thicket-clad crest of the cliff could hurl a boulder down on a car passing along the new stretch of road . . .

With sudden decision, Glanton wrenched the car into the old track, now a faint trace grown up in broom weeds and prickly pears.

Joan caught at him for support as she was thrown from side to side by the jouncing of the auto. Then as they swung around the slope and came back into the plain road again, behind and above them yammered a fiendish howling – the maddened, primordial shrieking of a baffled beast of prey which realises that his victims have eluded him.

'What's that?' gasped Joan, clutching at Glanton.

'Just a bobcat squalling in the brush on that knob,' he assured her, but it was with convulsive haste that he jammed his foot down on the accelerator and sent the car thundering down the road. Tomorrow, he swore, he'd raise a posse and hunt down that slavering human beast as he would a rabid coyote.

He could imagine the madman loping along the road after them, foam from his bared fangs dripping onto his bare, hairy breast. He was glad the lamp was burning in the parlour of his ranch house. It reached a warm shaft of light to them across the windy reaches of the night.

He did not drive the car into the shed that served as garage. He drove it as close to the porch as he could get it, and opened the car door in the light that streamed from the house, as old Juan Sanchez, his Mexican man-of-all-work, opened the front door.

Glanton was briefly aware of the bareness of his residence. There had been no time to adorn it in his toil to build his spread. But now he must have a front yard with a fence around it and some rose bushes and spineless decorative cacti. Women liked things like that.

'This is my wife, Sanchez,' he said briefly. 'Señora Joan.'

The old Mexican hid his astonishment with a low bow, and said, with the natural courtliness of his race: '*Buenas noches*, señora! Welcome to the *hacienda*.'

In the parlour Glanton said: 'Sit down by the fire and warm yourself, Joan. It's been a cold drive. Sanchez, stir up the fire and throw on some more mesquite chunks. I'm going to call up John Bruckman. There's something he ought to know – '

But even as he reached for the phone the bell jangled discordantly. As he lifted the receiver over the line came John Bruckman's voice, brittle with fear and more than fear – with physical agony.

'Emmett! Emmett Glanton! Tell them – in pity's name tell them that you've married Joan Zukor! Tell them I'm no longer responsible for her!'

'Tell who?' demanded Glanton, all but speechless with amazement.

Joan was on her feet, white-faced; that frantic voice shrieking from the receiver had reached her ears.

'These devils!' squalled the voice of John Bruckman. 'The Black Brothers of – aaagh . . . mercy!'

The voice broke in a loud shriek, and in the brief silence that followed there sounded a low, gurgling, indescribably repellent laugh. And Glanton's hair stood up, for he knew it was not John Bruckman who laughed.

'Hello!' he yelled. 'John! John Bruckman!'

There was no answer. A click told him that the receiver had been hung up at the other end, and a grisly conviction shook him that it had not been John Bruckman's hand who had hung it up.

He turned to the girl, who stood silent and wide-eyed in the middle of the room, as he snatched a gun from its scabbard hanging on the wall.

'I've got to go back to Bruckman's ranch,' he said. 'Something devilish is happening over there, and the old man seems to need help bad.'

She was speechless. Impulsively he took her hands in his and stroked them reassuringly.

'Don't be afraid, kid,' he said. 'Sanchez will take care of you till I get back. And I won't be gone long.'

Chapter 3. *Dead Madness*

As he drew the old Mexican out onto the porch a glance back showed her still standing dumbly in the centre of the room, her hands pressed childishly to her breasts, an image of youthful fright and bewilderment lost in an unfamiliar world of violence and horror.

'I don't know what the Hell's happened over at Bruckman's,' he said swiftly and low-voiced to Sanchez. 'But be careful. Joshua, the halfwit's gone on the rampage. He tried to kill me tonight, and he laid for us at the knob where the new road passes. Probably meant to brain me with a rock and kidnap Joan. Shoot him like a coyote if he shows his head on this ranch while I'm gone.'

'Trust me, *señor*!' Old Sanchez's face was grim as he fondled the worn butt of his old single-action Colt. Men had died before that black muzzle in the wild old days when Sanchez had ridden with Pancho Villa. Sanchez could be depended on. Glanton clapped him on the back, leaped into the Ford and roared away southward.

The road before him was a white crack in a black wall, opening steadily in the glare of the headlights. He drove recklessly, half expecting each moment to see the shambling figure of the maniac spring out of the blackness. Grimly he touched the butt of the pistol thrust into the waistband of his trousers.

Aversion to driving under that gloomy cliff was so strong in Glanton that again he swung aside and followed the dimmer, longer road that wound around the opposite side of the knob.

And as he did so he was aware of another roar, above that of his own racing motor. He caught the reflection of powerful headlights. Some other car was eating up the road, racing northward and taking the shorter cut. As he drove into the open road beyond the knob he looked back and glimpsed a rapidly receding tail-light. A nameless foreboding seized him, urging him to wheel around and race back to his own ranch.

But there was not necessarily anything sinister in a car speeding northward even at that hour. It was probably some ranchman who lived north of Glanton returning home from Skurlock, or some travelling salesman bound for one of the little cow towns still further north, and leaving the paved highways to take a short cut.

There was no light in the window of the Bruckman ranch house as Glanton approached it; only the glow of the fire in the fireplace staining the windows with lurid blood, crimsoning it without illuminating. There was no sound but the moaning of the ghostly wind through the dark junipers as Glanton went up the walk. But the front door stood open.

Pistol in hand, Glanton peered in. He caught the glimmer of red coals glowing on the hearth. The dry, toneless ticking of the clock made him start nervously.

He called: 'John! John Bruckman!'

No answer, but somewhere a moan rose in the fire-shadowed darkness, a low, whimpering of anguish, thick and gurgling as if through a gag of welling blood. And a steady drip, drip of something wet and sticky on the floor.

Panic clawed at Glanton's spine as he moved toward the smouldering hearth, instinct drawing him toward the one spot of light in the room. At the moment he did not remember just where stood the table with the oil lamp on it. He must have a moment to gather his wits, to locate it.

He groped for a match, then froze in his tracks. A black hand had materialised out of the shadows, faintly revealed in the light of the glowing embers. It cast something on the coals while Glanton stood transfixed.

Little tongues of red grew to life; the fire rose and the shadows retreated before the widening pool of wavering light. A face grew out of the darkness before Emmett Glanton – a grinning face that was like a carven mask somehow imbued with evil life. White pointed teeth reflected the firelight, eyes red as the eyes of an owl burned at him.

With a choking cry Glanton lifted his gun and fired full at the face. At that range he could not miss. The face vanished with a shattering crash and Glanton was showered with tiny particles that stung his hand.

But a low laugh rang through the room – the laugh he had heard over the phone! Whence it came he could not be sure, but in the flash of intuition that came to him, as it often comes to men in desperate straits, he realised the trick that had been played upon him, and wheeled with a gasp of pure terror. Point blank he fired, with the muzzle jammed against the bulk that was almost on him – the bulk of the fiend that had crept up behind him while he was staring at its reflection in front of him.

There was an agonised grunt and something that swished venom-ously ripped away the front of his shirt. And then the monster was down and floundering in its death throes in the shadows at his feet, and in a panic Glanton fired down at it again and again, until its thrashing ceased and in the deafening silence that followed the booming of the shots he heard only the dry tick-tock of the clock, the drip-drip on the floor and the moaning that rose eerily in the gruesome dark.

His hands were clammy with sweat when he found the oil lamp and lighted it. As the flame sprang up, sending the shadows slinking back to the corners, he glared fearfully at the thing sprawled before the hearth. At least it was a man – a tall, powerful man, naked to the waist, his shoulders and arching chest gigantic, his arms thick with knotting muscles.

Blood oozed from three wounds in that massive torso. He seemed to be stained with some sort of paint from his shaven crown to his fingertips. And the fingers of one hand were frightfully armed, with steel hooks that were hollow nearly to the points and slipped over the fingers, curving and razor sharp, making terrible, tiger-like talons.

The thick lips, drawn back, revealed teeth filed to points, and then Glanton saw that he was not painted all over, after all. In the centre of the breast a circle of white skin showed, and inside that circle there was a strange black symbol; it looked like a blind, black face.

An arrangement of mirrors fastened at right angles to the mantel and to the wall, one shattered by his bullet, revealed the trick by which he meant to take Glanton off guard. He must have made his arrangements, simple and easy enough, when he heard the car driving up. But it was diabolical, betraying a twisted mind.

From where he had been standing, Glanton could not see his own reflection in the mirror on the mantel, but only the reflection of the man behind and to one side of him, like a spectral face floating in the shadows.

What takes long in the telling flashed lightning-like through Glanton's mind as he looked down at the black man; and then he saw something else. He saw old John Bruckman.

The old man lay naked on a table, on his back, arms and legs spread wide, so that his body formed a St Andrew's Cross. Through each hand, nailing it to the wood, and through each ankle, a black spike had been driven.

His tongue had been pulled out of his mouth and a steel skewer was driven through it. A ghastly raw, red patch showed on his breast, where a portion of skin as big as a man's palm had been savagely sliced away. And that piece of skin lay on the table beside him and Glanton gasped at the sight of it. For it bore the same unholy symbol that showed on the breast of the dead man by the hearth. Blood trickled along the table, dripped on the floor.

Nauseated, Glanton drew forth the skewer from John Bruckman's tongue. Bruckman gagged, spat forth a great mouthful of blood and made incoherent sounds.

'Take it easy, John,' said Glanton. 'I'll get some pliers and pull these spikes out – '

'Let them be!' gurgled Bruckman, scarcely intelligible with his butchered tongue. 'They're barbed . . . you'll tear my hands off. I'm dying . . . they hurt me in ways that don't show so plainly. Let me die in as little pain as possible. Sorry . . . would have warned you *he* was waiting for you in the dark . . . but this accursed skewer . . . couldn't even scream. He heard your car and made ready . . . mirrors . . . always carry their paraphernalia with them . . . paraphernalia of illusion . . . deception and murder! Whiskey, quick! On that shelf!'

Though he winced at the sting of the fiery liquid on his mangled tongue, Bruckman's voice grew stronger; and a blaze rose in his bloodshot eyes.

'I'm going to tell you everything,' he panted. 'I'll live that long . . . then you set the law on them . . . blast them off the earth! I've kept the oath until now, even with the threat of death hanging over me, but I thought I could fool them. Curse their black souls, I'll keep their secret no longer! Don't talk or ask questions – listen!'

Strange the tales that dying lips have gasped, but never a stranger tale than that Emmett Glanton heard in the blood-stained room, where a dead black face grinned by a smouldering hearth, and a dying man, spiked to a table, mouthed grisly secrets with a mangled tongue in the smoky light of the guttering lamp, while the black wind moaned and crawled at the rattling windows.

'When I was young, in another land,' panted John Bruckman, 'I was a fool. And I was trapped by my own folly into joining a cult of devil-worshippers – the Black Brothers of Ahriman. Until too late I did not realise what they were . . . nor to what horrors my own terrible oath had bound me. I need not speak of their aims and purposes . . . they were foul beyond conception. Yet they had one characteristic that is so often lacking in many such cults . . . they were sincere – fanatic. They worshipped the fiend Ahriman as zealously as did their heathen ancestors. And they practised human sacrifice. Once each year, on this very night, between midnight and dawn, a young girl was offered up on the burning altar of Ahriman, Lord of Fire. On that glowing altar her body was consumed to ashes and the ashes scattered to the night wind by the black-painted priests.

'I became one of the Black Brothers. On my breast was tattooed indelibly the symbol of Ahriman, which is the symbol of Night – a blind, black face. But at last I sickened of the revolting practices of the cult, and fled from it. I came to America and changed my name. Some of my people were already here – the branch of the family to which Joan belongs.

'With the passing of nineteen years I thought the Black Brothers had forgotten me. I didn't know there were branches in America, in the teeming foreign quarters of the great cities. But I might have known they never forget. And one day I received a cryptic message that shattered my illusions. They had remembered, had traced me, found me – knew all about me. And, in punishment for my desertion, they had chosen my niece, Joan, for the yearly sacrifice.

'That was bad enough, but what nearly drove me mad with terror was knowledge of the custom that attends the sacrifice . . . since time immemorial it's been the habit of the Black Brothers to kill the man nearest the girl chosen for sacrifice . . . father, brother, husband – her "master" according to their ritual. This is partly because of a dim phallic superstition, partly a practical way of eliminating an enemy, for the girl's protector would certainly seek vengeance.

'I knew I couldn't save Joan. She was marked for doom, but I might save myself by shifting responsibility for her to somebody else's shoulders. So I brought her here and married her to you.'

'You swine!' whispered Glanton.

'It did me little good!' gasped Bruckman, his tortured head tossing from side to side. His eyes were glazing and a bloody froth rose to his livid lips. 'They came shortly after you drove away. I was fool enough to let them in . . . told them I was no longer responsible for the chosen maiden. They laughed at me . . . tortured me. I broke away – got to the phone . . . but they had ordered my death, as a renegade brother. They drove away, leaving one of them here to attend to me. You can see he did his work well!'

'Where – where did they go?' Glanton spoke with dry lips, remembering the big automobile roaring northward.

'To your ranch . . . to get Joan . . . I told them where she was – before they started torturing me!'

'You fool! You're telling me this *now*,' Glanton yelled.

But John Bruckman did not hear, for, with a convulsion that spattered foam from his empurpled lips and tore one of the bloody spikes out of the wood, the life went out of him in one great cry.

Chapter 4. *Crackling blue flame*

Like a drunken man, Emmitt Glanton left from that lamp-lit room where a black face on the floor grinned blindly at a blind white face lolling on the table. The black wind ripped at him with mad, invisible fingers as he ran in great leaps to his car.

The drive through the screaming darkness was nightmare, with the black wall splitting before him and closing behind him, horror hounding him like a werewolf on his trail, and the wind howling awful secrets in his ears.

He did not turn aside for the sombre knoll this time, but plunged straight on, thundered over the bridge and rushed past the black cliff. No boulder fell from above. Joshua must have left his ambush long ago.

Three more miles and his heart leaped into his throat and stuck there, a choking chunk of ice. He should be able to see the light in the ranch house window by now – but only the glare of his own headlights knifed the black curtain before him.

Then the ranch house bulked out of the night and on the porch he saw a strange pale spot of radiance glowing. There was no sign of the automobile that had come northward. But he checked his own car suddenly to avoid running over a shape that sprawled in the fenceless yard. It was the mad Joshua, lying face down, one side of his head a mass of blood. He had come only to meet death.

Glanton slid out of the car and ran toward the house, shouting Sanchez's name. His cries died away in the stormy clamour of the wind, and an icy hand gripped his heart.

His dilated eyes were fixed on the pale spot that grew in size and shape as he approached . . . a man's face stared at him – the face of Sanchez, weirdly illuminated. Glanton stole closer, holding his breath. Why should the face of Sanchez glow so in the darkness? Why should he stand so still, unanswering, eyes fixed and glassy? Why should his face be looking down from such a height?

Then Glanton knew. He was looking at Sanchez's severed head, fastened by its long hair to a pillar of the porch. Some sort of phosphorus had been rubbed on the dead face to make that eerie glow.

'Joan!'

It was a cry of agony as Glanton flung himself into the darkened house. Only the wind outside answered him, mocked him. His foot struck something heavy and yielding just inside the door. Sick with horror he found a match and struck it. Near the door lay a headless body, riddled with bullets. It was the body of Sanchez. And but for the corpse the house was empty. The match burned down to Glanton's fingers and he stumbled out of the house.

Out in the yard he fought down hysteria and forced himself to look at the matter rationally. Joshua must have been shot by Sanchez, while trying to sneak up on the house. Then it would have been easy for strangers to catch the old Mexican off-guard. He had not expected an attack from anyone except the halfwit, nor would he have been expecting enemies to come in a motor car. He would have come to the door at a hail from a stopping auto, unsuspectingly showing himself in the lighted doorway. A sudden hail of bullets would have done the rest. And then . . . beads of perspiration broke out on his body. Joan, alone and undefended, with those fiends!

He whirled, gun in hand, as he thought he heard a noise like something moving in the bushes north of the house. It diminished, ceased as he went in that direction. It might have been a steer, or some smaller beast. It might – suddenly he turned and strode toward the car.

The body that had lain there before was gone. Had dead Joshua risen and stalked away in the shadows, and was it he that Glanton had heard stealing northward through the bushes? Glanton did not greatly care. At that moment he was ready to believe any grisliness was possible, and he had no interest in Joshua, dead or alive.

He walked around the house, wiping the sweat from his face with clammy hands. The house stood on a rise. From it he could see the lights of any car fleeing northward, for several miles. He strained his eyes, but saw no distant shaft splitting the dark. The raiders must have already put many miles between them and the scene of their crimes. He must follow – but where? Northward, yes – but a few miles north of his ranch the road split into three forks, each leading eventually into a highway, one of which ran to New Mexico, one to Oklahoma, and one north into the Panhandle.

He twisted his fingers together in an agony of indecision. Then he stiffened. He had seen a light – yet not a distinct shaft like a car light. This was more like a blur in the dark – like the glow of embers not yet extinguished. It seemed to emanate from a spot somewhat east of the road which ran north, and this side of the forks. Night made sight and judgment deceptive, but tracing out that eerie glow was better than sitting in racking inaction.

Fixing the spot in his mind as well as he could, he ran to his car and drove northward. As soon as he had descended the rise on which his house stood he could no longer see the glare, but he drove on until he reached a spot which he believed was the point where the road most closely approached the spot where he had seen the glow. A long wooded ridge stood east of the road at that spot.

He left the car and toiled up the western slope of the ridge, scratching his hands and tearing his clothing on rocks and bushes. And nearly to the crest he heard something that stopped him in his tracks. The wind had dwindled to a fitful moaning, and somewhere ahead of him there rose a weird sound that set his flesh crawling.

Chanting! Beyond that black ridge men were chanting in an evil monotone that brought up shuddersome racial memories, old as time and dim as nightmares, of grim black temples where clouds of foul incense smoke rolled about the feet of bowing worshippers before a blood-stained altar. In a frenzy Glanton charged to the crest, tearing through the thickets by sheer force.

Crouching there he looked down on a scene that wrenched his horrified mind back a thousand years into the black night of the medieval when madness stalked the earth in the guise of men.

At the foot of the ridge, in a wide, natural basin glowed a ring of fire. He saw its apparent source – boulders had been rolled to form a solid circle and these boulders glowed with a blue-white light that was like an icy heat beyond human comprehension. From them rose a glow that hung like an unholy halo above the shallow basin. It was this light he had seen from his ranch. It might have been a glow from the slag-heaps of Hell. And devils were not lacking. He saw them, three of them inside the circle – tall, muscular men, naked, their heads hidden by grinning golden masks made like the faces of beasts.

They stood about a heap of stones which glowed with a dull blue radiance, and on that crude improvised altar lay a slender, unmoving figure.

Glanton almost screamed aloud at the sight. Joan lay there, stark naked, spread-eagled in the form of St Andrew's Cross, her wrists and ankles strapped securely. In that instant Glanton knew what it would mean to him to lose that girl – realised how much she had come to mean to him in the few hours he had known her. His wife! Even at this moment the phrase brought a strange, warm thrill. And now those devils down there were preparing, by some hellish art, to reduce that lovely body into ashes . . .

Madly he hurled himself down the slope, pistol in hand. As he went he heard the chanting cease, and was aware of a strange, yet curiously familiar humming in the air.

Whence it came he could not tell, but it sounded like the pulsing of a giant dynamo. Joan cried out. An edge of pain vibrated through her voice.

The halo over the circle mounted, grew more intensely blue. The rocks glowed with a fiercer light; pale tongues of flame licked up from them. The hue of the altar under the girl was changing. The blue was growing more pronounced, less dull. That the change in its colour was accompanied by painful sensations was evident from Joan's cries and the writhings of her bound body.

Glanton yelled incoherently as his feet hit level ground, and the black men turned quickly toward him. His lips drew back in a wolfish snarl and the old single-action gun went up in a menacing arc as he thumbed back the fanged hammer. He meant to shoot these devils down in their tracks, like so many mad dogs – then his out-thrust left hand touched one of the glowing boulders. Merely touched it, but the contact was like the jolt of a fork of lightning. Glanton was knocked off his feet and rolled, blind and dizzy with brief but stunning agony. As he staggered up, snarling and still gripping his gun, he recognised the truth.

Somehow those boulders had been made conductors of electricity. They were charged with a voltage terrific beyond his understanding. And so was the altar, though as yet the full force had not been turned on.

The rising hum that now filled the air told its own grisly tale. Joan was to die by electricity, not swiftly shocked to death as in an electric chair, but slowly, agonisedly, burned to a crisp – to white ashes to be scattered to the night wind.

With an inhuman yell he threw up his gun and fired. One of the masked men spun on his heels and fell sprawling, but the taller of the remaining two bent quickly and laid a hand on some sort of contraption at his feet.

Instantly the hum grew to a shriek. White fire danced around the ring, blinding and dazzling the man outside. He saw the tall black forms within it vaguely, through a dizzying blue-white curtain of flame.

Shielding his eyes from the glare, panic tugging at his soul, he fired again and again until the hammer fell with an empty snap. He could not hit them. The noise, the glare, bewildered him; everything was thrown out of its proper proportions; vision and perspective were distorted.

He hurled the gun at them and reeled toward the blazing barricade with his bare hands, knowing that to touch it would be death, yet choosing death rather than standing by and watching the girl die. But before he reached it a black shape hurtled past him, out of the darkness. Joshua! Blood clotted his scalp, but his primitive fury, his mad desire for the body on that glowing altar were undimmed.

Like a charging bull he came out of the dark, headlong at the barrier. Running hard and low he bent, gathered his thews and leaped! Only a beast or a madman could have made that leap. He cleared the barrier with a foot to spare; one instant he was etched in mid-air, black against the glare, arms wide and fingers spread like talons, then he hit catlike on his feet within the ring of death.

And as he struck he lunged. The priests were naked and weapon-less. The taller let go the lever he held, sprang aside, stooped and snatched up some object, even as Joshua struck his companion. It might have been a bull that smote and tossed the priest.

Plain above the lessening hum and crackle of blue flame sounded the snap of splintering bones, the shriek of the priest. He was whirled from his feet, a broken, dangling doll, lifted high in apelike arms above the bullet-head and dashed head first to the earth with such fury that the broken corpse rebounded before it lay still. Head down, the killer plunged at the taller priest's throat.

It had been a pistol this man had snatched up, and a raking blast of lead met the charging madman – met him, but did not stop him.

With bullets smacking into his body at close range, Joshua bell-owed with pain and swayed on his feet, but came on in an irresistible surge of fury and threw his arms about the body of his foe. He must have been dying even then, but the blind force of his rush was enough to carry the priest off his feet. Together they hurtled on – to crash full against the blazing ring of boulders!

A crack like a clap of thunder, a blinding spray of blue fire, one awful scream . . . then the reek of burnt flesh filled the air. In the swiftly dying glare, Emmett Glanton saw two hideous figures crump-led in a fused, indistinguishable mass against the dulling rocks.

Something had happened to the generator of that terrible power. The hum had ceased; the demon halo was dying. Already the stones of the altar had assumed their natural tint. But on it the girl lay limp.

As Glanton crawled over the barrier his heart was in his mouth. Tenderly he freed her and lifted her, grateful to feel warm, living flesh under his hands, but setting his teeth against what he might find . . . but her tender back and limbs showed none of the ghastly burns he feared.

Obviously no great amount of electricity had been turned into the altar. He saw wires running in all directions from the amazingly small, compact, black case-like thing that stood near the altar.

Before he carried Joan out of the ring he smashed the thing with a heavy rock. The Black Brothers knew secrets that were better kept from the world at large. Even clean science became hurtful black magic in their hands. That tiny dynamo, of a type undreamed of by the world, contained more energy than sane men conceived of – power to turn naked rocks into live wires. Such a secret could only be evil.

He whipped off his torn shirt and wrapped the girl in it, as care-fully he carried her down to the road.

As he went, he thought of Joshua, and the only logical explanation offered itself. The bullet that had struck the madman had not killed him, but only creased him and knocked him out. When he came to himself, he started on the trail of the woman his crazed brain desired, drawn either by the same glimpse of the distant fire that had drawn Glanton, or by dark, psychic instinct.

Glanton had almost reached the car when Joan opened her eyes, stared about her wildly, then clung to him.

'It's all right, kid,' he soothed her. 'You're not hurt. You just fainted. Everything's all right now. Joshua paid his debt, without meaning to, poor devil. Look, it's getting daylight. The night's past.'

He meant it in more than its literal sense. 'Take me home, Emmett,' she whimpered, nestling deep into his arms. Then, irrelevantly: 'Kiss me.'

And Emmett Glanton kissed his wife for the first time, just as dawn touched the eastern hills.

The Fire of Asshurbanipal

Yar Am squinted carefully down the blue barrel of his Lee-Enfield, called devoutly on Allah and sent a bullet through the brain of a flying rider.

'Allaho akbar!'

The big Afghan shouted in glee, waving his weapon above his head, 'God is great! By Allah, sahib, I have sent another one of the dogs to Hell!'

His companion peered cautiously over the rim of the sand-pit they had scooped with their hands. He was a lean and wiry American, Steve Clarney by name.

'Good work, old horse,' said this person. 'Four left. Look – they're drawing off.'

The white-robed horsemen were indeed reining away, clustering together just out of accurate rifle-range, as if in council. There had been seven when they had first swooped down on the comrades, but the fire from the two rifles in the sand-pit had been deadly.

'Look, sahib – they abandon the fray!'

Yar Ali stood up boldly and shouted taunts at the departing riders, one of whom whirled and sent a bullet that kicked up sand thirty feet in front of the pit.

'They shoot like the sons of dogs,' said Yar Ali in complacent self-esteem. 'By Allah, did you see that rogue plunge from his saddle as my lead went home? Up, sahib; let us run after them and cut them down!'

Paying no attention to this outrageous proposal – for he knew it was but one of the gestures Afghan nature continually demands . . . Steve rose, dusted off his breeches and gazing after the riders, now white specks far out on the desert, said musingly: 'Those fellows ride as if they had some set purpose in mind – not a bit like men running from a licking.'

'Aye,' agreed Yar Ali promptly and seeing nothing inconsistent with his present attitude and recent bloodthirsty suggestion, 'they ride after more of their kind – they are hawks who give up their prey not quickly. We had best move our position quickly, Steve sahib. They will come back – maybe in a few hours, maybe in a few days – it all depends on how far away lies the oasis of their tribe. But they will be back. We have guns and lives – they want both. And behold.'

The Afghan levered out the empty shell and slipped a single cartridge into the breech of his rifle.

'My last bullet, sahib.'

Steve nodded. 'I've got three left.'

The raiders whom their bullets had knocked from the saddle had been looted by their own comrades. No use searching the bodies which lay in the sand for ammunition. Steve lifted his canteen and shook it. Not much water remained. He knew that Yar Ali had only a little more than he, though the big Afridi, bred in a barren land, had used and needed less water than did the American. As Steve unscrewed the canteen cap and drank very sparingly, he mentally reviewed the chain of events that had led them to their present position.

Wanderers, soldiers of fortune, thrown together by chance and attracted to each other by mutual admiration, he and Yar Ali had wandered from India up through Turkestan and down through Persia, an oddly assorted but highly capable pair. Driven by the restless urge of inherent wanderlust, their avowed purpose – which they swore to and sometimes believed themselves – was the accumulation of some vague and undiscovered treasure, some pot of gold at the foot of some yet unborn rainbow.

Then in ancient Shiraz they had heard of the Fire of Asshurbanipal. From the lips of an ancient Persian trader, who only half believed what he repeated to them, they heard the tale that he in turn had heard from the babbling lips of delirium, in his distant youth. He had been a member of a caravan, fifty years before, which, wandering far on the southern shore of the Persian Gulf trading for pearls, had followed the tale of a rare pearl far into the desert.

The pearl, rumoured found by a diver and stolen by a shaykh of the interior, they did not find, but they did pick up a Turk who was dying of starvation, thirst and a bullet wound in the thigh. As he died in delirium, he babbled a wild tale of a silent dead city of black stone set in the drifting sands of the desert far to the westward, and of a flaming gem clutched in the bony fingers of a skeleton on an ancient throne.

He had not dared bring it away with him, because of an overpowering brooding horror that haunted the place, and thirst had driven him into the desert again, where Bedouins had pursued and wounded him. Yet he had escaped, riding hard until his horse fell under him. He died without telling how he had reached the mythical city in the first place, but the old trader thought he must have come from the northwest – a deserter from the Turkish army, making a desperate attempt to reach the Gulf.

The men of the caravan had made no attempt to plunge still further into the desert in search of the city; for, said the old trader, they believed it to be the ancient, ancient City of Evil spoken of in the *Necronomicon* of the mad Arab Alhazred – the city of the dead on which an ancient curse rested. Legends named it vaguely: the Arabs called it Beled-el-Djinn, the City of Devils, and the Turks, Kara-Shehr, the Black City. And the gem was that ancient and accursed jewel belonging to a king of long ago, whom the Grecians called Sardanapalus and the Semitic peoples Asshurbanipal.

Steve had been fascinated by the tale. Admitting to himself that it was doubtless one of the ten thousand cock-and-bull myths booted about the East, still there was a possibility that he and Yar Ali had stumbled onto a trace of that pot of rainbow gold for which they searched. And Yar Ali had heard hints before of a silent city of the sands; tales had followed the eastbound caravans over the high Persian uplands and across the sands of Turkestan, into the mountain country and beyond – vague tales; whispers of a black city of the djinn, deep in the hazes of a haunted desert.

So, following the trail of the legend, the companions had come from Shiraz to a village on the Arabian shore of the Persian Gulf, and there had heard more from an old man who had been a pearl-driver in his youth. The loquacity of age was on him and he told tales repeated to him by wandering tribesmen who had them in turn from the wild nomads of the deep interior; and again Steve and Yar Ah heard of the still black city with giant beasts carved of stone, and the skeleton sultan who held the blazing gem.

And so, mentally swearing at himself for a fool, Steve had made the plunge, and Yar Ali, secure in the knowledge that all things lay on the lap of Allah, had come with him. Their scanty supply of money had been just sufficient to provide riding-camels and provisions for a bold flying invasion of the unknown. Their only chart had been the vague rumours that placed the supposed location of Kara-Shehr.

There had been days of hard travel, pushing the beasts and conserving water and food. Then, deep in the desert they invaded, they had encountered a blinding sand-wind in which they had lost the camels. After that came long miles of staggering through the sands, battered by a flaming sun, subsisting on rapidly dwindling water from their canteens, and food Yar Ali had in a pouch. No thought of finding the mythical city now. They pushed on blindly, in hope of stumbling upon a spring; they knew that behind them no oases lay within a distance they could hope to cover on foot. It was a desperate chance, but their only one.

Then white-clad hawks had swooped down on them, out of the haze of the skyline, and from a shallow and hastily scooped trench the adventurers had exchanged shots with the wild riders who circled them at top speed. The bullets of the Bedouins had skipped through their makeshift fortifications, knocking dust into their eyes and flicking bits of cloth from their garments, but by good chance neither had been hit.

Their one bit of luck, reflected Clarney, as he cursed himself for a fool. What a mad venture it had been, anyway! To think that two men could so dare the desert and live, much less wrest from its abysmal bosom the secrets of the ages! And that crazy tale of a skeleton hand gripping a flaming jewel in a dead city – bosh! what utter rot! He must have been crazy himself to credit it, the American decided with the clarity of view that suffering and danger bring.

'Well, old horse,' said Steve, lifting his rifle, 'let's get going. It's a toss-up if we die of thirst or get sniped off by the desert-brothers. Anyway, we're doin' no good here.'

'God gives,' agreed Yar Ali cheerfully. 'The sun sinks westward. Soon the coolness of night will be upon us. Perhaps we shall find water yet, sahib. Look, the terrain changes to the south.'

Clarney shaded his eyes against the dying sun. Beyond a level, barren expanse of several miles width, the land did indeed become more broken; aborted hills were in evidence. The American slung his rifle over his arm and sighed.

'Heave ahead; we're food for the buzzards anyhow.'

The sun sank and the moon rose, flooding the desert with weird silver light. Drifted sand glimmered in long ripples, as if a sea had suddenly been frozen into immobility. Steve, parched fiercely by a thirst he dared not fully quench, cursed beneath his breath. The desert was beautiful beneath the moon, with the beauty of a cold marble Lorelei to lure men to destruction. What a mad quest! his weary brain reiterated; the Fire of Asshurbanipal retreated into the mazes of unreality with each dragging step. The desert became not merely a material wasteland, but the grey mists of the lost aeons, in whose depths dreamed sunken things.

Clarney stumbled and swore; was he failing already? Yar Ali swung along with the easy, tireless stride of the mountain man, and Steve set his teeth, nerving himself to greater effort. They were entering the broken country at last, and the going became harder. Shallow gullies and narrow ravines knifed the earth with wavering patterns. Most of them were nearly filled with sand, and there was no trace of water.

'This country was once oasis country,' commented Yar Ali. 'Allah knows how many centuries ago the sand took it, as the sand has taken so many cities in Turkestan.'

They swung on like dead men in a grey land of death.

The moon grew red and sinister as she sank, and shadowy darkness settled over the desert before they had reached a point where they could see what lay beyond the broken belt. Even the big Afghan's feet began to drag, and Steve kept himself erect only by a savage effort of will. At last they toiled up a sort of ridge, on the southern side of which the land sloped downward.

'We rest,' declared Steve. 'There's no water in this hellish country. No use in goin' on for ever. My legs are stiff as gun-barrels. I couldn't take another step to save my neck. Here's a kind of stunted cliff, about as high as a man's shoulder, facing south. We'll sleep in the lee of it.'

'And shall we not keep watch, Steve sahib?'

'We don't,' answered Steve. 'If the Arabs cut our throats while we're asleep, so much the better. We're goners anyhow.'

With which optimistic observation Clarney lay down stiffly in the deep sand. But Yar Ali stood, leaning forward, straining his eyes into the elusive darkness that turned the star-flecked horizons to murky wells of shadow.

'Something lies on the skyline to the south,' he muttered uneasily. 'A hill? I cannot tell, or even be sure that I see anything at all.'

'You're seeing mirages already,' said Steve irritably. 'Lie down and sleep.'

And so saying, Steve slumbered.

The sun in his eyes awoke him. He sat up, yawning, and his first sensation was that of thirst. He lifted his canteen and wet his lips. One drink left. Yar Ali still slept. Steve's eyes wandered over the southern horizon and he started. He kicked the recumbent Afghan.

'Hey, wake up, Ali. I reckon you weren't seeing things after all. There's your hill – and a queer-lookin' one, too.'

The Afridi woke as a wild thing wakes, instantly and completely, his hand leaping to his long knife as he glared about for enemies. His gaze followed Steve's pointing fingers and his eyes widened.

'By Allah and by Allah!' he swore. 'We have come into a land of djinn! That is no hill . . . it is a city of stone in the midst of the sands!'

Steve bounded to his feet like a steel spring released. As he gazed with bated breath, a fierce shout escaped his lips. At his feet the slope of the ridge ran down into a wide and level expanse of sand that stretched away southward. And far away, across those sands, to his straining sight the 'hill' slowly took shape, like a mirage growing from the drifting sands.

He saw great uneven walls, massive battlements; all about crawled the sands like a living, sensate thing, drifted high about the walls, softening the rugged outlines. No wonder that at first glance the whole had appeared like a hill.

'Kara-Shehr!' Clarney exclaimed fiercely. 'Beled-el-Djinn! The city of the dead! It wasn't a pipe-dream after all! We've found it – by Heaven, we've found it! Come on! Let's go!'

Yar Ali shook his head uncertainly and muttered something about evil djinn under his breath, but he followed. The sight of the ruins had swept from Steve his thirst and hunger, and the fatigue that a few hours' sleep had not fully overcome. He trudged on swiftly, oblivious to the rising heat, his eyes gleaming with the lust of the explorer. It was not altogether greed for the fabled gem that had prompted Steve Clarney to risk his life in that grim wilderness; deep in his soul lurked the urge to seek out the hidden places of the world, and that urge had been stirred to the depths by the ancient tales.

Now as they crossed the level wastes that separated the broken land from the city, they saw the shattered walls take clearer form and shape, as if they grew out of the morning sky. The city seemed built of huge blocks of black stone, but how high the walls had been there was no telling because of the sand that drifted high about their base; in many places they had fallen away and the sand hid the fragments entirely.

The sun reached her zenith and thirst intruded itself in spite of zeal and enthusiasm, but Steve fiercely mastered his suffering. His lips were parched and swollen, but he would not take that last drink until he had reached the ruined city. Yar Ali wet his lips from his own canteen and tried to share the remainder with his friend. Steve shook his head and plodded on.

In the ferocious heat of the desert afternoon they reached the ruin, and passing through a wide breach in the crumbling wall, gazed on the dead city. Sand choked the ancient streets and lent fantastic form to huge, fallen and half-hidden columns. So crumbled into decay and so covered with sand was the whole that the explorers could make out little of the original plan of the city; now it was but a waste of drifted sand and crumbling stone over which brooded, like an invisible cloud, an aura of unspeakable antiquity.

But directly in front of them ran a broad avenue, the outline of which not even the ravaging sands and winds of time had been able to efface. On either side of the wide way were ranged huge columns, not unusually tall, even allowing for the sand that hid their bases, but incredibly massive. On the top of each column stood a figure carved from solid stone – great, sombre images, half human, half bestial, partaking of the brooding brutishness of the whole city. Steve cried out in amazement.

'The winged bulls of Nineveh. The bulls with men's heads! By the saints, all the old tales are true! The Assyrians did build this city! The whole tale's true! They must have come here when the Babylonians destroyed Assyria! Why, this scene's a dead ringer for pictures I've seen – reconstructed scenes of old Nineveh! And look!'

He pointed down the broad street to the great building which reared at the other end, a colossal, brooding edifice whose columns and walls of solid black stone blocks defied the winds and sands of time. The drifting, obliterating sea washed about its foundations, overflowing into its doorways, but it would require a thousand years to inundate the whole structure.

'An abode of devils!' muttered Yar Ali, uneasily.

'The temple of Baal!' exclaimed Steve. 'Come on! I was afraid we'd find all the palaces and temples hidden by the sand and have to dig for the gem.'

'Little good it will do us,' muttered Yar Ali. 'Here we die.'

'I reckon so.' Steve unscrewed the cap of his canteen. 'Let's take our last drink. Anyway, we're safe from the Arabs. They'd never dare come here, with their superstitions. We'll drink and then we'll die, I reckon, but first we'll find the jewel. When I pass out, I want to have it in my hand. Maybe a few centuries later some lucky son-of-a-gun will find our skeletons . . . and the gem. Here's to him, whoever he is!'

With which grim jest Clarney drained his canteen and Yar Ali followed suit. They had played their last ace; the rest lay on the lap of Allah.

They strode up the broad way, and Yar Ali glanced nervously to right and left, half expecting to see a horned and fantastic face leering at him from behind a column. Steve him felt the sombre antiquity of the place, and almost found himself fearing a rush of bronze war chariots down the forgotten streets, or to hear the sudden menacing flare of bronze trumpets. The silence in dead cities was so much more intense, he reflected, than that on the open desert.

They came to the portals of the great temple. Rows of immense columns flanked the wide doorway, which was ankle-deep in sand, and from which sagged massive bronze frameworks that had once braced mighty doors, whose polished woodwork had rotted away centuries ago. They passed into a mighty hall of misty twilight whose shadowy stone roof was upheld by columns like the trunks of forest trees. The whole effect of the architecture was one of awesome magnitude and sullen, breathtaking splendour, like a temple built by sombre giants for the abode of dark gods.

Yar Ali walked fearfully, as if he expected to awake sleeping gods, and Steve, without the Afridi's superstitions, yet felt the gloomy majesty of the place lay sombre hands on his soul.

No trace of a footprint showed in the deep dust on the floor; half a century had passed since the affrighted Turk had fled these silent halls. As for the Bedouins, it was easy to see why those superstitious sons of the desert shunned this haunted city – and haunted it was, not by actual ghosts, perhaps, but by the shadows of lost splendours.

As they trod the sands of the hall, which seemed endless, Steve pondered many questions: How did these fugitives from the wrath of frenzied rebels build this city? How did they pass through the country of their foes – for Babylonia lay between Assyria and the Arabian desert. Yet there had been no other place for them to go; westward lay Syria and the sea, and north and east swarmed the 'dangerous Medes', those fierce Aryans whose aid had stiffened the arm of Babylon to smite her foe to the dust.

Possibly, thought Steve, Kara-Shehr – whatever its name had been in those dim days – had been built as an outpost border city before the fall of the Assyrian empire, whither survivals of that overthrow fled. At any rate it was possible that Kara-Shehr had outlasted Nineveh by some centuries – a strange, hermit city, no doubt, cut off from the rest of the world.

Surely, as Yar Ali had said, this was once fertile country, watered by oases; and doubtless in the broken country they had passed over the night before, there had been quarries that furnished the stone for the building of the city.

Then what caused its downfall? Did the encroachment of the sands and the filling up of the springs cause the people to abandon it, or was Kara-Shehr a city of silence before the sands crept over the walls? Did the downfall come from within or without? Did civil war blot out the inhabitants, or were they slaughtered by some powerful foe from the desert? Clarney shook his head in baffled chagrin. The answers to those questions were lost in the maze of forgotten ages.

'Allaho akbar!' They had traversed the great shadowy hall and at its further end they came upon a hideous black stone altar, behind which loomed an ancient god, bestial and horrific. Steve shrugged his shoulders as he recognised the monstrous aspect of the image – aye, Baal, on which black altar in other ages many a screaming, writhing, naked victim had offered up its naked soul. The idol embodied in its utter, abysmal and sullen bestiality the whole soul of this demoniac city. Surely, thought Steve, the builders of Nineveh and Kara-Shehr were cast in another mould from the people of today. Their art and culture were too ponderous, too grimly barren of the lighter aspects of humanity, to be wholly human, as modern man understands humanity.

Their architecture was repellent; of high skill, yet so massive, sullen and brutish in effect as to be almost beyond the comprehension of moderns.

The adventurers passed through a narrow door which opened in the end of the hall close to the idol, and came into a series of wide, dim, dusty chambers connected by column-flanked corridors. Along these they strode in the grey ghostly light, and came at last to a wide stair, whose massive stone steps led upward and vanished in the gloom. Here Yar Ali halted.

'We have dared much, sahib,' he muttered. 'Is it wise to dare more?'

Steve, aquiver with eagerness, yet understood the Afghan's mind. 'You mean we shouldn't go up those stairs?'

'They have an evil look. To what chambers of silence and horror may they lead? When djinn haunt deserted buildings, they lurk in the upper chambers. At any moment a demon may bite off our heads.'

'We're dead men anyhow,' grunted Steve. 'But I tell you – you go on back through the hall and watch while I go upstairs.'

'Watch for a wind on the horizon,' responded the Afghan gloomily, shifting his rifle and loosening his long knife in its scabbard. 'No Bedouin comes here. Lead on, sahib. Thou'rt mad after the manner of all Franks, but I would not leave thee to face the djinn alone.'

So the companions mounted the massive stairs, their feet sinking deep into the accumulated dust of centuries at each step. Up and up they went, to an incredible height, until the depths below merged into a vague gloom.

'We walk blind to our doom, sahib,' muttered Yar Ali. 'Allah il allah . . . and Muhammad is his Prophet! Nevertheless, I feel the presence of slumbering Evil and never again shall I hear the wind blowing up the Khyber Pass.'

Steve made no reply. He did not like the breathless silence that brooded over the ancient temple, nor the grisly grey light that filtered from some hidden source.

Now above them the gloom lightened somewhat and they emerged into a vast circular chamber, greyly illumined by light that filtered in through the high, pierced ceiling. But another radiance lent itself to the illumination. A cry burst from Steve's lips, echoed by Yar Ali.

Standing on the top step of the broad stone stair, they looked directly across the broad chamber, with its dust-covered heavy tile floor and bare black stone walls. From about the centre of the chamber, massive steps led up to a stone daïs, and on this daïs stood a marble throne. About this throne glowed and shimmered an uncanny light, and the awestruck adventurers gasped as they saw its source. On the throne slumped a human skeleton, an almost shapeless mass of mouldering bones. A fleshless hand sagged outstretched upon the broad marble throne-arm, and in its grisly clasp there pulsed and throbbed like a living thing, a great crimson stone.

The Fire of Asshurbanipal! Even after they had found the lost city Steve had not really allowed himself to believe that they would find the gem, or that it even existed in reality. Yet he could not doubt the evidence of his eyes, dazzled by that evil, incredible glow. With a fierce shout he sprang across the chamber and up the steps. Yar Ali was at his heels, but when Steve would have seized the gem, the Afghan laid a hand on his arm.

'Wait!' exclaimed the big Muhammadan. 'Touch it not yet, sahib! A curse lies on ancient things – and surely this is a thing triply accursed! Else why has it lain here untouched in a country of thieves for so many centuries? It is not well to disturb the possessions of the dead.'

'Bosh!' snorted the American. 'Superstitions! The Bedouins were scared by the tales that have come down to 'em from their ancestors. Being desert-dwellers they mistrust cities anyway, and no doubt this one had an evil reputation in its lifetime. And nobody except

Bedouins has seen this place before, except that Turk, who was probably half demented with suffering.

'These bones may be those of the king mentioned in the legend – the dry desert air preserves such things indefinitely – but I doubt it. May be Assyrian – most likely Arab – some beggar that got the gem and then died on that throne for some reason or other.'

The Afghan scarcely heard him. He was gazing in fearful fascination at the great stone, as a hypnotised bird stares into a serpent's eye.

'Look at it, sahib!' he whispered. 'What is it? No such gem as this was ever cut by mortal hands! Look how it throbs and pulses like the heart of a cobra!'

Steve was looking, and he was aware of a strange undefined feeling of uneasiness. Well-versed in the knowledge of precious stones, he had never seen a stone like this. At first glance he had supposed it to be a monster ruby, as told in the legends. Now he was not sure, and he had a nervous feeling that Yar Ali was right, that this was no natural, normal gem. He could not classify the style in which it was cut, and such was the power of its lurid radiance that he found it difficult to gaze at it closely for any length of time. The whole setting was not one calculated to soothe restless nerves. The deep dust on the floor suggested an unwholesome antiquity; the grey light evoked a sense of unreality, and the heavy black walls towered grimly, hinting at hidden things.

'Let's take the stone, and go!' muttered Steve, an unaccustomed panicky dread rising in his bosom.

'Wait!' Yar Ali's eyes were blazing, and he gazed, not at the gem, but at the sullen stone walls. 'We are flies in the lair of the spider! Sahib, as Allah lives, it is more than the ghosts of old fears that lurk over this city of horror! I feel the presence of peril, as I have felt it before – as I felt it in a jungle cavern where a python lurked unseen in the darkness – as I felt it in the temple of Thuggee where the hidden stranglers of Siva crouched to spring upon us – as I feel it now, tenfold!'

Steve's hair prickled. He knew that Yar Ali was a grim veteran, not to be stampeded by silly fear or senseless panic; he well remembered the incidents referred to by the Afghan, as he remembered other occasions upon which Yar Ali's Oriental telepathic instinct had warned him of danger before that danger was seen or heard.

'What is it, Yar Ali?' he whispered.

The Afghan shook his head, his eyes filled with a weird mysterious light as he listened to the dim occult promptings of his subconsciousness.

'I know not; I know it is close to us, and that it is very ancient and very evil. I think – ' Suddenly he halted and wheeled, the eerie light vanishing from his eyes to be replaced by a glare of wolf-like fear and suspicion.

'Hark, sahib!' he snapped. 'Ghosts or dead men mount the stair!'

Steve stiffened as the stealthy pad of soft sandals on stone reached his ear.

'By Judas, Ali!' he rapped; 'something's out there – '

The ancient walls re-echoed to a chorus of wild yells as a horde of savage figures flooded the chamber. For one dazed insane instant Steve believed wildly that they were being attacked by re-embodied warriors of a vanished age; then the spiteful crack of a bullet past his ear and the acrid smell of powder told him that their foes were material enough. Clarney cursed; in their fancied security they had been caught like rats in a trap by the pursuing Arabs.

Even as the American threw up his rifle, Yar Ali fired point-blank from the hip with deadly effect, hurled his empty rifle into the horde and went down the steps like a hurricane, his three-foot Khyber knife shimmering in his hairy hand. Into his gusto for battle went real relief that his foes were human. A bullet ripped the turban from his head, but an Arab went down with a split skull beneath the hillman's first, shearing stroke.

A tall Bedouin clapped his gun-muzzle to the Afghan's side, but before he could pull the trigger, Clarney's bullet scattered his brains. The very number of the attackers hindered their onslaught on the big Afridi, whose tigerish quickness made shooting as dangerous to themselves as to him. The bulk of them swarmed about him, striking with scimitar and rifle-stock while others charged up the steps after Steve. At that range there was no missing; the American simply thrust his rifle muzzle into a bearded face and blasted it into a ghastly ruin. The others came on, screaming like panthers.

And now as he prepared to expend his last cartridge, Clarney saw two things in one flashing instant – a wild warrior who, with froth on his beard and a heavy scimitar uplifted, was almost upon him, and another who knelt on the floor drawing a careful bead on the plunging Yar Ali. Steve made an instant choice and fired over the shoulder of the charging swordsman, killing the rifleman – and voluntarily offering his own life for his friend's; for the scimitar was swinging at his own head. But even as the Arab swung, grunting with the force of the blow, his sandaled foot slipped on the marble steps and the curved blade, veering erratically from its arc, clashed on

Steve's rifle-barrel. In an instant the American clubbed his rifle, and as the Bedouin recovered his balance and again heaved up the scimitar, Clarney struck with all his rangy power, and stock and skull shattered together.

Then a heavy ball smacked into his shoulder, sickening him with the shock.

As he staggered dizzily, a Bedouin whipped a turban-cloth about his feet and jerked viciously. Clarney pitched headlong down the steps, to strike with stunning force. A gun-stock in a brown hand went up to dash out his brains, but an imperious command halted the blow.

'Slay him not, but bind him hand and foot.'

As Steve struggled dazedly against many gripping hands, it seemed to him that somewhere he had heard that imperious voice before.

The American's downfall had occurred in a matter of seconds. Even as Steve's second shot had cracked, Yar Ali had half severed a raider's arm and himself received a numbing blow from a rifle-stock on his left shoulder. His sheepskin coat, worn despite the desert heat, saved his hide from half a dozen slashing knives. A rifle was discharged so close to his face that the powder burnt him fiercely, bringing a bloodthirsty yell from the maddened Afghan. As Yar Ali swung up his dripping blade the rifleman, ashy-faced, lifted his rifle above his head in both hands to parry the downward blow, whereat the Afridi, with a yelp of ferocious exultation, shifted as a jungle cat strikes and plunged his long knife into the Arab's belly. But at that instant a rifle-stock, swung with all the hearty ill-will its wielder could evoke, crashed against the giant's head, laying open the scalp and dashing him to his knees.

With the dogged and silent ferocity of his breed, Yar Ali staggered blindly up again, slashing at foes he could scarcely see, but a storm of blows battered him down again, nor did his attackers cease beating him until he lay still. They would have finished him in short order then, but for another peremptory order from their chief; whereupon they bound the senseless knife-man and flung him down alongside Steve, who was fully conscious and aware of the savage hurt of the bullet in his shoulder.

He glared up at the tall Arab who stood looking down at him.

'Well, sahib,' said this one – and Steve saw he was no Bedouin – 'do you not remember me?'

Steve scowled; a bullet-wound is no aid to concentration.

'You look familiar – by Judas! – you are! Nureddin El Mekru!'

'I am honoured! The sahib remembers!' Nureddin salaamed mockingly. 'And you remember, no doubt, the occasion on which you made me a present of – this!'

The dark eyes shadowed with bitter menace and the shaykh indicated a thin white scar on the angle of his jaw.

'I remember,' snarled Clarney, whom pain and anger did not tend to make docile. 'It was in Somaliland, years ago. You were in the slave-trade then. A wretch escaped from you and took refuge with me. You walked into my camp one night in your high-handed way, started a row and in the ensuing scrap you got a butcher-knife across your face. I wish I'd cut your lousy throat.'

'You had your chance,' answered the Arab. 'Now the tables are turned.'

'I thought your stamping-ground lay west,' growled Clarney; 'Yemen and the Somali country.'

'I quit the slave-trade long ago,' answered the shaykh. 'It is an outworn game. I led a band of thieves in Yemen for a time; then again I was forced to change my location. I came here with a few faithful followers, and by Allah, those wild men nearly slit my throat at first. But I overcame their suspicions, and now I lead more men than have followed me in years.

'They whom you fought off yesterday were my men – scouts I had sent out ahead. My oasis lies far to the west. We have ridden for many days, for I was on my way to this very city. When my scouts rode in and told me of two wanderers, I did not alter my course, for I had business first in Beled-el-Djinn. We rode into the city from the west and saw your tracks in the sand. We followed there, and you were blind buffalo who heard not our coming.'

Steve snarled. 'You wouldn't have caught us so easy, only we thought no Bedouin would dare come into Kara-Shehr.'

Nureddin nodded. 'But I am no Bedouin. I have travelled far and seen many lands and many races, and I have read many books. I know that fear is smoke, that the dead are dead, and that djinn and ghosts and curses are mists that the wind blows away. It was because of the tales of the red stone that I came into this forsaken desert. But it has taken months to persuade my men to ride with me here.

'But I am here! And your presence is a delightful surprise. Doubtless you have guessed why I had you taken alive; I have more elaborate entertainment planned for you and that Pathan swine. Now . . . I take the Fire of Asshurbanipal and we will go.'

He turned toward the daïs, and one of his men, a bearded one-eyed giant, exclaimed, 'Hold, my lord! Ancient evil reigned here before the days of Muhammad! The djinn howl through these halls when the winds blow, and men have seen ghosts dancing on the walls beneath the moon. No man of mortals has dared this black city for a thousand years – save one, half a century ago, who fled shrieking.

'You have come here from Yemen; you do not know the ancient curse on this foul city, and this evil stone, which pulses like the red heart of Satan! We have followed you here against our judgment, because you have proven yourself a strong man, and have said you hold a charm against all evil beings. You said you but wished to look on this mysterious gem, but now we see it is your intention to take it for yourself. Do not offend the djinn!'

'Nay, Nureddin, do not offend the djinn!' chorused the other Bedouins. The shaykh's own hard-bitten ruffians, standing in a compact group somewhat apart from the Bedouins, said nothing; hardened to crimes and deeds of impiety, they were less affected by the superstitions of the desert men, to whom the dread tale of the accursed city had been repeated for centuries. Steve, even while hating Nureddin with concentrated venom, realised the magnetic power of the man, the innate leadership that had enabled him to overcome thus far the fears and traditions of ages.

'The curse is laid on infidels who invade the city,' answered Nureddin, 'not on the Faithful. See, in this chamber have we overcome our kafar foes!'

A white-bearded desert hawk shook his head.

'The curse is more ancient than Muhammad. Evil men reared this black city in the dawn of the Beginnings of Days. They oppressed our ancestors of the black tents, and warred among themselves; aye, the black walls of this foul city were stained with blood, and echoed to the shouts of unholy revel and the whispers of dark intrigues.

'Thus came the stone to the city: there dwelt a magician at the court of Asshurbanipal, and the black wisdom of ages was not denied to him. To gain honour and power for himself, he dared the horrors of a nameless vast cavern in a dark, untravelled land, and from those fiend-haunted depths he brought that blazing gem, which is carved of the frozen flames of Hell! By reason of his fearful power in black magic, he put a spell on the demon which guarded the ancient gem, and so stole away the stone. And the demon slept in the cavern unknowing.

'So this magician – Xuthltan by name – dwelt in the court of the sultan Asshurbanipal and did magic and forecast events by scanning the lurid deeps of the stone, into which no eyes but his could look unblinded. And men called the stone the Fire of Asshurbanipal, in honour of the king.

'But evil came upon the kingdom, and men cried out that it was the curse of the djinn, and the sultan in great fear bade Xuthltan take the gem and cast it into the cavern from which he had taken it, lest worse ill befall them.

'Yet it was not the magician's will to give up the gem wherein he read strange secrets of pre-Adamite days, and he fled to the rebel city of Kara-Shehr, where soon civil war broke out and men strove with one another to possess the gem. Then the king who ruled the city, coveting the stone, seized the magician and put him to death by torture, and in this very room he watched him die; with the gem in his hand the king sat upon the throne . . . even as he has sat upon the throne . . . even as he has sat throughout the centuries . . . even as now he sits!'

The Arab's finger stabbed at the mouldering bones on the marble throne, and the wild desert men blenched; even Nureddin's own scoundrels recoiled, catching their breath, but the shaykh showed no sign of perturbation.

'As Xuthltan died,' continued the old Bedouin, 'he cursed the stone whose magic had not saved him, and he shrieked aloud the fearful words which undid the spell he had put upon the demon in the cavern, and set the monster free. And crying out on the forgotten gods, Cthulhu and Koth and Yog-Sothoth, and all the pre-Adamite dwellers in the black cities under the sea and the caverns of the earth, he called upon them – to take back that which was theirs, and with his dying breath pronounced doom on the false king, and that doom was that the king should sit on his throne holding in his hand the Fire of Asshurbanipal until the thunder of Judgment Day.

'Thereat the great stone cried out as a live thing cries, and the king and his soldiers saw a black cloud spinning up from the floor, and out of the cloud blew a fetid wind, and out of the wind came a grisly shape which stretched forth fearsome paws and laid them on the king, who shrivelled and died at their touch. And the soldiers fled screaming, and all the people of the city ran forth wailing into the desert, where they perished or gained through the wastes to the far oasis towns. Kara-Shehr lay silent and deserted, the haunt of the lizard and the jackal. And when some of the desert people ventured into the city they found the king dead on his throne, clutching the blazing gem, but they dared not lay hand upon it, for they knew the demon lurked near to guard it through all the ages – as he lurks near even as we stand here.'

The warriors shuddered involuntarily and glanced about, and Nureddin said, 'Why did he not come forth when the Franks entered the chamber? Is he deaf, that the sound of the combat has not awakened him?'

'We have not touched the gem,' answered the old Bedouin, 'nor had the Franks molested it. Men have looked on it and lived; but no mortal may touch it and survive.'

Nureddin started to speak, gazed at the stubborn, uneasy faces and realised the futility of argument. His attitude changed abruptly.

'I am master here,' he snapped, dropping a hand to his holster. 'I have not sweated and bled for this gem to be balked at the last by groundless fears! Stand back, all! Let any man cross me at the peril of his head!'

He faced them, his eyes blazing, and they fell back, cowed by the force of his ruthless personality. He strode boldly up the marble steps, and the Arabs caught their breath, recoiling toward the door; Yar Ali, conscious at last, groaned dismally. God! thought Steve, what a barbaric scene! – bound captives on the dust-heaped floor, wild warriors clustered about, gripping their weapons, the raw acrid scent of blood and burnt powder still fouling the air, corpses strewn in a horrid welter of blood, brains and entrails . . . and on the daïs, the hawk-faced shaykh, oblivious to all except the evil crimson glow in the skeleton fingers that rested on the marble throne.

A tense silence gripped all as Nureddin stretched forth his hand slowly, as if hypnotised by the throbbing crimson light. And in Steve's subconsciousness there shuddered a dim echo, as of something vast and loathsome waking suddenly from an age-long slumber. The American's eyes moved instinctively toward the grim Cyclopean walls. The jewel's glow had altered strangely; it burned a deeper, darker red, angry and menacing.

'Heart of all evil,' murmured the shaykh, 'how many princes died for thee in the Beginnings of Happenings? Surely the blood of kings throbs in thee. The sultans and the princesses and the generals who wore thee, they are dust and are forgotten, but thou blazest with majesty undimmed, fire of the world . . .'

Nureddin seized the stone. A shuddery wail broke from the Arabs, cut through by a sharp inhuman cry. To Steve it seemed, horribly, that the great jewel had cried out like a living thing! The stone slipped from the shaykh's hand. Nureddin might have dropped it;

to Steve it looked as though it leaped convulsively, as a live thing might leap. It rolled from the daïs, bounding from step to step, with Nureddin springing after it, cursing as his clutching hand missed it. It struck the floor, veered sharply, and despite the deep dust, rolled like a revolving ball of fire toward the back wall. Nureddin was close upon it – it struck the wall – the shaykh's hand reached for it.

A scream of mortal fear ripped the tense silence. Without warning the solid wall had opened. Out of the black wall that gaped there, a tentacle shot and gripped the shaykh's body as a python girdles its victim, and jerked him headlong into the darkness. And then the wall showed blank and solid once more; only from within sounded a hideous, high-pitched, muffled screaming that chilled the blood of the listeners. Howling wordlessly, the Arabs stampeded, jammed in a battling, screeching mass in the doorway, tore through and raced madly down the wide stairs.

Steve and Yar Ali, lying helplessly, heard the frenzied clamour of their flight fade away into the distance, and gazed in dumb horror at the grim wall. The shrieks had faded into a more horrific silence. Holding their breath, they heard suddenly a sound that froze the blood in their veins – the soft sliding of metal or stone in a groove. At the same time the hidden door began to open, and Steve caught a glimmer in the blackness that might have been the glitter of monstrous eyes. He closed his own eyes; he dared not look upon whatever horror slunk from that hideous black well. He knew that there are strains the human brain cannot stand, and every primitive instinct in his soul cried out to him that this thing was nightmare and lunacy. He sensed that Yar Ali likewise closed his eyes, and the two lay like dead men.

Clarney heard no sound, but he sensed the presence of a horrific evil too grisly for human comprehension – of an Invader from Outer Gulfs and far black reaches of cosmic being. A deadly cold pervaded the chamber, and Steve felt the glare of inhuman eyes sear through his closed lids and freeze his consciousness. If he looked, if he opened his eyes, he knew stark black madness would be his instant lot.

He felt a soul-shakingly foul breath against his face and knew that the monster was bending close above him, but he lay like a man frozen in a nightmare. He clung to one thought: neither he nor Yar Ali had touched the jewel this horror guarded.

Then he no longer smelled the foul odour, the coldness in the air grew appreciably less, and he heard again the secret door slide in its groove. The fiend was returning to its hiding-place. Not all the legions of Hell could have prevented Steve's eyes from opening a trifle. He had only a glimpse as the hidden door slid to – and that one glimpse was enough to drive all consciousness from his brain. Steve Clarney, iron-nerved adventurer, fainted for the only time in his chequered life.

How long he lay there Steve never knew, but it could not have been long, for he was roused by Yar Ali's whisper, 'Lie still, sahib, a little shifting of my body and I can reach thy cords with my teeth.'

Steve felt the Afghan's powerful teeth at work on his bonds, and as he lay with his face jammed into the thick dust, and his wounded shoulder began to throb agonisingly – he had forgotten it until now – he began to gather the wandering threads of his consciousness, and it all came back to him. How much, he wondered dazedly, had been the nightmares of delirium, born from suffering and the thirst that caked his throat? The fight with the Arabs had been real – the bonds and the wounds showed that – but the grisly doom of the shaykh . . . the thing that had crept out of the black entrance in the wall – surely that had been a figment of delirium. Nureddin had fallen into a well or pit of some sort – Steve felt his hands were free and he rose to a sitting posture, fumbling for a pocket-knife the Arabs had overlooked. He did not look up or about the chamber as he slashed the cords that bound his ankles, and then freed Yar Ali, working awkwardly because his left arm was stiff and useless.

'Where are the Bedouins?' he asked, as the Afghan rose, lifting him to his feet.

'Allah, sahib,' whispered Yar Ali, 'are you mad? Have you forgotten? Let us go quickly before the djinn returns!'

'It was a nightmare,' muttered Steve. 'Look . . . the jewel is back on the throne . . . ' His voice died out. Again that red glow throbbed about the ancient throne, reflecting from the mouldering skull; again in the outstretched finger-bones pulsed the Fire of Asshurbanipal. But at the foot of the throne lay another object that had not been there before . . . the severed head of Nureddin el Mekru stared sightlessly up at the grey light filtering through the stone ceiling. The bloodless lips were drawn back from the teeth in a ghastly grin, the staring eyes mirrored an intolerable horror. In the thick dust of the floor three spoors showed one of the shaykhs where he had followed the red jewel as it rolled to the wall, and above it two other sets of tracks, coming to the throne and returning to the wall – vast, shapeless tracks, as of splayed feet, taloned and gigantic, neither human nor animal.

'My God!' choked Steve. 'It was true . . . and the Thing . . . the Thing I saw . . . '

Steve remembered the flight from that chamber as a rushing nightmare, in which he and his companion hurtled headlong down an endless stair that was a grey well of fear, raced blindly through dusty silent chambers, past the glowering idol in the mighty hall and into the blazing light of the desert sun, where they fell slavering, fighting for breath.

Again Steve was roused by the Afridi's voice: 'Sahib, sahib, in the Name of Allah the Compassionate, our luck has turned!'

Steve looked at his companion as a man might look in a trance. The big Afghan's garments were in tatters, and blood-soaked. He was stained with dust and caked with blood, and his voice was a croak. But his eyes were alight with hope and he pointed with a trembling finger.

'In the shade of yon ruined wall!' he croaked, striving to moisten his blackened lips. 'Allah il allah! The horses of the men we killed! With canteens and food-pouches at the saddle-horns! Those dogs fled without halting for the steeds of their comrades!'

New life surged up into Steve's bosom and he rose, staggering.

'Out of here,' he mumbled. 'Out of here, quick!'

Like dying men they stumbled to the horses, tore them loose and climbed fumblingly into the saddles.

'We'll lead the spare mounts,' croaked Steve, and Yar Ali nodded emphatic agreement.

'Belike we shall need them ere we sight the coast.'

Though their tortured nerves screamed for the water that swung in canteens at the saddle-horns, they turned the mounts aside and, swaying in the saddle, rode like flying corpses down the long sandy street of Kara-Shehr, between the ruined palaces and the crumbling columns, crossed the fallen wall and swept out into the desert. Not once did either glance back toward that black pile of ancient horror, nor did either speak until the ruins faded into the hazy distance. Then and only then did they draw rein and ease their thirst.

'Allah il allah!' said Yar Ali piously. 'Those dogs have beaten me until it is as though every bone in my body were broken. Dismount, I beg thee, sahib, and let me probe for that accursed bullet, and dress thy shoulder to the best of my meagre ability.'

While this was going on, Yar Ali spoke, avoiding his friend's eye, 'You said, sahib, you said something about . . . about seeing? What saw ye, in Allah's name?'

A strong shudder shook the American's steely fray 'You didn't look when – when the – the Thing put back the jewel in the skeleton's hand and left Nureddin's head on the daïs?'

'By Allah, not I!' swore Yar Ali. 'My eyes were as closed as if they had been welded together by the molten irons of Satan!'

Steve made no reply until the comrades had once more swung into the saddle and started on their long trek for the coast, which, with spare horses, food, water and weapons, they had a good chance to reach.

'I looked,' the American said sombrely. 'I wish I had not; I know I'll dream about it for the rest of my life. I had only a glance; I couldn't describe it as a man describes an earthly thing. God help me, it wasn't earthly or sane either. Mankind isn't the first owner of the earth; there were Beings here before his coming . . . and now, survivals of hideously ancient epochs. Maybe spheres of alien dimensions press unseen on this material universe today. Sorcerers have called up sleeping devils before now and controlled them with magic. It is not unreasonable to suppose an Assyrian magician could invoke an elemental demon out of the earth to avenge him and guard something that must have come out of Hell in the first place.'

'I'll try to tell you what I glimpsed; then we'll never speak of it again. It was gigantic and black and shadowy; it was a hulking monstrosity that walked upright like a man, but it was like a toad, too, and it was winged and tentacled. I saw only its back; if I'd seen the front of it . . . its face . . . I'd have undoubtedly lost my mind. The old Arab was right; God help us, it was the monster that Xuthltan called up out of the dark blind caverns of the earth to guard the Fire of Asshurbanipal!'

Pigeons from Hell

Chapter 1. *The whistler in the dark*

Griswell awoke suddenly, every nerve tingling with a premonition of imminent peril. He stared about wildly, unable at first to remember where he was, or what he was doing there. Moonlight filtered in through the dusty windows, and the great empty room with its lofty ceiling and gaping black fireplace was spectral and unfamiliar. Then as he emerged from the clinging cobwebs of his recent sleep, he remembered where he was and how he came to be there. He twisted his head and stared at his companion, sleeping on the floor near him. John Branner was but a vaguely bulking shape in the darkness that the moon scarcely greyed.

Griswell tried to remember what had awakened him. There was no sound in the house, no sound outside except the mournful hoot of an owl, far away in the piney woods. Now he had captured the illusive memory. It was a dream, a nightmare so filled with dim terror that it had frightened him awake. Recollection flooded back, vividly etching the abominable vision.

Or was it a dream? Certainly it must have been, but it had blended so curiously with recent actual events that it was difficult to know where reality left off and fantasy began.

Dreaming, he had seemed to relive his past few waking hours, in accurate detail. The dream had begun, abruptly, as he and John Branner came in sight of the house where they now lay. They had come rattling and bouncing over the stumpy, uneven old road that led through the pinelands, he and John Branner, wandering far afield from their New England home, in search of vacation pleasure. They had sighted the old house with its balustraded galleries rising amidst a wilderness of weeds and bushes, just as the sun was setting behind it. It dominated their fancy, rearing black and stark and gaunt against the low lurid rampart of sunset, barred by the black pines.

They were tired, sick of bumping and pounding all day over woodland roads. The old deserted house stimulated their imagination with its suggestion of antebellum splendour and ultimate decay. They left the automobile beside the rutty road, and as they went up the winding walk of crumbling bricks, almost lost in the tangle of rank growth, pigeons rose from the balustrades in a fluttering, feathery crowd and swept away with a low thunder of beating wings.

The oaken door sagged on broken hinges. Dust lay thick on the floor of the wide, dim hallway, on the broad steps of the stair that mounted up from the hall. They turned into a door opposite the landing, and entered a large room, empty, dusty, with cobwebs shining thickly in the corners. Dust lay thick over the ashes in the great fireplace.

They discussed gathering wood and building a fire, but decided against it. As the sun sank, darkness came quickly, the thick, black, absolute darkness of the pinelands. They knew that rattlesnakes and copperheads haunted Southern forests, and they did not care to go groping for firewood in the dark. They ate frugally from tins, then rolled in their blankets fully clad before the empty fireplace, and went instantly to sleep.

This, in part, was what Griswell had dreamed. He saw again the gaunt house looming stark against the crimson sunset; saw the flight of the pigeons as he and Branner came up the shattered walk. He saw the dim room in which they presently lay, and he saw the two forms that were himself and his companion, lying wrapped in their blankets on the dusty floor. Then from that point his dream altered subtly, passed out of the realm of the commonplace and became tinged with fear. He was looking into a vague, shadowy chamber, lit by the grey light of the moon which streamed in from some obscure source. For there was no window in that room. But in the grey light he saw three silent shapes that hung suspended in a row, and their stillness and their outlines woke chill horror in his soul. There was no sound, no word, but he sensed a Presence of fear and lunacy crouching in a dark corner . . . Abruptly he was back in the dusty, high-ceilinged room, before the great fireplace.

He was lying in his blankets, staring tensely through the dim door and across the shadowy hall, to where a beam of moonlight fell across the balustraded stair, some seven steps up from the landing. And there was something on the stair, a bent, misshapen, shadowy thing that never moved fully into the beam of light. But a dim yellow blur that might have been a face was turned toward him, as if something crouched on the stair, regarding him and his companion. Fright crept chilly through his veins, and it was then that he awoke – if indeed he had been asleep.

He blinked his eyes. The beam of moonlight fell across the stair just as he had dreamed it did; but no figure lurked there. Yet his flesh still crawled from the fear the dream or vision had roused in him; his legs felt as if they had been plunged in ice-water. He made an involuntary movement to awaken his companion, when a sudden sound paralysed him.

It was the sound of whistling on the floor above. Eerie and sweet it rose, not carrying any tune, but piping shrill and melodious. Such a sound in a supposedly deserted house was alarming enough; but it was more than the fear of a physical invader that held Griswell frozen. He could not himself have defined the horror that gripped him. But Branner's blankets rustled, and Griswell saw he was sitting upright. His figure bulked dimly in the soft darkness, the head turned toward the stair as if the man were listening intently. More sweetly and more subtly evil rose that weird whistling.

'John!' whispered Griswell from dry lips. He had meant to shout – to tell Branner that there was somebody upstairs, somebody who could mean them no good; that they must leave the house at once. But his voice died dryly in his throat.

Branner had risen. His boots clumped on the floor as he moved toward the door. He stalked leisurely into the hall and made for the lower landing, merging with the shadows that clustered black about the stair.

Griswell lay incapable of movement, his mind a whirl of bewilderment. Who was that whistling upstairs? Why was Branner going up those stairs? Griswell saw him pass the spot where the moonlight rested, saw his head tilted back as if he were looking at something Griswell could not see, above and beyond the stair. But his face was like that of a sleepwalker. He moved across the bar of moonlight and vanished from Griswell's view, even as the latter tried to shout to him to come back. A ghastly whisper was the only result of his effort.

The whistling sank to a lower note, died out. Griswell heard the stairs creaking under Branner's measured tread. Now he had reached the hallway above, for Griswell heard the clump of his feet moving along it. Suddenly the footfalls halted, and the whole night seemed to hold its breath. Then an awful scream split the stillness, and Griswell started up, echoing the cry.

The strange paralysis that had held him was broken. He took a step toward the door, then checked himself. The footfalls were resumed. Branner was coming back. He was not running. The tread was even more deliberate and measured than before. Now the stairs began to creak again. A groping hand, moving along the balustrade, came into the bar of moonlight; then another, and a ghastly thrill went through Griswell as he saw that the other hand gripped a hatchet — a hatchet which dripped blackly. Was that Branner who was coming down that stair?

Yes! The figure had moved into the bar of moonlight now, and Griswell recognised it. Then he saw Branner's face, and a shriek burst from Griswell's lips. Branner's face was bloodless, corpse-like; gouts of blood dripped darkly down it; his eyes were glassy and set, and blood oozed from the great gash which cleft the crown of his head!

Griswell never remembered exactly how he got out of that accursed house. Afterward he retained a mad, confused impression of smashing his way through a dusty cobwebbed window, of stumbling blindly across the weed-choked lawn, gibbering his frantic horror. He saw the black wall of the pines, and the moon floating in a blood-red mist in which there was neither sanity nor reason.

Some shred of sanity returned to him as he saw the automobile beside the road. In a world gone suddenly mad, that was an object reflecting prosaic reality; but even as he reached for the door, a dry chilling whir sounded in his ears, and he recoiled from the swaying undulating shape that arched up from its scaly coils on the driver's seat and hissed sibilantly at him, darting a forked tongue in the moonlight.

With a sob of horror he turned and fled down the road, as a man runs in a nightmare. He ran without purpose or reason. His numbed brain was incapable of conscious thought. He merely obeyed the blind primitive urge to run — run — run until he fell exhausted.

The black walls of the pines flowed endlessly past him; so he was seized with the illusion that he was getting nowhere. But presently a sound penetrated the fog of his terror . . . the steady, inexorable patter of feet behind him. Turning his head, he saw something loping after him — wolf or dog, he could not tell which, but its eyes glowed like balls of green fire. With a gasp he increased his speed, reeled around a bend in the road, and heard a horse snort; saw it rear and heard its rider curse; saw the gleam of blue steel in the man's lifted hand.

He staggered and fell, catching at the rider's stirrup.

'For God's sake, help me!' he panted. 'The thing! It killed Branner – it's coming after me! Look!'

Twin balls of fire gleamed in the fringe of bushes at the turn of the road. The rider swore again, and on the heels of his profanity came the smashing report of his six-shooter – again and yet again. The fire-sparks vanished, and the rider, jerking his stirrup free from Griswell's grasp, spurred his horse at the bend. Griswell staggered up, shaking in every limb. The rider was out of sight only a moment; then he came galloping back.

'Took to the brush. Timber wolf, I reckon, though I never heard of one chasin' a man before. Do you know what it was?'

Griswell could only shake his head weakly.

The rider, etched in the moonlight, looked down at him, smoking pistol still lifted in his right hand. He was a compactly-built man of medium height, and his broad-brimmed planter's hat and his boots marked him as a native of the country as definitely as Griswell's garb stamped him as a stranger.

'What's all this about, anyway?'

'I don't know,' Griswell answered helplessly. 'My name's Griswell. John Branner – my friend who was travelling with me – we stopped at a deserted house back down the road to spend the night. Something . . . ' at the memory he was choked by a rush of horror. 'My God!' he screamed. 'I must be mad! Something came and looked over the balustrade of the stair – something with a yellow face! I thought I dreamed it, but it must have been real. Then somebody began whistling upstairs, and Branner rose and went up the stairs walking like a man in his sleep, or hypnotised. I heard him scream – or someone screamed; then he came down the stair again with a bloody hatchet in his hand – and my God, sir, he was dead! His head had been split open. I saw brains and clotted blood oozing down his face, and his face was that of a dead man. But he came down the stairs! As God is my witness, John Branner was murdered in that dark upper hallway, and then his dead body came stalking down the stairs with a hatchet in its hand . . . to kill me!'

The rider made no reply; he sat his horse like a statue, outlined against the stars, and Griswell could not read his expression, his face shadowed by his hat-brim.

'You think I'm mad,' he said hopelessly. 'Perhaps I am.'

'I don't know what to think,' answered the rider. 'If it was any house but the old Blassenville Manor . . . well, we'll see. My name's Buckner. I'm sheriff of this county. Took a prisoner over to the county-seat in the next county and was ridin' back late.'

He swung off his horse and stood beside Griswell, shorter than the lanky New Englander, but much harder knit. There was a natural manner of decision and certainty about him, and it was easy to believe that he would be a dangerous man in any sort of a fight.

'Are you afraid to go back to the house?' he asked, and Griswell shuddered, but shook his head, the dogged tenacity of Puritan ancestors asserting itself.

'The thought of facing that horror again turns me sick.

'But poor Branner . . .' he choked again. 'We must find his body. My God!' he cried, unmanned by the abysmal horror of the thing; 'what will we find? If a dead man walks, what – '

'We'll see.' The sheriff caught the reins in the crook of his left elbow and began filling the empty chambers of his big blue pistol as they walked along.

As they made the turn Griswell's blood was ice at the thought of what they might see lumbering up the road with a bloody, grinning death-mask, but they saw only the house looming spectrally among the pines, down the road. A strong shudder shook Griswell.

'God, how evil that house looks, against those black pines! It looked sinister from the very first . . . when we went up the broken walk and saw those pigeons fly up from the porch . . .'

'Pigeons?' Buckner cast him a quick glance. 'You saw the pigeons?'

'Why, yes! Scores of them perching on the porch railing.'

They strode on for a moment in silence, before Buckner said abruptly: 'I've lived in this country all my life. I've passed the old Blassenville place a thousand times, I reckon, at all hours of the day and night. But I never saw a pigeon anywhere around it, or anywhere else in these woods.'

'There were scores of them,' repeated Griswell, bewildered.

'I've seen men who swore they'd seen a flock of pigeons perched along the balusters just at sundown,' said Buckner slowly. 'A tramp was buildin' a fire in the yard, aimin' to camp there that night. I passed along there about dark, and he told me about the pigeons. I came back by there the next mornin'. The ashes of his fire were there, and his tin cup, and skillet where he'd fried pork, and his blankets looked like they'd been slept in. Nobody ever saw him again. That was twelve years ago. They say the pigeons are the souls of the Blassenvilles, let out of hell at sunset. The red glare in the west is the light from hell, because then the gates of hell are open, and the Blassenvilles fly out.'

'Who were the Blassenvilles?' asked Griswell, shivering.

'They owned all this land here. French-English family. Came here from the West Indies before the Louisiana Purchase. The Civil War ruined them, like it did so many. Some were killed in the war; most of the others died out. Nobody's lived in the Manor since 1890 when Miss Elizabeth Blassenville, the last of the line, fled from the old house one night like it was a plague spot, and never came back to it . . . this your auto?'

They halted beside the car, and Griswell stared morbidly at the grim house. Its dusty panes were empty and blank; but they did not seem blind to him. It seemed to him that ghastly eyes were fixed hungrily on him through those darkened panes. Buckner repeated his question.

'Yes. Be careful. There's a snake on the seat – or there was.'

'Not there now,' grunted Buckner, tying his horse and pulling an electric torch out of the saddle-bag. 'Well, let's have a look.'

He strode up the broken brick walk as matter-of-factly as if he were paying a social call on friends. Griswell followed close at his heels, his heart pounding suffocatingly. A scent of decay and mouldering vegetation blew on the faint wind, and Griswell grew faint with nausea that rose from a frantic abhorrence of these black woods, these ancient plantation houses that hid forgotten secrets of slavery and bloody pride and mysterious intrigues. He had thought of the South as a sunny, lazy land washed by soft breezes laden with spice and warm blossoms. But now he had discovered another, unsuspected side . . . a dark, brooding, fear-haunted side, and the discovery repelled him.

The oaken door sagged as it had before. The blackness of the interior was intensified by the beam of Buckner's light playing on the sill. That beam sliced through the darkness of the hallway and roved up the stair, and Griswell held his breath, clenching his fists. But no shape of lunacy leered down at them. Buckner went in, walking light as a cat, torch in one hand, gun in the other.

As he swung his light into the room across from the stairway, Griswell cried out – and cried out again, almost fainting with the intolerable sickness of what he saw. A trail of blood drops led across the floor, crossing the blankets Branner had occupied, which lay between the door and those in which Griswell had lain.

And Griswell's blankets had a terrible occupant. John Branner lay there, face down, his cleft head revealed in merciless clarity in the steady light. His outstretched hand still gripped the haft of a hatchet, and the blade was embedded deep in the blanket and the floor beneath, just where Griswell's head had lain when he slept there.

A momentary rush of blackness engulfed Griswell. He was not aware that he staggered, or that Buckner caught him. When he could see and hear again, he was violently sick and hung his head against the mantel, retching miserably.

Buckner turned the light full on him, making him blink. Buckner's voice came from behind the blinding radiance, the man himself unseen.

'Griswell, you've told me a yarn that's hard to believe. I saw something chasin' you, but it might have been a timber wolf, or a mad dog.

'If you're holdin' back anything, you better spill it. What you told me won't hold up in any court. You're bound to be accused of killin' your partner. I'll have to arrest you. If you'll give me the straight goods now, it'll make it easier. Now, didn't you kill this fellow, Branner?

'Wasn't it something like this: you quarrelled, he grabbed a hatchet and swung at you, but you dodged and then let him have it?'

Griswell sank down and hid his face in his hands, his head swimming.

'Great God, man, I didn't murder John! Why, we've been friends ever since we were children in school together. I've told you the truth. I don't blame you for not believing me. But God help me, it is the truth!'

The light swung back to the gory head again, and Griswell closed his eyes.

He heard Buckner grunt.

'I believe this hatchet in his hand is the one he was killed with. Blood and brains plastered on the blade, and hairs stickin' to it . . . hairs exactly the same colour as his. This makes it tough for you, Griswell.'

'How so?' the New Englander asked dully.

'Knocks any plea of self-defence in the head. Branner couldn't have swung at you with this hatchet after you split his skull with it. You must have pulled the axe out of his head, stuck it into the floor and clamped his fingers on it to make it look like he'd attacked you.

And it would have been damned clever . . . if you'd used another hatchet.'

'But I didn't kill him,' groaned Griswell. 'I have no intention of pleading self-defence.'

'That's what puzzles me,' Buckner admitted frankly, straightening. 'What murderer would rig up such a crazy story as you've told me, to prove his innocence? Average killer would have told a logical yarn, at least. Hmmm! Blood drops leadin' from the door. The body was dragged – no, couldn't have been dragged. The floor isn't smeared. You must have carried it here, after killin' him in some other place. But in that case, why isn't there any blood on your clothes? Of course you could have changed clothes and washed your hands. But the fellow hasn't been dead long.'

'He walked downstairs and across the room,' said Griswell hopelessly. 'He came to kill me. I knew he was coming to kill me when I saw him lurching down the stair. He struck where I would have been, if I hadn't awakened. That window – I burst out at it. You see it's broken.'

'I see. But if he walked then, why isn't he walkin' now?'

'I don't know! I'm too sick to think straight. I've been fearing that he'd rise up from the floor where he lies and come at me again. When I heard that wolf running up the road after me, I thought it was John chasing me – John, running through the night with his bloody axe and his bloody head, and his death-grin!'

His teeth chattered as he lived that horror over again.

Buckner let his light play across the floor.

'The blood drops lead into the hall. Come on. We'll follow them.'

Griswell cringed. 'They lead upstairs.'

Buckner's eyes were fixed hard on him.

'Are you afraid to go upstairs, with me?'

Griswell's face was grey.

'Yes. But I'm going, with you or without you. The thing that killed poor John may still be hiding up there.'

'Stay behind me,' ordered Buckner. 'If anything jumps us, I'll take care of it. But for your own sake, I warn you that I shoot quicker than a cat jumps, and I don't often miss. If you've got any ideas of layin' me out from behind, forget them.'

'Don't be a fool!' Resentment got the better of his apprehension, and this outburst seemed to reassure Buckner more than any of his protestations of innocence.

'I want to be fair,' he said quietly. 'I haven't indicted and condemned you in my mind already. If only half of what you're tellin' me is the truth, you've been through a hell of an experience, and I don't want to be too hard on you. But you can see how hard it is for me to believe all you've told me.'

Griswell wearily motioned for him to lead the way, unspeaking. They went out into the hall, paused at the landing. A thin string of crimson drops, distinct in the thick dust, led up the steps.

'Man's tracks in the dust,' grunted Buckner. 'Go slow.

'I've got to be sure of what I see, because we're obliteratin' them as we go up. Hmmm! One set goin' up, one comin' down. Same man. Not your tracks. Branner was a bigger man than you are. Blood drops all the way . . . blood on the banisters like a man had laid his bloody hand there . . . a smear of stuff that looks . . . brains. Now what –'

'He walked down the stair, a dead man,' shuddered Griswell. 'Groping with one hand – the other gripping the hatchet that killed him.'

'Or was carried,' muttered the sheriff. 'But if somebody carried him – where are the tracks?'

They came out into the upper hallway, a vast, empty space of dust and shadows where time-crusted windows repelled the moonlight and the ring of Buckner's torch seemed inadequate. Griswell trembled like a leaf. Here, in darkness and horror, John Branner had died.

'Somebody whistled up here,' he muttered. 'John came, as if he were being called.'

Buckner's eyes were blazing strangely in the light.

'The footprints lead down the hall,' he muttered. 'Same as on the stair . . . one set going, one coming. Same prints – Judas!'

Behind him Griswell stifled a cry, for he had seen what prompted Buckner's exclamation. A few feet from the head of the stair Branner's footprints stopped abruptly, then returned, treading almost in the other tracks. And where the trail halted there was a great splash of blood on the dusty floor . . . and other tracks met it – tracks of bare feet, narrow but with splayed toes. They too receded in a second line from the spot.

Buckner bent over them, swearing.

'The tracks meet! And where they meet there's blood and brains on the floor! Branner must have been killed on that spot – with a blow from a hatchet. Bare feet coming out of the darkness to meet shod feet . . . then both turned away again; the shod feet went downstairs, the bare feet went back down the hall.' He directed his light down the hall. The footprints faded into darkness, beyond the reach of the beam. On either hand the closed doors of chambers were cryptic portals of mystery.

'Suppose your crazy tale was true,' Buckner muttered, half to himself. 'These aren't your tracks. They look like a woman's. Suppose somebody did whistle, and Branner went upstairs to investigate. Suppose somebody met him here in the dark and split his head. The signs and tracks would have been, in that case, just as they really are. But if that's so, why isn't Branner lyin' here where he was killed? Could he have lived long enough to take the hatchet away from whoever killed him, and stagger downstairs with it?'

'No, no!' Recollection gagged Griswell. 'I saw him on the stair. He was dead. No man could live a minute after receiving such a wound.'

'I believe it,' muttered Buckner. 'But – it's madness! Or else it's too clever – yet, what sane man would think up and work out such an elaborate and utterly insane plan to escape punishment for murder, when a simple plea of self-defence would have been so much more effective? No court would recognise that story. Well, let's follow these other tracks. They lead down the hall . . . here, what's this?'

With an icy clutch at his soul, Griswell saw the light was beginning to grow dim.

'This battery is new,' muttered Buckner, and for the first time Griswell caught an edge of fear in his voice. 'Come on – out of here quick!'

The light had faded to a faint red glow. The darkness seemed straining into them, creeping with black cat-feet. Buckner retreated, pushing Griswell stumbling behind him as he walked backward, pistol cocked and lifted, down the dark hall. In the growing darkness Griswell heard what sounded like the stealthy opening of a door. And suddenly the blackness about them was vibrant with menace. Griswell knew Buckner sensed it as well as he, for the sheriff's hard body was tense and taut as a stalking panther's.

But without haste he worked his way to the stair and backed down it, Griswell preceding him, and fighting the panic that urged him to scream and burst into mad flight. A ghastly thought brought icy sweat out on his flesh. Suppose the dead man were creeping up the stair behind them in the dark, face frozen in the death-grin, blood-caked hatchet lifted to strike?

This possibility so overpowered him that he was scarcely aware when his feet struck the level of the lower hallway, and he was only then aware that the light had grown brighter as they descended, until it now gleamed with its full power – but when Buckner turned it back up the stairway, it failed to illuminate the darkness that hung like a tangible fog at the head of the stair.

'The damn thing was conjured,' muttered Buckner. 'Nothin' else. It couldn't act like that naturally.'

'Turn the light into the room,' begged Griswell. 'See if John – if John is . . . '

He could not put the ghastly thought into words, but Buckner understood.

He swung the beam around, and Griswell had never dreamed that the sight of the gory body of a murdered man could bring such relief.

'He's still there,' grunted Buckner. 'If he walked after he was killed, he hasn't walked since. But that thing . . . '

Again he turned the light up the stair, and stood chewing his lip and scowling. Three times he half lifted his gun. Griswell read his mind. The sheriff was tempted to plunge back up that stair, take his chance with the unknown. But common sense held him back.

'I wouldn't have a chance in the dark,' he muttered. 'And I've got a hunch the light would go out again.'

He turned and faced Griswell squarely.

'There's no use dodgin' the question. There's somethin' hellish in this house, and I believe I have an inklin' of what it is. I don't believe you killed Branner. Whatever killed him is up there – now. There's a lot about your yarn that don't sound sane; but there's nothin' sane about a flashlight goin' out like this one did. I don't believe that thing upstairs is human. I never met anything I was afraid to tackle in the dark before, but I'm not goin' up there until daylight. It's not long until dawn. We'll wait for it out there on that gallery.'

The stars were already paling when they came out on the broad porch. Buckner seated himself on the balustrade, facing the door, his pistol dangling in his fingers. Griswell sat down near him and leaned back against a crumbling pillar. He shut his eyes, grateful for the faint breeze that seemed to cool his throbbing brain. He experienced a dull sense of unreality. He was a stranger in a strange land, a land that had become suddenly imbued with black horror. The shadow of the noose hovered above him, and in that dark house lay John Branner, with his butchered head . . . like the figments of a dream these facts spun and eddied in his brain until all merged in a grey twilight as sleep came uninvited to his weary soul.

He awoke to a cold white dawn and full memory of the horrors of the night. Mists curled about the stems of the pines, crawled in smoky wisps up the broken walk. Buckner was shaking him.

'Wake up! It's daylight.'

Griswell rose, wincing at the stiffness of his limbs. His face was grey and old.

'I'm ready. Let's go upstairs.'

'I've already been!' Buckner's eyes burned in the early dawn. 'I didn't wake you up. I went as soon as it was light. I found nothin'.'

'The tracks of the bare feet . . . '

'Gone!'

'Gone?'

'Yes, gone! The dust had been disturbed all over the hall, from the point where Branner's tracks ended; swept into corners. No chance of trackin' anything there now. Something obliterated those tracks while we sat here, and I didn't hear a sound. I've gone through the whole house. Not a sign of anything.'

Griswell shuddered at the thought of himself sleeping alone on the porch while Buckner conducted his exploration.

'What shall we do?' he asked listlessly. 'With those tracks gone there goes my only chance of proving my story.'

'We'll take Branner's body into the county-seat,' answered Buckner. 'Let me do the talkin'. If the authorities knew the facts as they appear, they'd insist on you being confined and indicted. I don't believe you killed Branner . . . but neither a district attorney, judge nor jury would believe what you told me, or what happened to us last night. I'm handlin' this thing my own way. I'm not goin' to arrest you until I've exhausted every other possibility.

'Say nothin' about what's happened here, when we get to town. I'll simply tell the district attorney that John Branner was killed by a party or parties unknown, and that I'm workin' on the case.

'Are you game to come back with me to this house and spend the night here, sleepin' in that room as you and Branner slept last night?'

Griswell went white, but answered as stoutly as his ancestors might have expressed their determination to hold their cabins in the teeth of the Pequots: 'I'll do it.'

'Let's go then; help me pack the body out to your auto.'

Griswell's soul revolted at the sight of John Branner's bloodless face in the chill white dawn, and the feel of his clammy flesh. The grey fog wrapped wispy tentacles about their feet as they carried their grisly burden across the lawn.

Chapter 2. *The snake's brother*

Again the shadows were lengthening over the pinelands, and again two men came bumping along the old road in a car with a New England licence plate.

Buckner was driving. Griswell's nerves were too shattered for him to trust himself at the wheel. He looked gaunt and haggard, and his face was still pallid. The strain of the day spent at the county-seat was added to the horror that still rode his soul like the shadow of a black-winged vulture. He had not slept, had not tasted what he had eaten.

'I told you I'd tell you about the Blassenvilles,' said Buckner. 'They were proud folks, haughty, and pretty damn ruthless when they wanted their way. They didn't treat their slaves as well as the other planters did – got their ideas in the West Indies, I reckon. There was a streak of cruelty in them – especially Miss Celia, the last one of the family to come to these parts. That was long after the slaves had been freed, but she used to whip her mulatto maid just like she was a slave, the old folks say.

'Well, after the Civil War they died off pretty fast, livin' in poverty on the plantation which was allowed to go to ruin. Finally only four girls were left, sisters, livin' in the old house and ekin' out a bare livin', with a few blacks livin' in the old slave huts and workin' the fields on the share. They kept to themselves, bein' proud, and ashamed of their poverty. Folks wouldn't see them for months at a time.

'But folks knew about it when Miss Celia came to live with them. She came from somewhere in the West Indies, where the whole family originally had its roots – a fine, handsome woman, they say, in the early thirties. But she didn't mix with folks any more than the girls did. She brought a mulatto maid with her, and the Blassenville cruelty cropped out in her treatment of this maid. I knew an old man years ago, who swore he saw Miss Celia tie this girl up to a tree, stark naked, and whip her with a horsewhip. Nobody was surprised when she disappeared. Everybody figured she'd run away, of course.

'Well, one day in the spring of 1890 Miss Elizabeth, the youngest girl, came in to town for the first time in maybe a year. She came after supplies. Talked a little more, too, a bit wild. Said Miss Celia had gone, without leaving any word. Said her sisters thought she'd gone back to the West Indies, but she believed her aunt was still in the house. She didn't say what she meant. Just got her supplies and pulled out for the Manor.

'A month went past, and a black came into town and said that Miss Elizabeth was livin' at the Manor alone. Said her three sisters weren't there any more, that they'd left one by one without givin' any word or explanation. She didn't know where they'd gone, and was afraid to stay there alone, but didn't know where else to go. She'd never known anything but the Manor, and had neither relatives nor friends. But she was in mortal terror of something.

'It was a stormy spring night when Miss Elizabeth came tearin' into town on the one horse she owned, nearly dead from fright. She fell from her horse in the square; when she could talk she said she'd found a secret room in the Manor that had been forgotten for a hundred years. And she said that there she found her three sisters, dead, and hangin' by their necks from the ceilin'. She said something chased her and nearly brained her with an axe as she ran out the front door, but somehow she got to the horse and got away. She was nearly crazy with fear, and didn't know what it was that chased her . . . said it looked like a woman with a yellow face.

'About a hundred men rode out there, right away. They searched the house from top to bottom, but they didn't find any secret room, or the remains of the sisters. But they did find a hatchet stickin' in the doorjamb downstairs, with some of Miss Elizabeth's hairs stuck on it, just as she'd said. She wouldn't go back there and show them how to find the secret door; almost went crazy when they suggested it.

'When she was able to travel, the people made up some money and loaned it to her – she was still too proud to accept charity – and she went to California. She never came back, but later it was learned, when she sent back to repay the money they'd loaned her, that she'd married out there.

'Nobody ever bought the house. It stood there just as she'd left it, and as the years passed folks stole all the furnishings out of it. But they came after sunup and left long before sundown.'

'What did the people think about Miss Elizabeth's story?' asked Griswell.

'Well, most folks thought she'd gone a little crazy, livin' in that old house alone. But some people believed that mulatto girl, Joan, didn't run away, after all. They believed she'd hidden in the woods, and glutted her hatred of the Blassenvilles by murderin' Miss Celia and the three girls. They beat up the woods with bloodhounds, but never found a trace of her. If there was a secret room in the house, she might have been hidin' there . . . if there was anything to that theory.'

'She couldn't have been hiding there all these years,' muttered Griswell. 'Anyway, the thing in the house now isn't human.'

Buckner wrenched the wheel around and turned into a dim trace that left the main road and meandered off through the pines.

'Where are you going?'

'There's an old Negro that lives off this way a few miles. I want to talk to him. This old man is nearly a hundred years old. They say he's a voodoo man.'

Griswell shivered at the phrase, staring uneasily at the green forest walls that shut them in. The scent of the pines was mingled with the odours of unfamiliar plants and blossoms. But underlying all was a reek of rot and decay. Again a sick abhorrence of these dark mysterious woodlands almost overpowered him.

'Voodoo!' he muttered. 'I'd forgotten about that . . . I never could think of black magic in connection with the South. To me witch-craft was always associated with old crooked streets in waterfront towns, overhung by gabled roofs that were old when they were hanging witches in Salem; dark musty alleys where black cats and other things might steal at night. Witchcraft always meant the old towns of New England, to me . . . but all this is more terrible than any New England legend . . . these sombre pines, old deserted houses, lost plantations, old tales of madness and horror . . . God, what frightful, ancient terrors there are on this continent fools call "young"!'

'Here's old Jacob's hut,' announced Buckner, bringing the auto-mobile to a halt.

Griswell saw a clearing and a small cabin squatting under the shadows of the huge trees. The pines gave way to oaks and cypresses, bearded with grey trailing moss, and behind the cabin lay the edge of a swamp that ran away under the dimness of the trees, choked with rank vegetation. A thin wisp of blue smoke curled up from the stick-and-mud chimney.

He followed Buckner to the tiny stoop, where the sheriff pushed open the leather-hinged door and strode in. Griswell blinked in the comparative dimness of the interior. A single small window let in a little daylight. An old Negro crouched beside the hearth, watching a pot stew over the open fire. He looked up as they entered, but did not rise. He seemed incredibly old. His face was a mass of wrinkles, and his eyes, dark and vital, were filmed momentarily at times as if his mind wandered.

Buckner motioned Griswell to sit down in a string-bottomed chair, and himself took a rudely-made bench near the hearth, facing the old man.

'Jacob,' he said bluntly, 'the time's come for you to talk. I know you know the secret of Blassenville Manor. I've never questioned you about it, because it wasn't in my line. But a man was murdered there last night, and this man here may hang for it, unless you tell me what haunts that old house of the Blassenvilles.'

The old man's eyes gleamed, then grew misty as if clouds of extreme age drifted across his brittle mind.

'The Blassenvilles,' he murmured, and his voice was mellow and rich, his speech not the patois of the piny woods darky. 'They were proud people, sirs – proud and cruel. Some died in the war, some were killed in duels – the menfolks, sirs. Some died in the Manor . . . the old Manor . . . ' His voice trailed off into unintelligible mumblings.

'What of the Manor?' asked Buckner patiently.

'Miss Celia was the proudest of them all,' the old man muttered. 'The proudest and the cruellest. The black people hated her; Joan most of all. Joan had white blood in her, and she was proud, too. Miss Celia whipped her like a slave.'

'What is the secret of Blassenville Manor?' persisted Buckner.

The film faded from the old man's eyes; they were dark as moon-lit wells.

'What secret, sir? I do not understand.'

'Yes, you do. For years that old house has stood there with its mystery. You know the key to its riddle.'

The old man stirred the stew. He seemed perfectly rational now.

'Sir, life is sweet, even to an old man.'

'You mean somebody would kill you if you told me?'

But the old man was mumbling again, his eyes clouded.

'Not somebody. No human. No human being. The gods of the swamps. My secret is inviolate, guarded by the Big Serpent, the god above all gods. He would send a little brother to kiss me with his cold lips . . . a little brother with a white crescent moon on his head. I sold my soul to the Big Serpent when he made me maker of zuvembies . . . '

Buckner stiffened.

'I heard that word once before,' he said softly, 'from the lips of a dying man, when I was a child. What does it mean?'

Fear filled the eyes of old Jacob.

'What have I said? No – no! I said nothing.'

'Zuvembies,' prompted Buckner.

'Zuvembies,' mechanically repeated the old man, his eyes vacant. 'A zuvembie was once a woman   on the Slave Coast they know of them. The drums that whisper by night in the hills of Haiti tell of them. The makers of zuvembies are honoured of the people of Damballah. It is death to speak of it – it is one of the Snake God's forbidden secrets.'

'You speak of the zuvembies,' said Buckner softly.

'I must not speak of it,' mumbled the old man, and Griswell realised that he was thinking aloud, too far gone in his dotage to be aware that he was speaking at all. 'No man must know that I danced in the Black Ceremony of the voodoo, and was made a maker of zombies and zuvembies. The Big Snake punishes loose tongues with death.'

'A zuvembie is a woman?' prompted Buckner.

'Was a woman. She knew I was a maker of zuvembies . . . she came and stood in my hut and asked for the awful brew – the brew of ground snake-bones, and the blood of vampire bats, and the dew from a nighthawk's wings, and other elements unnameable. She had danced in the Black Ceremony – she was ripe to become a zuvembie – the Black Brew was all that was needed . . . the other was beautiful . . . I could not refuse her.'

'Who?' demanded Buckner tensely, but the old man's head was sunk on his withered breast, and he did not reply. He seemed to slumber as he sat. Buckner shook him. 'You gave a brew to make a woman a zuvembie . . . what is a zuvembie?'

The old man stirred resentfully and muttered drowsily.

'A zuvembie is no longer human. It knows neither relatives nor friends. It is one with the people of the Black World. It commands the natural demons – owls, bats, snakes and werewolves – and can fetch darkness to blot out a little light. It can be slain by lead or steel, but unless it is slain thus, it lives for ever, and it eats no such food as humans eat. It dwells like a bat in a cave or an old house. Time means naught to the zuvembie; an hour, a day, a year, all is one. It cannot speak human words, nor think as a human thinks, but it can hypnotise the living by the sound of its voice, and when it slays a man, it can command his lifeless body until the flesh is cold. As long as the blood flows, the corpse is its slave. Its pleasure lies in the slaughter of human beings.'

'And why should one become a zuvembie?' asked Buckner softly.

'Hate,' whispered the old man. 'Hate! Revenge!'

'Was her name Joan?' murmured Buckner.

It was as if the name penetrated the fogs of senility that clouded the voodoo-man's mind. He shook himself and the film faded from his eyes, leaving them hard and gleaming as wet black marble.

'Joan?' he said slowly. 'I have not heard that name for the span of a generation. I seem to have been sleeping, gentlemen; I do not remember – I ask your pardon. Old men fall asleep before the fire, like old dogs. You asked me of Blassenville Manor? Sir, if I were to tell you why I cannot answer you, you would deem it mere superstition.'

As he spoke he was reaching across the hearth for a piece of firewood, groping among the heaps of sticks there. And his voice broke in a scream, as he jerked back his arm convulsively. And a horrible, thrashing, trailing thing came with it. Around the voodoo-man's arm a mottled length of that shape was wrapped, and a wicked wedge-shaped head struck again in silent fury.

The old man fell on the hearth, screaming, upsetting the simmering pot and scattering the embers, and then Buckner caught up a billet of firewood and crushed that flat head. Cursing, he kicked aside the knotting, twisting trunk, glaring briefly at the mangled head. Old Jacob had ceased screaming and writhing; he lay still, staring glassily upward.

'Dead?' whispered Griswell.

'Dead as Judas Iscariot,' snapped Buckner, frowning at the twitching reptile. 'That infernal snake crammed enough poison into his veins to kill a dozen men his age. But I think it was the shock and fright that killed him.'

'What shall we do?' asked Griswell, shivering.

'Leave the body on that bunk. Nothin' can hurt it, if we bolt the door so the wild hogs can't get in, or any cat. We'll carry it into town tomorrow. We've got work to do tonight. Let's get goin'.'

Griswell shrank from touching the corpse, but he helped Buckner lift it on the rude bunk, and then stumbled hastily out of the hut. The sun was hovering above the horizon, visible in dazzling red flame through the black stems of the trees.

They climbed into the car in silence, and went bumping back along the stumpy trail.

'He said the Big Snake would send one of his brothers,' muttered Griswell.

'Nonsense!' snorted Buckner. 'Snakes like warmth, and that swamp is full of them. It crawled in and coiled up among that firewood. Old Jacob disturbed it, and it bit him. Nothin' supernatural about that.'

After a short silence he said, in a different voice, 'That was the first time I ever saw a rattler strike without singin'; and the first time I ever saw a snake with a white crescent moon on its head.'

They were turning in to the main road before either spoke again.

'You think that the mulatto Joan has skulked in the house all these years?' Griswell asked.

'You heard what old Jacob said,' answered Buckner grimly. 'Time means nothin' to a zuvembie.'

As they made the last turn in the road, Griswell braced himself against the sight of Blassenville Manor looming black against the red sunset. When it came into view he bit his lip to keep from shrieking. The suggestion of cryptic horror came back in all its power.

'Look!' he whispered from dry lips as they came to a halt beside the road. Buckner grunted.

From the balustrades of the gallery rose a whirling cloud of pigeons that swept away into the sunset, black against the lurid glare . . .

Chapter 3. *The call of Zuvembie*

Both men sat rigid for a few moments after the pigeons had flown.

'Well, I've seen them at last,' muttered Buckner.

'Only the doomed see them perhaps,' whispered Griswell. 'That tramp saw them . . . '

'Well, we'll see,' returned the Southerner tranquilly, as he climbed out of the car, but Griswell noticed him unconsciously hitch forward his scabbarded gun.

The oaken door sagged on broken hinges. Their feet echoed on the broken brick walk. The blind windows reflected the sunset in sheets of flame. As they came into the broad hall Griswell saw the string of black marks that ran across the floor and into the chamber, marking the path of a dead man.

Buckner had brought blankets out of the automobile. He spread them before the fireplace.

'I'll lie next to the door,' he said. 'You lie where you did last night.'

'Shall we light a fire in the grate?' asked Griswell, dreading the thought of the blackness that would cloak the woods when the brief twilight had died.

'No. You've got a flashlight and so have I. We'll lie here in the dark and see what happens. Can you use that gun I gave you?'

'I suppose so. I never fired a revolver, but I know how it's done.'

'Well, leave the shootin' to me, if possible.' The sheriff seated himself cross-legged on his blankets and emptied the cylinder of his big blue Colt, inspecting each cartridge with a critical eye before he replaced it.

Griswell prowled nervously back and forth, begrudging the slow fading of the light as a miser begrudges the waning of his gold. He leaned with one hand against the mantelpiece, staring down into the dust-covered ashes. The fire that produced those ashes must have been built by Elizabeth Blassenville, more than forty years before. The thought was depressing. Idly he stirred the dusty ashes with his toe. Something came to view among the charred debris – a bit of paper, stained and yellowed. Still idly he bent and drew it out of the ashes. It was a note-book with mouldering cardboard backs.

'What have you found?' asked Buckner, squinting down the gleaming barrel of his gun.

'Nothing but an old note-book. Looks like a diary. The pages are covered with writing . . . but the ink is so faded, and the paper is in such a state of decay that I can't tell much about it. How do you suppose it came in the fireplace, without being burned up?'

'Thrown in long after the fire was out,' surmised Buckner. 'Probably found and tossed in the fireplace by somebody who was in here stealin' furniture. Likely somebody who couldn't read.'

Griswell fluttered the crumbling leaves listlessly, straining his eyes in the fading light over the yellowed scrawls. Then he stiffened.

'Here's an entry that's legible! Listen!' He read: '"I know someone is in the house besides myself. I can hear someone prowling about at night when the sun has set and the pines are black outside. Often in the night I hear it fumbling at my door. Who is it? Is it one of my sisters? Is it Aunt Celia? If it is either of these, why does she steal so subtly about the house? Why does she tug at my door, and glide away when I call to her? Shall I open the door and go out to her? No, no! I dare not! I am afraid. Oh God, what shall I do? I dare not stay here – but where am I to go?"'

'By God!' ejaculated Buckner. 'That must be Elizabeth Blassenville's diary! Go on!'

'I can't make out the rest of the page,' answered Griswell. 'But a few pages further on I can make out some lines.' He read: '"My sisters are dead. I know they are dead. I seem to sense that they died horribly, in fear and agony. But why? Why? If someone murdered Aunt Celia, why should that person murder my poor sisters? Joan – "' He paused, scowling futilely.

'A piece of the page is torn out. Here's another entry under another date – at least I judge it's a date; I can't make it out for sure.

' " – the awful thing that the old Negress hinted at? She named Jacob Blount, and Joan, but she would not speak plainly; perhaps she feared to – " Part of it gone here; then: "No, no! How can it be? She is dead – or gone away. Yet – she was born and raised in the West Indies, and from hints she let fall in the past, I know she delved into the mysteries of the voodoo. I believe she even danced in one of their horrible ceremonies – how could she have been such a beast? And this – this horror. God, can such things be? I know not what to think. If it is she who roams the house at night, who fumbles at my door, who whistles so weirdly and sweetly – no, no, I must be going mad. If I stay here alone I shall die as hideously as my sisters must have died. Of that I am convinced." '

The incoherent chronicle ended as abruptly as it had begun. Griswell was so engrossed in deciphering the scraps that he was not aware that darkness had stolen upon them, hardly aware that Buckner was holding his electric torch for him to read by. Waking from his abstraction he started and darted a quick glance at the black hallway.

'What do you make of it?'

'What I've suspected all the time,' answered Buckner. 'That mulatto maid Joan turned zuvembie to avenge herself on Miss Celia. Probably hated the whole family as much as she did her mistress. She'd taken part in voodoo ceremonies on her native island until she was "ripe", as old Jacob said. All she needed was the Black Brew – he supplied that. She killed Miss Celia and the three older girls, and would have gotten Elizabeth but for chance. She's been lurkin' in this old house all these years, like a snake in a ruin.'

'But why should she murder a stranger?'

'You heard what old Jacob said,' reminded Buckner. 'A zuvembie finds satisfaction in the slaughter of humans. She called Branner up the stair and split his head and stuck the hatchet in his hand, and sent him downstairs to murder you. No court will ever believe that, but if we can produce her body, that will be evidence enough to prove your innocence. My word will be taken, that she murdered Branner. Jacob said a zuvembie could be killed . . . in reporting this affair I don't have to be too accurate in detail.'

'She came and peered over the balustrade of the stair at us,' muttered Griswell. 'But why didn't we find her tracks on the stair?'

'Maybe you dreamed it. Maybe a zuvembie can project her spirit – hell! why try to rationalise something that's outside the bounds of rationality? Let's begin our watch.'

'Don't turn out the light!' exclaimed Griswell involuntarily. Then he added: 'Of course. Turn it out. We must be in the dark as' – he gagged a bit – 'as Branner and I were.'

But fear like a physical sickness assailed him when the room was plunged in darkness. He lay trembling and his heart beat so heavily he felt as if he would suffocate.

'The West Indies must be the plague spot of the world,' muttered Buckner, a blur on his blankets. 'I've heard of zombies. Never knew before what a zuvembie was. Evidently some drug concocted by the voodoo-men to induce madness in women. That doesn't explain the other things, though: the hypnotic powers, the abnormal long-evity, the ability to control corpses – no, a zuvembie can't be merely a mad-woman. It's a monster, something more and less than a human being, created by the magic that spawns in black swamps and jungles – well, we'll see.'

His voice ceased, and in the silence Griswell heard the pounding of his own heart. Outside in the black woods a wolf howled eerily, and owls hooted. Then silence fell again like a black fog.

Griswell forced himself to lie still on his blankets. Time seemed at a standstill. He felt as if he were choking. The suspense was growing unendurable; the effort he made to control his crumbling nerves bathed his limbs in sweat. He clenched his teeth until his jaws ached and almost locked, and the nails of his fingers bit deeply into his palms.

He did not know what he was expecting. The fiend would strike again – but how? Would it be a horrible, sweet whistling, bare feet stealing down the creaking steps, or a sudden hatchet-stroke in the dark? Would it choose him or Buckner? Was Buckner already dead? He could see nothing in the blackness, but he heard the man's steady breathing. The Southerner must have nerves of steel. Or was that Buckner breathing beside him, separated by a narrow strip of darkness? Had the fiend already struck in silence, and taken the sheriff's place, there to lie in ghoulish glee until it was ready to strike? – A thousand hideous fancies assailed Griswell tooth and claw.

He began to feel that he would go mad if he did not leap to his feet, screaming, and burst frenziedly out of that accursed house – not even the fear of the gallows could keep him lying there in the darkness any longer . . . the rhythm of Buckner's breathing was suddenly broken, and Griswell felt as if a bucket of ice-water had been poured over him. From somewhere above them rose a sound of weird, sweet whistling . . .

Griswell's control snapped, plunging his brain into darkness deeper than the physical blackness which engulfed him. There was a period of absolute blankness, in which a realisation of motion was his first sensation of awakening consciousness. He was running, madly, stumbling over an incredibly rough road. All was darkness about him, and he ran blindly. Vaguely he realised that he must have bolted from the house, and fled for perhaps miles before his overwrought brain began to function. He did not care; dying on the gallows for a murder he never committed did not terrify him half as much as the thought of returning to that house of horror. He was overpowered by the urge to run – run – run as he was running now, blindly, until he reached the end of his endurance. The mist had not yet fully lifted from his brain, but he was aware of a dull wonder that he could not see the stars through the black branches. He wished vaguely that he could see where he was going. He believed he must be climbing a hill, and that was strange, for he knew there were no hills within miles of the Manor. Then above and ahead of him a dim glow began.

He scrambled toward it, over ledge-like projections that were more and more taking on a disquieting symmetry. Then he was horror-stricken to realise that a sound was impacting on his ears – a weird mocking whistle. The sound swept the mists away. Why, what was this? Where was he? Awakening and realisation came like the stunning stroke of a butcher's maul. He was not fleeing along a road, or climbing a hill; he was mounting a stair. He was still in Blassenville Manor! And he was climbing the stair!

An inhuman scream burst from his lips. Above it the mad whistling rose in a ghoulish piping of demoniac triumph. He tried to stop – to turn back – even to fling himself over the balustrade. His shrieking rang unbearably in his own ears. But his will-power was shattered to bits. It did not exist. He had no will. He had dropped his flashlight, and he had forgotten the gun in his pocket. He could not command his own body. His legs, moving stiffly, worked like pieces of mechanism detached from his brain, obeying an outside will. Clumping methodically they carried him shrieking up the stair toward the witch-fire glow shimmering above him.

'Buckner!' he screamed. 'Buckner! Help, for God's sake!'

His voice strangled in his throat. He had reached the upper landing. He was tottering down the hallway. The whistling sank and ceased, but its impulse still drove him on. He could not see from what source the dim glow came. It seemed to emanate from no central focus. But he saw a vague figure shambling toward him. It looked like a woman, but no human woman ever walked with that skulking gait, and no human woman ever had that face of horror, that leering yellow blur of lunacy – he tried to scream at the sight of that face, at the glint of keen steel in the uplifted claw-like hand . . . but his tongue was frozen.

Then something crashed deafeningly behind him; the shadows were split by a tongue of flame which lit a hideous figure falling backward. Hard on the heels of the report rang an inhuman squawk.

In the darkness that followed the flash Griswell fell to his knees and covered his face with his hands. He did not hear Buckner's voice. The Southerner's hand on his shoulder shook him out of his swoon.

A light in his eyes blinded him. He blinked, shaded his eyes, looked up into Buckner's face, bending at the rim of the circle of light. The sheriff was pale.

'Are you hurt? God, man, are you hurt? There's a butcher's knife there on the floor – '

'I'm not hurt,' mumbled Griswell. 'You fired just in time – the fiend! Where is it? Where did it go?'

'Listen!'

Somewhere in the house there sounded a sickening flopping and flapping as of something that thrashed and struggled in its death convulsions.

'Jacob was right,' said Buckner grimly. 'Lead can kill them. I hit her, all right. Didn't dare use my flashlight, but there was enough light. When that whistlin' started you almost walked over me gettin' out. I knew you were hypnotised, or whatever it is. I followed you up the stairs. I was right behind you, but crouchin' low so she wouldn't see me, and maybe get away again. I almost waited too long before I fired – but the sight of her almost paralysed me. Look!'

He flashed his light down the hall, and now it shone bright and clear. And it shone on an aperture gaping in the wall where no door had showed before.

'The secret panel Miss Elizabeth found!' Buckner snapped. 'Come on!'

He ran across the hallway and Griswell followed him dazedly. The flopping and thrashing came from beyond that mysterious door, and now the sounds had ceased.

The light revealed a narrow, tunnel-like corridor that evidently led through one of the thick walls. Buckner plunged into it without hesitation.

'Maybe it couldn't think like a human,' he muttered, shining his light ahead of him. 'But it had sense enough to erase its tracks last night so we couldn't trail it to that point in the wall and maybe find the secret panel. There's a room ahead – the secret room of the Blassenvilles!'

And Griswell cried out: 'My God! It's the windowless chamber I saw in my dream, with the three bodies hanging – ahhhhh!'

Buckner's light playing about the circular chamber became suddenly motionless. In that wide ring of light three figures appeared, three dried, shrivelled, mummy-like shapes, still clad in the mouldering garments of the last century. Their slippers were clear of the floor as they hung by their withered necks from chains suspended from the ceiling.

'The three Blassenville sisters!' muttered Buckner. 'Miss Elizabeth wasn't crazy, after all.'

'Look!' Griswell could barely make his voice intelligible. 'There – over there in the corner!'

The light moved, halted.

'Was that thing a woman once?' whispered Griswell. 'God, look at that face, even in death. Look at those claw-like hands, with black talons like those of a beast. Yes, it was human, though – even the rags of an old ballroom gown. Why should a mulatto maid wear such a dress, I wonder?'

'This has been her lair for over forty years,' muttered Buckner, brooding over the grinning grisly thing sprawling in the corner. 'This clears you, Griswell – a crazy woman with a hatchet – that's all the authorities need to know. God, what a revenge! – what a foul revenge! Yet what a bestial nature she must have had, in the beginnin', to delve into voodoo as she must have done . . .'

'The mulatto woman?' whispered Griswell, dimly sensing a horror that overshadowed all the rest of the terror.

Buckner shook his head. 'We misunderstood old Jacob's maunderin's, and the things Miss Elizabeth wrote – she must have known, but family pride sealed her lips. Griswell, I understand now; the mulatto woman had her revenge, but not as we'd supposed. She didn't drink the Black Brew old Jacob fixed for her. It was for somebody else, to be given secretly in her food, or coffee, no doubt. Then Joan ran away, leavin' the seeds of the hell she'd sowed to grow.'

'That – that's not the mulatto woman?' whispered Griswell.

'When I saw her out there in the hallway I knew she was no mulatto. And those distorted features still reflect a family likeness. I've seen her portrait, and I can't be mistaken. There lies the creature that was once Celia Blassenville.'